"I'M NOT AFRAID OF YOU, MY LORD."

Even in the soft light of the stables, Brynna could feel the force of Brand's gaze. "I am a cold hearted, ruthless bastard who sees what he wants and takes it. Is that not so?" He stepped closer to her, too close. His voice, no longer tender, was like the growl of a hungry wolf.

"Nay, I . . ." Brynna's words caught in her throat somewhere between a sigh and a gasp as he traced the soft contour of her jaw with his fingertip.

"You think that I cannot be gentle." Brand traced his lips against her temple. He slipped his hands around her waist, pulling her against him. "And you think that I don't want you." He ran his fingers over the pulse beat of her throat, cupping her face in his hands. His lips found hers in a hungry kiss that searched and demanded until he took the breath from her body. He withdrew so slowly that Brynna nearly collapsed into his powerful arms.

"But I do."

LORD OF DESIRE

Paula Quinn

WARNER
FOREVER

NEW YORK   BOSTON

Warner Forever is a registered trademark of Warner Books.

Cover design by Diane Luger
Cover art by Alan Ayers
Hand lettering by David Gatti
Book design and text composition by Stratford Publishing Services

Warner Books

Time Warner Book Group
1271 Avenue of the Americas
New York, NY 10020
Visit our Web site at www.twbookmark.com

Printed in the United States of America

First Paperback Printing: August 2005

10 9 8 7 6 5 4 3 2 1

To my children, Danny, Samantha, and Hayley . . . thank you for all your sacrifices. I love you. To my husband, Dan . . . this is the result of your unending support and encouragement. You are my inspiration. You are . . . my William.

Acknowledgments

SPECIAL THANKS TO my dearest friend, Suellen Marita, for patiently listening to all my stories and loving my characters as much as I do. Brand is yours. And to Butchie DeMarco for supplying me with endless reams of paper. I know I drove you crazy; thank you for letting me. To my brilliant editor, Devi Pillai, thank you from the very bottom of my heart for believing in me. Andrea Somberg, my wonderful agent, you worked so quickly, my head is still spinning. Special thanks to my mom for always encouraging me, and to you Daddy . . . the first knight in my life. I love you both.

Prologue

PORTHLEVEN, ENGLAND
SUMMER 1064 A.D.

The carriage came to a halt on the side of the dirt road. Lady Brynna Dumont peeked her head out of the small, curtained window to see why her troupe had stopped. Her hand, holding back the velvet curtain, was delicate. Her skin was smooth and white against the bright red of the lush fabric.

"Derrick, why have we stopped?"

"There is a fallen tree up ahead, m'lady. We must move it before we can continue. It will be a while, I'm afraid."

Frowning at the delay, but willing to make the most of such a magnificent day, Brynna flung open the carriage door, eager to explore her surroundings. Layers of blue linen cascaded over a dainty slipper before she stepped out onto the forest floor. Her eyes, as green as the leaves that sang in the soft breeze, scanned the surrounding woods dense with summer growth. She breathed in the fresh scent of morning dew just as Sir Nathan rode past her on his snorting black destrier.

"Get back inside the carriage," he commanded, swinging

his mount around to face her. "It could be dangerous out here."

Brynna narrowed her eyes on the permanently furious face of her uncle Robert's most trusted guard. Sir Nathan sat tall and menacing in the saddle, the glint in his hard gaze attesting to the fact that he ached to take her over his knee and whip her into dutiful submission. She huffed at him just thinking of it. Never.

"I will be fine, Sir Nathan." She offered him a cheeky smile. "Just see to the tree. I am anxious to return home to my father."

She felt his smoldering eyes on her back as she walked away, but she ignored him and tilted her face to the canopy of leaves above her. She closed her eyes and drew in a deep breath. Lovely, she thought as a slight breeze kissed her cheeks and sent a silky wisp of copper hair across her face. She swept the lock back with one long, elegant finger and cast a quick glance over her shoulder at Nathan. He was busy barking orders to his men. Brynna's feet were light, and no one watched her as she slipped through the trees.

Brynna strolled through the forest, ducking around the ancient branches and pushing at vines that clung to her gown. Somewhere behind her, she could hear Sir Nathan still bellowing orders on the proper way to hoist a fallen tree from the road. Happy to be out of his sight, she began to hum. The cantankerous knight had been in her uncle Robert's service since God spoke the first words of creation. Sir Nathan was highly respected, even by her father, but that hadn't stopped Brynna from arguing with him at every opportunity. Of course, she wasn't the one who picked the fights. Nathan was a crusty old soldier who didn't believe ladies should ride horses, wear boots, or speak until spoken to. She was still undecided if the summer spent arguing with her uncle's commander had been ghastly, or exhilarating. The daughter of Lord Richard Dumont, mightiest warrior in England, loved a good fight, same as her father.

None of it mattered now. She was finally going back home to her father and she couldn't wait. Well, she corrected herself, she could wait a little while longer just to enjoy this splendid day.

Nathan's harsh voice pursued Brynna through the trees and into a small glen, where it finally blended with the call of blue jays overhead. Carpeted with yellow jasmine and blue linseed, the splendor of the meadow washed over her. Brynna smiled and lifted her skirts to run through the luxuriant field. She dropped to her knees beneath the shade of an old willow tree and then lay down in the tall grass, delighting in the delicate yellow and blue petals that tickled her cheeks.

An odd sound captured her attention. At first she thought she was dreaming. She sat up and looked around. She was alone in the glen. The beguiling laughter drifted across the fragrant air and, like a siren's song, drew her toward a large cluster of currant bushes. The man's laughter was so wonderfully inviting. It was most definitely a man's voice, for the tones were deep and rich. But unlike the gravelly pitch of the men's voices in her uncle Robert's garrison, this voice was not rough to her ears.

Kneeling before the dense bushes with bated breath, Brynna parted the branches.

It was definitely a man. He floated on his back, just a few feet away, in a lagoon painted with sunshine and discarded dogwood blossoms. The sight of his naked body made Brynna's cheeks burn and her lips part. Golden columns of light glistened off the corded muscles that sculpted his chest and upper arms. Dipping his head backward, he gathered a mouthful of water, then shot it from his lips like a fountain.

Brynna sighed, looking at the scene before her. All around the small pool pink and white dogwood trees, which shed their dainty blossoms at the slightest breeze, grew. Like snowflakes in summer, hundreds of tiny petals drifted through the air, many coming to rest upon the water, covering its surface. And there, in the middle of paradise, was the most breathtaking man Brynna had ever seen. Though he swam alone in the lagoon, he played as though others were enjoying the day with him. He dived deep into the crystal blue ripples, entering a world known only to him. Down he went like a sun-kissed fish, deeper and deeper into his private world.

Moments stretched as Brynna watched the sun-dappled surface for any sign of him. Alarmed, she stood up, surrendering her hiding place amid the foliage. She wanted to jump in, but hesitated, since she didn't know how to swim. He suddenly burst through the surface with a thunderous splash of jet-black curls and diamond-crystal droplets. He rocketed out of the water until Brynna saw his whipcord tight belly . . . and beyond. With a swift turn of his body, he vanished again, only to come back up.

Brynna felt that she was watching a merman. Mayhap, beneath the water snaked a great, scaled tail, powerful and iridescent.

Indeed, he looked happier in his aqua playground than any human had the right to be. Joy filled his face; his smile was ecstatic, heating Brynna's skin, her muscles, her blood. Never had she seen such erotic, intoxicating pleasure in a man's face. The water was his lover, kissing every part of his body at once; he closed his eyes, surrendering himself to the sheer delight that consumed him. When he opened them again, he lifted his face to the sun.

Heart stilled, Brynna gaped at the color of his eyes gazing into the heavens. Eyes that absorbed the rich blues of the sky while reflecting the depthless green of the sea. She wanted to stay there forever and watch him caught in his private fantasy. She was heated in places she had just discovered existed.

The sound of a horse approaching from the opposite end of the lagoon startled Brynna out of her delicious reverie. She snapped her head in the direction of the intruder.

A woman seated atop a white gelding appeared out of the trees, a dream coming to life. Pale blond hair fell in silky splendor down her back, reaching her saddle. Her face was beautiful, her form as delicate as the sprouts freshly sprung from the grass that grew around the lagoon.

When he saw her, the man in the water smiled. "Colette, you're late," he called out.

"I'm surprised you noticed." The beauty threw him a teasing smile that did not reach her eyes before she dismounted and tied her horse to a nearby tree.

Brynna gasped when the woman slipped her cotton gown off her shoulders. The dress tumbled to the earth as if an angel had shed its gossamer wings. And all the while the swimmer watched her, gliding toward her so effortlessly not a single ripple wavered around him.

Oh, dear God, what should I do? Brynna beseeched. She could tell by the raw hunger in the man's voice that the couple was not just going to swim together. How could she escape now without being discovered? Would she have to watch? Oddly enough, the thought both intrigued and troubled her. She wanted to dream that she had discovered this merman, that he was hers alone. She could swim with him, travel to his world below the surface, and share the ecstasy that impassioned him.

"Is it cold?"

"I will warm you," the merman promised silkily. His voice was the softest breeze on a sweltering day, lulling in its gentleness, calming Brynna's anxious heart.

The girl stepped over her clothes with a grace that made Brynna feel like a towering oaf, and made her way, naked, to the edge of the lake.

He swam toward her. And then to Brynna's shock and mortified delight, he stepped out of the lake. Water cascaded down his glistening back, over hard, round buttocks, down muscular thighs and strong calves. He wasn't a merman after all, Brynna thought, biting her lower lip. Taking his lover's hands, he walked backward into the water, gently pulling her along. She protested, gasping when the cold water licked her feet, but he laughed merrily and pulled her in deeper. When the water reached his waist, he let himself go, falling backward into his liquid lover's embrace while holding the woman in his arms, keeping her barely afloat on top of him.

Brynna wanted to turn away, to run, but she couldn't. She had fallen under a spell, enchanted by the sound of his laughter, the hungry way his fingers stroked the wet body resting on his chest.

He disappeared beneath the surface, releasing his lover. She followed, and Brynna waited, counting seconds in her mind. It was too long. They should have come up. Brynna waited, anxious to see his face again.

An instant passed, and then another, drawing on Brynna's nerves until she could barely stand it, and then the surface broke and the couple exploded upward like a geyser. The man held his lover's waist, bringing her up first. The woman's mouth was open, sucking in a life-giving breath, as though it were her last. Held closely in the masculine strength of his arms, she smiled as she slipped down his body.

Brynna could see the passion in his face. Oh, she could see it, so intense it vibrated and rippled outward like the water around them. His lips curled into a wide, hungry grin as he drank in the woman's face.

"I love you."

The words were clear to read upon his lips, to see in his eyes. Brynna groaned softly, wishing they were being said to her.

He kissed his lover's neck, blazing a fiery trail to her breasts.

Brynna stopped breathing.

He disappeared again under the water and the maiden threw her head back as her lover had done before, alone in the water, in euphoric ecstasy.

Biting her lip, Brynna tried to imagine what he was doing to the beauty under the surface that caused her to gasp and groan, and then cry out.

He surfaced again, this time behind his flaxen-haired lady. He wrapped his arms around her chest and whispered into her ear—words that made her smile as radiantly as the sun itself. Then he lifted her slightly onto him and lowered her again.

Thankfully, Brynna caught the groan before it could escape her lips. But the fire he had ignited in her could not be quenched, and she knew she would never forget it.

Chapter One

Brynna paced her bedchamber, creating a worn path in the rushes. When she could not take another moment of waiting, she slapped her palms against her thighs and turned her tight, frowning lips on her handmaiden.

"What can possibly be taking them so long?"

Alysia watched her mistress from the edge of the bed. She shook her head, afraid to say a word. Lady Brynna was a good-natured woman, though at times she sported a temper hotter than fire. Today was one of those times. Still, Alysia never had seen her this furious before. But then, so much had changed since the lady's father, Lord Richard Dumont, had returned from battle, defeated. Alysia knew that her mistress's only concern was that her father had returned alive, but the Norman bastard had beaten him. It was a shock to all who lived at Avarloch, for no one had ever defeated Lord Richard. All their lives were about to change with the arrival of Lord Brand Risande. The victor was coming to lay claim to the castle and Lord Richard's title. But even worse than having a Norman lord rule Avarloch were the rumors that he had been spoiled by betrayal. Whispers had reached as far north as Aberdeen about the dark knight, how his heart had turned cold and cruel. Poor Alysia had spent many a night with the other maidens and with the serfs and vassals of the castle fretting over what would become of them when Lord Richard and Lady Brynna were cast out like unwanted baggage. But Brynna did not worry. She just grew angrier by the day, vowing never to leave her home no matter what manner of beast moved in.

When the witan, a council of the Anglo-Saxon nobles, arrived this morn to counsel with Lord Richard, they forbade Brynna from attending their meeting. Alysia sat quietly for most of the day while Brynna spewed forth curses and accusations that made the swarthy handmaiden cringe in her own skin.

"It's treachery, Alysia." Brynna fumed. "Our king, who is himself a Saxon, conspired against my father."

"But why?" Alysia asked.

"Because my father has gone to the church to voice his displeasure with the way King Edward rules England. Edward is weak and has placed too much of this country's fate into the hands of his brother-in-law, Harold of Wessex." Brynna's auburn hair was loose, save for two strands braided at her temples and pinned to the back of her head. When she whirled in her pacing, thick waves shimmered and fanned outward like flames around the waist of her organdy gown. "Edward is a coward who would turn this land over to a Norman rather than stand up to my father's scrutiny."

Alysia remained quiet, not daring to suggest that Brynna spoke treason. Not that anyone in Avarloch would betray her for the like. Her mistress was well loved here, as was Lord Richard.

"Now my father has lost his home and my fate is being decided by a council of men I scarcely know. Well, I will tell you this." Brynna pivoted around once more. "If the Norman swine thinks he's going to come here and take my home, he is in for an unkind awakening. I will tear the eyes from his head, I swear it!"

Alysia gulped. It was a slight sound, but Brynna heard it and glared at her, eyes blazing like fire within emerald stones.

"What? I should not kill the bastard?" she demanded.

Alysia shook her head again. "I—I did not say anything, my lady."

"You think I should just leave my home without a fight?"

Alysia had no choice; she had to say something now. "Mayhap he is . . . not s-so bad," she stammered, wringing the edge of Brynna's bedsheets in her fingers. "I heard tell that he is quite handsome and tall and strong and—"

"I care not if he is as tall as Goliath!" Brynna shouted. Then seeing Alysia cower, she lowered her voice and came to kneel before her. "Forgive me, Alysia. I did not mean to raise my voice to you. It is just that . . . that . . ." She didn't finish. Her lips quivered for just an instant before settling into a hard, determined line.

The door opened and one of her father's guards stuck his head inside the chambers. "You can go down now, my lady. The council awaits you."

Brynna cast the guard a dark glare, though he had nothing to do with her father's betrayal, then rose to her feet. "Thank you, Sir Martin." Her voice was suddenly soft, her expression, a mask of calm she wished she felt.

"What will become of you, m'lady?" her young handmaiden asked, twisting her hands in her lap.

Brynna looked down at Alysia with a beautiful smile and reached for her handmaiden's hand. "Fear not. I will do whatever I must to remain here. I will not leave you."

Brynna entered the great hall with all the grace and elegance of a queen . . . much to Lord Richard Dumont's delight. She smiled at her father when his eyes met hers across the crowded table. God's breath, she loved him. He was the most handsome man in the room, but since the men sitting around him at the long trestle table looked like fat hams ready for the roasting, it wasn't saying much. Brynna scanned every face, her lovely smile growing tighter on her lips with each face she passed.

Formed in the time of King Alfred, the witan were a group of nobles who ruled in consultation with the king. They gave grants of land, administered justice, and decided matters such as war and peace, with the consent of their king.

Lord Richard stood up from his seat when his daughter reached him. He took her hand and lifted it to his lips for a tender kiss. "My sunshine," he whispered, and offered her the chair beside his.

Before she sat, Brynna spotted her uncle Robert seated next to Sir Nathan. The cranky knight nodded at her silent appraisal.

"My dear," her uncle began, and shifted uncomfortably in his seat. "You know why we are here."

"To decide my fate," Brynna told him. She kept her expression neutral, though in truth she wanted to tell them all to rot in hell. No one was going to force her to leave her home.

"I wish it were so, child," he said quietly. "I would have you come back to my home until your father arranged a proper marriage for you." Sir Nathan grumbled under his breath and Brynna was tempted to smile at him before returning her attention to her uncle. "I'm afraid your fate was already decided when the Norman defeated your father."

Brynna raised a perfectly arched brow. "What do you mean, Uncle?"

"Brynna," her father answered for him. It was most difficult to look into her eyes when she turned to him, but he wanted to be the one to tell her. It was his fault for losing to the Norman—a regret he would live with forever. "The council refuses to forfeit this land to the Normans."

"But what can we do?" She turned and searched the faces staring back at her. "Will the king allow my father another battle with this Norman?"

"Nay, daughter," Richard said, shaking his head. "The council has demanded that the Norman warrior marry you. Having a Saxon wife is the only way to assure that the land partially remains under Saxon rule."

"Wife?" Brynna almost choked on the word. She felt the blood draining from her face and fought to regain control of her senses when the room began to spin. "But I . . ."

"You are ten and nine now, Brynna," her uncle reminded her gently. "Well past the age when a lady should take a husband."

She wasn't ready to become a wife. She didn't want to marry the man who defeated her father in battle. She hated the Norman already. How was she supposed to honor and obey him when she wanted to command him to

Hades? She wanted to protest, but when she opened her mouth, only a soft moan came out. She realized this was probably the only way to remain at Avarloch.

"The king sides with the Normans in many things because of his kinship with Duke William," her uncle explained, though it was clear he was growing impatient with his task. His niece should be embroidering a tapestry, not sitting with men, discussing politics. "Lord Brand Risande does not wish to marry, but the king has agreed to enlist the aid of Duke William in the matter. Risande was trained under the duke's tutelage and our king assures us that he will obey William's command to marry you."

"Our king?" Brynna's temper finally flared. She narrowed her eyes on her uncle first, and then on the others. "Do you mean the same king who signed a decree giving away ownership of Avarloch to any noble who battled against my father and won?—a king who did not counsel with you as the law requires before he did this grievous thing? And, why, after he conspired to remove my father from his land, would Edward agree to help us?"

"Because," a gravelly voice answered her, and Brynna shifted her gaze to Sir Nathan, "we will bring battle to Avarloch if the Norman refuses you."

"Nay!" Brynna almost leaped from her chair. Her father's hand on her shoulder stopped her. She turned to him. "Father, you cannot agree to this."

"We don't believe it will come to that, Brynna," her father assured her. "Edward may be many things I detest, but he's not simple-minded. If the council comes against Lord Risande, the Normans will surely take offense, especially now that we have involved Duke William. It could start a war." Lord Richard smiled and patted Brynna's hand when she shook her head. "Don't you see, sweeting? If there is war here, Edward must side with the Saxons, and he will lose all alliances with Duke William if he does. He has to help us. He may not want a Dumont in Avarloch, but now he has no choice. As for Duke William, he has already sent me a missive stating that he will arrive here sometime within the next sennight. He made a request to the king that I remain here until he arrives. I don't know why he wants me to stay, but I am certain he doesn't want to go to war over a single castle in England. So you see? There will be no fighting here. The duke will convince his man to take you as his wife. You will not have to leave your home, and Avarloch will remain, in part, a Saxon holding."

Brynna's heart hammered in her chest at the thought of battle in Avarloch. The very idea of her vassals losing their lives made her want to weep. Images of her home destroyed at the hands of warring men hardened her resolve to do whatever she must to ensure that it never happened. And what choice did she have? None. Her fate had indeed been decided when her father lost to Lord Brand Risande. She had to marry the Norman. She turned to face the many nobles who watched her. Her delicate shoulders squared with determination. "I will not let Avarloch be destroyed. Whatever you command of me, I will do. But I will never forget King Edward's treachery against my father. He is undeserving of your fealty and he will never have mine."

A flurry of murmurs went up in the great hall. Beating the king at his own underhanded deeds was one thing, treason was quite another. Sir Nathan, who wore a frown of disgust, shook his head at Brynna.

"You speak treason at your own peril, young girl. If you were my daughter, I would have you flogged."

In that moment the sun fled. Rays of light that had been filtering through the arched windows in the great hall vanished. It seemed the sun sensed her father's wrath and shrank away. Darkness filled Avarloch as Lord Richard slowly rose to his feet.

"Sir Nathan, we have known each other for many years. And mayhap you think that gives you leave to speak to my daughter with such disrespect. You are wrong." Richard's eyes were as sharp as daggers. "I will grant you mercy because you are a good friend to my brother. But never think to lay your hands on my daughter, else I will dismember you and leave your parts scattered upon the moors." Richard's challenging gaze swept over his other guests.

"My daughter speaks her mind as I have taught her to do. You know Risande was sent by order of my own king to kill me. The Norman spared my life, though I know not why. A fierce warrior, he fought like no one I have ever seen, save for rumors of William of Normandy himself. Edward's efforts to rid England of me have placed one even more dangerous in my stead. The king will realize it soon. When he decides to send someone to battle the Norman warrior, he will need a man whose arm is swifter than the wind and whose heart beats to the sound of a battle drum. And still, I doubt any can beat him. I could not, and now my daughter must pay for my defeat. But this I promise, if she is harmed in any way by King Edward's continued treachery, I will come back from hell if I have to and kill him." He waited for a moment, and when no one spoke, Lord Richard took his daughter's hand and led her out of the great hall.

Brynna returned to her room and threw herself on her bed. Alysia was gone. The hearth fire had died down to glowing embers and her bedchamber was cold. Winter would come early; the Norman was bringing his hated cold with him. Brynna shivered at the thought. She was willing to do anything to save Avarloch and her people from strife, but how would she be able to give her life and her body to a man she did not love?

Her thoughts drifted, as they always did, to a cloudless day two summers ago, when she was in Porthleven; to a man whose eyes were the color of heaven and earth; a man whose heart sang with the pleasures of life. She would never forget the passion in his smile and the way it warmed her loins.

She sighed deeply against her pillow. If only it were him, her magnificent merman, she was going to marry.

Chapter Two

❋

Brynna stood on the parapet overlooking the vast fields
and distant forest that belonged to her father.

Nay, not anymore.

He was coming. Brynna could feel him, sense him on
the wind that made the distant treetops dance. The Norman knight was coming to take her home, and there was
naught she could do about it. Indeed, naught anyone
could do. Not even her father. Was the Norman so savage
that Lord Richard Dumont had surrendered to him? The
thought of it still stunned Brynna. Her father had never
lost a battle.

Lord Richard was a warrior known by every Saxon
since his days as King Edward's commander. He fought
against Godwin, father of Harold of Wessex, who planned
an unsuccessful rebellion against the king after Edward
promoted a Norman bishop to archbishop of Canterbury.
The Godwins were banished, but returned a year later and
gained the popularity of the people. King Edward returned his favor to Harold and, for fighting against the
Godwins, exiled Richard to a year of living among the
Turks. It was meant to be a punishment, but Brynna's father became a friend to the Seljuk Turks when he fought

on their side against their enemies, the Byzantines. He returned home to Brynna in her tenth year with riches of damask silks and a new handmaiden named Alysia to serve Brynna's mother.

Lord Richard was a great warrior and would live to fight other battles, of that Brynna was certain. His Saxon blood ran deep . . . as did hers. But his fight for Avarloch was over. He had lost, and now he had to leave.

Brynna cast her gaze over her land. "I, on the other hand, will never leave," she declared defiantly, glaring into the distant forest as if the Norman could somehow hear her. "I will never surrender to you." Hugging herself, she raised her chin in defiance of the cold that answered her. Her woolen tunic felt flimsy against the wind.

She knew naught about him, save the gossip she heard from her handmaidens. He was dubbed "Brand the Passionate" by his longtime friend Duke William of Normandy because of his zeal for life. It was said that he never lost a battle because his hunger for victory was greater than any opponent he faced.

What would betrayal do to a man like him? Brynna wondered. The way Lily and Alysia told it, Lord Brand's betrothed was caught in the throes of passion with a man from Brand's own guard. Brynna's handmaidens worried over rumors that their new Norman lord had turned cold. Brynna would have felt pity for him if she didn't hate him.

He brings the cold.

The weight of a hand on her shoulder broke through her thoughts and Brynna turned to smile at her father.

Lord Richard took a step forward and looked out into the distance, pulling his daughter closer under his arm.

"I cannot protect you from this, Brynnafar."

"I know," she answered quietly, resting her cheek against his broad shoulder. Even at the age of forty and two, her father was an imposing man, a warrior, savage in his own right. But, Brynna thought painfully, not savage enough.

"Is he horrible, Father? Does he have long, straggling hair and sharp fangs?"

Lord Richard laughed softly, tightening his arm around her. "Nay, daughter, he has no fangs. He is quite comely for a Norman." He paused, remembering the man he fought with in battle. "Odd." The word rolled off her father's tongue; it was riddled with curiosity and something that Brynna couldn't quite put her finger on.

"What is it, Father?" She lifted her head, expecting him to inform her that her betrothed had a forked tail.

"The Norman . . . he was an odd rogue. After I was captured, I was taken to a small clearing with the rest of my men. The Norman was approaching, and there was another man with him. I am told 'twas the Norman's brother, a powerful knight who felled many of my men with his blade. They spoke together and Lord Brand laughed. For a moment my mind could not comprehend that this was the same man who had defeated me."

"Why not?" Brynna asked, caught up in the trancelike sound of her father's voice.

"He seemed"—Lord Richard shook his head, helpless to find the right words to describe the warrior—"innocent, almost childlike, as if he did not know what hatred was, nor anger. There was nothing hard or calculating in his smile. And then that innocence was gone when his eyes met mine, and I knew that it was indeed him whom I fought on the battlefield. It struck me as odd that one could look that way and fight so mercilessly." Her father angled his head to look at her. "His face is deceiving, Brynnafar. Let caution guide you with this man."

"I will, Father," she promised, straightening her body to gaze over the parapet again.

Lord Richard studied his daughter with eyes that were lined with creases and regret. "If there was any way I could stop this marriage from taking place . . ." His voice trailed off and he turned toward the wooden doors leading to the castle. "King Edward is already here to make sure the Norman weds you, and Duke William should be arriving this night."

Brynna squared her shoulders, making her father want to embrace her again. She was his daughter, proud and fearless in the face of any danger, but her attempt at bravery for his sake broke his heart.

"I will do whatever I must to remain in my home, Father. He will never take Avarloch from me. Mother still lives here, in the herb garden, in the mews. I can still sense her sewing and spinning in the solar. I grew up with many of the people here. Remember when I was seven and Cook let me help her prepare supper? I used some of mother's herbs for the stew and near poisoned everyone in the castle."

"Aye, your hemlock stew. How could I forget?" Her father laughed.

"And old Gavin, the smith, who taught me how to make my first horseshoe?"

Her father nodded. "You tried to put it on my stallion and the beast kicked. He missed you, but you fell backward and hit your head on a shovel."

"Poor Gavin wept for a week." Brynna smiled, recalling her life at Avarloch.

Another icy breeze riffled through her long, russet-streaked hair and she lifted a slender finger to swipe it out of her eyes. "I will survive this man, just as I survive the harsh winters here."

"Come inside, Brynna." Her father took her hand to comfort her. But she shook her head.

"Nay, I want to see him when he comes," she told him with the hard edge of defiance slicing her words. "I want him to feel my presence here. I will send my hatred to him on the wind." She kept her eyes on the distant canopy of trees. Her father knew better than to argue. She had a strong mind, and if she intended the Norman to feel her hatred, then feel it he would.

Sir Luis watched Brynna's father disappear down the hall before stepping out onto the parapet. The young English knight had arrived with King Edward days before. He knew when he saw the fair Brynna Dumont that he would forever regret the day he did not go into battle with Lord Richard himself and win the hand of this fiery creature before him, and her castle along with her.

He moved silently, studying her from behind before making his presence known. Her hair flowed in thick wavy cascades down her back. Her legs were long and shapely in black woolen hose with leather riding boots reaching up to her calves. She wore no gowns for the coming of her bridegroom, but fought to conceal her beauty.

Luis smiled wolfishly behind her. Her attire failed at its duty miserably.

Brynna turned, though Luis had made no sound. And seeing him, she rolled her eyes, allowing her contempt for the English knight to spill forth freely. She did not like this man, who seemed always to be lurking in the shadows watching her with his tiny dark eyes. He was tall and lanky and wore extra padding under his hose in an attempt to make his manhood appear indecently large.

"Go away," she ordered dully.

Luis took another step forward. "Are you so eager to gaze upon your Norman warrior that you stand freezing in the cold?"

Brynna did not answer him, for though he did his best to sound concerned for her well-being, she heard the slight sarcastic edge in his voice that she had come to know so well in these last few days.

"He does not want you, you know." Luis came to stand beside her. He rested his back against the parapet railing and soaked in her beauty with beady black eyes.

"That matters not to me," Brynna replied curtly without looking at him.

The knight lifted a bushy eyebrow. "Oh?" he asked, amusement curling one corner of an upper lip hidden beneath a thin mustache. "It does not offend you that this man is going to be forced to marry you? Lord Brand has made it quite clear that he does not wish to be your husband. Why, the king had to summon the duke of Normandy here in an effort to avoid battle." Luis studied the soft, milky contours of Brynna's face while he spoke and smiled slightly at the minute furrow of her dainty brow. "He would rather battle the Saxons than marry you, my lady, and you mean to tell me that does not offend you?"

"That was my reply." Brynna's expression had not changed, nor had the frigid tone of her voice. Why should she care if the savage wanted to marry her or not? But although she tried to deny it, she did wonder why the Norman lord would rather fight than be her husband. Did he hate the Saxons so? Did his refusal have anything to do with the infidelity of his betrothed?

"Your fingers are curling, my lady." Luis purred, inching his face closer to hers. "Does the thought of bedding the Norman repulse you?"

Unable to stand the sound of his voice another moment, Brynna spun on her heel to face him fully. "Nay, it is *you* who repulses me, Sir Luis."

The English knight's eyes smoldered for a moment before he grabbed her by the shoulders. "You would not say that once you felt my manhood plunge deep within you." He tried to kiss her, but Brynna pulled her head back and fought furiously until she broke free of his grasp. Her hand came around her shoulder to crack him across the face with all the force she could muster.

"I will inform my father and the king immediately of your behavior and see to it that you are punished." She spat at him.

Ignoring the stinging pain in his face, Luis motioned for her to do as she pleased. "I will tell him that you begged me to take you away from here, or that you used your feminine guile to bewitch me into bedding you. No marriage would take place if the king thought we had coupled. You would lose your precious land." Luis smiled at her, but his eyes seethed. "Do not ever strike me again, for if you do, I will take what I want and leave you for the other knights to find." He began to walk back to the castle but stopped and turned to look at her once again. "I might just do that anyway."

Brynna watched him leave. A ribbon of fear drifted down her spine. She turned back to the trees after making sure the loathsome knight was gone. Good Lord, she prayed silently that the Norman savage was nothing like Sir Luis.

Chapter Three

Brynna narrowed her eyes toward the trees as a figure emerged. As if appearing from flames, he came cloaked in a crimson mist. He rode a huge destrier, tinted in crimson as well. Stallion and man seemed one, invincible, permeating the air with male power and authority. Other riders followed the first. Out of the trees they rode like thunder on the storm's heel, pennants of blue and gold snapping in the cold. But Brynna could not look away from the lone knight. So proudly he rode. Fearless. His back arrow straight, his chin lifted slightly upward as though he could see her standing there alone on the parapet, her bronze hair blowing across her face. As he loomed closer, larger, Brynna noticed the crimson that covered him was not a mist, but a long cloak. It fell over his broad, chain-mailed shoulders and swirled around the stallion's haunches in heavy woolen folds. Confidence surrounded him, echoed in the way he carried his helm under his arm while steering his mount easily with one hand.

King Edward's men were already riding out to meet the advancing troupe with the king himself in the lead. Brynna watched while the Norman called a halt and waited for the king's party to reach him.

Suddenly, as if he could feel her bold green gaze burning into his flesh, the warrior lifted his face and set his eyes directly on her.

Brynna staggered backward.

It was him! The man from the lake! The man she longed for in her dreams. *Nay, it couldn't be.* Brynna's mind reeled. Was this the beast who fought and defeated her father? The one who would be her husband? She lifted a trembling hand to her mouth to stifle her gasp. Many nights had she dreamed about him, ached to see him, but surely this was not the same man. The face below her was hard. Cerulean eyes, radiant when they had gazed up at the sun, were now as cold as the stones beneath her feet. The staggering power of his gaze made her want to take a step back. She fought for control as her senses were bombarded by the beauty of his face, the chiseled lines carved from granite, the strong, straight nose, and full, pursed lips while he studied her. He was pure, unrelenting strength under a shock of raven curls. But something had changed. No longer was he the rhapsodic creature who had captivated her with his joy. There was no trace of happiness in his icy gaze. Emptiness filled him, as vast and as dark as the sea under the velvet sky.

Brynna gathered her courage around her like a cloak and gazed directly into his eyes.

He stared at her for a moment before looking away.

"He would rather battle the Saxons than marry you."

The words echoed in Brynna's ear. Her heart hammered in her chest. What happened to the flaxen beauty from the lake? The woman he so clearly loved? Was she the woman who betrayed him?

Forcing herself to remember that this was the Norman savage who was taking her home, throwing her father out, and possibly her as well, Brynna cast her fantasies of her merman away. She spun on her heel, her long hair whipping the air as she turned to leave the parapet. Avarloch meant more to her than any dream, and she would not let this man refuse her and allow her home to be destroyed.

Brand lifted his eyes again, catching a glimpse of the rich, auburn hair that fanned outward over the railing.

King Edward's horse had reached Brand and his men by now and Edward followed his gaze upward. "Richard's daughter, Lady Brynna Dumont."

"She's beautiful," a man to Brand's right noted. He sat on a warhorse so big it made the king's stallion look like a pony.

"A bit pale," Brand replied succinctly.

"She's probably frozen solid by now," Edward told them. "She has been up there all day awaiting your arrival."

Brand turned his stoic gaze on the king. "Mayhap to pierce me through the heart with an arrow."

Edward folded his beringed fingers over his saddle horn and cast a narrowed look at Brand. "Let me assure you, Lord Brand, Lady Brynna is quite harmless. She bears no ill feeling for you, but has come to terms with her position like a true lady of her station." The king did not want a confrontation with this man. Duke William had made it perfectly clear in his missives that he wanted Lord Brand Risande treated with respect. Edward cursed his bad fortune for the hundredth time for allowing a Norman noble to fight Richard. This rogue was too close to William. Surely all his careful plans would come to naught now.

"What position might that be?"

The king regarded the man on the huge destrier beside Brand. "Who is addressing me?" he asked with a haughty tip of his chin.

"I am Sir Dante Risande." He flicked a silver gaze toward Brand. "This knave's brother."

Two of them! King Edward thought sourly. His luck couldn't get any worse. He drew his mouth into a tight slit when Dante had the audacity to raise his brows waiting for an answer to his question. "She is to become your brother's wife."

"As I've told you, I have no need of a wife."

Edward turned back to Brand. "And as I've told you, the Saxon nobles will consider it an offense simply to toss Lady Brynna by the wayside. . . ."

"They do not consider it an offense that you plotted her father's death?" Brand asked casually while raising a curious eyebrow over the king's shoulder.

The girl was marching toward them, taking long, forceful strides while her woolen cloak flowed out behind her. Her face was set. Her eyes fixed on Brand like two blazing gems. "She looks about to kill me," Brand said with the tiniest trace of a smile curling one corner of his mouth. Long copper waves danced around her face and cascaded over her full bosom. Her windburned cheeks added an alluring spark to the brilliant green of her eyes. Brand let his gaze drift slowly to her shapely legs and strong thighs as she strode toward him, and then upward to her slender waist accentuated by the thick belt cinching her olive tunic.

"Strange attire for a lady," he remarked.

Looking forward to the confrontation he knew was about to commence, Brand relaxed on his mount and met her challenging gaze with a mildly amused one of his own.

The king turned on his horse just as Brynna reached them. He was about to announce her when her voice cut him off.

"I am Lady Brynnafar Dumont." She looked up at the dark lord, and then at the blue flag snapping behind him. The single gold lion would soon replace her father's griffin in the halls of Avarloch. She lifted her chin defying every Norman soldier there. "I welcome you and your company to Avarloch Castle, *my* home." She waited. No response, just that slightly amused expression. She had the sudden urge to slap it off the Norman's face if she could have reached it.

Brand stared down at her for a long time without saying a word, until Brynna began to squirm under his scrutiny. Dante shook his head feeling sorry for the woman. He recognized his brother's expression. As curious and patient as it was, Brand was about to finish her the way he did on the battlefield. It was a calculating gaze, the kind a tiger used to size up its prey before it attacked, only Brand's luminous eyes made the victim believe they were looking at a puppy, rather than a predator.

Suddenly Brand leaped from his stallion. The two separated with the ease of a feather falling from a wing. His mantle flared around his legs when he landed softly, only inches away from Brynna. Hell, she was beautiful, he admitted to himself. Being harsh with her would be difficult, but he had no other choice. Taking her as a wife would make them both miserable. Bowing politely, he swept his frosty gaze over her a moment before he reached for her dainty hand and held it to his lips. "I am Lord Brand Risande of Dover, lord of Graycliff Castle."

His voice was a husky caress. She wasn't certain if her warm cheeks were the result of his mouth gliding over her knuckles or the subtly sexy Norman-French inflection he spoke with. With a mere slant of his lips, he had made her forget her anger, made her remember only the joy she had seen on his face once before. She found herself aching to reach out and touch him if only to convince herself that he was real. Beneath the sweep of sooty lashes, blue-green eyes captivated her as he kissed her hand.

"My men are at your disposal, mademoiselle . . ."

Caught up in his tender trap and by the intoxicating smile he offered, Brynna blinked and bit her lower lip. She couldn't let herself forget why he was here. "My lord, I—"

"To help you pack your things." The finality of his words and the flat tone in which he spoke fell upon her like an ax. He lowered her hand with controlled tenderness and turned to reach for the reins of his mount, ignoring the shock that made her eyes blaze. He cast a smoldering look of his own at King Edward; then, he looked over his shoulder at Dumont's daughter, his gaze a direct challenge. "If you need an escort to wherever it is you're going, I would be happy to provide my best men."

As if he had been holding his breath the entire time his brother spoke, Dante released an explosive sigh followed by a few expletives spoken in French as Brand led his horse toward the castle. No one said another word; even the king's mouth was hanging to the ground.

Brynna turned to watch him leave. She wanted to go after him, plead with him to change his mind and avoid battle at Avarloch. But buoyed by a stubborn rush of pride, she clenched her teeth instead. How could she have been such a fool to fall under his spell again? Was she so weak-spirited that a mere glance from this man could shake her to her core? Blinking back a rush of tears and a string of blasphemies, she looked up at another brute, whose dusky gray gaze softened on her. She turned to glare at Sir Luis, who sat upon his mount beside the king. His broad grin only fanned her fury.

Biting her tongue to keep her temper in check, Brynna spun on her heel and stormed away toward her garden.

Left with her fury firing the air, Dante lifted his eyes in time to catch Sir Luis's satisfied smirk. Dante had seen the same hunger in the eyes of Sir Alexander when the traitor had looked at Colette, the wench who betrayed his brother. But since this woman was leaving in the morn, it mattered not. Still, Dante's eyes were like molten steel when Luis finally met his gaze, and then Brand's younger brother put the spurs to his horse and followed Brand to his new home.

Brynna walked until her legs ached, until she reached her garden, where she fell to her knees in the cold grass.

What kind of man was Brand Risande that he could cast her out of her home without even a hint of regret in his expression? How could his touch be as tender as if he were stroking the cheek of a newly born babe, and then strike with the lethal calculation of a serpent?

"Oh, Mother," she whispered, and closed her eyes to see Lady Tanith's face. "He is the man I've dreamed about from the lake, and the coldhearted savage I've hated for the past fortnight. How can I fight him? If he forces me to leave, there will be bloodshed here. What should I do?"

Brynna opened her eyes at the sound of a robin singing

overhead. She looked around the garden and wiped the tears from her eyes. She saw her mother planting her precious seeds, lovingly picking sweet violet and rosemary to flavor her husband's supper. She saw herself as a child giggling at the way her mother stroked her husband's bristly jaw when he had come to the garden to bring them home. She remembered her mother's dulcet laughter, and Brynna knew what had to be done. She must put away her anger at the Norman the way her mother had put away her resentment when she married Lord Richard.

But could she forgive Brand for taking over her home? He was victorious over her father, but he hadn't killed him. God's fury, there had to be something good in him. Brynna wondered what had happened to him in the year that passed. How could his eyes be so breathtaking, and yet be so cold, so void of emotion? He could not be the same man who had stirred up such languid heat in her when she saw him in the lake. How could she reach him? She knew she had to. She couldn't leave Avarloch.

Chapter Four

❋

Brand entered Avarloch Castle with the power and authority of one who had lived there all his life. Vassals leaped to attention, handmaidens scurried along the softly lit halls like rodents fleeing from the shadow of a falcon overhead. His heels tapped the floor lightly sprinkled with fresh rushes. The sound echoed throughout the long halls. Avarloch was well cared for. Every bronze bowl and gilded candle stand was polished until it sparkled like fine gold. There were freshly cut, late-blooming flowers neatly arranged in bouquets everywhere he set his eyes.

Her.

Brand studied the walls richly adorned with tapestries depicting battles between men dressed in crude armor that he did not recognize.

"The Celts fought bravely for their land."

Brand looked over his shoulder. Lord Richard stood a few feet away, watching him.

"I thought you would be gone by now," Brand replied flatly, turning back to survey the tapestries.

"As did I. But Duke William requested that I stay until he arrives."

Brand offered the tapestries a cool smile. "So William

is coming here? No doubt to join Edward in their campaign to have me wed your daughter."

"Have you met her?"

Sighing, Brand finally turned to look at the man he had conquered in battle. They were not enemies. Facing a warrior on the battlefield was quite different from meeting your defeated opponent in his own home. Brand clenched his teeth at the pang of sympathy he was now feeling for Lord Richard.

"She is lovely, Lord Richard, but I have no desire to take a wife." Brand regarded the older knight curiously. Here in his own surroundings, dressed in simple cote and surcoat, his dark hair and beard closely clipped, the famous Lord Richard looked anything but savage. He was simply a father concerned for the welfare of his daughter. "I do not want a wife," Brand repeated quietly.

Lord Richard Dumont was once again struck by the gentle nature of this warrior. Never in all his years of battle had he encountered anyone so skilled, merciless, powerful, yet here he stood, mindful of offending the same man whose blood he was sent to spill just a fortnight ago.

Richard's eyes drifted over Brand's shoulder to the elaborate tapestry that covered the entire west wall. "My wife's people," he pointed out, smiling as if he could see her standing before him. "When I first came here, Tanith hated me, though I had naught directly to do with the slaughter of the Celts centuries ago. I was a Saxon and that was enough."

"You were forced to marry a Celtic woman?" Brand asked incredulously.

Brynna's father chuckled softly. "Forced? Nay, I loved

her from the moment I clapped eyes on her. She was a breathtaking flame that burned within my soul. She was passionate even in her hatred, and when I finally won her love, I thought her passion would consume me."

Brand listened silently, understanding what it meant to love another so completely. But he also knew the torment of love betrayed. He shifted uneasily, running his hand through his black curls. He did not want to remember love, nor did he want to hear of it. If Lord Richard was trying to convince him that his daughter could someday forgive the fact that he was a Norman soldier and come to love him, then his words were being wasted. Brand needed to tell him before he went any further.

"Sir Richard, I mean no harm to your daughter. You have my word that she can stay here until she finds a husband, but that husband will not be me."

Richard bowed slightly. "I respect your desire to remain unwed, Lord Brand. I will not ask you to take my daughter for your wife again. You do know by now that there will be fighting here. It will break my daughter's heart. Brynnafar loves Avarloch dearly."

Scowling, Brand met Richard's steady gaze. Hell, he didn't care about battles, but how could he force a young woman to leave the only home she had ever known?

"This matter will be discussed at length later with the king," Brand tossed at him, and with two long strides, he reached the narrow staircase. He stopped suddenly, one boot poised on the first step. Haunted by the memory of Richard's face when he had spoken of his wife, drawn by a morbid kind of curiosity, mayhap to ease the pain of his own heart, he turned to look at the older knight once more.

"Tell me, Sir Richard, does your wife's love still consume you?"

Only Dante, entering the castle, heard the sorrow that laced Brand's question, only he recognized the pain infused with anger in his brother's dark gaze.

"Aye, it does." Lord Richard nodded. "Even from the grave it does."

"The grave?" Brand's eyes widened, shock and an even deeper torment now shown clearly on his face.

"Tanith was killed while traveling south three summers past," Richard said quietly. His gaze drifted back to the large tapestries that hung on the walls. "But her fire still burns within me. And it burns in Brynna as well." Slowly he turned his gaze to Brand. "My daughter was born with the pride of her father and the passion of her mother in her blood. Only a man with great control and a will of iron could resist her. 'Tis that kind of man I pity, for never will he be drenched in warmth by a kiss from the sun when she smiles at him. Nor, will he feel the promise of spring unleashed after a long, harsh winter when she looks upon his face."

Silence clung to the three men like the veil of a thick fog. Then, as abruptly as lightning slices through the clouds, Brand turned on his heel and left the hall to the hollow echo of Lord Richard's words. Anger and regret filled him as he climbed the stairs. He felt sorry for the former lord of Avarloch Castle who had lost such a love, but he wanted no part of those delusions. For no matter how sweet they were, they were just that, delusions.

His thoughts drifted to Colette and the day he found her in the grove not far from Graycliff Castle. Her hair spilled down her slender back; a shroud to cover her nakedness. She waited with her arms crossed demurely over her breasts for the man approaching her from behind. Would that it had been another man and not his friend Alexander who bent to lick Colette's honeyed shoulder. Mayhap if it had been a stranger making love to her, the cold that reached its long, gnarled fingers into his heart would not have been so complete.

"Damn you both," Brand growled as he climbed the winding steps. Everything he knew about trust and loyalty was snatched from him that day, leaving him empty and uncertain if he could trust anything he had ever believed in.

Taking the last three steps in one, he strode down the long corridor. Torches danced as he passed rows of doors on either side of him. There were flowers on the second-floor landing as well, and Brand's blood seared his veins when he looked at them. Colette had filled Graycliff with freshly cut flowers, permeating the air with the scent of rose and gardenia.

Why did she betray him? He had asked that question millions of times, but there was never an answer. Had he not given her everything? And still, he would have given her more. Anything . . . anything she wanted. But she wanted Alexander. He whirled in a circle as if he were trapped in a place too small to house his great anger and torment. "What blasted room should I take?" he shouted at the doors that surrounded him.

"Sir?"

The young woman stood on the stairs, her back pressed against the wall and her trembling hands pressed to her heart. The dark knight before her was terrifying in his anger, standing there seething and as impenetrable as the battlements that surrounded the castle. His hands clenched at his sides as he spun around to face her, his mantle sweeping around his leather boots.

"I am terribly sorry for not showing you to your room directly. I—"

"It's all right." Brand held his hand up to quiet her. "I am not angry with you." He smiled slightly, trying to ease the fear so plainly etched in her huge sable eyes. "What is your name?"

"Alysia. I—I am a handmaiden to Lady Brynna." Cautiously the girl studied his smile. A moment ago he looked about to tear the walls down with his bare hands. Where had all those emotions just gone? A moment ago she had seen fury mixed with a sorrow so deep and so harshly contained it frightened her. He wore a mask now, a mask that could melt the flesh clean off her bones. When he angled his head and offered her a curious look, she blushed over being caught in her thorough examination of him.

"You are the new lord of Avarloch, are you not?" she asked quietly, not moving from her place against the wall.

"*Oui*, lady."

Alysia smiled at the title he so graciously bestowed upon her. She smiled softly at first, and then it grew as his lips mirrored hers in a wide grin. So radiant was his smile that the handmaiden nearly stumbled when she took another step up the staircase.

"Do you want the master's room, m'lord?"

Brand was about to decline when his brother came barreling up the stairs and called his name.

Dante slowed when he saw the dark-haired beauty. Whatever he wanted to tell his brother drifted away as he gazed into the handmaiden's wide eyes. He was a big man and had to angle his body against Alysia's to squeeze past her.

From his position Brand couldn't see his brother's face, but Alysia's expression of numb wonder told him that if Dante wasn't pressed so snugly against her, she would have melted down the stairs.

He was right. Alysia's bones turned to pudding. The stranger had to be the most powerfully built man she'd ever clapped eyes on, and the most handsome. His hair was as inky black as his brother's, but longer and without the curl. His eyes were a mesmerizing shade of pale gray sprinkled with shards of green. His muscles were hard and warm while he lingered against her. Then he moved away, taking a step up to the landing. Somewhere in the back of Alysia's mind, she heard Brand introduce the man as his brother.

"Enchanté." His slow grin and the beguiling dimple it produced made Alysia's pulse race on an uneven breath.

"Did you want to tell me something, Dante?" Brand asked, growing impatient while his brother's enthralled gaze lingered on the smooth black mane that fell over Alysia's shoulders.

"Pardon?"

"You nearly ran the lady Alysia down in your haste to tell me something. What was it?"

Dante turned to face his brother, his trance shattered for the moment. "Duke William is here. He has just entered the bailey."

Dante wasn't certain what Brand's response was. His eyes fell back to Alysia as if they had a mind of their own.

Brand brushed past them and was about to tell Dante to

follow him downstairs, but noticed his brother and the handmaiden smiling at each other again.

"Mayhap he has come for our heads," Brand called out before he descended the stairs. He smiled when Dante happily agreed.

Chapter Five

Duke William of Normandy was agitated.

With predatory dominance he roamed the floor, his eyes taking in every movement, cataloging what he saw. For the servants of Avarloch Castle, he was a frightening sight indeed. The very air around him was charged, revealing his power and supremacy over everyone in the castle, including the king, who sat quietly near the great hearth watching him with thick wrinkles creasing his brow while his foot tapped nervously against the floor.

Though dressed in heavy chain mail over a thick woolen tunic and trousers, the muscles that corded the duke's body could be seen rippling against his clothing. His long mane of chestnut hair dangled carelessly over his massive shoulders and framed his heavy brow and bearded jaw. He wore no rings on his fingers, though he was as rich as a king. His wealth was revealed in the fine leather of his boots and the thick fur lining of his mantle, which was carefully slung over the back of a chair.

"William," Brand called from the stairs. With the casual grace of one who had all day to get to where he was going, he made his way down.

The dark gray eyes that turned to assess Brand were

unblinking, hard, and ruthless. Then they crinkled at the corners as the duke of Normandy smiled at his dearest friend.

"What are you doing here?" Brand asked suspiciously, turning to glance at the king with a pointed look.

"Is this how I am greeted in your new home, Brand?" William's smile widened and he lifted his great arms to meet Brand at the bottom of the stairs. "Not even a, 'How was your journey, *mon seigneur*?'" Arms like tree trunks came around the younger knight as William gave his former squire a few hard slaps on the back for good measure. "I knew I should never have allowed you to live in England for so long. Your manners are atrocious."

Brand smiled. It was good to see his friend, even if his suspicions as to why the duke had come were correct. "How was your journey, my lord?" he conceded graciously.

"Ugh, 'twas dreadful! The sea was angry and I lost a horse on the way." William growled, then brightened quickly. "But it was worth it all to see this fine country again." He cast his razor sharp eyes at Edward. "Someday, when I am crowned king of England, this will all be mine. You cannot live forever, Cousin," he added with a rueful smile.

"I have no wish to live forever, William," Edward retorted somewhat flatly. "But as far as being crowned after I am gone, that is a matter you will have to take up with Harold of Wessex."

"I intend to." The Norman duke's eyes gleamed with the hunger of a savage warrior eager for battle. Deadly, unspoken promises permeated the air, and Edward shifted in his seat, knowing his cousin only too well.

In the same instant it took William to blink, he turned his attention back to Brand. "So why didn't you kill Richard?"

The question was direct and Brand was unprepared for it, but his gaze did not falter under William's controlled scrutiny. "His death was not part of the decree."

"Witnesses to the decree would disagree with you, Lord Brand," Edward said benignly. "As usual, you did not do what was ordered, and took it upon yourself to let Richard live."

"That's correct." The smile that graced Brand's lips was so charming and so perfect in its sincerity that King Edward almost smiled back at him. Brand let his soft expression fade before he attacked. "Lord Richard Dumont stands defiantly against a king who cannot rule his own country, but lets someone else do it for him. I respect him. He's not weak as you are. Why, then, should I kill him?"

Edward's eyes raked over Brand with black contempt. "Now you go too far. I—"

"He's right, Edward, and you know it," William interrupted, not bothering to hide his amusement. "Harold rules England. You speak for him as though his hand was a permanent fixture up your arse. Personally, I welcome battle with the Saxons. I am only here because I know what contemptuous fools you Saxons really are, and I don't want what happened to Richard to happen to Brand as well."

Before Edward could recover, William set his heavy gaze back to Brand. "Whether you respect Richard or not, do you think letting him live was wise?"

"I was on the battlefield. It was my decision to make." The hard edge in Brand's voice told William that despite

Brand's lingering smile, he would not tolerate being questioned. Even from the Norman duke.

William laughed, the sound drifted through the halls like a robust song. Brand was the only man that William knew who did not yelp with his tail between his legs when confronted by him. And William would not have it any other way.

"Very well," he said with a quick wave of his beefy hand. "In truth, I'm pleased that Richard still lives. He's fought many battles with courage and great skill, which is why I asked him to remain here."

"Your request has put me in a most uncomfortable position," Brand said stiffly.

"I was willing to risk it." William tossed him a stealthy grin and seated himself in a high-back chair beside the king. "But we will not discuss that now." He snapped his lips together and looked around the great hall. "Is there no ale in this place?"

Brand turned to one of the servants standing nearby and the man jumped to attention, then scurried from the hall.

Curling his lips in a satisfied grin, Duke William nodded. "*Oui*. The true master of his house needs not speak a word."

Brand took a seat across from William and sank into its thick brocade cushion. "I am happy to see you, William. Trustworthy friends are hard to come by." He gave the duke a long, thoughtful look. "I know why you're here."

"I was summoned," William said bluntly, and met Brand's gaze, then glanced at the king. "Dismiss your servants, Brand, we should speak privately." Before Brand could lift a hand, the few remaining servants took off in all directions.

"Your Majesty?" Duke William used Edward's title with measured respect. "I would speak to my friend alone." He smiled. *"S'il vous plaît."*

Edward's eyes opened wide to reveal his shock at being dismissed as if he were a servant instead of the king of England. But without another word, he, too, left the hall.

When they were alone, William leaned forward in his chair. The smile on his face was laced with venom. "I am quite fond of you, Brand, but if you ever dismiss me like that when I am king, I shall have your head."

Brand's genuine smile was sorely missed by the duke and a pleasure to see again. "How are you, *mon ami*?" William asked more seriously.

"I am well." Brand stretched his long legs out in front of him and clasped his hands together in his lap.

Across from him, gray eyes narrowed like finely polished swords. "Chivalry requires honesty, Brand. You're a poor liar."

Turning his face toward the great hearth, Brand studied the flames pensively. After a long time, he blinked and fire reflected in his turquoise gaze. He had not spoken of Colette since he sent her away, but William knew his heart. When Brand opened his mouth, the words spilled off his tongue.

"She was my whole life, William," he said quietly. "We were going to be wed in the spring. Do you expect that I should forget what she did so quickly?"

"Je sais. I know." The hefty duke sighed. "But that part of your life is over, Brand. 'Tis time to mend."

The servant returned carrying a tray laden with various fruits and cheeses and two goblets of ale to wash it down.

He handed the drinks over and laid the tray on a small wooden table before the two men, then bowed and left the hall before Brand could thank him.

When the servant turned the corridor, he nearly pounded straight into Brynna. She knit her brows at him and held a finger to her lips so that he would not reveal her presence; then she motioned with her hand for him to leave. She had already heard most of the conversation and had no intention of leaving now. She pressed her cheek against the cool wall and listened once again.

"By mending, do you mean marrying Lady Brynna Dumont?" Brand asked, setting his careful gaze on his friend and confirming his suspicions.

"Right now 'tis what you must do," William replied gently.

"I cannot."

"And why not? Colette is gone."

"I know that!" Brand snapped at him. "Do you think I want her back after what she did?"

"Do you?" William raised a dark eyebrow.

"Non." Brand shook his head. *"Oui. Non."*

"Sounds like your mind is made up." The Norman grumbled and began to gnaw on an apple.

"I don't want her back."

William ignored Brand's black glare because he understood the depth of his friend's pain, but William had come here to prevent Brand from having the Saxons turn against him. And that was exactly what would happen if he turned the lady out into the cold. Still, William spoke gently, letting his concern for his favored knight be heard. "If you do not want Colette back, then what prevents you from marrying the Saxon woman?"

"I simply do not want to marry her."

"Why?" William pressed.

Flames flickered and sent long shadows across the walls when Brand rose from his chair. He paced the large hall, running his fingers through his inky curls. "I could never love her."

"Love has naught to do with this. Even she knows that," William replied easily, and tossed the apple core into the flames.

"I don't . . ." Brand stopped pacing and closed his eyes. Silence stretched on; all that could be heard was the crackling of flames while they devoured the remains of William's discarded fruit.

"You don't want to be hurt again." William finished the sentence for him. Brand opened his eyes to search his friend's gaze against the soft glow of the hearth.

"I *won't* be hurt again," he corrected scathingly.

Aged wooden floors creaked on the other side of the wall and William's head snapped up, swift and wolflike. He sniffed the air for a moment, then held up a finger to quiet Brand.

"The witan have informed the king that they will burn Avarloch to the ground if you turn the girl out." William winked when Brand offered him a puzzled look.

Both men heard the sharp gasp from behind the wall. Brand started toward the sound to see who the eavesdropper was, but William, already suspecting who it was, rose from his chair, stopping his advance.

"They must have an answer, Brand. Do the Saxons burn Avarloch?"

"Nay!" Brynna left her hiding place on the other side of the wall on feet that brought her crashing straight into

Brand's unsuspecting arms. "Nay, please!" she begged him, her tear-filled eyes glimmered like emeralds in seawater. "I will demand naught of you, I swear it, my lord. Make me your wife and I promise to give you heirs and never complain. I will submit to your will, do anything you say. Don't let them burn Avarloch, I pray you. This is my home!"

Brand wanted to be angry with her for listening to their private conversation. But he couldn't, not when her face was so close to his, her lower lip soft and trembling. Her thick coppery hair spilled over his fingers, her creamy face wet with tears. God's blood, her face was beautiful, her lush mouth, a Cupid's bow tempting him into decadent thoughts of what he'd like to do to them. Brand's gaze moved over her face, brooding, with a hint of menace that had nothing to do with letting Avarloch burn. Her eyes glimmered with fear, searching his own for mercy. But there was strength as well in those vividly verdant gems, strength and life that ignited a tiny spark and warmed Brand's blood. She smelled wonderful too, and she was soft. Hell, he'd almost forgotten how soft a woman could be.

"Lady, I—"

"How *dare* you spy on us like a common wench!" William's voice cracked the air like a peal of thunder, slicing through Brynna's nerves like no voice ever had before. He was quite pleased to see that it had the exact effect he had planned. The lady disappeared into Brand's chest, clinging there as if for her life.

"Who are you?" William blasted through her eardrums. "That I may know whose head I take at first light!"

Brynna couldn't look at him, hadn't seen him at all in

her flight into Brand's arms, but she was sure he was a monster. She kept her face pressed into Brand's mailed chest, trembling in his arms.

"Answer me!"

She could not. Indeed, if Brand had not been holding her so tightly, she would have fainted dead away.

"Enough William! She is frightened half to death." Raw command echoed through the hall. Brynna heard the strength in Brand's voice, felt the power in his arms as they tightened around her and she marveled at it. Was he daft speaking in that tone to this . . . this barbarian?

"And well she should be." The Norman brute huffed, quite happy with himself now that he had Brand protecting her. "If she were in Normandy right now, she would be beaten to within an inch of her life for such treachery."

"She's not in Normandy." Brand's warm breath stirred the curls at Brynna's ear.

"*Non,* but it would solve all your problems, would it not?" William asked with a sparkle in his steel gray eyes and a bright, victorious smile stretching his lips. "Let us kill her and we will inform the witan council that she took her own life rather than wed Norman swine."

"That's enough, William," Brand admonished. "You have had your play with her."

Play? Brynna heard the word, but she thought she must be dreaming. No one could be so cruel. She tightened her fingers around Brand's mantle.

"Lady?" Brand's voice was an intoxicating blend of silk and smoke as he withdrew his arms slowly and held her away to look at her. "It's all right. He will not harm you."

Brynna lifted her face to his. Tender concern filled his aqua gaze. Concern mixed with . . . amusement.

"Are the Saxons going to burn Avarloch if you do not marry me?" Brynna asked in a quiet voice as understanding and fury washed over her.

Basking in the beautiful facets of her eyes, Brand quite literally had to tear his gaze away from her to cut William a hard look. Brynna caught the look they exchanged with each other and her blood began to boil. The Duke chuckled. Brynna turned to him slowly, no longer caring how frightening he might be. Her eyes blazed and shot fire hotter than molten lava. Her lips tightened, her teeth clenched, and stepping away from Brand, she balled her hands into fists as if to strike the hefty beast to her right.

"You rotting pile of devil spit!" she seethed, stepping closer to William.

Behind her now, Brand's eyes opened wide and he quickly suppressed the urge to laugh.

The duke of Normandy towered over her, but Brynna raised her face fearlessly to his. "How *dare* you jest so lightly about my home? If I were a man, I would kill you where you stand, you spineless rake! But death would be too good for you. I would make you suffer at my sword until you begged for mercy, and then I would slice your wicked throat from ear to ear and the smile on my face would be the last thing your wretched soul remembered as it descended into hell!"

William shifted his astonished gaze to Brand, who mirrored his friend's expression of shock and amused admiration.

"By God, you have to marry her, Brand!" William exclaimed.

As if remembering Brand suddenly, Brynna spun on

her heel to face him with just as much contempt and venom as she had poured out on William.

"And you! Clearly my home means naught to you. When you turn me out and the nobles send their soldiers to attack, I hope they kill you first." She whirled on her heel again and Brand caught the fresh scent of jasmine on her hair as her thick locks struck his face. His nostrils flared slightly, breathing her in as she stormed out of the hall.

When she was gone, Brand cast a sly, sideward glance at William. "You're a bastard."

William nodded and sat back down in his seat. "*Oui,* that is what they tell me. Though I do believe my father loved my peasant mother." Staring in the direction Brynna had taken to leave, William's voice softened and slowed to a husky purr. "If my mother had one spark of the fire Richard's daughter possesses, I cannot blame him." Looking in the same direction, Brand agreed, but said nothing. "What spirit!" William continued breathlessly. He turned back to Brand. "This place means more to her than her own life."

Brand nodded slowly, knowing William was right. "How can I make her leave?"

"You cannot! You must marry her. I command it. You still answer to me, even though I allow you to forget it," William added haughtily when Brand looked like he might either protest at the command, or laugh at it. "Besides, I will not have you die at the hands of the Saxons. I would have you live, and I've a feeling that woman can remind you what living means."

Chapter Six

Brynna stormed up the stairs to her room. Candle flames whipped and danced as she passed them. Barbarians! She fumed. The whole lot of them! To treat her with such callous disregard . . . wasn't it bad enough that the council threatened to bring battle here? To suggest the witan would burn Avarloch down was unforgivable. Lord Brand cared naught for Avarloch. It was just another conquest, his prize for defeating her father in battle. She hated him, hated them all, especially the knight's hairy friend. What kind of man would jest about cutting off a woman's head? At the thought, Brynna wrapped her fingers around her throat and swallowed hard. And yet . . .

The memory of Brand's rich baritone voice filled her before she finished her next thought.

Lord Brand Risande had defended her, hadn't he? She had felt safe in the strength of his arms. Nay! She had to remember that he was sending her away at first light. He cared not whether she lived or died. Protect her? Brynna laughed bitterly at herself. He would be the first one to throw her to the wolves.

She slammed the door shut to her room.

Unclasping the emerald brooch at her throat, she flung

her cloak across the room and threw herself on her bed. She hated him. She shook her head at the memory of Lady Tanith's laughter in the garden. Of course, her mother had been able to find the good in Lord Richard and come to love him. Brynna's father was a kind, honorable man. He was nothing like the heartless wretch downstairs. She should hate him. But the memory of Brand's passionate smile in the lake still haunted her.

God's mercy, he is real. His masculine scent clinging to her clothes attested to it. Against her will she remembered his armored chest cold against her face, hard and impenetrable just like his heart. And now she knew why.

"She was my whole life."

Torment, like ghostly echoes in an old battlefield, had permeated the air of the castle when the Norman warrior spoke of his love. Lord Brand had adored the woman in the lake. Brynna had seen it, had tried to forget it, but it was real. She pulled her pillow over her face trying to forget the images of the two in the lake, caressed by the kiss of summer. He had been so alive that day, but his heart was wrenched from his body, leaving him a cold remnant of who he once was.

But, Brynna told herself, his eyes were anything but cold when they gazed into hers. Warm concern and tender compassion had filled them. Could she penetrate his frigid defense, warm the heart of this warrior? She knew she must if she was going to remain at Avarloch . . . or if she ever wanted to feel his arms around her again.

Brand found Dante exiting a room on the second-floor landing not too far from the room where Brynna lay on her bed thinking of him at that moment. Like a small dark shadow, Alysia clung to Dante's arm and smiled up at him with a look of veneration lighting her face.

"Brand!" Dante blurted as if his brother were the last person he expected to see at Avarloch Castle.

Brand smiled softly at the flushed cheeks of the handmaiden when she spun around to face him. "I was just showing Sir Dante to his room," Alysia explained, avoiding Brand's gaze.

"Have you found a room for me yet, Alysia?" Brand asked gently.

Her swarthy complexion paled. "Nay, my lord, I . . . I . . ." She cast Dante a desperate look, but the handsome knight only smiled and lifted a finger to her dark hair.

"I'm afraid I have kept her from her duties, brother." Dante defended her, though he knew there was no need. Brand rarely grew angry with the serfs and vassals of Graycliff, and besides Alexander, Dante had never known of anyone punished or harmed while in his brother's service. Of course, Alysia didn't know what Dante knew. But at that moment, with Dante's smoky eyes and sultry smile directed at her, she forgot Brand was even standing next to her until Dante finally lifted his gaze from her.

"No matter, I'm sure there is a perfectly acceptable room for me. . . ."

"Oh!" the handmaiden gasped, breaking free of her trance. "Forgive me, I will show you to a room right away." She pushed past the two men and scurried down the long corridor, leaving Brand and Dante to exchange a quick grin behind her.

Alysia stopped at the end of the hall and swung open the heavy wooden door. "It belonged to Lord Richard's father. 'Tis the only room in the castle, besides Lord Richard's and Lady Brynna's, with a private bath."

"Perfect," Brand said, stepping past her to enter the chambers. "A bath was my next request."

"Shall I tend to you, my lord?" Alysia asked shyly, knowing her duties to the new lord. Though bathing Lord Brand would not be in any way unpleasant, the only man she wanted to tend to at that moment was Dante.

"Non." Brand answered casually, surveying the enormous room with king-size canopied bed and massive stone hearth. Against the west wall there stood a deep walnut wardrobe large enough to house every article of clothing he owned. A trestle table beside it was adorned with a thick vase of wild roses and a fine golden bowl for hand washing. There was an elegant screen reaching as high as Brand's shoulders concealing the private bath Alysia spoke of. The room was airy enough and would serve him quite well. With a nod that suggested his acceptance, Brand turned to Alysia again. "Have my things brought up and send someone to start the fire—and get rid of these flowers."

Alysia curtsied with lowered head and turned to leave, but Brand took two long strides and reached for her hand. "You do not have to curtsy every time I open my mouth." His smile eased the handmaiden's nerves. All the fretting she and the others had done was for naught, Lord Brand Risande was wonderful.

"Will there be anything else, m'lord?" she asked, eager to tell the others.

Brand released her hand and continued to investigate the room. *"Oui,* advise the cooks that I want the last meal served every evening one hour after sunset. I would like a cup of warm mead each morning." He paused, examining the roses that blossomed like hearts overflowing with promises of love. He swept his finger over a delicate petal, aching to breathe in its sweet, familiar scent. "And inform Lady Brynna that I would like to see her at my table."

Alysia's eyes lit up and Brand guessed that talk of whether or not Avarloch's lady would be thrown out was a deep concern to the people here. Either that, or the handmaiden had learned quite well how to eavesdrop from the lady of the house.

Unwittingly, he smiled at the memory of Brynna's spitfire tongue. Her father was right, she was a passionate woman, full of fire and life and . . . Quickly, he erased the thought of her from his mind. He would marry her if he must. He would take her to his bed. But he would never lose his heart to her.

He strode to the edge of the enormous bed and tested the down mattress with his fingers. "One more thing." He lifted his aqua gaze to the dark, exotic handmaiden. "Tell Duke William that I have requested your company in my bed this eve." He sat on the soft bed and removed his boots. He looked up again, registering her stunned silence. The curl of his lips assured her there was a reason for his words.

"Although he is married, the duke does enjoy his women and his wine—when he is not fighting, that is. He will request you tonight if I haven't already, and refusing the duke of Normandy would not be wise," Brand explained, rising from the bed once again. "Sleep where you will tonight, *ma cher,* but if you don't want it to be with Duke William, then you must tell him that you will be with me."

Alysia stared into her new lord's eyes unable to believe what she was hearing. Did he hold the feelings of a simple handmaiden so high that he would protect her from the warrior downstairs?

She curtsied for want of anything to say to express her gratitude and Brand sighed exhaustively, then smiled at Dante over her head.

Closing his arm around the young handmaiden, Dante escorted her out of the room.

The moment the door closed behind them, Alysia tugged on Dante's sleeve. "Will he accept Lady Brynna as his wife, then?"

"I don't know what he has decided yet, but I can't imagine him just throwing her out."

"Nay," Alysia agreed breathlessly. "He is wonderful, so kind and soft-spoken." How wrong they had all been to worry so.

"Alysia," Dante said softly, seeing the light of hope in her eyes. It was good that Brand would be liked here, but Dante did not want anyone in Avarloch to mistake Brand's kindness for weakness the way Alexander did. "My brother is a fair man. He demands respect and will give it in return. But tell the others that their new lord is a warrior above all else."

She nodded, looking at the door where, inside, the new lord of the castle was readying for his bath. She remembered the power in his honey-smooth voice and the fierce blazing in his eyes when she had first come upon him in the hall. "I will tell them, m'lord."

Dante cupped her chin in his hand and lifted her face to his. "I will see you this evening, at supper."

"Supper? Nay, I do not dine with . . ."

Dante nodded, stilling her words. "From now on, we all dine together."

Once again, Alysia's eyes gleamed. She offered him her most radiant smile, then ran, holding her skirts above her ankles down the stairs to inform the others.

Ten minutes later, five wooden chests of various sizes were delivered to Brand's room, as well as the water for his bath, which was hot enough to send silvery vapors whirling above the tub as it was poured.

Dante threw himself on Brand's bed after returning to have a word with his brother. "So what is the duke doing here?" he asked while Brand undressed and tossed his clothes onto the trestle table now bare of any flowers.

"Edward sent for him to convince me to marry Lady Brynna."

"And has he?"

"*Oui.* He commanded it." Brand ignored his brother's rueful smile and stepped behind the screen and into the tub. He slid down into the steaming water, threatening to send the water overflowing to the floor.

"My bed is not this comfortable." Dante frowned a moment later, kneading a pillow before resting his head on it.

"Strange," Brand called out as he began to soap his chest. "I was sure the handmaiden would have given you the most comfortable bed in the castle. Since, after all, she will be spending so much time in it," he added with a lazy smirk.

Dante opened his mouth to protect her honor, but then thought of Alysia's cool black hair spreading over her olive shoulders and decided that Brand was probably right, at least if Dante had his way. He folded his hands behind his head and sighed instead.

Brand laughed softly at the wistful sound and slid farther down in the water, submerging his head. He returned a moment later with a force that sent water flying.

"Tell me what you think of your bride-to-be," Dante asked him.

"I think she's got quite a tongue on her." Brand scooped up a handful of creamy soap scented with spice and lathered his black curls and face.

A slow, lazy grin spread over Dante's face. "A tongue can be quite an advantage to a man."

Brand stopped scrubbing for a moment, a certain image being conjured up in his mind by his brother's reply. He dunked his body under again, rinsing the soap from his head and trying to douse the fire that suddenly heated his blood.

The door to his room burst open. William towered in the doorway. The duke looked at Dante, who pointed to the screen.

William strode toward the barrier and knocked it away with a swipe of his hand. He stared down at Brand soaking in his bath. "I will give you ten men for the dark beauty Alysia!" the brutish Norman implored.

"*Non,*" Brand replied simply, stepping out of the steaming water. Water cascaded down his lean body and gathered in a puddle at his feet. He caught the drying towel Dante tossed him from the edge of the bed and cloaked his dripping torso.

A heavy frown creased the duke's face, making him look more like an agitated wolf than a pouting warrior. "An hour ago you did not want one woman, now you want two?"

"I did not want a wife, William," Brand reminded him,

sorting through one of the many chests he had brought with him from Graycliff Castle. "I never said anything about not enjoying a woman in my bed." He chose thick black hose and a long-sleeved dark blue shirt embroidered with golden swirls. He tossed the shirt onto the bed and pulled on his hose.

"Selfish bastard." William growled, allowing his defeat to come easily. He turned his attention to Dante, who was now sitting on the bed, smiling at the playful feud.

"Dante!" William rushed toward him; arms extended for a great bear-hug greeting that Brand's brother braced himself for. "*Merde,* you're twice as big as when you left Normandy! I should never have let you come to England to live with this rogue." William gestured with his chin toward Brand, who smiled, then threw his towel at him.

"Who else can teach me how to please two women at once?" Dante teased.

William cast him a shrewd smile and pounded him on the shoulder. "From what I've heard, there has been no shortage of women in your bed, Dante. *Oui,* your reputation with the fairer sex has reached even Normandy." He narrowed his eyes. "What are you now, twenty years?"

"Twenty and four."

"Ah, you are in your prime, son. Come back to Normandy with me and I'll give you your own harem. This one is twenty and eight and afraid to be wed."

"And you are too old to hear the mocking giggles of your harem wenches when you leave them," Brand countered.

"Look at him," William said with pity lacing his voice. He ignored Brand's insult while he shook his head at him.

"You call that muscle? Why, the legs of barn chickens have more muscle than you."

"They are strong enough to crush you under my feet, old man," Brand taunted cheerfully, realizing how much he had missed parrying with his dearest friend.

With one giant step William reached him again and tossed his arm around Brand's neck, stopping him like a linked iron chain when Brand tried to pull away. William grew serious suddenly, taking Brand's face in his huge hand. "I worry about you. You are like a son to me. At least your brother keeps his heart out of his pants."

"I'm fine," Brand assured him quietly.

William studied Brand for another moment, then slapped his cheek. "All right, then, marry the girl and give her many children, and if you ever need me, I will be at your side."

Brand bowed with genuine respect and affection. "Thank you, William." He smiled. "Now get out and let me get dressed. And take Dante with you."

"Very well, but I warn you, the next beautiful wench I see this night will be mine," William called out as he left, a massive arm thrown over Dante's shoulder.

When they were gone, Brand crossed his chambers and reached for his belt and scabbard. There came a knock at the door while he tied the heavy leather band to his waist. "Come," he called, barely looking up.

Brynna pushed open the door, but instead of stepping inside, she waited beneath the frame. Her eyes scanned the subtle changes Brand made in the room, then came to rest on him. Damn him, he had no right looking so brutally handsome and so alive in a room that held the memory of her dead grandsire for so long. And as if those blasted black glistening curls dangling over his eyes wasn't bad enough, the sight of his bare chest made her completely forget why she had come to his room in the first place. Her mouth went dry. He was still wet. Crystal droplets dripped down the smooth, sleek muscles of his arms and down his neck, forming a thin rivulet that drew her eyes farther down to his sculpted belly.

"Lady Brynna." He crossed the room and sat down on the bed. He reached for his boots and looked up at her again, finally realizing that she hadn't spoken a word yet. "It's nice to see you again," he offered, deciding to treat her more gently than he had when he arrived. After the way William had bellowed at her, she deserved a kinder tone.

"Is it?"

"Nice to see you?" He lifted an eyebrow while he pulled his boots on. She nodded, watching him so closely he thought she might be calculating the best angle in which to come at him with a dagger. His gaze fell to her hands. She held no weapon, but her fingers were clenched into fists. That made him smile, remembering the hellcat that attacked the duke of Normandy after he tricked her. "Why wouldn't it be?" he asked mildly.

She shrugged her delicate shoulders. "Because my hair is red, mayhap?"

Brand cast her a look before he stood to his feet again and snatched his shirt off the bed. "You have beautiful hair, lady. But what the hell does that have to do with anything?"

Brynna watched him while he dressed. She did her best to keep her voice steady, but the hard lines of his body muddled her thoughts. "I'm not leaving Avarloch," she blurted. He ran his hand through his wet curls to clear them from his face. Brynna licked her dry lips. "You—you cannot take everything from me and throw me out of the place I've lived my whole life."

"Can I at least convince you to step inside? You're drawing a crowd."

Brynna spun around and blushed at the servants huddling behind her. She shooed them away, entered the room, and slammed the door shut. "There," she fired at him. "Are you happy now?"

Brand leaned up against the hearth mantel and studied her. *Enfer,* but she was lovely. He never expected his prize to be such a fiery little hellwitch with eyes that promised sweet pursuits. He was enjoying the challenge that sparked her temper so much that he decided not to tell her just yet that she was staying. He gazed boldly over her body in the same way her eyes had surveyed him. He smiled when she blushed again, but his eyes revealed something far more feral than humor. "You have no relatives with whom you can live? A sister or brother? Aunt or—"

"I said I am not leaving Avarloch, you simpleton. Are you hard of hearing?"

Lord Brand took a step toward her. "You're cheeky for a woman with no choice."

The room grew smaller as he came closer. Brynna had the urge to draw her hand to her throat; he had the look of a wolf, dark and hungry for blood. "I have a choice, Lord Brand." Her heart pounded hard in her chest when he reached her. So close was he now that she could feel the warmth of his breath on her cheek. She looked at his chin rather than into those beautiful, deceptive eyes. But she quickly discovered her mistake when she noticed the sexy dimple in his chin. A dimple that accentuated his sinfully full lips.

"What choice is that?" His voice was low, husky, and infuriatingly arrogant.

Brynna braced herself and tipped her head back to meet his gaze. Her head spun and her breath grew heavy. When she'd seen him in the lake, she had been too captivated by his pleasure to realize the full impact of his features. His clean, male scent hadn't covered her the way it covered her now. When she spied on him, she had no idea of the sheer, dominating size of him and the effect it would have on her senses standing so close. She bit her lip, determined not to lose herself to a dream. This man was real, and he was going to make her leave her home. "I will fight you for Avarloch," she told him, managing to lift her chin in defiance of the power he had over her.

For a moment Brand looked too stunned to speak. Then he laughed right in her face.

"You rogue!" Brynna fumed at him. "You think because I'm a woman I cannot fight you? Sir Nathan thought the same thing until I smashed Aunt Gertrude's vase over his head and then he had a different tune to sing, I'll tell you that! You are no different than he. Why, you're nothing but a low—"

His arm snaked around her waist, snatching her clean off the floor.

"What do you think . . ." Brynna's eyes opened wide, but once again her words were halted, this time by a long, hard, demanding kiss that halted her breath as well.

"How dare you!" Brynna said with such gusto when

he withdrew, and after her head cleared, that he had no choice but to smile at her belligerence. "You knave!" His smile fanned her fury even more and she lifted her hand to strike him.

Brand caught her by the wrist, his blood fired up as well by her wonderful temper. Before she had time to wonder how she'd arrived there, her back was shoved against the door behind her. He yanked her wrist over her head, then brought the other one up to meet it. He didn't say a word, and it was worse than if he had. For he simply stared down at her with excitement lighting his eyes. His breath wasn't as heavy as Brynna's, but his mouth curved into a half smile so salacious and challenging, Brynna grew frightened. He moved up against her. His body hard and warm. His lips brushed her throat, as feathery and beguiling as a faerie's wings. When she groaned against his body, Brand dipped his mouth to hers and kissed her almost brutally, letting her taste the passion that still raged beneath his iron control.

When he withdrew, he did so only enough so that they still shared breath. His breath came as hard and heavy as hers now. Brynna licked her swollen lips and his eyes dipped there. He leaned down and brushed her lips with his, tasting her again and leaving his indelible mark on her.

Brynna stared into his eyes, breathless by the color and intensity. She would have staggered if she wasn't pressed so tightly against him. "You're despicable," she whispered.

"Surely, then"—his smoky baritone voice encased her like a warm mist—"you wouldn't want to remain at Avarloch with such a man."

"I could pretend you don't exist," Brynna promised, and then looked away from him when he lifted an eyebrow at her.

"Somehow I doubt that," he pointed out.

Brynna huffed at his arrogance and pushed away from him. He stepped back and watched her eyes blaze at him. "I am not leaving Avarloch, of that you can be sure. And if ignoring you does not work"—she lifted her lips in a wicked smile to match the one he was giving her—"I could just kill you in your bed."

Brand offered her a slow, heart-wrenchingly sensual grin. "That sounds very tempting."

Brynna blushed to her roots, realizing what he meant, and then yanked the door open and ran out of his room.

Brand thought her emerald eyes were filled with a fire matched only in their fury by his own, and her hair danced against the light like flames streaked with gold. Her jasmine scent on his tunic made him draw a deep breath. Lord Richard's daughter was delicate in his arms, passionate against his mouth, and Brand found himself savoring the thought of her body, soft yet unyielding. Her strength of spirit exhilarated him, sparked something within him that he had almost forgotten existed. He wanted her, but was she strong enough to have him? He knew that if he took her, it would be different than it had been with Colette. He would not be gentle. He would devour her until she was completely his, until she knew that no one else could fill her the way he could.

The more Brand thought about it, the more the idea of marrying Brynna Dumont appealed to him. She was certainly beautiful. Would he be making such a poor choice of brides with her? He didn't love her and he never would, but that was no reason to deny his body the exhilarating pleasure he felt when he kissed her, or the ache he felt when he had held her in his arms, an ache he had thought he would never feel again.

Chapter Seven

Brand stepped out of his room and shut the door softly behind him. When he looked up, he spotted Lord Richard heading for the stairs. He didn't know why William wanted the Saxon warrior to remain here, but he intended to find out. It was damned difficult having to cast a man from his home when the man was still in it. Even worse, Lord Richard was not just a warrior, but a father who was being torn away from his daughter. Tightening his jaw, Brand readied himself to the task of speaking to the seasoned commander.

"Lord Richard," he called out before the older knight reached the stairs. Brand quickened his pace a bit to catch up with him.

"Lord Brand." The two men regarded each other in silence for a moment before Brand spoke.

Brand was a bit taller and broader of shoulder than Brynna's father, but Lord Richard was no less imposing as he stood at the edge of the stairs, his hand resting comfortably on the hilt of his sword at his side.

"Your daughter will be staying here as my wife."

Richard blinked, then nodded slightly. "Brynna will be pleased that she will be allowed to remain at Avarloch."

Pleased, Brand thought. She will be pleased. It was not the reaction he had ever expected when he made a woman his wife, but why should it be anything else? She did not love him. They barely knew each other. As a matter of fact, he thought sourly, she wouldn't even *be* pleased. She was willing to become his wife to remain at Avarloch and to avoid bloodshed. He guessed that was as good a reason as any.

"I thought you didn't want a wife," Richard said, wondering, as he had for the last fortnight, if he should just take his daughter with him wherever God saw fit to lead him. It only took him an instant to decide. He was a soldier. Battle followed him like the wind. What kind of life could he give his daughter without even a home to rest her feet?

"I don't," Brand replied simply. "But the man I swore to obey wants me to have one. Your daughter also made it quite clear to me how much Avarloch means to her. I would be naught but a heartless savage to make her leave it. And I am not a savage."

Richard narrowed his eyes. After facing Lord Brand Risande in battle, Brynna's father had to disagree with that declaration. Would the Norman treat his daughter kindly? Richard wondered, searching Brand's eyes. Or was the dark knight letting him know that Brynna meant naught to him but a means to avoid another battle?

"Brynnafar is easy to love, Lord Brand," Richard declared softly, trying to contain the fear and anger he felt growing inside him. "As I am sure you will come to realize."

Brand's eyes were like endless seas when Richard looked into them. Emotions tossed about like waves battering Brand's heart. What was it? Richard beseeched silently. Why did the vastness in the Earl's gaze fill him with such unease, as though he was gazing into depth after depth of nothing but turquoise emptiness?

"I will never love her." Brand's reply was spoken with a haunting certainty that left Brynna's father cold. "I will not mistreat her or cast her out, but I will never love her."

"As you say." Richard's voice was barely a whisper. He looked away from the infinite emptiness staring back at him. Many fathers gave their daughters away for so much less than love, but Richard had wanted his only child to experience what he and his Tanith had shared. What fate was decided for his daughter when he had surrendered to this man? Without another word he stepped away from Brand and descended the stairs alone.

Watching him leave, Brand thought to go after him. He should say something more. He wanted to assure the dignified knight that his daughter would be safe here, but it was not enough, and Brand knew it. He clenched his jaw, restraining promises he knew he could not keep, and finally traced Richard's path to the great hall.

Brynna leaned against the wall and closed her eyes to stop the pounding of her heart. She had entered the hall moments after Brand called her father, and with only a faint trace of guilt, she had listened to their conversation. Now she was sorry she had. His vow had hit her like a blast of frigid air until she shivered from the hopeless echoes it carried with it. She thought after he kissed her that she might try to win his favor. She didn't need to. He was going to marry her. She should have been joyful that she was staying at Avarloch, ecstatic that she was going to be his wife. But he was being forced to marry her.

"I will never love her."

His promise charged through her like a sword, but, as was usually the case, Brynna's pride and hot temper were victorious over her heart. She straightened her shoulders and left the wall that seemed to be holding her up.

I will make you feel something, Lord Brand Risande. She was fuming. *There must be something you can still feel.*

With a new determination igniting a glint in her eyes, Brynna charged back into her room and pulled her tunic over her head. She tore her hose away and ran her fingers through her hair, sending shimmering cascades down her bare back. Rushing to the tall chest beside her bed, she smiled to herself as she slipped into a thin cotton chemise. She would make him feel something if it killed her. She remembered her merman and the man who had kissed her so thoroughly in his chambers. He might be a cold, ruthless warrior, but there was no shortage of sexual heat in the man. Of that, Brynna was certain. Aye, she knew exactly what that something should be.

The gown she chose was fashioned of turquoise silk so fine it looked as if it were spun by faeries. So rare was the silk that her father had nearly been killed for the skeins he had carried home from the Turkish lands of the Seljuks. Lady Tanith had fashioned the gown herself, delicately embroidering silver thread around the low-cut neckline and tapered cuffs. It flowed across Brynna's fingers as softly as a child's sigh. She slipped the gown over her head. Whispers that promised victory clouded her thoughts as silk clung to her breasts and buttocks in a thin, taunting layer that felt deliciously feminine. She moved, and the fabric seemed to breathe, pulsate, and beckon to be touched.

She brushed her long hair to a molten copper finish and wrapped it neatly in a silver netted veil that shimmered down her back.

Brynna wanted Brand to desire her, but she had no idea of the power she possessed, or the effect her raw beauty had on men. Her strong will and stubborn nature kept most suitors from courting her a second time. She rarely dressed to please. Since her father and his men were off fighting so much, there were few, if any, visitors at Avarloch. But now the halls were brimming with men, Norman and English alike. Brynna felt her cheeks flush when a Norman soldier, summoned from his duties for supper in the great hall, nearly walked straight into the wall when he saw her. Two of King Edward's knights stopped, frozen in their places, when she graced them with a smile and bid them good eve.

She looked down at herself twice before she reached the stairs, making certain nothing indecent was exposed. Satisfied that everything was in place, she shrugged her shoulders and made her way on light, slippered feet to the place where her newly betrothed would be waiting for her.

The great hall overflowed with people. Brynna had never seen so many Normans gathered in one place. They were loud and boisterous, and most looked drunk already, though the evening meal had just begun. She scowled while her eyes flitted around the room searching for the Norman's dark lord. She spotted Lord Brand sitting at the high dais, his cold, calculating gaze drifting over the hall taking in everything and everyone around him. Gone was the rhapsodic merman whose thick, rich laughter made even dogwood blossoms dance. The merman was gone, and in his place was a statue of a warlord carved from ice. And still, his beauty silenced her heart.

From the dais where he sat with Dante, Brand lowered a tankard of wine from his lips and stared at the breathtaking goddess who had just entered the hall. She moved, causing the silk that clung so delicately to her to brush against her soft curves underneath. Brand found his breath coming harder between clenched teeth. With ruthlessly feral eyes he watched the firm bounce of her breasts, the sensuous glide of the taut buds that pushed against two thin layers of gossamer fabric, the way her hips danced when she walked, taunting . . . promising. Fire burned, igniting raw desire in him as the thin silk caressed her. Silk that would tear easily at his touch.

One of King Edward's knights moved in front of Brynna, blocking Brand's view. Cursing tightly under his breath, Brand tried to recall the name of the rogue.

". . . like him." Dante leaned forward in his chair, studying the knight who was speaking to Brynna.

"What?" Brand asked his brother, coming out of the heated spell he had fallen into.

"The knave speaking to Lady Brynna," Dante repeated. "I don't like him."

"Why not?" Brand strained to see past the dozens of serfs and squires obscuring his view. He caught a glimpse of Brynna's sleeve and then her shoulder behind the dark English knight. It looked to Brand as if she was trying to pass him, but was unable.

"This afternoon, after you left her outside, he was watching her in a way that I have seen before," Dante told Brand.

Brand said nothing but turned to Dante with narrowed, lethal eyes. "Where have you seen it before?"

"In Alexander." Dante regretted his words as Brand rose slowly from his chair, his eyes, like blue-green glaciers, on the man now clutching Brynna's arm.

"I'll be right back," Brand announced with a growl.

He cut through the crowd like a wolf stalking its prey, slowly, carefully, and with a single purpose. He watched, with an intensity that deepened his aqua eyes to flame blue, every movement the English knight made. Stepping around knights and ladies, who were neither seen nor heard by him, Brand finally stood only inches away from Brynna. He could hear the stinging venom in her voice, the harsh snap of her words as she warned the knight to let her pass. And he saw the surprise and relief in her eyes when she spotted him over the knight's shoulder.

Sir Luis saw the surprise as well and turned just as Brand stepped around him to stand at Brynna's side.

"Ah, Lord Brand." Edward's knight greeted him cheerfully, deceived by Brand's serene smile. "The lady and I were just discussing you."

Brynna almost staggered backward when Brand turned his radiant smile on her. It was not his startling beauty that made her heart falter, but the unrelenting frost in his eyes that no smile, no matter how luminous, could conceal. So close to him, she felt the menace of his big, powerful body and she shook from it.

"Lady," Brand's voice dripped like sweet acid as he laced her hand through his arm, "what is this rogue's name?"

For the space of a single breath, Brynna stared into Brand's eyes. Fear shot through her, coiling her nerves, and suddenly she understood how this man could have defeated her father.

"He is Sir Luis of—"

"I am one of King Edward's royal knights," Luis interrupted. A mixture of shock and anger now replaced the smile he had offered Brand a moment earlier. "I am no rogue, sir, and I take offense at being called one."

Brand's lips curled into a grin of such savage hunger, his betrothed feared he might leap at Sir Luis's throat in the next instant. "It's better that I call you a rogue than a corpse, is it not?" Brand asked smoothly, then waited with dreadful patience while Sir Luis shifted uneasily and wiped the tiny beads of moisture from his forehead.

"Are you threatening me, sir?" Luis asked. The confidence he usually spoke with had faded into a weak whisper.

"Non," Brand uttered softly as though he felt sorrow for the man who stood before him. "If you touch Lady Brynna again, I will kill you. That is a fact."

Luis's dark eyes shot to Brynna, disbelief sweeping across his face.

"Do not look at her!" Brand snapped sharply, his anger now fully unleashed.

Brynna's face paled. Her hands trembled at the suppressed violence he no longer bothered to conceal. She was afraid to look at him, knowing his smile was vanished. She did not want to see what replaced it.

Sir Luis, on the other hand, found it impossible to look anywhere else. The piercing, terrifying promise of violence in Brand's eyes held him paralyzed; Luis was afraid even to open his mouth in defense.

"Know this," Brand warned with a growl, inching closer to Luis. "No one will be able to save you if you go near her again, not even your king will stop me. I vow it." His eyes were as hard as granite, daring the English knight to challenge him. When no challenge came, Brand closed his hand over Brynna's and led her away without another word.

Gripped with fear that nearly paralyzed her steps, Brynna's gaze swept over the strong fingers tenderly covering her own. She was acutely conscious of the gentle pressure Brand applied and the tremor that coursed through her body when he ran the pad of his thumb over her skin, as though testing its texture. Suppressing a sudden urge to sigh, she wondered how his touch could be so like a caress just a moment after he was willing to kill with this same hand. She shivered from the chill that danced up her spine.

Still afraid to see the fury in his crystalline gaze, but aching to look at him, Brynna slanted her eyes slowly, cautiously, toward his face. His gaze was set straight ahead to the table where Dante sat waiting for him. Only a trace of the fire that had darkened his eyes remained. She studied him. Her gaze lingered over curls blacker than a starless sky, yet as luminous as moonlight upon the sea. His brow and torturously long lashes were just as dark, casting shadows into his eyes.

Shadows that whisper for me to peer closer into them, to find the light that once set him ablaze with rhapsodic ecstasy.

Forgetting her fear now, she drank in the strong lines of his Norman nose, the hard angles of his jaw where faint dark-colored shadows remained, no matter how closely he shaved. The relaxed line of his lips was decadently full and inviting. She sighed looking at him, and remembering the way he had kissed her. He was a beautiful, dark warrior. A warrior who could change his appearance with a simple smile and become an angel.

Cool, deep eyes regarded her when Brynna lifted her gaze from his lips. She almost smiled, lost in the feral, yet strangely poignant, beauty of him. She caught herself quickly and looked away, but not before a warm flush raced across her cheeks. How long had he been watching her drink him in? Was it amusement she saw in his eyes, or tenderness? Brynna tried to pull her hand away but he coiled her arm more securely around his own.

"You look even more beautiful tonight," Brand said suddenly, setting his gaze straight ahead once again.

More beautiful? Brynna thought, letting herself look at him again, but only for an instant. "Thank you, m'lord." She smiled, pleased after all that she had chosen this gown to wear. "You are not going to force me to kiss you again, are you?" she added with a spark of Dumont fire glinting her eyes.

Brand snorted and tilted his head to look at her. "Force? Mademoiselle, if I recall, you were as eager for my kiss as I was to give it."

"You recall incorrectly, m'lord," she replied insolently.

When they reached the table, Dante rose from his chair and was promptly offered Brynna's hand for a kiss, which he gave her tenderly while lifting an eyebrow enviously to his brother.

"I have informed the king that I will marry you," Brand said, pulling out a chair for Brynna beside his. "So you will be sitting with me from now on."

Brynna froze at the arrogance in his voice. Fool! She had almost forgotten what a cad her merman had turned out to be. She turned away from Dante to glare at her newly betrothed, her eyes ablaze.

"I am humbled by your graciousness, m'lord," she

seethed, offering him a slight bow. "But since *I* was not informed of your kindness, I already made arrangements to sit with my father." The challenge in her scalding gaze pierced his, and she realized just how quickly the luminous depths of his eyes could shift from flame to frost. She didn't care. Fear did not exist in her when anger charged through her veins, as it did now. How could she have wasted so many nights dreaming of the beast?

"What you decide is of little importance to me, lady," Brand said coolly. "My wife will sit with me at my table."

"Until I *am* your wife," Brynna countered just as coolly. "I will sit where I please." She stood defiant, ready to battle him.

But the battle was over before it had begun. Brand smiled and stepped aside to let her pass on her way back to her father.

Recognizing that his smile was his most disarming weapon, Brynna hesitated for a moment before leaving him. Would he kick her in the backside as she left? Gut her with another one of his merciless statements while she stormed away?

Oh, but he was more gallant than that she quickly learned. Sweeping his arm across his waist, he offered her a clear path to take. "You are free to go to your father," he said with icy contempt lacing his chivalrous offer. "Leave with him too . . . if you so wish."

Fury swept over Brynna as she whipped past him. If the fate of Avarloch were not at stake, she would march upstairs to her chambers, pack away her belongings, and leave with her father. Even living with her uncle and cranky Sir Nathan would be better than spending another moment with Brand. She wanted to laugh at herself, but a sob rose in her throat. She couldn't leave. No matter what kind of inconsiderate ogre moved in. She loved Avarloch and everyone in it. She wanted to love the man from the lake, but he was gone. Just as her father would be gone. She couldn't lose her home as well.

Left alone to stare after her, Brand ripped his chair from its place under the table with such gusto it nearly flew out of his hand.

"I see what you mean about her tongue." Dante carefully hid the humor in his voice as Brand sat down next to him. "She will make an interesting wife."

"If I don't have her flogged first," Brand threatened, and took a slow swallow of his wine. His eyes followed Brynna over the rim of his goblet.

"She's playing with you." William slid into the chair that should have been Brynna's.

"I know." Brand growled and his gaze on Brynna hardened as she bent to kiss her father.

"She is . . . *magnifique*." The duke sighed dreamily, dropping his chin into his hand. "And from the choice of dress she wore tonight, I think she will be a willing bride."

"Games can be dangerous." Brand fumed without taking his eyes off her. "At this moment I don't care if she's willing or not."

There came a loud crack of laughter from the man seated beside him, and then a sharp slap on the back. "Good," William cajoled. "She has got you panting already."

The duke rose from his seat, still chuckling, but Brand did not watch his friend leave. Blazing, hot fury filled him with each moment that passed. He should not have allowed her to go. Her place was beside him and now he looked like a fool sitting next to an empty chair. He would let her have her victory tonight, but it would be her last.

Brynna could feel Brand seething from where he sat, and she was quite pleased with herself. But when she tilted her head over her shoulder to glance at him, she noted his anger had changed. A masculine calculation gleamed in his eyes and made her uneasy. Tightly coiled energy made his muscles ripple beneath the blue linen of his shirt. He looked like a hunter ready to eat her alive.

Brynna squared her shoulders but looked away from the strength of his gaze.

The food was finally served, and Brynna watched in astonishment as serfs broke bread with the knights and nobles.

Was this the act of a cold man?

"What is he doing, Father?" Brynna asked, leaning in close to Lord Richard's ear.

"Lord Brand made the announcement before you arrived," her father replied, ripping at his bread. "Everyone will be dining together from now on." Lord Richard looked up briefly at Brand, but the new lord of Avarloch was not in his seat. Richard shrugged. "I told you he was odd."

Brynna thought it was a marvelous idea. Most of these people were her friends, men and women whose company she enjoyed for many years. Gerald, the gardener, sat opposite her and Brynna gave him a warm smile. Dennis and Peter, the stable hands, were there, along with Blythe and Lily, her handmaidens. They were all here, some looking uncomfortable in their chairs, while others smiled and laughed with the knights as they ate. Brynna's eyes scanned the room, smiling at the many familiar faces. When her gaze came to rest on the dark sneer of Sir Luis, she looked away, momentarily sorry that she had left Brand's side.

Thinking of him, she could not stop her eyes from returning to the dais. She was surprised to find Brand's chair empty. She looked around the hall and found him leaning over her handmaiden Rebecca's chair. One of his hands was planted on the table in front of her while the other hand rested on the girl's back. . . . Over hair as pale as an angel's wings, Brynna thought bitterly. His head was bent to the beautiful maiden and Brynna cursed herself for not looking away when Rebecca giggled at something he said. He moved to Alysia's chair next. He leaned close to her ear to tell her something and both the new lord of Avarloch and Brynna's dearest friend turned to watch Dante making his way toward them with a half a pheasant in one hand and his goblet in the other. Brand smiled at what seemed to be some secret jest he shared with Alysia. He turned to look at the duke of Normandy next and laughed quietly.

Everything in the room changed for Brynna in that moment. His laughter was warmth caressing her, that siren song that drew her to him a year before. The chill vanished from Avarloch Castle. For a moment her merman had returned. But now he was quiet, shy, and intriguingly sensual. The hard lines of his face flowed into an amused smile that made him appear almost tender and undefended. His luminous beryl eyes transformed him. Pure, masculine innocence poured forth from his gaze, from his guileless smile. Brynna sat completely mesmerized by his radiance, as did every other woman in the great hall, not excluding Alysia, whose dark olive skin blushed an even darker shade of burgundy when he turned his smile back on her.

Brynna curled her fingers into her palms. Was this what her life would be like? Cursed with a husband who cast his breathtaking grin on the handmaidens of the castle while his wife sat a few feet away? Unwittingly, Brynna slapped her palms against the table; then she pushed her chair out from under her and stood up.

When she rose, Brand lifted his gaze to look at her and Brynna glared at him. She bid her father a hasty good night before she stormed toward the doors to leave.

Was she some beast of burden not even worthy of a smile, a tender look? Surprisingly, the barbarian *was* capable of human emotions, just not for her.

Suddenly a hand shackled her wrist, stopping her progress to the stairs.

"Where are you going?" Brand's voice was harsh against her ear as he spun her around.

"To—my—room." She bit off each word with bitter contempt.

His fingers tightened around her wrist, his eyes seared into her flesh like burning coals. "You already left me to sit alone after I informed the king of our marriage. You will not leave the dining hall now as well."

"You informed the king. Did informing me ever cross your mind?"

"Why should it?" Brand arrogantly arched an eyebrow at her. "It is your duty."

"Aye." Brynna's gaze met his with matched strength. "It is." Then she smiled grimly. "Pity for me that I shall never love you."

For an instant Brand wanted to smile at her audacity.

She had eavesdropped again when he had spoken with her father earlier, and now she wanted to win the battle. He was amused at the daring look she cast him and decided to play her game a little longer.

Pride. Fire. Beauty.

He remained quiet for a long time, studying her with a predatory curiosity Brynna now recognized and braced herself against.

"It's better with no love between us, Brynna," he finally said. "We will both be much happier."

Brynna's cheeks burned. Why was she so hurt by his blasted promise not to love her? "Take your hands off me, Lord Brand," she shot back hotly, gathering what was left of her pride. "My handmaiden awaits you, go to her."

Looking away, Brynna ached not to feel the strength of his hand any longer. She longed to be as cold and numb as he was. But from the moment she first saw the hunger for life sparking his sea blue eyes, giving music to his deep laughter, Brynna knew she could fall in love with him. She had dreamed of him for over a year, wished with all her heart that it was her he held that day in the water. She never expected to see him again and she had accepted it. It would have been better if she never had. There was no way to reach him. Aye, his kiss was passionate, but it meant naught to him but a way to show her that he was in control. She would spend the rest of her life with a man who cared not whether she lived or died. And suddenly, for the first time since her mother died, Brynna felt a deep well of sadness overwhelm her. She had dreamed of his smile, fallen under a spell that day as she watched him swim. But fantasies were for children, and the dream was over.

Brand narrowed his eyes on her, tilting his head as if trying to read her. The soft tremble of her lower lip told him the battle was finished for now. Brynna's defeat was real. And seeing it, Brand's defenses fell. It was not this fair maiden's doing that he was being forced to marry her. It was not she who deceived him. She was caught in the middle of Edward's treachery, the same way her father was, the same way he had been caught in it. She was innocent, but she was willing to fight him for her home. He recalled her promise when William tricked her into thinking that Avarloch would be burned to the ground if he didn't marry her. She was willing to become his wife and bear his children. Her sacrifice drew him, not to mention those lips he found himself aching to kiss again.

"Lady?"

"What?" She blinked her eyes slowly, looking toward the people inside the great hall instead of at him.

He caught her chin in his fingers and angled her head to examine her face. "I request that you stay at Avarloch and be my wife. What say you?" The tenderness in his voice pulled Brynna's eyes back to him, shock and amazement parting her lips.

The brilliant gaze that met and captured hers was alive with emotion. Human, wonderful emotion. Brand seemed to be set ablaze with light, not just the hunger she had seen in his eyes when he kissed her earlier, but radiant emotion. His eyes were seas of passion, inviting and serene. Sorrow, joy, anguish, compassion, fury, and a lustful hunger so powerful that it emanated from his every pore. And there was something else, a mere shadow of what used to give life to all these emotions. But it was there, waiting in the darkness, waiting to be set free.

"Aye." The word rolled off Brynna's tongue breathlessly. "I will be your wife."

She had glimpsed beyond the darkness of the thing that was trying to destroy him. What had changed for him in this one passing moment? She had just seen his heart when he asked her to be his wife and her nerves were still tingling. She smiled because there was some light still left in him.

Brand ran his fingers lightly down her arm to her hand, lacing his much larger fingers through hers. Brynna's body jolted at his tender touch as though he were made of lightning. She had dreamed for so long of just touching him. She had dreamed that it was her being loved so passionately by a man so charged with life.

Slowly, thoughtfully, he bent his head forward, parting his full lips. God help her, he was about to kiss her again, and this time she was ready for it. Unable to resist, Brynna watched him until she could feel the warmth of his breath on her face. His tongue slid across her lips just before he captured her gasp with his mouth. Her spine melted. He pulled her closer and her legs grew weak as his kiss became more passionate. In the space of each new breath, his tongue searched more longingly, drank her in more deeply, while his arms snaked around her waist, pulling her closer still until she felt completely and utterly consumed by him. He flooded her senses. She could hear him breathing, smell the earthy scent that clung to him, taste the wine that sweetened his breath. She was being swept away, drowning in the endless waves that were Brand's passions until she ceased to know herself, and knew only him.

When he finally withdrew, she felt more alone than

ever before. He claimed her with his kisses, both passionate and meaningful, and she knew that she would never feel complete again unless she belonged to him.

He laughed softly at the dreamy smile she wore. The sound was like his voice—low, silky, and very male. "What?" he asked when she bit her lower lip.

"You are smiling at me." Brynna blushed. "It's the first time you have smiled at me without some other meaning hidden behind your eyes."

"I don't believe my eyes hid the fact that I wanted to kiss you earlier," Brand said deeply. He lifted his hand to her hair and fingered the copper strands, unable to help himself. "But I will admit if I had known how beautiful happiness looked upon your face, I would have asked you to marry me sooner."

This is who he is, Brynna told herself, remembering what she had seen in his face at the lagoon, what it was that made her want to know him. He was fire, uncontainable, insuppressible, and passion the thing he hungered for, devouring it insatiably, always wanting more, needing it to survive. What had happened to him? Sadness washed over Brynna's face and she reached out to touch his smile.

"What did she do to destroy you so?"

Her hand stopped before she reached his lips. For Brand's smile had vanished, just as the light that had burned in him for a few moments was now extinguished, leaving only shadows behind.

"She made me love her," Brand answered quietly.

Chapter Eight

Brand escorted Brynna back to his table, where she agreed to sit for the rest of the night. He announced their betrothal to everyone in the great hall and there was a chorus of toasts from Brand's knights, as well as from William's and Edward's men. But Brynna was sure the people of Avarloch cheered the loudest.

She took her seat beside him, and though she did not see any part of him that resembled affection again that eve, her betrothed's mood had definitely brightened. He cheered when Dante challenged Sir Henry LeForre, a high knight in William's guard, to a game of who could drink the most ale and still throw a dagger twenty feet at the makeshift target set up by William. Brand lifted his goblet in a silent toast graced by a carefree, luminous grin to a victorious Dante sometime later. After that, Brand moved around the hall talking quietly to almost every person present on his first night as Avarloch's lord. While he spoke to his new vassals, his eyes found Brynna's on more than one occasion to share a quiet glance and a quick, sensuous smile that made her heart falter every time she saw it.

"It seems you will be well accepted by my people,

Lord Brand," Brynna told him when he finally made his way back to the table sometime later. He sat beside her as she cast her sharp gaze over the endless faces that filled Avarloch's great hall. "Especially by the handmaidens. Alysia, most obviously," she added, noticing how the maiden smiled shyly when the new lord looked at her.

Amusement made Brand's eyes dance when he cast Brynna a long, sideward glance. "Alysia's eyes follow my brother only."

Brynna doubtfully lifted an eyebrow. "Is that why she smiles at you that way?"

Brand's gaze settled squarely on hers for a moment, just a pause that showed his surprise; then one corner of his mouth lifted with mirth. "Jealousy is hard to see in your beautiful green eyes, lady."

"I assure you I am not jealous!" Brynna huffed indignantly. "I have no reason to be."

"*Non,* you don't." He turned completely in his chair to face her fully, the fierceness of his gaze softened only by his satin voice. "I will make sure there is never a reason for you to find pleasure in the bed of another." His eyes raked over her like waves in a tempest sea and Brynna wasn't sure if she should smile or fear this man who would be her husband. His voice was deep, smooth, and filled with a hunger that sent its scorching breath across her breasts and then downward, igniting tiny fires within her. The heat was familiar to her, having felt it whenever she remembered him. *Surely this man can be gentle when he chooses to be,* Brynna told herself. But he was gentle with the serfs as well. He was gentle with those who wanted naught from him but a place to live and food to fill their bellies. As long as one did not ask for his heart in return, Lord Brand Risande would be the perfect lord of Avarloch.

Could she live her life with him knowing he would never love her? And what about sharing his bed? The thought of it thrilled Brynna and terrified her. Brand's alluring promise to please her in bed did little to assure her that he wouldn't give the same pleasure to any woman who offered herself to him. Brynna was surprised at the depth of her anger over that idea. She would never tolerate a mistress. Her father never kept one, but then, Lord Richard had loved his wife. Dear God, what if she fell in love with the scoundrel? Brynna shook her head slightly and chastised herself for entertaining such childish notions of love. But even as she did, the memory of being in Brand's arms invaded her thoughts, and she knew that loving him would never be enough. She wanted to be loved by him as well.

Brand rose from his seat, looking past Brynna to William, who was signaling for Brand to join him at a long table besieged by drunken Norman guards. Brand nodded reluctantly, then sat back down and sighed looking at Brynna.

"I am needed," he said earnestly.

Brynna couldn't help but smile. She wanted to tell him that indeed he was. "Of course, m'lord," she answered instead.

For a moment she thought he had changed his mind and would stay. For he moved closer to her, so slightly that if she hadn't been watching him with such intensity she would not have noticed.

"Excuse me, then, fair lady," he whispered, and as he stood to leave, Brynna understood why he had moved closer. He intended to leave her fighting to control the shiver that washed over her spine when his breath touched her and the scent of him filled her lungs. He wanted her to ache to have him closer, feel the heat that flowed from his body and reached her.

Studying his gait as he walked to where William sat with men who looked as savage as the duke himself, Brynna decided that everything about Lord Brand Risande was sensuously masculine, even the sorrow he tried so hard to conceal.

It would do no good to dwell on any of it now, she decided, then turned to gaze out at the many faces who filled Avarloch's hall. Knights, vassals, and serfs alike were out of their chairs mingling. Laughter echoed in the great hall, filling Brynna with a sense of wonder at what the new lord of Avarloch had done. Serfs usually fought for their lords in battle, but it was only out of necessity, to remain under the lord's protection in time of need. Looking around, Brynna realized that soon the men of Avarloch would follow Brand out of loyalty and love. Every moment another face searched the new lord out, smiling brightly when their eyes met his. He made them equals here, respected each man whether knight or serf, and his respect would be returned.

Brynna spotted her father standing with one of his knights in the far corner of the hall and rose from her seat to go to him. Even here, among the king and his company, even among the savage knights of Normandy, Lord Richard Dumont stood out from among the rest. Avarloch was still his, if only for a few more nights.

"Brynnafar." Her father offered her a warm smile while holding his hand out to receive her when she reached him.

He turned to the knight at his side who studied Brynna with a long, measuring smile. "That will be all, Eldred," Richard barked with a hovering glare.

When the knight was gone, Brynna's father offered her a dark scowl. "That gown could prove dangerous for you, daughter."

Brynna touched her father's arm, easing the small lines around his eyes. "Fear not, Father. With you here to protect me, no man would dare cause me harm."

Tender emotion played across her father's handsome face, reminding Brynna that she was about to lose the only man who would ever love her. Sorrow claimed her suddenly, clawing at her throat with warm fingers, threatening to choke her until nothing remained of her but a flood of tears. "I will miss you terribly," she said in a voice plagued with grief.

With a sigh that burdened Brynna's heart even further, her father drew her into his arms and stroked the back of her netted hair. "And I will miss you, my dear, dear Brynnafar," he told her. He withdrew from their embrace to look at her. "But we must remain strong. A new fate calls to us, daughter, and we must embrace it, not fight it."

"But where will you go?"

He turned his head in the direction of William's table, glancing briefly at the small congregation of men sitting together. "Brynna." Lord Richard stepped away from his daughter and held her at arm's length. When he spoke, he looked directly into her eyes, calling for her attention and her understanding. "Duke William has offered me a place among his men. He is discussing the arrangements right now with Lord Brand."

Confusion shadowed Brynna's emerald eyes as she

searched her father's face. "You're going to Normandy?" she asked quietly, bringing her hand to her chest when he nodded. Her eyes grew large with tears. "I thought you would remain in England, Father."

It had been difficult enough being the daughter of a warrior, waiting and praying while he went off to battle that he would return to her and her mother. He always had. Now he was going to Normandy and she might never see him again. "What else will the Normans take from me?"

"Brynnafar." Her father's eyes glistened against the soft firelight of the hearth. His voice was low, deep, and broken with sadness. "Norman rogues killed your mother. 'Tis wrong to hate them all."

"But, Father, I don't—"

"Your mother taught me forgiveness. My people ravaged the Celts, destroyed whole villages, took what did not belong to them and did what they wanted with it all. We made them our servants. Your mother hated me at first because of what I was, but she understood after a time that I had naught to do with what happened to her people. She was able to love me. We cannot grow cold toward all because of what a few have done." Tears fell down Brynna's cheeks and her father wiped them with the back of his fingers. "Lord Risande is an honorable man, Brynna. That is more important than what country he came from or whose blood flows in his veins."

Laughter erupted from William's table and Brynna lifted her head to behold the man she was going to wed.

"Mother would have liked him, I think." She gazed at the knight. "Everyone here seems to like him."

Her father agreed, following her gaze. "He is lethal on

the battlefield, but he is spoken of very highly at Graycliff Castle in Dover." Richard returned his gaze to his daughter and smiled softly. "You will learn to love him as your mother learned to love me."

Brynna wanted to ask her father, what would become of her if her love was never returned? How could she tell him that she spied on a man swimming naked, that she grew captivated by the love he shared with another woman? And even if her father was not shocked by her scandalous behavior, how could she admit to him that she wanted to be loved by Lord Brand the Passionate?

"I know my duty; I always have," she said. There was no point in telling her father what troubled her. Lord Brand the Passionate no longer existed. She sighed, then managed a smile for her father. "Good heavens, you're going to be a Norman!"

Her father chuckled softly. "Fighting on William's side will not change who I am. And besides, Edward is not well and I've a feeling Harold will vie for the throne when the king dies. You know how I feel about Harold."

"Aye. I just want you to be happy."

"I will be," Lord Richard reassured her. "William is a great warrior. My only regret is that I will not be able to see my daughter."

"As is mine, Father." Brynna watched Brand and William together and motioned to her father to look at them. "Mayhap we will not be apart as much as we fear. They are great friends. I imagine the duke of Normandy will visit Avarloch often. A fact I was not pleased with . . . until now."

"Then let us hope that Lord Brand finds the arrangement agreeable as well."

"What does it matter if he agrees or not?" Brynna's eyes changed from quiet resignation to flashing indignation. "Has he not taken enough from you already? Why should he have any say in your future?"

"He wouldn't if I chose to go anywhere but Normandy," her father explained. "'Tis a code of honor, Brynnafar. Some men would take offense to their lord if he hired someone they had defeated in battle."

Brynna listened with one eye on the two men now approaching, the scruffier of the two with his muscular arm tossed around his friend's shoulder.

Brand's eyes never left Brynna, and the closer he and William came to her, the more arrested he became by her beauty. Her hair, encased in the gossamer silver net, cascaded down her back in thick waves of russet, bright gold, and traces of brown. Soft copper curls ended where the sensual curves of her buttocks began. Silken threads of silver and gold softly framed the contours of her face making her straight nose softer, her defiant chin more compliant, and her eyes greener than spring unleashed. He watched her with a gaze that burned, and when William finally slapped Lord Richard on the back upon reaching him, Brand offered his betrothed a smile that revealed his silent thoughts and made her blush to her roots.

"Well, Lord William, which way do I travel when I leave Avarloch?" Richard asked boldly.

"Toward Normandy of course!" William's grin was as wide as his shoulders and Brynna almost smiled looking at him. Then she remembered the cruel joke he had played on her earlier and she turned away from him to kiss her father.

"This is what you want. I am happy for you, Father."

"Of course," William taunted with a quick wink to Lord Richard, "we will have to take two of your fingers—your being a Saxon and all."

Clenching her teeth, Brynna pinned the knavish duke with a scathing stare. Her voice sliced sharp through the air. "You waste your pathetic humor trying to intimidate me, Your Grace. Your cruel jests about my home and my father's well-being prove you naught but a cad. Aye, and a tiresome cad at that!"

Lord Richard Dumont stood frozen in his spot, his mouth slack against his chin. Brand lowered his head to hide the deep grin and quiet amazement he wore on his face. And William, the savage duke of the Normans, stared, stricken with awe and admiration at the fiery woman before him. His voice was deep and wistful when he spoke to her.

"You are an incredible woman."

Brand's shoulders shook softly and Brynna knew he was laughing. She almost stomped her foot. She was too angry to speak so she spun on her heel, storming out of the great hall for the second time that night.

Brand did not follow her, elbowing William in the side instead, while trying to contain the laughter he was sure offended her father. "Bastard," he whispered to William, then grew serious quickly when he looked at Lord Richard. "The duke is completely void of morals. Are you sure you wish to go with him?"

Lord Richard was still too stunned by his daughter's dangerous outburst to reply, but William patted him on the back to reassure him that he was not angry. "I'm afraid I have had a little too much fun at your daughter's expense, but she is quite remarkable. Was her mother the same?"

"Aye, she was." Richard drew in a great cleansing breath and let it out slowly, watching the path his daughter took out of the great hall. "She was."

"Then you are a man truly blessed by God," William said in a low voice made serious by the tales he knew to be true of the crazed Saxon noble who massacred the men responsible for murdering his wife three years earlier.

"You told me your wife was killed, Sir Richard," Brand said, touched by the quiet sorrow in Richard's eyes. "Did you ever find out who it was that took her from you?"

"Aye." Brynna's father said, glancing at William. They had agreed not to tell Brand how Lady Tanith Dumont died, fearing he would use Brynna's hatred for Normans as an excuse not to marry her. It no longer mattered.

William placed his large hand on Richard's shoulder, but his steely gray gaze was set on Brand. "We did," he answered quietly, and then walked away.

❋

Brynna had almost made it to her room when she stopped dead. Sir Luis stood in her path, a smile as dark as midnight contorted his face.

"It would appear that your gown did the trick, my lady. Your Norman will not go into battle after all." While he spoke, his eyes washed over her breasts with a hunger that made Brynna want to slap his face.

"Step aside, sir," she warned him through clenched teeth.

Sir Luis obliged, clearing her path. But as she passed

him, he spoke again. "Pity your handmaiden will know Lord Brand the Passionate before you do."

Brynna stopped and whirled around to face him. "What do you mean?"

"Alysia." A smile that looked more like a sneer hovered at one end of his mouth. The stench of sour ale seemed to ooze from every pore. As if to reaffirm why he disgusted her so thoroughly, Luis wiped a drop of spittle off his lips with the back of his hand. "She was overheard telling the duke of Normandy that she could not visit his bed tonight because the new lord had requested her in his."

"You lie!" Brynna snapped, but she was already remembering the way Brand had leaned over Alysia's chair, smiling so tenderly. "Nay," she blurted out, dismissing the image. "Alysia fancies Sir Dante."

"His brother had better watch his back in that case." Luis snickered. "Sir Alexander LaRouche, a dear friend of your lord Risande, felt the cold steel of a blade through his heart when he took what Risande wanted. Your betrothed cares for no one. He kills friends and enemies alike."

"Nay." Brynna twisted her hands through her gown. None of this was true. Why was she even listening to this scoundrel? "You are a liar!" She took a step closer, gritting her teeth at him. "I warn you, Sir Luis, if you come near me again, I will go to the king."

Luis shrugged coolly. "Do what you wish. But while you're filling the king's ears, your betrothed will be filling your handmaiden with his seed."

"It matters not. I don't care what he does," Brynna retorted hotly. Her insides churned, her nails dug into the skin of her palms, but she would not let the rogue see her pain. "I would still rather give my body to Brand after he has had a hundred of my handmaidens than give it to you."

Brynna gave the knight a tight smile and escaped to her room. Fury boiled her veins by the time she threw herself on her bed. Alysia! Her dear friend of all people! Oh, how could she have believed Brand? She'd seen his tender smiles aimed at her sultry handmaiden, their secret whispers, and at poor Dante's expense. Did Brand and Alysia laugh at her as well? Would they be laughing tonight when he took Alysia to his bed? How could she have been so weak to fall under the rogue's spell again? She shook her head frantically, driving the image of his sensual smile away. Did he really kill his friend? Nay, her mind rebuked the idea. Luis was a liar. He had to be. It would mean that the man she remembered was truly just a dream, that the man she was going to marry was a cold, calculating, emotionless barbarian who killed his own friends. But her father had warned her that the Norman was dangerous. He had told her Brand's angelic smile was misleading. And she had seen it firsthand. How could she have been so daft? He must not have loved the woman in the lake either. Surely he cast his beguiling spell on her as well.

But I saw it. I saw his love for her.

There had to be an explanation for all of this. Brynna refused to doubt what she had seen that day. She could not allow herself to doubt it. Her marriage would be completely hopeless if she did. She sprang from her bed and raced for the door. She had to talk to him, ask him about Alysia and this "friend" he supposedly had killed. She had to look into his eyes and see something besides the deadly cold. She left her room and bounded down the stairs, holding her gown above her ankles as she went.

The halls of Avarloch were empty, but laughter still rang out from the great hall ahead. She slowed her pace, suddenly remembering William of Normandy. She had to curb her tongue around the savage who seemed to derive intense pleasure from watching her lose her temper.

Brynna sensed, rather than heard, movement behind her. She stopped and turned to look over her shoulder.

Shadows danced on the walls from the many torches lit along the long corridors and from the fire in the great central hearth. The wooden floor creaked. She could feel eyes watching her like vultures over a dying animal. Suddenly her skin began to crawl under the silk of her gown. She moved her feet to run. A shadow moved and hands sprang around her mouth and waist like demons from the vast darkness of hell. She couldn't breathe from the tightly clamped hand over her mouth and part of her nose. She clawed at the face behind her, but it was as if pain were nonexistent to the force that bound her. She was half dragged, half carried down the long corridor to the small, private garden outside. Her assailant pushed her up against the stone wall, then spun her around so that his face became visible under the torches that flared above her.

"I told you this morn that I would take you." Luis pushed his palm against her mouth to stifle her screams. His face was close to hers. Hot breath, soured by wine and ale, made Brynna's stomach churn. "I am sick of your defiance." He growled, squeezing her cheeks with his fingers. "You parade around the castle dressed like a wench and expect men to keep their desire controlled in their pants?" He laughed, using his other hand to grope at her breasts. "Every knight in Avarloch wants you, dear Brynna. Every knight except Lord Brand." He tore at her gown and the chemise underneath exposing her milky breasts.

Brynna fought him wildly, but to no avail. She twisted her head away from his hand and for an instant her mouth was free. "You are a dead man. My father will—"

His hand came back, but this time it closed around her throat until blackness threatened to overtake her.

Brand left the great hall, stricken with the knowledge that Normans had killed Brynna's mother and angry that the information had been kept from him. Brynna had many reasons to hate him, he realized, climbing the stairs. She had been given a choice to either accept a husband who didn't know how to love anymore or be thrown out of her home. *Merde,* how did she cast her eyes upon him without pure hatred spilling from her heart? She had every right to hate him.

He moved silently along the hall to her room. When he reached her door, he raked his hand through his hair. He wanted to tell her he knew about her mother and ask her forgiveness for what his people had done.

Brynna did not answer the door when Brand knocked. He tried again, then looked down the hall. She must have returned to the great hall and he had missed her.

He was taking a wife he did not love and who would never be able to love him. He was used as a pawn to rid England of Lord Richard, but the price was high indeed,

Brand thought dryly as he made his way back down the stairs. He should have mercy on her and bid her farewell. But where would she go now that her father was going to Normandy with William? The idea of Lord Richard fighting on the Norman side still surprised Brand. The man held naught against the people who bore his wife's murderers. How had his heart ever healed from that? Brand wondered as he reached the first-floor landing.

He looked down the long, silent corridor. A chill swept through him, but he shook the feeling away and entered the great hall. Aqua eyes scanned the immense hall, but there was no trace of Brynna. With a growing sense of dismay, he entered the halls once again and looked around. Silence. Where was she? He wanted to call her name, but whispers from his dreams invaded his thoughts. He knew Brynna would not answer him, just as Colette never did when he searched the endless corridors of Graycliff in his dreams. His lips tightened around his teeth instead.

The floor creaked beneath his boots. Doors beckoned to him on either side of the long passageway, but he opened none of them. He looked straight ahead as he walked toward the garden doors, knowing somehow that he would find Brynna when he reached the end of the corridor.

Brand pressed his palm against the cold wood. A blast of fresh air assailed his senses when he pushed the door open and entered the garden.

He heard a muffled cry and turned his head slowly toward the sound.

Brynna was pinned against the wall, struggling heedlessly against a shadow that clawed at her gown and dipped its dark head to her breasts.

Rage, so black it threatened his very soul, gave Brand speed, agility, and power. It only took him an instant to reach them. His hand shot out with the swiftness of an arrow and closed around the back of Sir Luis's head. With one swift, seemingly effortless tug, Brand yanked the knight away from Brynna and then smashed Luis's face into the wall just above her shoulder.

Blood from Luis's forehead, nose, and mouth splashed onto Brynna's face, but it was only when she gazed upon her rescuer that she felt a scream well up inside her.

The English knight's body melted after the blow, but Brand would not allow Luis to sink to the floor. Pulling him up by the collar, Brand spun him around. With a fist that flew like a hammer, he sent Luis's teeth to the floor.

Luis collapsed at his attacker's feet, and as Brynna watched in absolute terror, the Norman released his sword from the scabbard at his side. The sound of metal leaving leather went on forever in Brynna's mind. Then the sword was free, flashing against the moonbeams and the torchlight in the garden. Brand lifted his arms high over his head, readying for the final blow.

Large, powerful hands caught his wrists in midair.

"What are you doing? What has happened here?" It was William. His savage eyes darted past Brand to Brynna, now huddled in the corner against the wall. "Do not do it, Brand," William warned, still struggling to keep the sword from falling upon Luis.

Almost unrecognizable in his wrath, Brand's eyes were wide and burning with such terrible power when they turned on the duke, William almost let him go. "He was trying to rape her."

"Let me take him to the king. 'Tis his man, Brand," William pleaded quickly, his voice low.

"Release me, William." A warning growl. The distant rumble of thunder.

"*Non!* You avoid battle by marrying her. Will you go to war now over killing one of the king's knights? The lady is unharmed. Look at her." William's eyes did not leave Brand's when he spoke to her. "Did he take you, lady?"

For a moment Brynna could not answer as fear wound itself around her throat.

"Did he take you?" the duke demanded harshly.

"Nay."

"There, you see?" William insisted.

Brand leveled his arctic gaze on his friend. "I warn you for the last time, William. Let me go."

"Fine. We can duel in the morning, but I won't have you imprisoned over killing this pile of filth. *Now put down your sword!*"

Brynna sank to the floor, covering her ears against the terrible thunder of William's voice that echoed through the garden. She began to cry.

Brand's eyes darted to her, then at the bloodied, terrified face of Luis. Brand wanted to kill him. He cared not about prison, or war, or anything else. He could smell Luis's blood on the air and wanted to finish him.

Suddenly, and with a force that sent William hurling backward, Brand yanked his arms free and swiped his blade smoothly across Luis's throat, all in the space of an instant. When it was done, he turned his icy gaze on the duke before tossing his sword to the floor. "No man will take what is mine ever again, or even attempt it in my house."

The duke of Normandy nodded slowly, looked once more at Brynna, then silently left the garden.

A low whimper drew Brand's attention back to Brynna. He fell to his knees in front of her. Her head was lowered. Her silver net had been torn in her struggles against Luis and bronze hair fell over her bare shoulder into her lap. "Are you injured?" he asked gently, reaching to smooth the fiery tresses away from her face. "Brynna?"

Lifting her head, her eyes sparkled with fear and tears. She stared at Brand's dark, beautiful face, where only moments before, the passion that ruled his heart was unleashed into something completely terrifying. And though traces of it remained, tender concern filled his aqua gaze now.

"What demons possess you?" she asked him quietly.

Brand recoiled back as if she held a flaming torch to his flesh. "What?"

Sliding her back up along the wall, Brynna rose to her feet. She pulled the torn fabric of her gown over her exposed breast and kept her arms there to keep it in place. "You are so cold. You fear nothing. Not Duke William, nor the king. Not even war—"

"He was about to take you!" Brand shouted, rising to his feet.

"Aye! And then you killed him before my eyes!"

"And that upsets you after what he did?"

"I am not a barbarian like you, m'lord," Brynna announced quietly, flatly.

Ice, pure and crystal blue, raked over her, over the creamy flesh that peeked from behind her fingers. "Mayhap you are disappointed that I arrived when I did."

Brynna's hand whipped the air. Her fingers stung as they met Brand's cheek.

His face turned slightly from the force of the blow; then his eyes returned to her, cold, but no longer frozen. He stared at her for a moment. Then without a word he turned and left the garden.

Chapter Nine

Dawn filtered into Brand's room spreading golden light over his bed. He opened his eyes, erasing the images of Colette's face from his mind. For a moment he lay still on his belly. Nothing moved as reality settled over him. Blinking, he looked through the shaft of sunlight beside his bed.

Why did you betray me? Brand wanted to scream the words out. He wanted Colette to tell him how he could have been so terribly wrong about her. How had he allowed himself to become so blinded by love that he did not see his own feet in front of him as they carried him into the jaws of a jackal? He had always trusted his instincts. Being a warrior made it imperative that his instincts be correct. The simplest error could cost him or his men their lives. It had cost Alexander his.

Wearily he sat up, slinging his bare legs over the side of the bed. He had dreamed again of falling off the edge of a high precipice. He raked his fingers through his curls and swore under his breath. He had been so sure of his steps, and yet he fell. How could he ever trust his instincts again?

He went to the chair where his hose and thin linen

braies draped the arm, and with another mumbled curse, he snatched them up.

There was a knock at the door. Alysia with his mead, Brand thought gratefully. "Come."

The door burst open and William's gleeful grin lit up the room, making Brand recoil.

"Good morn!" William looked at the bed, then around the room. His smile faded. "Where's the girl?"

"What girl?" Brand drawled. He was not in the mood for his cheerful friend this morning.

"Alysia."

"With Dante probably," Brand said with a scowl. He slipped his legs into soft woolen hose that fit snugly over muscular thighs, and tied his braies at his hips. He sat on his bed, pulled his boots on, and looked up at William over dark brows. "I should not have let her stay with Dante. It's freezing in this blasted room and she's late with my drink."

"With Dante?" William repeated in wide-eyed disdain. "You gave her to Dante after I requested her?"

Brand left the bed and rummaged through his wardrobe for a tunic. He sighed. "She was never coming to my room in the first place. I only told you that because she fancied Dante and I didn't want you bedding her."

William closed the door behind him and fell into a chair with a heavy thud, hurt etching his face. "You merely had to tell me Dante wanted her. You did not have to deceive me."

Brand slammed the door of his wardrobe shut without finding a suitable tunic. "No one can 'just tell you' anything. You're a pushy bastard who does not take no for an answer."

"That didn't stop you last eve."

Brand threw open the lid of a trunk not yet unpacked from Graycliff and glanced briefly over his shoulder at William. "You should not have involved yourself. This is *my* castle and that worthless filth was forcing himself on *my* betrothed."

"And it would have been the *king's* castle, and someone *else's* betrothed within a week, had I not spoken to Edward on your behalf, Brand. Like it or not, there is a law about killing the king's guard. Sir Luis was one of Edward's personal knights."

"A fact I would not boast about, were I King Edward," Brand said dryly while examining a scarlet velvet tunic.

A faint smirk lifted one side of William's mouth. "That's what I like about you, Brand. You don't give a rat's arse if the king threatens to toss you into the dungeons. Which he will not do now that he and I have had our little talk. Still, he awaits you in the solar to give an account of what happened last eve."

"You have my gratitude," Brand sneered, eyeing William before he slipped the tunic over his head.

"You know"—William tossed his leg over the arm of his chair, his battle-worn boot swinging in midair— "when I am king, I won't tolerate disobedience, even from you."

Curls crowned the opening of the tunic before Brand's face appeared wearing a sardonic smile. "Don't make up daft rules and you won't have to."

William sighed, shaking his head, because he knew that daft or not, Brand would only obey those laws he chose to obey, no matter whose laws they were.

"Arguing with you is fruitless," the duke conceded, ignoring Brand's innocent smile laced with victory.

There was another knock at the door.

"Enter," William called casually over his shoulder.

Dante entered the room carrying a clay goblet. He was about to explain to Brand why he was bringing the drink instead of Alysia when he spotted William and snapped his lips together.

"Thank the saints!" the duke bellowed, leaving his seat. He plucked the goblet from Dante and handed it to Brand. "His mead has finally arrived. But wait, what's this?" William studied Dante's face. "You are not Alysia. Where is the lovely handmaiden this morn, rogue?"

Unsure of what to answer, Dante glanced over William's shoulder at his brother, but Brand merely smiled at him. Left on his own, Dante shrugged his broad shoulders and met William's level gaze. "Alysia is . . . indisposed."

"Ah, indisposed." William brooded, throwing himself back into the chair. " 'Tis perfectly understandable then why you have taken up her duties. At least you are more honorable than your lying brother." He glared at Brand while he grumbled, then gave his attention back to Dante. "It also explains why you were not at my side last eve when your brother killed Sir Luis."

"You killed him?" Dante's expression changed from amusement at his sulking liege lord to disbelief.

"He was trying to have his way with Brynna."

"*Enfer!* I told you I didn't like the bastard."

"Do not encourage him, Dante." William shook his head at them. "Where did you both learn to be so dishonest and bloodthirsty?"

"From you," Brand and Dante answered at the same time.

William's hard features relaxed into a wide, thoroughly satisfied grin. "I've done well with you both then."

"Now tell me"—William leaned forward in his chair and offered Dante a sly smile—"what you meant by 'indisposed'?"

Dante rolled his moonlit eyes toward heaven, then looked at his brother for assistance when William pressed him for an answer.

Brand raised his eyebrows and humor curled a corner of his mouth while he, too, waited for Dante's reply.

❋

Brand left his room with William and Dante at his side. Squires and handmaidens busy with the day's chores bowed to the three men as they passed, but Brand barely noticed them. He had picked up the faint scent of jasmine on the air and an image of bronze hair filled his head. He must have just missed her. Good thing, he thought sourly, for the lady would have surely fainted dead away at the sight of such a heartless beast.

Brynna looked up from her chair when the three men entered the solar. Her heart hammered in her chest as it usually did when she saw Brand. The rich scarlet tunic he wore made him look especially handsome this morn. The deep ruby velvet gave the illusion of warmth to his penetrating eyes. His curls were tousled carelessly about his forehead and made him look charming and playful. Brynna reminded herself to breathe while she assessed the self-confident gait of her betrothed. He was tall, lethally quick, broad-shouldered, and strong. He possessed the lean grace of a wolf rather than the muscular density of a bear like the brutish Duke William.

But no amount of luxurious fabric could soften the hard angles of his features when Brand's gaze passed Lord Richard and found the king, where he sat in a golden velvet-lined chair. His brooding gaze lingered there for a moment before his eyes moved over Edward like a brush-fire and settled on Brynna.

King Edward stood up. He looked the Norman knight over, frowning at the slight bow he received from him, a gesture given more in scorn than respect. Edward fumed that he had listened to William and not had the rogue knight seized last eve.

"Please sit down, Lord Brand," the king said through tight lips.

William growled low in his throat, giving Edward a deadly look as he passed him and took a seat beside Lord Richard.

Brand chose the chair closest to Brynna. "Lady," he greeted coolly before he sat, his eyes blazing, nostrils slightly flared. Was she here to rebuke him before the king? he wondered. She would regret her decision to stay at Avarloch if she did.

Brynna could feel Brand's strength next to her like a molten steel shield covering him. She nodded curtly, twisting uneasily in her chair. She crossed her legs and tossed her thick copper braid over her shoulder. Unable to ignore his potent presence, she shifted her green eyes under a thick fringe of dark lashes to peek at the soft black linen that sheathed his leg. His thigh was thick with muscle. His bent knee extended far in length, making her own leg appear frail and tiny in comparison. *He is a man,* a tiny voice in her head taunted. *Raw power, warrior hard. His body, a weapon capable of killing anything that threatens what is his.* But Brynna could not stop the memory of his caress when she clung to him after being discovered by the Norman duke on his first day at Avarloch. Her betrothed's protection could also come in the form of a tight yet tender embrace.

"Lord Brand," the king's voice pulled Brynna back to the present. "What do you have to say for yourself in defense of your actions last eve?"

Brand's lazy smile was somehow more dangerous than a snarl. "I was possessed by demons, Sire."

Beside him, Brynna shut her eyes, stifling a sigh. The anger from Brand stung her to her heart.

"I want the truth, not an explanation made out of fear," Edward warned, dismissing, with a flick of his hand, a servant who had carried a tray of ale into the hall. The servant looked at Brand, and the lord of Avarloch Castle shook his head, dismissing the servant gently.

"I want to know what happened with the lady, Lord Brand," the king demanded again.

Brand sat casually with his elbows resting on the arms of his chair, his fingers steepled together. He blinked slowly, like a cat watching a mouse he had all day to kill. "I don't speak out of fear." A dark mist rolled over the blue-green of his eyes, but his voice was silky smooth. "After the man ate in my castle, he attacked my betrothed. He was fortunate I cut his throat as quickly as I did."

King Edward simply stared at Brand, then turned his gaze to William. "This man is a monster. A monster *you* will have to deal with someday."

"So be it," William replied dully.

"And I am a monster as well," Lord Richard interjected. "For had I caught your knight forcing himself on my daughter, I would have killed him myself."

"As would I, my new friend." William grinned jovially at Richard.

"You are three coldhearted madmen," Edward sneered in contempt.

"And that is why we fight in battle while you simply watch and give orders from a well-guarded position," Brand added impatiently. Then with barely measured control, "This castle belongs to me as you decreed with your own hand. I will protect everyone in it with my life and without fear of the consequences."

"And he should not have to defend his actions, Edward," William added tightly.

Edward ignored William, realizing that the duke's presence here was useless. He cursed himself for even thinking his Norman cousin would ever take up his side over Lord Brand Risande. The king turned to Brynna finally, hoping that the lady would somehow give him a civilized account of what had happened.

"Were you in danger from Sir Luis, my lady?"

Brand stiffened, waiting for her reply.

Brynna knew this could be her chance to regain Avarloch. But how long would it be before the king had her father taken out of the way, and this time with no chance of mercy? The king's hard eyes bore naught but hatred for Brand, and if she said what he wanted to hear, her betrothed would be imprisoned. She remembered the insult in Brand's eyes when she called him a barbarian after he saved her from being raped. She did not understand the ways of men, but she did understand honor, and although

Brand's fury frightened her, she knew that she would never again question him when he was protecting her.

"Aye, Sire, I was in fear of my life," Brynna began quietly. "Sir Luis tore my gown and was choking me when Lord Brand found us. Sir Luis said he was going to take me, and that every knight in the keep wanted to . . . except my betrothed."

The room went still with a silence that was so great, flames could be heard crackling against candle wax. Brynna turned her head to look at Brand. She hadn't meant to say it, but now that she had, she was glad. There was no use hiding it any longer. Everyone knew that Lord Brand would have rather fought a battle than marry her. They probably all knew that he took her handmaiden Alysia to his bed last night as well. Brynna's eyes dropped to her hands, wringing the folds of her saffron gown in her lap. "Even though he does not wish it to be so, I am to be Lord Brand's wife, Sire," she stated, trying to ignore the ice that poured from her betrothed as he looked at her. "He was merely protecting what belongs to him"—she let herself look up into Brand's eyes—"as any warrior would."

Her merman smiled, but he was anything but pleased with her response. Indeed, he looked ready to slice her throat. Nay, Brynna thought quickly, catching something else in the slight curve of his lips. He was not angered by her answer because he thought she was playing some coy game with him, and he was readying to take up the challenge.

"Your Majesty," Brynna continued more carefully, hoping to convince Brand of her sincerity, "I am thankful to my betrothed for saving me from your knight, and I am offended by your questions here today. Mayhap, instead of berating him, you might want to question your men about their honor."

The king's eyes softened with resignation, knowing he had just lost this battle. How could he punish the defiant knight without it looking as if the safety of his own people did not matter to him? "Very well." He sighed. "Because you are to be his wife, and because Sir William has requested it"—he shot the duke a meaningful look—"I will question Lord Brand no further."

Brynna nodded, smiling softly. She ached to look at Brand to see if there was still pain in his sea blue gaze.

She didn't have to.

He stood up abruptly, pushing his chair from under him. "Are we through, Sire? I have other matters to attend to."

Edward waved him away with his hand, and before Brynna could look up, Brand was gone. She looked at William instead. The duke was striding toward her with long, lithe steps and a wide grin spread across his face. Behind him, Edward and Richard rose to leave the solar.

"Lady Brynna"—he leaned over her chair and took her hand in his—"you are truly a worthy bride for Brand." He planted a rough kiss on her delicate hand, flashed her a pearly white smile, and left the room.

Brynna sighed heavily. She had said the right thing to protect Brand, and William was delighted. But she admitted to playing a dangerous game with her betrothed at the same time, and it had fallen apart on her.

Dante rose from his chair next, but instead of following Brand, he took his brother's seat next to Brynna. His full mouth slanted into an easy smile that softened his diamond-colored gaze. "My brother can be obnoxious and overbearing."

Brynna nodded in agreement. "And don't forget brooding and insensitive." She expelled a loud sigh that made Dante laugh.

"*Oui,* he can be those things," he told her, growing serious. "But he is so much more. I fear he has forgotten, or mayhap he is afraid to be who he was before."

Brynna remembered the man in the lake. "Will you tell me what happened, Dante?" she asked gently, laying her hand on his.

Dante looked at her long, elegant fingers and then lifted his eyes to hers. "He loved her, *ma dame.* But his love was betrayed," he began.

※

"Lord Brand!" Brynna's father caught up with the dark warrior in the hall. "Please let me express my gratitude for saving my daughter from that bastard, and for guarding her honor. She remains untouched."

Brand's jaw tightened. His betrothed was a virgin. And why should that surprise him? Not every woman in England spread her knees so easily the way Colette had. "He died too quickly," he replied in a soft but thoroughly chilling voice.

Richard nodded his agreement. "I must admit, I was worried you would not treat my daughter kindly."

"I would never harm her," Brand argued, his irritation at the insult was obvious in his tone.

"But you would never care for her either."

Brand frowned, his eyes growing dark. "I know what I told you, sir, there is no need to toss my words back at me.

Brynna will be my wife, and as your daughter has herself stated, I will protect what is mine as any warrior would. On this I give you my word. That is all that should concern you."

"Aye, she did say that." Richard eyed him narrowly. He remembered the frosty glint in this man's eyes when Brynna suggested that the only reason he would protect her was because she belonged to him. "And it seemed to vex you, why?"

Shifting restlessly, Brand offered Richard a wry smile. "I care not what she thinks of me. Whatever you thought you saw, you were mistaken."

"Truly?" Richard asked doubtfully.

"Truly," Brand answered, almost growling at him.

"Very well. I was mistaken then." Richard smiled and proceeded cautiously. "But I am not wrong when I say that my daughter needs love as well as protection."

Brand grunted, dropped his eyes for a moment, then looked up again. "Then mayhap she does not belong at Avarloch after all."

Chapter Ten

The bracing tingle of winter air bit Brynna's face when she stepped out into the bailey. She pulled her cloak tighter, shielding herself from the cold that pulled straws of hay loose from the neatly piled bales against the east wall. Dante's words rang in her ears like the howling wind.

"His love was betrayed. . . ."

"Lady Colette de Marson . . ." Dante had given the flaxen-haired beauty a name, and he spoke it almost breathlessly. While Dante told her of Brand's beloved, his eyes darkened to a smoky charcoal gray. "Her hair spilled down her back like a golden waterfall. Her voice was sweeter than any nectar touched by God's own hand. Everyone loved her. But Alexander desired her. We all knew it. We should have told Brand. Mayhap it would not have happened. But Alex was a loyal soldier and a trusted friend. We never thought . . ."

Brynna narrowed her eyes looking toward the distant forest crowned in a myriad of late-autumn colors. A bitter wind snapped her cloak around her legs, snatched wisps of molten bronze hair out of her braid, and blew locks across her face.

Brand brought the cold with him, she thought again. Cold that replaced the passion that once gave him life. Cold that protected his heart from the anguish and betrayal placed on him by people he loved, people he trusted.

"He cries out for her in the night," Dante had told her. "I can hear him from my room. He doesn't say her name, though, when he awakens. He never speaks her name." Regret raked Dante's voice and Brynna thought he may have forgotten she sat right beside him while he spoke. "Mayhap he should not have sent her away." Dante had whispered his thoughts aloud.

"Why are you telling me this?" Brynna had asked him, not wanting to hear any more.

Dante had shrugged his shoulders as though the weight of his brother's sorrow was too much for him to carry alone. "Mayhap you can make him forget her. I wanted you to understand him. He lives with promises he made, but can never fulfill."

Brynna shivered, pulling her cloak tighter. So, there was truth to the rumors. Brand had discovered Colette and her lover together. As she made her way to the stables to check on her pregnant mare, images of Brand and Colette together came to life in Brynna's mind. She pushed them all aside, save for the memory of his smile. It belonged to Colette de Marson. How many times had the woman seen it? How often had it been bestowed upon her like the giving up of his heart?

"Good morn, Peter." She greeted the young stable boy as she pushed open the heavy wooden doors of the stable.

Peter ceased his sweeping of the hay and looked up. A bright smile crossed his fresh face while a gust of wind blew into the stable, blowing the hay into swirls at his feet.

"Good morning to you, my lady." Peter dropped his broom and helped her close the doors. "Winter will be upon us soon. 'Tis a good thing the foal will be born soon, else its tender flesh would freeze."

Emerald eyes adjusted to the soft light of candle flames and thin beams of sunlight that streaked through cracks in the aged wooden walls. Brynna's gaze fell on the large chestnut mare in her stall, her belly swollen to twice its size. "How is she?" Brynna asked, already walking toward the mare.

"Well, she won't be going today. She is still standing." Peter took up his sweeping once again.

Brynna ran her hand down the velvety white diamond patch between the mare's eyes. "I envy you," she whispered to the horse. "To give life to another is a wondrous thing indeed."

The doors creaked on their hinges and bright morning light invaded the stable again as Brand entered with a blast of cold air.

"My lord." Peter's smile faded at the sight of the man before him.

Brand took a few steps toward Brynna. His gaze on her was as intent as an eagle's that had just spotted its prey. "Leave us." There was a raw demand in his voice that made Peter drop the broom where he stood and run from the stable, pulling the door closed behind him.

"What are you doing in here?" Brand asked her. His very presence made her swoon. God's teeth, but he was as raw as the harshest winter, and as beautiful as a lone black wolf upon a field of freshly fallen snow. She could hardly catch her breath as he took a step closer to her.

"He cries out for her in the night. . . ." Brynna heard over the cool edge of his voice. "My mare—she's pregnant.

I c-came to c-check on her," she stammered as Brand came closer, his eyes pouring over her lips and neck while she spoke.

Thankfully, his powerful gaze left her before she melted all over him. He lifted his hand to stroke the mare's soft coat.

"Ssh . . . it is all right," Brand soothed as the mare snorted, throwing her head back at the stranger's touch. Brand's voice was smooth, his breath as soft as a whisper. He praised the mare's beauty, her fine lines, and the roundness of her belly. He was patient while the horse huffed and kicked out behind her, but it was not long before she brought her head back to him, calmed by his gentle voice, eager for the touch of such a tender hand.

Brynna watched him, touched by the almost poignant way he spoke to her mare, as if he understood the beast's fear. But how could he? Brynna knew this man feared nothing.

"You ease fear well, m'lord."

Brand turned his eyes on her while he stroked the mare's face. "But not yours," he pointed out silkily.

Brynna laughed. The sound was high-pitched and forced. "I'm not afraid of you, m'lord."

He lazily cocked a brow, studying her. "I'm a warrior possessed by demons, lest you forget."

Even in the soft light of the stable, Brynna could feel the force of his gaze. His jaw was aggressive, his mouth so sensual when he offered her a frankly male grin. She dropped her eyes to the floor. "I—I did not mean . . ."

"You meant what you said." He stepped closer to her, very close, in fact. He watched her with eyes that probed her soul. "I am a coldhearted, ruthless bastard who sees what he wants and takes it. Is that not so, Brynna?" His breath touched her face. His voice deepened, no longer tender.

"Nay, my lord. I . . ." Brynna's words caught in her throat somewhere between a sigh and a gasp as he traced the soft contour of her jaw with his fingertip.

"And you think I don't want you." He was close enough to inhale the scent of her hair, but he moved closer still, until his hard chest brushed against her heaving breast. He traced his lips against her temple. "But I do."

Closing her eyes, Brynna let his warm breath wash over her. God help her, it ignited a burning fire somewhere below her belly. It was a fire that exploded upward straight to her heart. His lips sent a scorching flame down the side of her face to her neck, where he kissed the slight fluttering of her pulse.

"You think I cannot be gentle." His mouth came back up, finding hers in a hungry kiss that searched and ached until he took the breath from her body. He slipped his hands around her waist, pulling her against the hardness of his large male form, pulling her closer . . . closer until she thought she would meld into him. He ravaged her mouth with cruel expertise. His tongue swept over hers softly, confirming that he could be gentle with her. When he ran his hot palms up her sides, over the beat at her throat, Brynna moaned into his mouth. He withdrew so slowly she nearly collapsed in his powerful arms. His breath was heavy and ragged.

"You are so beautiful," he whispered. He lifted one hand and sighed at the silkiness of her hair as he smoothed it over her forehead. He had forgotten how good it felt to hold a woman in his arms, and Brynna's body, yielding without resistance under his touch, sent hot shafts of fire through his blood. He wanted to cover her softness with the hard, hungry heat of his body.

His desire devoured her, his touch so tender against her skin made her want to weep for herself. She wanted to be loved by this sensual man. Unable to look into his beautiful eyes and not see the emotion she longed for, Brynna lowered her eyes, leaving him to gaze at the sooty velvet of her lashes.

He whispered her name, bending his head to kiss the seam of her mouth. "Lay with me now."

God help her, she wanted him. She had wanted him from the first moment she saw him. Raw passion gripped her, shocking her. She had never been with a man before, but the memory of his ecstasy while he swam had heated her in places that sent its burning traces to her cheeks. How would she survive his touch, his passion? His strength consumed her, made her utterly weak in his arms, yet she was sure he would take her tenderly, soothing the temporary pain of his passion with his honey voice. She ached for him, longed to feel his strength covering her . . . but she wanted more. She wanted him to look at her the way he had looked at his angel. She wanted to make him smile the way Lady Colette had. She wanted to mean everything to him, and she wanted to see it in his eyes, to feel it when he caressed her.

And so, with all the strength Brynna could muster, and all the pain she could endure, she resisted him, pulling away.

"Nay."

"Brynna . . ." He reached for her again.

"Nay!" She took a step backward. "I will be no more than Alysia was to you last night."

Brand stopped, astonishment and a sudden flare of anger filled his eyes. "I did not bed Alysia! I only told William—"

But Brynna's voice overrode his. "I will be more than a handmaiden to you, Lord Brand," she insisted . . . demanded.

His eyes hardened. His smile was a drawn sword ready to slice, his voice dropped to a provocative purr. "*Oui*, you will be more, lady," he promised with a razor edge in his voice. "You will be my wife, and then I will no longer ask you. I will only take." His fingertip glided over her mouth, wiping the moisture her tongue left there when she licked her lips nervously. She watched him helplessly while he brought his finger to his mouth. His cerulean eyes clouded with sensuality tasting her, his sculpted lips so dangerously alluring. "I will take what I want like the demon-possessed savage that I am."

❋

Frosty air rushed into Brand's lungs when he left the stable. He sucked in a deep breath, letting the bitter chill sweep across his heart. Brynna's mind was made up about him. He was a heartless bastard who bedded her maidens one night and her the next. He clenched his teeth. *Oui,* she was right. He would never be blinded by love again. This time he would keep his eyes directly ahead of him and never fall over the edge of that cliff. He knew he had to be careful with this woman. He could get lost in those enticing flashes of temper and tenderness he saw in her eyes. Unlike the calculating control hidden behind Colette's coy smiles, Brynna's smile was as guileless as her charm. It wouldn't be difficult to fall victim to the sultry warmth in her gaze and the innocent passion of her kiss. He had to keep himself guarded, prepare for this marriage the way he prepared for battle, donning armor fully resistant to Cupid's bow. Lady Brynna Dumont was a dangerous opponent.

Exiting the mews, Peter saw Brand coming toward him and instantly felt the urge to run back inside. But it was too late to run. The wolf had seen him. Stark eyes stared at him as if he were a tender morsel.

"You!" Brand barked, pointing a finger at Peter. "What is your name?"

The stable boy swallowed his heart and stopped dead in his tracks. "P-Peter, my lord."

"Peter, keep an eye on the mare. If there is any change in her condition, I want to be advised immediately." Brand never slowed while he spoke but continued on toward the castle as if on a quest.

That's it? Peter thought, still shaking. He was not going to be eaten whole?

"Aye, m'lord," the stable hand called out. The dark mantle that flowed outward behind Brand looked like dark wings on a falcon about to swoop down on Avarloch Castle and devour everyone inside.

❊

A bird was not the first thing that came to William's mind when Brand stormed through the front doors a few moments later. But he would have agreed with Peter that the new lord of Avarloch looked like he was about to sink his teeth into someone.

The Norman duke was resting comfortably before the massive hearth in the great hall, a leather-clad leg thrown lazily over the arm of his chair, a goblet of ale in his hand, and a dark-haired maiden in his lap.

Brand moved swiftly toward him, his eyes hard and his jaw set. "When are you leaving?" he asked, unclasping the silver pin at his throat.

William whispered something into the girl's ear, then dismissed her with a tender smile and a lecherous wink.

"Why? Are you so anxious to see me off?" The duke watched the gentle sway of the maiden's hips as she left the hall.

"Non." Brand tossed his mantle over the back of a chair and began pacing the hall. "As a matter of fact, I want you to postpone your departure for a few days without telling the king."

Now William turned to give Brand his full attention. Hard granite glinted in his eyes. "Why?"

"You're invited to my wedding."

William laughed. "Your wedding! First you don't want to wed the girl and now you're rushing into it like a man whose pants are on fire." Brand remained silent while his friend laughed, until understanding washed over the duke's face. His smile faded. "Ah, your pants *are* on fire." William sighed heavily. Then, "Why don't you just take her now? Make sure she is worthy of your marriage bed."

Brand thought about the way her fingers clenched his mantle and the way her eyes closed with languid desire when he kissed her. "She is worthy," he said.

Flinging himself into a chair, he signaled for a servant. "Something hot to drink," he called out, and watched the man disappear to his task. "She thinks I bedded her handmaiden Alysia," he said dryly without turning back to William.

"Ah! She is jealous and withholds her affections."

Brand cast his steely gaze into the flames and the

firelight danced and flickered across the surface of his eyes. "It is not her affections I want."

The duke shrugged his massive shoulders. "You think just because you wed her, she will be more willing?"

"Willing or not, I will have what I want." Brand's voice was as empty as a broken promise.

Dark, steel gray eyes studied him narrowly. "And what is it that you want, Brand—besides her flesh beneath you, of course?"

Silence, then, "I expect naught from this marriage."

William chuckled softly and downed his ale. "Sometimes we are pleasantly surprised by what we least expect."

Sighing impatiently, Brand relaxed in his chair and folded his arms across his chest. "Spare me your riddles, William, and say what is on your mind."

The duke belched loudly and threw Brand a cheerful smile. "You are a refreshing bastard, do you know that? Everyone is always rushing around eager to kiss my arse, but not you . . . and not her. Lady Brynna Dumont is going to make your life many things, *mon ami.* Happy, I hope. Miserable, I'm sure." William held his empty goblet up to a passing squire and waited for the space of a breath it took the squire to run to him, receive the goblet, and refill it.

"You see what I mean?" William grinned wolfishly and sipped his drink. "You are still waiting for your drink."

Brand had to laugh, and when he did, it was as if sunlight lit the great hall, shining especially on him. Years faded in the light. Eyes as large and luminous as a child's danced with carefree abandon and joyous enthusiasm.

Watching him, William realized with a sore heart how much he missed experiencing life with his dearest friend, Lord Brand the Passionate.

"She will bring you back your life," William said quietly as a wave of sorrow for all his friend had lost gripped him. Then he drew in a quick, great breath, replenishing his normally cheerful soul. "She is a fiery angel, your lady Brynna. Would that I was twenty years younger. I would fight you for her."

"You would lose."

More laughter, this time from both men. The sound was rich and filled with merriment; everyone who passed them in the hall smiled upon hearing the sound.

"Will you stay, then?" Brand asked him.

"Of course." Warmth flowed once again from the brutish duke when he smiled at Brand. "I was hoping you would ask. I like it here and I am not looking forward to the journey home in this weather."

"But you have Viking blood, surely a few tempestuous waves do not frighten you," Brand taunted.

"They do not frighten me," William replied with a curt grin. "They make me sick to my stomach."

"So stay until spring, then."

"*Non*. But I will stay for a while." William's face grew serious. "I must ready my men for battle."

Brand realized his drink had not yet come and looked around the hall for the servant. "Whose land is it that you dream of ruling now?" he asked impassively, knowing that a day did not pass when the Norman duke was not either fighting or thinking about it.

"Edward's."

Brand turned to him in shock and surprise. "England?"

William grinned. He examined a fingernail and Brand was struck, as he had been many times before, by the ferocity in the warrior's eyes. By the soft glow of the firelight, William looked like a lion excited about a kill.

"You have jested about it many times, but I never thought you were serious."

"Why not?" William lifted his gaze. "Edward has promised the throne to me. Harold of Wessex will contest it, I am certain. He makes decisions for England already and Edward does naught because he fears the little bastard. But I will have Harold's head. And then I will have all of England."

"I'm glad I am not the king." Brand sighed, leaning back in his chair. "To have so many planning my funeral before I am even dead."

"Edward is not a young man and he's not well, in case you haven't noticed."

"I haven't," Brand mumbled dryly, and William cast him a sly smile out of the corner of his mouth before he continued.

"I must plan my future."

"Surely you have a few months before the man croaks," Brand suggested icily.

"If I stay, it will mean Lord Richard stays as well."

Brand nodded. "I know. I think he should be here for his daughter's wedding. When he isn't hanging about my feet making certain I am not mistreating Brynna, he can be pleasant enough." His eyes narrowed on the blazing flames of the hearth. "I wonder how long it will take before Edward sends someone to battle against me as he did to Lord Richard."

"Are you worried?" William asked fiercely.

The smile Brand offered him made the duke laugh again. William rose from his chair and slapped Brand hard on the back. "Does this mean the king is not invited to your wedding?"

Brand threw his head back and laughed and William was pleased. For though his favored knight was every bit as merciless as he in battle, his laughter could charm even his most hated enemy.

The duke left Brand a few moments later and searched the corridors for his promised lover, then burst into hearty laughter when he heard the tight, almost pleading howl from the great hall.

"All right, where in the name of God is my blasted drink?"

Chapter Eleven

Brynna plucked a sprig of mint from the ground and tasted it. Frosty dew melted on her tongue. She was going to have to collect as much of her herbs as she could before the frigid weather destroyed most of her garden. The rosemary and thyme could be hung in the cellars to dry, and most of her parsley could be saved if she worked fast enough. Her marigolds were already dying, though. Looking at the withering petals, she frowned.

She had risen from her bed just after sunrise in order to get an early start and to find some time alone before the castle bristled with people. God's blood, but she couldn't remember when Avarloch had been so crowded. She could barely walk through its halls without bumping into a soldier or a soldier's squire. Even her handmaidens had left their embroidery in favor of catching the attention of a Norman or an English guard.

Brynna longed for some peace and quiet to gather her thoughts, which were mainly centered around her future husband. She hadn't seen him again after he kissed her in the stable yesterday, and it was a good thing too. Her reaction to him every time she set eyes on him disgusted her thoroughly. Was she no better than a cat in season the way she near mewled at his hungry kisses? She found herself thinking about him all the time. Why, she even insulted the king last eve when he tried to carry on a conversation with her at supper. She had enough wits to realize King Edward's droning voice would have plunged her into semiconsciousness even if she hadn't been searching out Brand's face amid the inhabitants of the great hall. A face she hadn't found and sulked over until she retired to her chambers.

Most likely her betrothed was bedding another one of her handmaidens, Brynna thought, and ripped a spray of mint from the cold earth. What she needed was a brisk slap to return her to her senses.

She heard a sound behind her and turned, then realized that there was no hope of her senses ever coming back.

Brand stood there, simply staring at her, while her resolve wilted right along with the cabbage around his feet.

"How did you find me?" She managed to speak when he took a step toward her. She didn't want to be alone with him. She couldn't trust herself not to fling herself into his arms if he but asked her for another kiss.

"Your father told me you might be here."

She looked up at him when he reached her. She would have asked him *why* he found her if she had the courage to withstand his reply. And if the wind had stopped playing with his thick curls, making them dance around his temples.

"This was my mother's garden," she told him, and lowered her lashes in defense of his cool gaze. "I came here to save what I could before the frost . . ." Her words stalled in her throat when he suddenly squatted beside her.

"I'm sorry for the loss of your mother." His voice was a mixture of velvet and steel.

Brynna lifted her gaze to his, then cursed herself for doing so. His nearness scattered her thoughts and warmed her blood enough to make her forget winter altogether.

"I . . ." Blast him. She couldn't remember what she wanted to say. She scowled at him for making her so daft. He replied by giving her a smile that sent her pulse racing. How would she ever get anything accomplished now that he intruded upon her thoughts like a ray of sunshine piercing the gloom? "What do you want?" she snapped at him.

"You."

"You already have me, m'lord," Brynna said, trying hard to ignore the alluring promise of complete possession in his voice. "You saw to that with your victory over my father."

"I didn't even know you existed when I fought your father," Brand argued.

But she knew he existed. *Stop it, Brynna,* she chided herself, recalling the raw, radiant emotion that gave him his nickname, the Passionate. That man was gone. She shrugged her shoulders and stuffed a handful of leaves into a pouch hanging from her side.

"What's done is done. We will have to learn to hate each other with a little more discretion, though. I would not have my people know how miserable we are." She glared at him when he threw his head back and laughed. "I fail to see the humor in this, Lord Brand."

"I was just thinking how invigorating your father's life must have been raising you. It's no wonder he is such a great warrior. He had years of practice fighting a lioness."

Brynna balked and swiped a strand of hair away from her eyes, leaving a smudge of dirt across her cheek. "I rarely gave my father any trouble at all! He must have told you about the time I set the duchess of York's hair on fire. I can assure you, I was only holding my candle so close to her face because I thought there was a spider crawling across her nose. How was I supposed to know it was a mole?"

Brand stared at her for a moment and then burst into laughter again. Brynna wanted to be angry with him, but she found herself smiling instead. His laughter was contagious, sensual, and completely intoxicating. She found herself staring at him even after he sobered enough to smile at her with something other than humor.

He lifted his fingers to her cheek and brushed away the dirt there. "You're quite irresistible." His gaze captured hers for a moment before a shadow drifted across his eyes. He sat down fully in the grass, crushing some of her mint, and hugged his long legs to his chest. A waiting silence settled over the garden while he contemplated something that carved his features in ruthless lines.

"Our wedding will take place in three days."

"So soon, then?" Brynna hadn't meant to sound like the idea of being his wife utterly repulsed her. True, it was a forced marriage for both of them, and indeed, she was afraid to promise her life to him in the eyes of the Almighty. She had no idea what her life would be like and thought she would have at least a fortnight to ponder it.

Brand's somber gaze slid to hers. "Edward is leaving tomorrow. William will be leaving soon as well. I thought it would please you to have your father here on your wedding day."

"Forgive me." Brynna touched his sleeve. "I'm grateful for your consideration. I just thought I would have more time to prepare." He nodded and cast his eyes on the distant treetops. He suddenly looked as miserable as Brynna claimed him to be a few minutes earlier. His brother had told her that Brand was a difficult man to understand, but his eyes were like open doors, exposing his core. He still loved Colette de Marson. He wished it were her he was going to marry instead of Brynna. It was a tragedy really, she thought while unwanted tears misted her eyes. Not only would her husband never love her, but he loved someone else.

There was no reason to cry over it. She simply would never allow herself to fall in love with him. Then she wouldn't care to whom his heart belonged.

With that thought strengthening her mettle, Brynna decided to make peace with him here in her mother's garden. They could at least be friends, couldn't they? She left him and crossed the garden to where her prized wild roses still bloomed. She reached for a red rose, then changed her mind, since red represented love. She looked at the rest and finally smiled, deciding on white for purity. She wasn't the woman he loved, but at least she would never betray him.

Returning to Brand, she knelt before him and handed him her offering. She watched his unrelenting expression dissolve into one of quiet wonder. And then, when she positioned his broad fingers around the fragile stem to keep him from getting hurt by its thorns, his face transformed with a smile of such heart-wrenching appreciation Brynna knew trying not to fall in love with him was going to be impossible.

❈

From her window Brynna watched King Edward's company grow smaller as the distance between them and Avarloch grew. She was glad they were leaving. Pity the duke of Normandy was not leaving as well, she thought as the wind ripped through her hair. Lord William frightened her, though she would never let him see her fear again. But at least his staying meant her father would remain as well. She was thankful, and surprised, that Brand had invited her father to stay for her wedding. He seemed unaffected by her father's presence at Avarloch, but Lord Brand Risande knew his place here. Her father's former position did not threaten him in the least.

Leaving the window with a long, drawn-out sigh, Brynna went to her bed and stared at the wedding gown strewn across the mattress. Her poor handmaidens had worked day and night to have it ready in time. She touched the sheer white silk and bit her bottom lip. Had Brand rushed the ceremony so that her father could attend? Or was he taking her as a wife in haste so that he could bed her? He would not let her refuse again. Would he ever care that she wanted his passionate whispers to be real? Their union meant naught to him. She meant naught to him. Brynna remembered the way he had spoken to the mare, telling the horse of her beauty only moments before he told Brynna of hers. She might as well have *been* a horse; it mattered not to him. She was not Colette. She pushed the gown aside and plopped down on her bed with a great sigh. Why did it matter to her? A few days ago she was content to marry for peace, not for love. Even after learning that her future husband was the man she dreamed about, she had resigned herself to wedding him while knowing he would never love her. What had changed?

Lord Brand the Passionate was a man held prisoner by his own heart and Brynna ached to free him. But how? How could she break through the shield, reach down into the darkness? And if she could, did she dare touch his sorrow? Would it devour her as she tried to pull it out of him? Should she even try? Even as she plagued herself with questions, another arose in their place. What would it be like to be loved by him, treasured, cherished beyond imagination?

She lifted her wedding gown and held it to her chest. She would not refuse him, nor would she fight him when he took her. She would accept him as her husband and try to teach him to love her.

She did not leave her room for the rest of the day, and when night came, she advised her handmaiden Lily to bring her supper to her room. When supper arrived, though, Brynna was surprised to find Alysia serving her.

"Where is Lily?" Brynna asked from her bed. The sharp edge in her voice went unnoticed by the dark handmaiden.

"Sir William has requested that she dine with him. It is the fourth night in a row now," Alysia added with a knowing arch of her brow.

"Poor girl," Brynna mumbled blandly, fingering the thick quilted blanket that covered her bed.

Alysia giggled, laying the tray on a nearby table. "We were frightened that Lily would be found in the duke's bed drained of all her blood . . . or at least her energy, but the girl has not looked so fresh and healthy since she was a babe!"

Brynna eyed the young handmaiden, trying to discern

if she, too, looked "fresh and healthy" from spending her nights with Brand.

Oblivious to her mistress's scrutinizing stare, Alysia glanced at the open window and drew her arms around herself against the cold. "There is a storm coming on the eve of your wedding."

Brynna's eyes narrowed. "Do you think it is an omen, Alysia?"

"Nay, my lady, just unfortunate on such a wonderful day."

"Wonderful day?" Brynna questioned suspiciously.

"Oh, aye!" Alysia spun around to face her, happiness lighting her exotic features. "Lord Brand will make a fine husband. He is so handsome, so kind." Alysia grew serious, almost sad while looking at Brynna. "I know that you do not love him, m'lady, but I believe he will make you happy. He is such a gallant knight, a true lord, a—"

"Mayhap you should marry him instead of me," Brynna interrupted scathingly.

"And so I would if I were the lady of Avarloch, and if I did not fancy Sir Dante so," Alysia announced with all the enthusiasm of a girl ten years her junior.

"Sir Dante?" Brynna blinked back her surprise.

Alysia cast her mistress a long, slanted charcoal gaze and nodded. "Have you ever seen such a marvelous man?" she asked while she poured warm mead into a goblet and handed it to Brynna.

Her mistress stared at her, unable to speak; then she knit her brows together and shook her head, trying to clear the confusion that settled over her. "And Dante does not take offense that his brother took you to his bed?"

"What bed?" Alysia's head shot up and the goblet

almost slipped from her fingers. Brynna grabbed the cup just before the mead spilled into her lap, then fixed her eyes on her handmaiden.

"Lord Brand's bed, of course."

"M'lady!" Alysia gasped, throwing her hands to her chest as if the shock were just too much for her. "I never went to Lord Brand's bed!"

"But you told the duke—"

"Nay! Lord Brand told me to tell the duke that he had requested me so that I may be kept from William's bed. I swear to you, I have not bedded your betrothed."

Brynna's face paled. "I believe you, Alysia. It's all right," she comforted, seeing the glassy tears suspended upon the woman's long black lashes. "He tried to tell me in the stables," Brynna said more to herself than to Alysia, remembering Brand's anger toward her when she accused him of sleeping with her handmaiden.

"And you did not believe him?" Alysia sat down on the bed beside Brynna and, still trembling, reached for Brynna's hand.

"I did not even give him a chance."

"Oh, m'lady." The handmaiden sighed. "His eyes follow no one but you already."

Brynna looked up from her grim reverie. "What do you mean?"

"You must see it," Alysia insisted.

"See what?"

Alysia made a noise that sounded like a snort, but her smile turned radiant. "He watches you all the time with burning eyes. Why, Sir Conrad nearly sliced off your betrothed's arm when you passed the fence the day before last. Your Brand spotted you, you see, and he all but ceased his practice just to watch you stroll by. Surely you see the way he looks at you."

Brynna frowned. "That means naught. I am but a possession to be watched over."

"Oh, nonsense!" Now the handmaiden huffed loudly, impatient with her mistress's stubbornness. "When a man cannot keep his eyes off you, it means more than your being a possession to him."

Aye, it means that he wants me, that is all.

"Where is he now?" Brynna asked, proving to her quickening heart that her betrothed did not care for her.

"Dining with the duke and everyone else in the castle."

"Has he asked for me?"

"Nay, but—"

"There, you see?"

"M'lady," Alysia said softly, seeing the carefully shielded disappointment in Brynna's green eyes. "He is with all his men and Duke William. Men have pride. He would not reveal his eagerness for your company and be laughed at when told you would rather eat alone."

Brynna only sighed, her shoulders sagging. "Lord Brand does not care what others think of him, men or dukes, or even kings."

Alysia studied Brynna closely, a slow smile curling her lip as understanding washed over her. "You care for him."

Brynna was about to protest, but she suddenly felt so tired of denying her heart. She nodded, staring into her goblet. "I believe I do, but he will never care for me."

"That is not true—"

"It is." Brynna's voice overrode Alysia's. "But it does not matter, Avarloch must always come first." She rose from the bed and went to the window to watch night fall upon Avarloch. "Go find your knight, Alysia, and when you do, tell him of your love. Look into his eyes and let your heart speak for you."

"Oh, m'lady." Alysia went to her, but Brynna turned, smiling.

"Go. I will be fine. I have much to do to prepare for the morrow."

"Let me tend to you," her handmaiden pleaded softly.

"Nay, I am fine. Truly," Brynna reassured her, making her voice lighter.

Alysia sighed, not wanting to go, but when Brynna turned again toward the window, the handmaiden touched her arm and quietly left the room.

Brynna stared into the darkness of the bailey and beyond, to the distant forest, wishing that Alysia were right about Brand. *He probably does not even realize I am not there*, Brynna told herself.

With a resigned sigh she picked up her wedding gown and placed it carefully over a high-backed chair near her bed. She stripped down to her gauze chemise and climbed into bed without touching her dinner. She would not think about it anymore. She would not think at all.

Sometime later there came a knock at her door. Guessing it was one of her ladies, Brynna did not bother to robe herself when she left her bed.

Brand's expression was as dark as his raven curls when Brynna gasped seeing him on the other side of the door. He wore a black tunic and trousers, but the darkness that covered him did naught to dilute the glorious turquoise of his eyes. He was big and powerful against the frame of her door and the scent of the woods covered him. Brynna thought he looked more untamed than ever as his eyes scorched over her. She suddenly realized that the gauze chemise that covered her was as sheer as her finest lace. She felt warm in every place his eyes raked over her, as though flames licked softly over her body, tightening, burning her flesh beneath the smoldering caress of his gaze. She knew she should cover herself from his penetrating stare, but she liked how it made her feel.

"Are you ill?" he asked suddenly with a harsh edge to his voice.

"Nay, m'lord." She looked up into his eyes and blinked.

His nostrils flared slightly at her reply and his eyes grew more intent as they glared into hers. "From now on, Brynna, you dine with me. If you refuse, I will come get you myself."

"Why?" Brynna stared up at him.

"Why?" he repeated, addled by her question. When she nodded her head and repeated her question, he blinked. "Because your place is beside me." He watched her lower her eyes and sigh as if his words had somehow injured her. "And," he added, "because you make having to sit among William's blithering imbeciles more bearable. *Oui.*" He nodded as if just realizing the fact for himself, and then ran his fingers through his hair because what he discovered made him uncomfortable. "You make the night more pleasant."

Brynna almost melted right there in her spot. She raised her eyes to him and offered him a smile that made him groan. And then she did what she had wanted to do for the past year. She threw her arms around his neck and kissed him. The rest of her thoughts were snatched away when he slipped his arms around her waist and exchanged her innocent kiss for one more meaningful. He claimed her mouth with complete possession and dominance, hard and yet exquisitely tender. His tongue swept deep into her mouth, devouring her. His body grew harder and more tense. Before Brynna had time to go limp, he released her with the same zeal. He lingered there for just another instant, clenching his jaw and looking so untamed Brynna thought he might rip the chemise from her body and have his way with her without caring if they reached the bed or not.

"You will sit beside me every night while we dine and not ask me for the reasons again. Do you understand, Brynna?"

"Aye," she answered breathily, perfectly willing to do as he commanded. He nodded once before storming away.

Brynna closed the door and leaned against it, a hopeful grin spread across her face just before she leaped into her bed.

❋

Cursing angrily under his breath, Brand slammed the door to his room and kicked off his boots. Heat, like scalding flames, coursed through his veins. He told himself that it was anger that made his heart beat so furiously. Anger at being left to sit alone again beside a chair reserved for the lady of the castle. But he knew by the hard ache and the fierce throbbing below his navel that raw passion was the true culprit. Images of Brynna's body clouded his thoughts. The swell of her breasts, the way her nipples tightened beneath her sheer chemise without even a touch from him. And God's fury, he had wanted to touch her. He wanted to tangle his hands in her thick locks, bend her to meet the fervor of his desire. He wanted to bite her sensuously full lips, rake his teeth across her neck until he found the twin jeweled peaks of her lush breasts. Brand cursed under his breath, willing the memory of her to flee his thoughts. But her face remained, etching itself in his mind. Her smile was so honest, even when she was challenging him, her spirit so refreshing that he missed her when he wasn't with her.

"Damn you woman, what are you doing to me?" Brand seethed, yanking his tunic over his head. Not even Colette had heated his loins this way. He paced inside his chambers, trying to control his need to go take her. When he failed, he wrenched the door open and stormed out of his room. He wanted Brynna in his bed, wanted her more than any woman he had ever known. And she wanted him, he was certain of it. If not, she would never have tempted him so ruthlessly. *Oui,* her glorious emerald eyes seduced him, her smile teased him, and her body reacted to him whether she wanted it to or not.

When he reached her door, he pounded on it with his fist. Blood rushed through his veins, flooding his loins, and making his heart accelerate. The door opened. Brynna stood on the other side looking surprised to see him again. Her lips parted as if she meant to say something, but Brand closed the short distance between them, kicked the door closed, and hauled her into his arms. His mouth fastened on hers and his hands were rough when he fit them under her derriere and lifted her off her feet.

Instinctively, Brynna wrapped her thighs around his waist to hold on. She had no time to be frightened of the hungry gleam in his eyes, no time to wonder what had brought him back to her, this time bare-chested and too tempting to deny. Instead, she felt drunk on wine, light-headed while his tongue delved deep within her mouth, one hand cupping her bottom while his other arm pinned her tight against his muscular frame. She circled her arms around his neck and moaned a tight, little sound that made Brand's body snap with uncontrolled desire.

He rounded on his heel and pushed her back against the door, never letting her go, without breaking their kiss. He wanted to take her this way, his muscles, his every nerve ending screamed for him to take her this way, hard, fast, and rough. He spread her thighs and pressed his potent arousal to the sweet notch between her legs. He tugged at the hem of her chemise, trying to lift it over her hips, but the fabric was tangled between their aching bodies. His impatient fingers rose to the fringes of her neckline, but instead of tearing away the thin gauze, he fit his palms over her breasts and delighted in the feel of her. When the bud of her nipple grew taut beneath his thumb, Brand bent his head and closed his lips around her, tugging gently through the fabric.

Someone knocked and, not for the first time, Brand cursed William and himself for allowing Richard Dumont to remain at Avarloch when he heard Brynna's father calling to her on the other side of the heavy door.

Brynna gasped and panic filled her eyes. Brand found it so enchanting that she would be mortified at being caught this way, even though she was to become his wife in the morn, he almost laughed.

"A moment please, Father!" she called out breathlessly, and cast Brand a murderous glare when she caught the humor in his expression. "Release me," she whispered frantically.

He felt his lips slant into a devilish grin; then with a slow, relentless movement that nearly made her groan loud enough for her father to hear, Brand surged against her one last time before he slid her down his body. Her feet touched the ground, but he found the dreamy way she stared up at him quite satisfying.

Lord Richard's voice behind the door jolted Brynna to move. She pushed Brand away, using her palms on his chest. He barely budged. "Scoundrel," she flung at him in a tight whisper. Then, more brightly, "Coming, Father." She patted her hair back into some semblance of neatness and gave the wrinkles in her chemise a quick brush before she pulled open the door.

Richard stared at his daughter, who looked quite flustered and a bit befuddled, before his dark eyes swept over her shoulder to the man standing in his daughter's room as if he belonged there. "Lord Brand?" Richard said, not really certain what his reaction should be.

"Lord Richard, I was just leaving." Brand offered him a cool smile and then turned his gaze to Brynna. He lifted his thumb to her mouth and dragged it over her bottom lip. "I look forward to the morning." When she blushed a fresh shade of claret, he laughed softly and with sincere affection that made her heart thud dully in her ears.

"I came to bid you good night," Richard said, dragging his daughter's attention away from the man walking down the hall. He did not ask what Brand was doing in his daughter's chambers on the eve of their wedding. He thought it better not to know. "Good night, daughter." Richard kissed her forehead and then cast his gaze toward

Brand's door one last time. He wanted to feel relief that
the Norman lord had finally found favor in his heart for
Brynna. Richard ached for that relief, especially when his
daughter didn't answer him but sighed happily and shut
the door to her room.

Chapter Twelve

Lily and Alysia fastened the many buttons of Brynna's wedding gown with deft fingers.

Fashioned in old Saxon style, the gown was crafted in a layer of sheer white silk that fit close to the skin and cinched a little bit below the waist by a single silver cord of braided silk. The fabric was thin, meant to please the husband by falling softly over the swell of breasts, hinting at the pink buds underneath. To cover the bride from all other eyes, there was a mantle lined in satin and embroidered on the outside with swirling Celtic knots. The fabric flowed in thick, glossy folds to the floor.

"You are the vision of a virgin a dragon would give his life for." Alysia stood back to examine her mistress after tying the silver cord at Brynna's waist.

Brynna knit her delicate brow, then laughed. "And you, Alysia, are a hopeless romantic with dreams of times long dead."

"That may be so, but surely you will drive your husband mad with desire when he beholds you later this evening," Alysia replied while Lily brushed Brynna's hair to a burnished copper sheen, then fit a circlet of tiny white daisies braided into a cord of fine silver over her forehead.

Someone knocked at the door and Alysia motioned for

Lily to open it while she reached for the satin mantle. She was just beginning to tie the mantle closed when Lord Richard entered the room.

The Saxon lord stood at the doorway, simply gazing at his daughter, as Alysia stepped away from Brynna. "You look just like your mother." He breathed each word with a tight chest.

"Thank you, Father." Brynna smiled, then looked down at herself. "I hope it pleases Brand."

"Brynnafar." He went to her and took her hands in his. "If he is not pleased, then there is no hope at all and I will take you to Normandy with me."

"Father, I could not—"

He smiled, holding his hand up to quiet her. His eyes softened with emotion. "I jest, daughter. You are a rare beauty and your betrothed knows it, just as I did when I married your mother. He will be pleased beyond anything he has ever known, though I would prefer not to think about *that*," he added with an unpleasant scowl. He pulled the folds of his daughter's mantle closer together, then smiled tenderly. "I remember mine and your mother's wedding night. . . ." His voice trailed off and Brynna's eyes grew warm with tears, watching warmth and love soften her father's handsome face.

"You will be happy with this man, Brynnafar," he reassured her, wiping the tears from her eyes with the backs of his fingers. "I have spent the last week with him and come to find that I like him." Richard moved closer to her and whispered so that her handmaidens wouldn't hear. "Although if he wasn't going to be your husband today, I would have taken my sword to him last eve." He winked at his daughter before she could reply.

Lord Richard pulled her into the circle of his strong arms and kissed her cheek softly. "Now come, before William frightens away our chaplain and the marriage cannot take place after all."

Brynna laughed and laced her arm through her father's, letting him lead her out the door.

Candlelight danced along freshly polished mahogany pews. Incense permeated the castle's church, sending thin white wisps upward. A row of Brand's men lined the eastern stone walls while Lord Richard's men stood like silver statues against the west. William's men sat among the guests.

Brand's armored vest flashed against the thousands of flickering flames while his sea blue eyes stared, unblinking at the great carved wooden doors that led to the castle. He was about to begin a new life with a woman who considered him a cold, ruthless bastard. But then, he had never given her a reason to think otherwise. How would he ever make her happy? he wondered solemnly. And how was it that Brynnafar Dumont had found a way to make him care about her happiness at all?

He thought about the many moments they had spent together since he arrived at Avarloch. God's teeth, she was a passionate woman. That those passions usually sparked the hottest when she was angry only attracted him to her more. But he had also tasted her fervent kisses. *Oui*, she did naught to deny the fact that she desired him as much as he desired her. That bit of knowledge had served in keeping him awake for many hours after he left her the night before. He smiled softly in the warm glow of the candlelight, addled by the effect the woman had on him.

Merde, he had to be daft, but she'd given him a rose and then kept its thorns from pricking his skin. How had that simple act affected him so? He had no more time to think about it. When the gentle sound of a harp rang out in the church, he drew in a deep breath.

"You are not thinking of running, are you?" William whispered close to his ear.

Brand's smile widened into a grin. "*Non,* though I've no doubt you would leap into my spot the moment I was gone."

"Most assuredly," the Norman duke agreed with a hard slap on Brand's back.

Standing behind them, the chaplain cleared his throat. The sound was more like a grunt, and when William turned to look at him, the pious man glared.

"He is expecting me to gut someone any moment now," William said with a tight smile curling the corner of his mouth. "My reputation precedes me."

"Not entirely," Brand corrected him. "Remember Lady Winifred's wedding? You left her a widow before she could complete her vows."

The duke narrowed his eyes, recalling the fateful wedding. "Ah, *oui,* now I remember!" His face grew dark for a moment, then brightened again. "Well, we need not worry about that happening today." He slapped Brand on the back again and peered over his shoulder with a menacing grin for the chaplain.

A hush went through the church as the bride appeared at the entrance, accompanied by her father.

William heard the man at his side draw in another deep breath as though readying himself for an execution, but when he looked at Brand, he saw awe in Brand's eyes. The duke of Normandy smiled softly and stepped away from his dearest friend.

Flames shifted, causing shadows to dance along the dark walls and casting Brynna in a strange tawny golden light. Watching his fiery goddess, Brand didn't see anything but her eyes. Lord Richard handed his daughter over with a smile of genuine warmth, but Brand barely saw. As if Brynna were too lovely to behold without sighing, her betrothed swallowed and slanted his gaze away from her.

Vows were spoken, echoing promises of obedience, honor, and love. As Brand spoke them, his heart ached. He wanted to keep them. He wished with all his heart that he could.

Listening to Brand promise to love her, Brynna heard the hope that laced his words. She thrust her chin forward, squaring her shoulders. She was the daughter of a warrior. She did not care how long it took, this man's heart would be hers. She would conquer the cold emptiness that had laid siege to her merman. And she would bring him back. She had to, for the good of her heart depended on it.

When it came time to kiss her, Brand slipped his hands around her small waist, beneath the mantle to the thin fabric that awaited him. Delight curled his lips and hunger bent his body to hers. Brynna parted her lips, eager for his kiss. It came so slowly, so tenderly, that it made her tremble against him. As his arms came around her fully, his mantle gathered her up like the wings of a great black bird and cheers rose up from the knights and vassals surrounding them. But the loudest cheer came from William.

Brand withdrew finally. A smile as unexpected as a summer rain washed over his face and Brynna touched his cheek, once again fearing that he was not real and he might vanish if she but closed her eyes.

"Your people approve." His voice against her ear sent chills down her spine.

Brynna's eyes ran over the many smiling faces of his knights. "As do yours, m'lord."

"Then we must not disappoint them." His lips were already drawing near hers again and his breath was as hot as the passion in his eyes.

❊

Keeping one hand against the small of his wife's back, Brand led Brynna to the great hall, where the feast was about to begin. Long trestle tables, lined up along the length of each wall, were adorned with bouquets of fresh, late-blooming roses. Thick silver plates and goblets were set before every chair. Ale and mead waited in barrels for silver jugs to dip and fill. There was fresh baked trout and salted herring, pigs roasted whole and dressed in a myriad of fruit, fresh fowl and breads flavored with spices that warmed the soul. Minstrels filled the air with the sweet sound of harp and lute, while knights escorted ladies to the chairs beside the many serfs and vassals of Avarloch.

Brynna stared at the lavishly decorated hall in wonder as they made their way toward the dais. "Where did we get all this food? I know that the larder is half-empty from the early frost."

"Dante and I spent most of yesterday hunting so that the food would be fresh, and then we traveled to the village to do some trading." Brand cast her a playful side-long glance. "Did you not miss me? I wasn't here all day."

"You went yourself?" Brynna asked in astonishment, cataloging the vast amount of food strewn along the tables. "Why did you not send the cooks to do the trading?"

Brand shrugged his muscular shoulders. "I just wanted to make sure everything would be pleasing to you."

Brynna finally turned and stared up at him. "You did all this for me?"

Stopping, Brand met her awe-filled gaze. *"Oui,"* he said simply, as if she should have expected it.

"Thank you." It was a whisper. She could manage nothing more. Such consideration from a man who did not even love her. Saints, but she could not imagine what he would have done for her if he did.

Lord Richard was the first to offer his blessings to the couple by swallowing his daughter up in a great embrace. When he threw his arms around Brand next, the dark warrior looked over a massive shoulder at his wife in wide-eyed disbelief. A moment later William stepped around Brand and took Brynna's shoulders in his hands.

"May I kiss the bride?" the duke implored wolfishly.

"By all means." Brand lifted Brynna's hand and held it in front of the duke's face.

William looked at the offering as though it were diseased; then he glared at Brand. "That is not what I had in mind."

"But it is all you will get," Brand responded with a sweet smile.

Glowering, the duke pecked her hand, mumbling even before he lifted his head that his dearest friend did not even trust him with his wife.

Brynna watched the mighty duke slink away in self-pity and she finally bestowed a smile on the brutish warrior, though he did not see it. "He is a pussycat with large deadly fangs," she decided out loud, then slid her green-eyed gaze at her husband. "As are you."

Turning to her with a silky smile curving his mouth, Brand grazed his thumb across her lower lip. "Sometimes getting bitten can give you intense pleasure, wife." He added the last word with a fierce, sensual glint in his eyes.

Brynna licked her lip, where his finger had been, and Brand watched her, his blood beating a savage path to his loins. "Mayhap even inviting one to bite back . . . husband," she countered.

The expression on Brand's face was both surprised and delighted. He bowed to her slightly, staring into her eyes with predatory intensity from below dark lashes. "A fierce opponent makes for a more interesting battle. One that could last all night . . . even until the morn." He parried with a devastating grin and his cerulean eyes glowed with heat that made Brynna's mouth go dry. She was unable to stifle her sigh when a quivering burst of fire blazed through her. She took a bold step closer to him as he straightened and directed his hidden hand to the beguiling curve of her buttocks. She could feel the fullness of him as she lifted her lips to his neck.

"A long battle brings sweeter victory, warrior." She purred against his skin, then stepped back, looking up into his eyes with a triumphant smile. But Brand dragged her back against him, using only the hand firmly clamped on her beloved bottom. He squeezed, lifting her hips to a hardness that made her eyes open wider.

"Or a merciless defeat." His voice was a low, throaty growl. He was surprised by the savage need that raked him, made him feel about to burst if he didn't take her quickly. Never had he wanted a woman so badly. He could think of nothing else but the misty drenching of her most passionate place closing tightly around him, accepting his fullness. To taste her eager breasts and drink from the hard, erect buds he wanted to devour the night before.

Burning from the heat of his body, the driving hunger in his eyes, Brynna realized suddenly that this man was indeed what she had called him . . . a warrior. If she chose to play this dangerous game of seduction with him, she must be prepared to withstand the strength of his arm, the onslaught of fire that drove him, and the endurance that always brought him victory. Looking into his eyes, being crushed up against his lithe, hard body, Brynna knew she had to try. She was falling in love with him and she intended to have him love her back.

"You have already fought a Dumont in battle and won. You challenge his daughter now, and though we will meet on another type of battlefield, I assure you this time the defeat will be yours." Her eyes danced with the challenge at the same time a provocative smile slid across her lips. With a careful tug, she broke free of his grasp and walked off, looking over her shoulder to relish the state she had left her husband in.

Brand watched her, diamond-hard eyes grazing slowly over her body from head to foot. He rubbed the tips of his fingers together, remembering the feel of the sheer silk between them. His wife was playing another game with him, and this time she would lose. His smile tightened at the thought of defeating her.

His feet moved, bringing him to her quickly. In one swift instant Brynna was hoisted into his arms.

"What are you doing?" she cried out, frightened by the strength of him and the animallike hunger in his gaze.

"The battle," he said as he strode toward the stairs, "has begun."

Chapter Thirteen

❋

"Put me down! Everyone is watching!" Brynna's eyes darted quickly around the hall and then she blushed profusely at the shocked faces of their guests. "Brand . . ." She looked at him, pleading for him not to humiliate her this way, but his gaze was hard, demanding, and voracious.

"You play dangerous games, lady, and have sparked my curiosity." The corners of his mouth lifted into a savage curl. "I truly hope you can live through your challenge."

Brynna's heart pumped furiously in her chest. Live through it? Why would he say such a thing? Had she gone too far? She had ached for him so many times after seeing him at the lake, wearing nothing but a smile that resembled an angel in sinful ecstasy. But he was with a woman he loved that day. This was different, for though she was now his wife, Brynna knew that he felt naught for her but heated passion. How heated? She wondered as panic filled her eyes. Would he punish her for playing a game she knew naught about? She chewed her lip, worrying over her self-induced dilemma.

"Are you frightened?" Brand whispered. His eyes

burned with pure masculine power . . . and a sparkle of amusement.

"Should I be?"

He nodded. Brynna's pulse ticked wildly at her throat and he stroked it softly with his tongue as he carried her up the stairs. The taste of her skin made him ache for her all the more. He buried his face in her neck.

"I have never . . . ," Brynna started to say.

"I know," he whispered against her flesh.

Kicking the door open, Brand carried her into his room and stopped before the enormous bed. "The battlefield? Or someplace more neutral?" he offered, motioning toward a thick brown bearskin rug on the floor beside the roaring fire of the hearth.

Brynna swallowed. Both places seemed equally frightening. Indeed, she had gone too far with this man, promising him pleasure she knew not how to give. He would be angry, impatient, take her without tenderness. She had thought about this moment with him so many times that she felt confident she would know what to do, how to please him. But now, with the hearth fire warming the fur rug, the huge bed waiting to commence the passionate battle, and his hands clenched tightly around her, a fresh wave of panic invaded Brynna's nerves. She looked up at him, hoping to find comfort in the beauty of his blue-green gaze. She saw only raw hunger.

"Where, Brynna?"

"I—I . . . ," she stammered.

For a moment his eyes softened. "Neutral, then," he decided, taking three steps to the rug. He set her down as if she were a newborn babe. Her slippers disappeared into the luscious fur. He hooked his mouth into a half smile;

then he turned and headed for a small trunk at the other end of the room, tossing his mantle carelessly onto the bed as he went. He squatted, rummaging through the trunk. Brynna watched him, amazed that even in her panicked state she would notice the tight muscles in his thighs as he bent.

Besieged with images of his naked body dripping with water, she closed her eyes as silky threads of fire singed her somewhere deep within. Loving him frightened her even more than her husband's icy passion. What if he truly could never love her? The thought of it made Brynna want to run from the room. Nay, she thought defiantly, she would stay. She would let her husband fill her, gently, slowly, the way he filled her in her dreams.

She pulled at the laces that tied her mantle closed. The satin fell away into a feathery heap at her feet.

Finding what he was looking for, Brand rose to his feet, but when he turned around to face Brynna again, he stopped, arrested by the very sight of her. The firelight shimmered behind her, illuminating the silhouette of her body beneath the sheer silk. Fine curves and luscious lines beckoned him, ignited the smoldering fire in his body to the point of bursting. He sighed, looking at her, but it sounded more like a growl to Brynna and she tried desperately to calm the pounding of her heart.

"You are beautiful," he said in a low, powerful voice as he came toward her. Drawing in a deep breath, he slipped his hand through her hair, closing his eyes in delight when her fiery tresses wound around his fingers as if they were alive and answering the call of his desire. He caressed her scalp and turned her around so that her back was facing him.

Holding her breath, Brynna expected him to tear the thin gown from her body. She was surprised when his fingers slid down the back of her neck as softly as a sigh. He drew her hair away from the creamy flesh of her neck. He kissed her nape with a sweet, lingering tenderness that made her quiver as another thread of fire licked her spine.

She felt something cool touch her skin and instinctively put her hand to her throat just as Brand finished clasping the emerald choker at her neck.

She gasped. "What is this?"

"A wedding gift." His lips fluttered over her earlobe before he turned her to face him again. He stepped back to admire his gift. "And still your eyes are greener." He bathed in her glory.

She stood before him, her breathing suspended. He was tall and warrior hard, but it was the intensity of his eyes that made her doubt she could ever conquer the cold. She went to him, reaching up to touch a raven curl dangling over his eyes. "I have naught to give you."

"But you do," he corrected deeply, slipping one hand around her waist.

"Brand." Brynna sighed, her eyes full of meaning. "I want . . ."

"What?" He brought his mouth close to hers, cupping her face in his hand. "What do you want?"

"I want to please you." It was not a lie, but it was not what she meant to say. She could not tell him that she wanted his heart—his love. She would have to win it, the way he had won Avarloch from her father.

"You will please me, Brynna. Just looking at you pleases me." His hungry mouth found hers. His tongue entered smoothly, finding and then stroking hers like a heated flame. He gathered her closer, tighter, into his arms while his tongue worked gently, then darted deeper and withdrew.

Brynna was consumed by the strength of his body, and with every thrust of his tongue, she grew weaker. He claimed her with his mouth, biting with exquisite care, licking, drinking her in a way she never thought possible.

"I love you," she whispered while he licked fire down her neck. He stiffened, and Brynna cursed herself for blurting out in her passion what her heart had to conceal.

He stepped back. His hands dropped to his sides. "Brynna . . ."

"Ssh." She stepped close to him and held her finger to his lips. "I am sorry." She ran the tip of her finger down the slight dimple in his chin, then to his shoulders, where she began working the metal clasps of his armored vest. The silver metal fell away with a heavy clang to the floor and Brynna kicked it away without lifting her fingers from her husband's body. With tender care she untied the laces of his tunic while her heart beat wildly within her ribs.

Brand closed his eyes when she kissed his chest. His nostrils flared slightly as the scent of her hair floated upward. She pulled the tunic up over his arms, savoring the strength in his arms as they lifted above his head, then the height of him when she realized she could not reach his head to disrobe him. He finished for her, tossing the tunic to the floor.

Burning with a desire that even Brynna's dreams had not prepared her for, she ran her fingers down the tight, sleek muscles in his arms, then farther, caressing his corded belly. Brand groaned, unable to subdue the throbbing, wonderful pain his wife was causing him. And finally, when he felt her teeth against his skin, he ripped the buttons from her gown and tore the sheer fabric from her body as if it were paper. He dropped to his knees and began kissing her smooth, milky belly. So gently did he trace his fingers down her back and over the full luscious curves of her buttocks that she trembled in his arms. Then she stiffened when his tongue and teeth traversed an aching path to the silky mound below her navel.

Closing her eyes, Brynna felt his body quake as though she had caused him pain. Suddenly he rose to his full height and lifted her up in his arms. He kissed her breasts, lifting his head briefly to admire them with savage, sultry eyes before returning to run his tongue over the hard peaks that grew even tighter from his touch. He tugged on them gently with his lips while pleasure snapped his body taut at the slight breathless moan that was ripped from his wife's throat. He lifted his face again and looked at her. The sight of her head thrown back in languid ecstasy made him fear he could not be gentle taking her. He clenched his teeth as passion inflamed him, drove him to lay her down on the fur so that he could free himself from the confines of his trousers.

Brynna fell silent as she beheld the fully aroused warrior poised over her. Shadows danced over his sinewy muscle while firelight played seductively upon heated, glistening flesh.

"Brand, I am frightened."

He knelt beside her and stroked her hair. "*Non,* I will not hurt you."

"But how will it ever fit?" she lamented.

He smiled at her sweet innocence. "It will fit," he

whispered, kissing her. "I will help it go in smoothly. I will go slowly, Brynna."

"But you said—"

He leaned over her. The heat from his body warmed her. His eyes held hers captive with a strange force that was as powerful as the muscles that danced in his arms. "I meant to take you without a care, truly I did. But you are as delicate as a flower, more beautiful than a thousand sunrises." He moved his thumb over her nipple and then caressed the full swell of her breast. His touch was softer than a whisper and Brynna bit her lip as fire exploded between her legs. "Your beauty overwhelms me." He slid his tongue over her lower lip. "Your eyes are more radiant than the rarest of gems. They are filled with passion yet to be discovered. I want to bury my face in the warmth of your hair and lose myself in the scent that beckons me. And these breasts"—he moved his face down the valley between them—"so full and firm and beautiful." His mouth found the tight rose tips and his tongue slid over them while he cupped their fullness in his hands. "Ah, I meant to be rough. Make you never forget, but I cannot. I want to savor each caress. I want to take you slowly, feel every embrace, and make you cry out with delight and pleasure so intense your body will ache for more every moment that I am not inside you."

Brynna heard his sultry promises echoing in her mind. She wanted to tell him that she was aching already, but his body was so hot as it moved over hers she could say naught, save the utterances of passion from deep within her throat.

He slid down her body, spreading her legs apart with his hands. Brynna groaned and gasped as his gentle fingers parted the soft folds of her secret lips. She gripped the fur beneath her in tightly clenched fingers as wet heat began to pulse and pump her blood.

"A tender bud that will soon blossom into a ravishing flower," she heard him say before his face disappeared between her thighs.

She was being bathed in warmth, consumed by a fire so controlled she ached for it to engulf her, to feel it consume her fully. He lifted her in an undulating dance amid a myriad of waves that rocked her to and fro while light burst and showered her in delicious heat. Her breath came in hard gasps as the pink buds that crowned her breasts reached toward the heavens. His lips, his tongue, his teeth, worked to drive her into delighted oblivion. She cried out as more waves washed over her. Shamelessly she opened her legs wider, reaching down to grasp the cool black curls that brushed against her thighs.

Flames licked and cracked the wood in the hearth, but Brand's mouth was hotter. His hands gripped her hips with strength that frightened even him. His tight control was fading with each heated movement of her body, with every soft moan he pulled from her. He ached to ravish her, to take her with the primal fervor of an untamed beast. But he held on with the last thread of restraint he possessed. Then, slowly, he lifted himself over her. She was ready, and the aching in his loins was enough to make him forget his whispered promises and plunge deep within her.

The taste of her own sweet passion lingered on Brand's lips as they stole over her mouth. "I fear I will die if I don't have you." He groaned. Brynna trembled, for his voice was savage and hard.

She stared into his sea blue eyes as his pulsing manhood glided over the moist entrance of her body. He entered slowly, as he had promised, though she could read in the tight line of his lips that it took every ounce of self-control not to thrust himself inside her. He gazed into her eyes with a tenderness that surprised her, yet the passion in them threatened to overwhelm her.

As Brand suspected, her body gripped him, clenching tightly to accept him. He groaned from deep within, lifting his head like a beast about to howl. He filled her more completely than Brynna would have believed possible. Searing heat ripped through her, stretched her until she cried out. But the sound faded within the softness of his kisses. He whispered to her, told her how she felt inside, warm and tight and so silky sweet. And then he began to move.

Brynna thought she could not survive his thrusts. But the pain ebbed and pleasure took its place as the velvet rhythm of his slow plunges moved her body against the fur beneath her. Throbbing tremors built within until they were unbearable and she lifted her legs around him to answer the call of his driving hunger. She gasped, moaned, moistened her lips with her tongue and Brand thrust harder, deeper. Ecstasy, so complete it made her innocence a thing long forgotten, pushed her until she dug her fingernails heedlessly into his muscles.

"Your strength consumes me. You are so hard, so rigid."

Brynna's voice was like a whip across Brand's back. His body tightened, aching to explode within her. He felt he could not fill her enough. His body wanted more and more. He retreated, slowly, torturously, almost to exiting her, then filled her again, so slowly, Brynna moaned with long, languid heat. He withdrew again and smiled almost sinfully at her response to feeling the full length of him. He slid into her again, relishing every tight spasm her body used to grip him.

The ground beneath Brynna pitched and rocked as the smooth slide of Brand's body took her again and again. She arched her back. He closed his eyes, plunging harder, driven mad by the sensuous movements of her body under his, pulling, aching, and accepting him fully. He caught her wrists and held them over her head. She looked at him and saw that he was smiling, not the rhapsodic delight she had seen once before, but the molten heat in his eyes told her that his pleasure was about to be set free.

He pursed his lips slightly, drawing in a deep breath. "My defeat comes quickly, Brynna." He breathed tightly, then threw his head back. Cords strained his neck as a harsh groan permeated the air. Brynna felt his honey liquid rush into her like a tidal wave.

He caused spasms to convulse her body, exploding into fantastic color before her eyes. Her fingernails dug into his hands with careless abandon and she cried out, again and again, as waves of pleasure devoured her, rendering her weak under him.

Brand's weight fell upon her, encasing her with delicious, dominating heat as he kissed her neck, found her lips. "You surprised me, wife." He lifted his head and stared into her eyes with a passion that still lingered.

"Does this mean I won, m'lord?" Brynna lay in languid relaxation beneath him.

"*Oui*, you won." Passion darkened his eyes. "But it was only the first assault. My sword is still hungry for battle." His hands moved over her breasts, claiming with his fingers the nipple he brought back to life.

Brynna's eyes widened. "You cannot mean . . . again?" But even as she asked the question, she felt the rigid sword inside her begin its second attack.

This time Brand ravaged her, his passion fully unleashed. The muscular thrusts of his body were like thunder while his hands roamed roughly over her breasts, along her thighs, lifting her hips higher. He cupped her buttocks in his palms, kneading them with his fingers, pushing her to meet him further so that his devouring, slow plunges went deeper. He stroked her neck, licked her lips, and then bit them softly, and all the while he watched her as if the very sight of her drove him, rather than the silky spasms that clenched him.

"It fits well, does it not, lady?" A sound was ripped from him after he spoke that made Brynna arch her back.

"Aye, warrior, it fits perfectly."

Brand took her the way he took all things, with a driving need that gave him his nickname, the Passionate. He savored her as though it were the last time he would ever take her, delighting in her body the way he delighted in the water, the way he battled on the field. And in the end he was victorious, though Brynna's defeat came sweetly as he tasted her, savoring the salt of her skin and whispering promises of pleasure so complete that she would not only surrender, but also die to have him in her again and again. And she did, giving her life to the warrior who took her until the morning came.

Chapter Fourteen

✳

The sun crept over the horizon, as though sensing the battle that raged within Brand while he lay beside his new wife. He watched her while she slept. Part of him wanted to take her in his arms, run his fingertip along the thick fringes of her lashes, trace the full outline of her lips. He wanted to know her, discover the things that sparked that fiery temper. What made her smile? What brought tears to her beautiful eyes? His gaze swept over a copper curl that had fallen across her cheek. He wanted to touch that curl and kiss her alabaster cheek, but a tightness settled in his chest at the thought. She was his wife. He had made love to her all night long, yet he found it difficult to touch her so intimately now. It was as if doing so would somehow tear open his chest and lay his heart bare before her. Even if he wanted to allow Brynna to touch that raw, wounded part of himself, he couldn't let her. The sting of betrayal still pricked like thorns. Colette had taken too much from him. Still, Brynna was the kind of woman battles were fought over. Passionate, spirited, gloriously beautiful, sexy as hell, compassionate, and kind. She radiated heat and perfection, and Brand raised his hand to her hair, wanting her, wanting to lose himself in the warmth that clothed her. He groaned, then turned away from her peaceful face.

Raking his hands through his hair, he rose to his feet, dressed quickly, and left the room.

William stopped him on the stairs, a wide grin brightening his harsh face. "You missed a spectacular feast, my friend," he announced, then offered Brand a wicked smile. He had seen Brand carry his bride off the day before and the hungry gleam in both their eyes. "But I'm sure you had one of your own, eh?" He slapped the younger knight on the back. "I'm pleased to see that you've not lost the fire that burned your loins before that de Marson wench entered your life."

"It does no good, William," Brand answered quietly, lifting his eyes to William's before he left. "I've lost something far more priceless. I don't want to love her."

William was left staring at the flash of black curls against a swirl of crimson as Brand hurried down the stairs. Understanding washed over the duke's face and regret filled his gray gaze. He was the one who had taught Brand that anything of value could be gained with a good enough fight. William looked at the door to Brand's room. A spark of determination glinted in his eyes as he headed for it. Now it was time to teach that lesson to his wife.

Brynna's clothes had not been brought into Brand's chambers yet, so she had to find something of her husband's to wear when she heard the urgency in the rapping at the door. She slipped into black hose that fit her quite well, save for the gatherings at her ankles. The tight fit made her think about how deliciously snug they were on her husband. The buff-colored tunic she pulled from his wardrobe was quite another story. It sagged on her shoulders and fell to her knees until she cinched it at her waist with the silver cord from her torn wedding gown.

When she finally opened the door, she was surprised to see William towering over her on the other side.

"We need to talk," he said, pushing himself into the room.

"What is it? Where is Brand?" Brynna was startled by the seriousness in the duke's voice. Her heart hammered in her chest when she realized that the sun had just come up and her husband was already gone.

"He just left. That is what we need to talk about."

Brynna studied the savage man taking a seat in a chair beside the cold hearth. "Is there something wrong, m'lord?" she asked him, bringing her hand to her chest.

His eyes met hers, and for a moment something passed between them; there was a warmth that reached beyond Brynna's anger and William's callous taunting, a warmth and love they both shared for the same man.

"Your husband is lost and 'tis up to you to bring him back to us."

Brynna nodded. If there was a way to break through Brand's thick defenses, she wanted to know how to do it. The strength in Duke William's eyes made her feel like she could. She sat at his feet and looked up at him. "Tell me what to do. How do I make Brand forget Colette and the pain she caused him?"

"Ah, you know about the wench, then?"

"Dante told me," Brynna said. She saw no reason to tell the duke that she had seen Brand with his love.

"She is a quiet seductress with roving, sultry eyes," William told her. "A spoiled brat whose own father was so relieved to be rid of her that he agreed to let her live with

Brand, even though they were unwed. I visited the girl's father, Lord Fredric de Marson, at his home only to find that Colette had run off the week after she was returned. My men and I found her several days later living a few leagues away with another man. Lady Colette is a vision of beauty, and she knows how to lure men into her clutches. I dragged her home to her father once again. The wench begged me the entire way to return her to Brand, even offering herself to me for recompense. I was tempted to take her, for she is finer than the most sought-after land, but her beauty is deadly, beguiling in its soft innocence."

"She sounds wretched."

"Indeed, she is. Though I don't believe she ever showed that side of herself to Brand until the end. She needed him too much to escape the tight rule of her father."

"How can I fight her?" Brynna asked. The duke smiled at her, a soft, gentle smile that Brynna was surprised to see.

"I'm not certain it is Colette you must fight, but more what she did to him. You care for him," William said with knowing certainty. "'Tis clear to see in your eyes, *ma cher*."

"Aye, I do."

"Then be patient and understanding. Do not push him too quickly. You have already conquered much, for he was so set against taking a wife that the king had to drag me all the way from Normandy to convince him. But it was you who changed his mind, not I. He only obeys my commands when he wants to." William had risen to his feet then and took her hands in his, pulling her to her feet. "Fight for him, Brynna. You have warrior blood in you. Fight for him. Once, he lived his life with a passion. Help him live that way again and his love will be worth the battle."

⁂

Brand rode swiftly on his horse, though he knew not where he was going. He rode like one pursued by demons, his breath hard and heavy. The earth trembled beneath his stallion's black hooves. He rode over lush grass and then past trees of chestnut and oak. In the forest he could hide himself away from the anger and pain that followed him. Thick brush and dense wood could conceal him from the demons that plagued him with uncertainty for enjoying his wife, for wanting to be with her, for wanting to smell the clean scent of her. And the forest, with its gnarled branches that reached up toward the sun for the life-giving warmth that was being snatched away from it by the coming winter, could understand the cold emptiness he felt because he did not want to love her.

He stopped his horse finally when he came to a small steppe overlooking a lake that was beginning to freeze over. Even here he could not escape.

Dismounting, he dropped the reins carelessly and looked out over the surface of the lake.

He thought he had prepared himself enough to marry Brynna, to guard against her ever reaching him. He was no longer certain he had succeeded. Why would he be so daft to let another woman into his heart? Hadn't he learned his lesson well enough? Alexander was dead because Brand allowed himself to be blinded by what wasn't even real. And what was real? He didn't know anymore, and that was what worked at destroying him. He closed his eyes against the sunlight and saw Brynna's face. She seemed real enough. Her eyes were so easy to read. Her expressions, so open. She loved her father, and her love and loyalty for Avarloch were perfectly clear when she offered to fight him for it. Even more when she married a cold cad to avoid a battle she would not be there to witness. But even that wasn't enough for him. How could he trust his judgment when he'd been so wrong before? Still—and hell this was the worst of it—she had wrenched his heart from its place when she gave him that damned rose. Did she even know the effect it had on him when she saved his flesh from being pierced by a thorn? Would she protect his heart with such care?

His thoughts turned to the night before and a warm shaft of heat licked his spine. How had she managed to ignite such raw desire in him? He had wanted to make Brynna ache for him. He wanted her to yearn for his passion so much that she could never be satisfied by anyone else. But he was the one aching for her. And it scared the hell out of him. He knew that no woman would ever satisfy him the way Brynna did. In his mind he could see the vivid green of her eyes—sultry, teasing eyes that danced when she laughed and burned as hot as her temper when she was angry.

Brand had no idea how long he sat looking at the lake. Nor did he feel the cold that bit at his muscles, making them stiff. And he almost did not hear the voice that called his name.

Turning, he spotted Brynna leaving the trees. She walked with her cloak pulled tightly around her, leading her father's mount by the bridle over roots and rocks to reach him.

As their eyes met, his wary gaze stole her breath

away. She said nothing but simply sat beside him in the grass.

Her long hair draped her shoulders and Brand ached to touch it, to find his warmth within its bronze masses. "What are you doing here?" he asked, turning his turquoise gaze away from her.

"I don't want you to be alone."

"I want to be alone," he replied with less conviction than he'd felt in the past year. He stared at the sunlit surface of the water, remaining silent.

"I know about her, Brand," Brynna admitted, breaking the silence that stretched across his haunted eyes. "I know about Colette. Dante and William told me."

His shoulders tightened and then sagged when he shook his head. "They should not have told you. She means naught to me."

"Means naught?" Brynna asked incredulously. "You are still in love with her. How can that not mean anything?"

He blinked slowly, still watching the cold, crystalline water that matched his eyes. "You must forget what they told you."

Brynna's eyes narrowed on him. "How can I forget that my husband loves another?"

"This is not about love, Brynna. You and I did not marry for love," he answered dully.

Brynna's eyes filled with tears, but she did not let them fall. "But I do love you, Brand," she whispered.

"*Non,* you don't." He sighed. "You love how I made you feel last eve. Do not confuse the two."

Pain wrenched at her heart. He certainly did not confuse the two, she was sure of that. Well, she didn't care what he thought. It was high time he knew the truth of it. "Nay, I love you, husband. You claimed my heart the first time I saw you."

Brand finally looked at her then with a slight, doubtful smile. "You wanted me dead when I arrived at Avarloch."

"Nay, my beloved," she corrected, searching his eyes for the merman she longed for. "I saw you in Porthleven, swimming in a lagoon much like this one." She turned toward the freezing lake and her gaze lingered there as she remembered that wonderful day. "You were alone at first and I watched you. Then she came. I saw her Brand." Brynna brought her gaze back to him. "I saw you with her. . . ." Her voice trailed off and she lowered her eyes from his penetrating stare.

"You saw us?" It was all he could say, too shocked by her confession to say anything else. Brynna nodded. Confusion tore at his mind. He wanted to be angry with her because she never told him that she knew about Colette all along. He searched for his anger wherever anger lay hidden in the soul, but he could not find it. Odd, he thought, anger always lurked close to his heart when he thought of Colette. He did his best to produce a good, meaningful scowl to let her know that he didn't approve of her spying, eavesdropping ways. "What were you doing in Porthleven?" At the same moment he asked, he noticed that she was wearing his clothes and he fought not to smile.

"I was visiting my uncle. My company passed Porthleven on the way home and I wandered off alone when our carriage was stopped on the road by a fallen tree." Dear God, it felt cleansing telling him. "I saw you, so beautiful and in love with life, and I never forgot you, Brand."

Her words finally began to settle on him and he simply stared at her. Brynna forced herself to hold his gaze. But then he blinked and his eyes softened on her with such melting tenderness she thought she might just faint. "But I took your home," he reminded her quietly. "Your father is leaving Avarloch because of me."

"I know." She barely breathed.

"My people killed your mother, Brynna."

"Aye."

"And still you think you love me?"

"I know I do."

Brand studied her. He even angled his head trying to discern if she was telling him the truth. "You knew about Colette all along," he said rather then asked her, fully understanding what she had seen now. He knew the day she spoke of.

"I knew there was someone in your life whom you loved. Forgive me for not telling you," she answered, watching him turn to spread his thoughtful gaze over the water. She thought she saw the edges of his mouth lift in a slight smile.

"What did you see . . . exactly?" he pondered carefully.

Brynna sighed, remembering. "Everything. You were naked, letting the water wash over you in gleeful bliss. And then she arrived and I couldn't leave. I was trapped there behind those blasted bushes, dying with fright that I might be discovered."

Her husband's face broke into a wider smile, and as he turned that wondrous smile on her, the shadows that haunted his eyes faded.

It was a smile like the one Brynna had seen before—amused, happy, unexpected, and utterly radiant. "What do you find so humorous?" she asked, already blushing and breathless.

"I'm pleased that the sight of my body could enchant you so." His eyes danced with humor and affection, and Brynna's heart leaped. His smile was real and not calculated, innocent yet mischievous.

"I assure you, sir, it was your face—I mean, the happiness in your face that captivated me, not your body."

"It was my body," he insisted, moving in closer to her. He bent his head until his lips hovered just over hers. "You were enraptured by the sight of me." He laughed softly when Brynna rolled her eyes and tried to shove him away. "Admit it," he persisted, breathing in the scent of her hair.

"I admit nothing," Brynna said indignantly. She folded her arms across her chest and tried to turn away from him, but he took her chin in his hand and lifted her face to his.

"Thank you for last eve." Then he added with a lecherous grin, "And for this morn."

In the sunlight his eyes were bright aqua, sea blue wonders, and as Brynna gazed into them, she thought she saw something in the vastness, something full of meaning. She stroked his rough cheek. "You need not thank your wife for her duty, sir."

"It was more than duty," he whispered, and ran his lips over her mouth. "Was it not, Brynna?"

"Aye," she responded breathily just before he kissed her. Oh, it was so much more, she thought as he pulled her down and untied her cloak.

✳

They returned to the castle to find William standing in the front bailey watching intently while Dante fought against one of the duke's knights. Swords clashed and sparked, making Brynna gasp on her horse, but when she saw Alysia clapping frantically and jumping up and down in her spot, Brynna turned to her husband with a look of wonder.

"This is practice?"

Brand smiled slightly, shaking his head at the Norman duke, who was now bellowing at his man for losing. "Some might call it that," he told her with an exasperated sigh. "William is very competitive. He does not like to lose at anything, so even practice becomes competition. And right now it looks like he is losing." Brand cast her a long, sideward glance speckled with mischief just before he flapped his reins and galloped forward.

"Come on," he called out after her.

William barely looked his way when Brand called him, but continued to admonish his defeated knight.

"A little friendly competition, William?" Brand grinned, reining in.

Dante smiled, exchanging a quick, knowing glance with his brother.

"How many of his men have you beaten so far?" Brand queried, knowing the number must be high for William to be taking it so seriously.

Dante tossed his long blade over his shoulder and slid his gaze toward William; amusement curled his lips into a victorious smile. "Seven."

Brynna eyed the muscular warrior from her horse with admiration arching her brow. Dante defeated seven men and he was barely winded. And what a roguish smile he possessed, she decided when one of her handmaidens shouted something about Hercules and Dionysus. Brynna had to agree that Lord Dante Risande was an extremely handsome man. That, coupled with the way the sun's rays gleamed off his chain-mailed chest, made him look as if he had indeed just stepped off Mount Olympus.

"This is not over yet," William announced to them all.

From atop his horse Brand skeptically lifted an eyebrow. "I don't know, it looks over to me, Will."

Now the duke smiled like a wolf about to pounce. "Your brother has one more man to fight before he is named champion."

Brand dismounted, handing the reins over to Peter. He went to Brynna next and helped her off her horse, winking before he turned to William.

"And who might that one more man be? You, William?"

The duke returned Brand's dark smirk and shook his head. "*Non,* 'tis him." He pointed to Lord Richard, who was just exiting the gatehouse, fitting a thick leather gauntlet over his hand. Cheers rose up from Avarloch's vassals and Brynna joined in the revelry by throwing her father a kiss when he winked at her.

"Very well," Brand called out as William made his way toward the lists. "But if Dante wins, you must bow down before us all and kiss my arse."

"*Oui,*" William agreed. "And if Richard wins, you will bow down before your wife and kiss my . . ." He glanced at Brynna and winked.

Brand turned away and went to Brynna's side. His shoulders shook slightly as he chuckled, knowing it would drive William mad.

It did.

William barked orders for everyone to stand aside and make way for his champion knight as Richard strolled casually toward Dante—his massive blade flashing against the sun.

Folding his arms across his chest, Brand watched with an amused expression.

"You think my father will lose?" Brynna asked, and pinched his arm.

"I don't know, my lovely. Dante is a powerful warrior, but I know firsthand how skilled your father is. Whatever the outcome, Dante will put enough doubt in William's heart to make him cringe. . . . I want to be here to see it. By the way, who is Nathan?"

He asked the question so casually, Brynna was completely unprepared for it. "What? How do you know about Sir Nathan?"

Her husband laughed at William when the duke bellowed for everyone's silence, then turned back to her. "You said you smashed your aunt Gertrude's vase over his head when he thought you could not fight him. Was he someone your father promised you to?"

"Oh, good Lord, nay." Brynna laughed and then shivered at the thought. "Sir Nathan is one of my uncle's guards. A cantankerous fool who threatened to flog me."

Brand didn't flinch but turned his cool gaze back to the fight. "Did you damage him when you smashed this vase over his head?"

"Aye. He received a nasty slice just over his right eye."

"Good," her husband said quietly. Brynna could see the satisfaction in his profile and she smiled. And why had he suddenly asked her about a man she mentioned over a sennight ago? She smiled because he hadn't asked her about Nathan sooner. She would never betray him as Colette had done, but it was nice to find that her husband was beginning to feel jealousy.

Dante and Richard faced off, lifting great swords over their heads. They fought for a long time, longer than even Brand expected. And to Brand's delight, William paced nervously back and forth, lifting his steel gray eyes to Brand every few seconds.

Dante's swing was precise, savage, and wrought with devastating power. He parried brilliantly and dodged massive blows to his head, but Richard's experience ultimately won him the title of champion.

William cheered, exalting in his man's victory. He turned to seek out Brand, but his friend was nowhere to be found. Scoundrel, William thought triumphantly, and was about to make his way toward Richard when he felt cold, hard steel between his legs. He stiffened, and then a smile snaked across his face.

"The deal is off," came a low snarl from behind him, close to his ear. "I wouldn't kiss your hand, let alone that wee excuse for manhood that my sword threatens at this very moment."

"Pity," the duke replied, feigning pining. "I was hoping your wife would fulfill your end of the bargain."

Brand inched the sword closer and William flinched. "Take the sword, William, for I'm quite sure she would have bitten it off when the time came. And take that smirk off your face, you did not win."

Immediately William began to protest, but Brand hushed him with a slight jerk of his blade. "If this were a real battle, you would be dead. And an army without its leader is quickly defeated. I, my friend, have beaten you."

Brand withdrew his sword and stepped back. William pivoted around slowly, offering a dangerous glare to the man he trained to be so devious.

Brand offered him his most radiant smile in return and bowed low, trusting William not to lop off his head.

"You are ruthless," the Norman duke sneered.

Brand touched his heart with his hand. "Thank you." His eyes searched for Brynna as they always did when she was not near him, a fact his mind could not understand. He found her lost under the weight of her father's arm. His smile grew as he reached them.

"William has trained you and your brother well," Richard admitted after Brand complimented him on his victory. "I haven't fought against such skilled men since I faced the Byzantines in battle."

"We owe the duke much." Brand focused on Brynna and the way her hair blazed beneath the sun.

Richard cut a quick, sidelong glance at his daughter. "Brynna looks quite beautiful the day after her wedding, does she not?"

His son-in-law nodded. "*Oui,* she does."

"The wedding night went well, then?" Lord Richard asked.

Brand's eyes opened slightly wider, his smile froze on his face. "It was fine, thank you for asking." He stumbled over his words, disbelief at her father's query shadowing his eyes.

Richard did not notice Brand's unease. He smiled brightly and slapped the knight on the back as William would have done. "That is a good start," he advised before leaving the newlyweds to stare at him while he strode off toward William.

"Warriors lack tact. I am sorry." Brynna laced her arm through her husband's.

"He is your father! Why would he want to know something like that?"

Brynna shrugged. "He was worried you would beat me."

Turning to her with a sudden, darkly sensuous air, Brand lifted her hand to his mouth. "I did."

Brynna opened her mouth to protest, but Brand kissed her, passionately, senselessly, leaving her breathless before she could say a word; then he, too, strolled away from her.

"Where are you going?" she called out to him.

"To bed." He turned, walking backward to smile at her . . . and then at her father. "After last night I can hardly stand."

Brynna watched him go and shivered at the raw masculinity he possessed; then she smiled to herself and headed for the stable to check on her mare.

Chapter Fifteen

Brand climbed the winding stairs with a heart that felt lighter than it had in months. He smiled to himself thinking of how Brynna had looked standing in the bailey wearing his clothes. Even in a tunic that was twice her size, his wife delighted him and charmed his soul. He shook her image away. He was too tired to get aroused again, which, he smiled upon realizing, always seemed to happen when he thought of her.

He had almost reached the top of the stairs when he saw Brynna's handmaiden Rebecca on her way down. Her pale yellow hair hung loose like a silken mist around her shoulders, bouncing as she descended.

Brand went still.

For an instant he was back at Graycliff Castle watching Colette, waiting for her to reach him so that he could gather her up in his arms after returning from a battle.

"Good day, m'lord," the pale beauty greeted, then stopped as she passed him, realizing that the new lord was staring at her. "Is something wrong, m'lord?"

Blinking back to the present, Brand smiled at her. "*Non.*" He started his ascent but then stopped again and turned to her. "Please find squire Kennet and have him bring water for my bath."

"Surely, m'lord." Rebecca sighed quietly, watching him leave. Good Lord, but the man was handsome, she thought as she set out to find Kennet.

When Brand entered his room, the first thing he saw was Brynna's torn wedding gown strewn across the bearskin rug. He went to it and picked it up, bringing the delicate fabric to his nose.

The sound of William's boisterous laughter from the bailey below drew Brand to the window, still clutching the gown to his nose. The duke's arm was tossed over Richard's shoulder and there was a devious glint in William's eye, which Brand could see from his window. He laughed, guessing his friend was planning some sort of retaliation against him.

Watching the knavish duke, Brand's heart warmed. William always made him laugh, even after Colette. And Brand loved him for it. They had shared life the same way. They hungered for it, savored it with a passion that drove them in battle, love, and simple everyday things that others took for granted. They were men who would rather die than never again feel the glorious warmth of the sun on their faces or the wind biting their skin as they rode like thunder into battle. But Brand had changed, he had watched the world become dull and colorless—until he saw the color of spring in Brynna's eyes.

He inhaled her scent from the gown just as the water for his bath arrived, steaming hot. He watched from his place by the window as the screen was folded neatly away from his bath and four young squires poured water into his tub.

Rebecca waited by the door until they finished, then glanced at Brand, who was still clutching his wife's gown in his hands. "Shall I tend to you, sir?" she asked after she dismissed the squires.

"Where is Kennet?"

"I could not find him."

Brand looked out the window. He would much rather have Brynna tend to him, but she was nowhere in sight. Besides, he needed some sleep and knew if his wife's hands touched his body, he would be awake for at least another hour. "All right," he said. "I'm tired and fear I may fall asleep and drown in the water." He flashed a grin at the handmaiden, unaware of the effect it had on her. He tossed Brynna's gown onto his bed, then began to undress.

Rebecca watched him from beneath long lashes while she prepared his soap and drying cloths.

"Hand me one of those, please," Brand requested, and she handed him a fresh cloth to cover himself. To her delight, though, he did not do so until after his trousers were off. His back was facing her and the handmaiden's spine tingled as she eyed his sculpted buttocks and strong thighs.

Brand stepped into the water with a groan as thick as the steam that rose around him. Just before he sat, he tossed the drying cloth to the floor with the rest of his clothes.

Rebecca suddenly remembered to breathe. In fact, she exhaled so explosively, Brand turned to look at her. "Are you ill?"

"N-nay, m'lord." She went to the tub and knelt beside it, reaching for a small cloth to bathe him.

"Just my back and arms," he told her. "I will do the rest. And wash my hair as well." He slid down the back of the tub, lowering his head into the water to wet his hair.

Rebecca positioned herself behind him when he came back up and began to lather his thick black locks. She rubbed, working her fingers into his scalp. He moaned and the handmaiden closed her eyes in a dreamy fantasy behind him. After a few minutes he submerged again to rinse. When he came up, he shook his head powerfully, spraying the handmaiden with warm, soapy water.

"Oooh!" she squealed, holding her hands up to block more water from soaking her.

"Hell, apologies," Brand blurted, turning to look at her. Her pale tresses were a shade darker now and hung limply around her face with water dripping from every strand. He smiled, softly at first, and then threw his head back and began to laugh.

Brand was surprised by his laughter, but it felt wonderful and he let his mirth come, releasing himself to the happiness he missed so much.

Brynna was just about to enter the room when she heard the wonderful sound. The deep, robust music of her husband's laughter filled the halls and echoed through Brynna's heart, making her smile. She opened the door, expecting to find Brand and his brother sharing a toast. Her smile vanished quickly when she saw Rebecca.

Brynna's heart clamored in her chest, but she remained still, unseen by the two as they laughed together now.

"You are very different from Lord Richard," the flaxen-haired beauty complimented as she slid the wet, soapy cloth over Brand's arms, slow enough to make Brynna seethe. "It was never any fun bathing him."

"That feels good." Brand sighed heavily.

"You are so tense, so tight. What you need is a good massage with some medical oils."

"Um." Brand groaned. "That sounds wonderful."

That was it! Brynna could not stand to hear another word. She marched toward the bath, her hands balled into fists at her sides. "If you would like some oils"—her voice raked the air in a mixture of honey and strychnine—"I would be happy to fetch them for you."

Rebecca was so startled by the sound and the presence of her mistress that she fell backward onto her buttocks as if someone had given her a hard shove.

"Oh!" Brynna reached for her. "Did I frighten you, dear girl? I am so sorry." She yanked Rebecca up by her arm and glared at her and then down at Brand, then at the cloth lying on the floor beside the tub. "You dropped this." She bent swiftly, snatching the wet cloth in her hand, only to fling it at her husband.

"Brynna!" Brand's voice was like ice, but she ignored him and glared at her frightened handmaiden.

"Now you can finish bathing my husband, and when you are done, you can go help Peter clean the manure from the stables."

Rebecca's eyes filled with tears as she ran from the room.

When the girl was gone, Brynna turned her blazing emerald glare on Brand. He was standing now, dripping water from every part of his body, all traces of laughter vanished from his eyes.

"Pity, now you shall have to bathe yourself," Brynna spat venomously.

"Watch your tongue, wife," Brand warned menacingly.

"Are you angry that I interrupted you, you—you foul piece of insect dung?"

His eyes opened wider, darkened by the fury welling up in him. "Don't be a fool, Brynna."

"But I *am* a fool, rat spit! A fool to love you and to think there was a chance—"

"There wasn't." His words cut her off as blue fire poured from his eyes.

For an instant Brynna almost staggered backward by the crushing pain of his cold declaration, but she caught herself, vowing not to let him see the hurt he just caused her.

Her eyes narrowed, shooting green daggers. "Truly, you are a cold and heartless beast. It matters not whose flower blossoms in your fingers, whether mine or a hand-maiden's, we both mean the same to you."

Brand nodded. "Truly," he confirmed with an icy smile. But he did not mean it. Never had anyone aroused him the way she had, the way she did even now, spitting hatred at him. Her fire made him feel alive as passion's talons tore at his loins, passion he fought to control before he grew hard before her eyes. "It matters not to a savage who screams out beneath him, as long as they scream out wildly and for mercy. But none shall be given."

Brand's words frightened her, but they angered her as well, and her anger, like her mother's, always conquered her fear. Brynna squared her shoulders and met her husband's penetrating gaze.

"You shall *never* hear a scream from my lips, neither from passion, nor from fear. I swear it to you, you filthy lout." She whirled around on her heel to leave, but his hand shot out instantly and closed around her wrist. He stepped out of the bath and pulled her into his arms. There was nothing gentle in his actions, nor in his eyes, just fury and passion unleashed and raging. "This is the second time you have accused me falsely. Never do it again, unless you actually see me thrusting myself into one of your hand-maidens. As for screaming, I swear to you, wife, I will not only make you scream underneath me, but you will beg for more. You will beg pitifully until I fill you again and again, and it will never be enough." His breath was hot against her face, his body hard and ready to take her.

"Never!" Brynna spat, trying furiously to squirm free of his embrace, but he swooped down upon her and lifted her off the floor.

With three giant strides Brand carried her to his bed, ignoring the curses spewing from her lips. He dropped her onto the mattress with careless disregard.

She bounced back up like a spring. "I am leaving this room, Brand."

"*Non,* you are not. Not until I'm finished with you." He growled. "Get your clothes off before I rip them off you myself."

"I will not!" Brynna declared acidly, slinging her legs over the side of the bed.

He was upon her instantly.

They were his own clothes that she wore, but he ripped them off her nonetheless. Brynna wanted to scream, but she swore she would not.

"I will never surrender myself to you again, Norman scum!" she spat through clenched teeth as her husband threw the clothes to the floor and pushed her down on the bed.

"Then the battle begins again." His voice stung her ears as powerfully as his hands pinned her to the bed.

"I *welcome* it." Brynna lifted her head off the pillow to shout into his face, but he only smiled pleasantly.

"I thought it was my imagination"—he offered her an

infuriating grin—"but, truly, you are even more beautiful when you are spitting mad, Brynna. If you knew what you were doing to me right now, I'm sure you would become submissive quickly."

"Never, liar!" She fought wildly beneath him, but his grip was like a vise, his body covering hers like steel. She could feel his aroused flesh against her thigh and was surprised that he still had any desire left in him at all. She did not care. She ignored the eager throbbing, the ravishing hunger in his eyes.

"Does this make you feel like a man?" she hissed at him.

A corner of his full mouth hooked into a lecherous half smile. "Why don't you tell me?" He gripped her hand firmly and slid her palm down the length of his body, shifting his weight upon her. She bit her lip as he brought her fingers past the tight steel of his belly, then to his aching shaft. His voice was hoarse with restraint when he closed her fingers around him. "What does it feel like to you?"

Brynna gasped at the life pulsing within her fingers. Swelling, throbbing heat flowed from him and seemed to fill her even against her will.

Brand groaned. He grasped her nipple between his teeth, laving it inside his mouth with his tongue. The pink bud rose in his mouth even as she fought him. His tongue bathed the growing hardness, and then sucked fiercely. Pain, then startling pleasure, drove Brynna's hand farther down on him. She wanted to cry out, but she could not— she had vowed it. He released her hand and she did not move it away from his rigid flesh. He slid his fingers along her inner thigh, his touch teasing her, stroking, provoking her to squeeze his hardness within her fingers.

"Are you ready for me, wife?" he whispered huskily.

"You are a savage," Brynna answered breathlessly.

Suddenly his finger delved deep within her, rotating, stroking delicately and bringing her into an ecstasy that was alive with fire. She panted, arching her back. Brand bit her neck, forcing himself not to split her in two with the hardened lance about to explode in her hand. He stroked the crest of her desire with his thumb and Brynna was assaulted with wave upon wave of sexual ecstasy. It was so intense she wanted to scream, cry out, beg him to enter her and fill her with his powerful flesh.

"Never," she choked out, answering herself aloud. Brand grinned above her.

"*Oui,* now," he corrected, taking her hand once again so that she could guide him. "Now, Brynna," he whispered, and she pulled him, took him into herself, and then released him as he thrust fiercely, grunting in his power.

Brynna shuddered violently as pleasure spasms ripped through her body. Any thoughts she had of denying that she did not want this man's passion without his love slipped away like fallen leaves on the autumn wind. She wanted everything he was giving her. She wanted to be filled utterly by him, just as he was doing now. She found that she loved the weight of his body on hers, the roughness of his jaw as it brushed against her delicate cheek. The way his body moved hers in perfect rhythm with his own drove her to lift her hips higher and gyrate with more pressure until the fires—lapping her flesh, licking her spine, and exploding within her moist cavern, where pleasure burned—became almost unbearable.

Brand's passion was as turbulent as the sea in a raging storm. He rode Brynna with a feverish pitch, no longer caring about tenderness but only pleasure, hot and sweet and savage in its hunger. He wanted to consume her, be consumed *by* her. The tight bands of her desire caressed his manhood and Brand felt every delightful one of them pulling him back when he retreated, while outside, her velvet folds stroked him like wet lips.

Ecstasy peaked, sweeping through Brynna. She bit into his shoulders, raking her fingernails over his back. She clung to him shamelessly, moving with him as he commanded. He lifted her with a surge of power so great that all control was lost and she met the ardor of his mouth with an urgency that matched his own. And then she heard a sound from him that was unlike anything she had ever heard before. It was the sound of pleasure becoming audible, tangible. It was sensual and erotic, masculine and raw. Not a groan, but a series of husky whispers, primal, almost wicked. Brynna wasn't sure if it wasn't the sound alone that caused her to cry out as rapture overtook her.

She opened her eyes to see the face she had longed for, and it was there. Exhilaration—strangely angelic in its fiery, rhapsodic ecstasy—curved his lips into a wide smile. His eyes were closed as he filled her to her womb, rocking in the waters of her body. He curled his lips, sucking in air as if it were a delight to his lungs; then he tightened them, driving himself deeper into her. His passion was tangible, touchable, manifesting itself in his heated, savage smile, in the intoxicated delight that turned into sound while he breathed.

Brynna dug her nails into his flesh as color exploded within her in infinite, orgasmic convulsions she thought would never end. Groaning, choking back cries of ecstasy that threatened to spill forth like a waterfall, she washed him in her sweet juices, again and again, drowning him in her feminine liquid.

And her erotic merman remained, tossing his head back like some beautiful, primitive fantasy come to life. His lips curled into a grimace and a harsh, guttural cry tightened his neck to bursting before issuing forth from his mouth. Then he collapsed into her arms, spent and completely exhausted. He wanted to say something, but he couldn't. He rolled off her, pulled her into his arms, and was asleep within seconds.

Brynna lay beside him, clutching her chest and squeezing her eyes shut in an effort to halt the tears that threatened to drown her. The man from the lagoon still existed. He was here with her now. She had sent Brand over the edge of what passion was believed to be, the way the water had done to him the day she first saw him. Only it was a different passion, though no less intense.

His passion—things he experiences—consume him. Whether it is happiness, hate, lust, or love, it consumes him, Brynna told herself, lying next to her merman. And she knew in that moment that no matter how wonderful his desire was for her, she needed to see the passion of his love this way. She needed to feel it, touch it, live it.

Her thoughts drifted to earlier that day when the duke of Normandy had come to Brand's room to speak with her. He had asked her to be patient. He made her promise to try, swearing to her that her husband was a good man worth fighting for.

"Worth the battle."

Brynna heard Duke William's words playing over in her mind while she lay in bed with Brand, gazing at the black fringe of his lashes against his cheek. She knew she had no choice but to fight. Luckily, it was something she knew how to do well. Somehow she must win the love of this warrior. She had to find a way to melt his frozen heart.

"Worth the battle."

"Aye, that he is," Brynna whispered, and stroked his raven curls. "And, my beloved warrior husband, I shall win."

Chapter Sixteen

Brynna was awakened in the night by a sound of torment laden with grief. The blazing hearth fire had died down to weak embers, but there was enough light to see her sleeping husband when she sat up in bed.

"Colette!"

Brynna whispered his name in the darkness. Her heart broke into slivers that pained her chest. "Brand, wake up." Tenderly she called him. Cautiously, as if touching his skin might wound her, she laid her fingertips on his shoulder. "Awaken, please, my love."

His eyes opened with the stark awareness of waking to reality. He turned his head to look at Brynna and she recoiled at the haunting emptiness that plagued his gaze.

"Brynna." Strong, sure hands now trembled as they cupped her face. Blue-green, turbulent oceans searched her eyes for a moment; then, as if not finding what they needed, he turned away from her.

Tossing his blanket off, Brand left the bed. His naked body moving in the dying firelight of the hearth appeared almost luminous in the paleness of the sorrow he clothed himself in.

Brynna watched him leave her, pulling the blanket to her neck. "Brand, please don't go."

But he seemed not to hear her.

Finding his crimson mantle, he tossed it over his bare shoulders and went to stand before the fire. She watched him silently while he held his hands out to warm himself. He bent to feed wood to the dying embers. Flames licked and cracked, then sprang up with renewed strength, giving more light to the room as well as warmth. Brand straightened, as if growing out of the hungry fire, and held his hands out to warm them once again. His shoulders, so broad and powerful, sagged as the heat soothed him the way Brynna could not.

Seeing it all made Brynna weep. She longed to go to him. But what would she say? She was not Colette de Marson—and Colette was the woman Brand wanted.

"I hate her, Brand," Brynna barely whispered. "I hate her, but I understand that you love her still."

"Non." His voice was as deep as the shadows. "I do not love her anymore. Love makes fools of men." He did not turn to Brynna when he spoke but stared blankly into the flames. "I have always let my heart rule me, Brynna." He paused, remembering the anguish of his betrayal reflected in Alexander's terrified gaze just before he died. "I made choices that I must live with for the rest of my life. I will never make that same mistake again."

What could penetrate the frost that defeated her merman and encased his passionate heart? Brynna wanted to go to him, to hold him in her arms and promise him things he could trust and believe in. But it was his own emotions that had betrayed him.

She left his bed, needing to reach him. "Let me teach you to trust what your heart knows is right," she said quietly, drawing a step closer to him. "Let me heal you, husband." Her knees trembled as she went, hoping, praying, that he would not reject her. She stood before him. His silhouette was a carved masterpiece, stiff with uncertainty. She lifted her hands to his arms and traced the length of his sleek muscles.

He dipped his head and moved his lips along her temple, thrilling her with the slight groan he left there. His arms came around her, slowly at first, resistant to what she offered him. Then he hauled her against his body and captured her mouth in a kiss that was hotter than any amount of ice could withstand.

❈

Brand was gone by the time the morning sun cast its light on Brynna's face. She dressed slowly, thinking of the night she shared with him. Images of his face, a beautiful mask of pure, exotic, ecstasy, flashed in her mind. She traced her breast with her hand, remembering how his mouth felt there. He was hot, passionate, and purely male, so fierce that the mere memory of him devoured her. But he was wounded also, scared by love tainted with deceit and blood.

She knew the battle would be a difficult one, but she had Dumont blood coursing through her veins. She would fight to save Brand the Passionate. She knew, as she raced to her room and tore through her gowns, that it was not Brand she must battle, but what loving Colette de Marson had done to him.

She smiled victoriously, finding the gown that matched her eyes so perfectly. It was lovely. Emerald green velvet softer than the petal of a rose fell like liquid to her feet. Creamy pearls adorned the chevron bodice that pushed her breasts up into an exaggerated cleavage of milky promises. The skirt was full and fluid, with slits up both sides of her legs, reaching her knees. Underneath, two layers of cream-colored chiffon breathed over her flesh, hinting at her shapely legs.

With hope sparking her eyes, she clasped the emerald choker Brand had given her around her neck. She combed her hair away from her face, holding a handful back with a large emerald pin, while the remainder fell down her back. The battle wore on and her merman was worth every blow she consumed.

She slipped her dainty feet into golden slippers and left the room with a delicate bounce in her step.

William was the first to notice Brynna when she entered the great hall. Or at least, Brand thought, his bold friend was the only one with the courage to groan at the sight of her.

"By God, do I envy you, man!" the duke breathily commented, lowering the goblet he held to his lips. "If I did not love you so, I would kill you for her."

Seated beside William, Dante snorted out a laugh. "You're far too vain to offer her a smile without complimenting yourself first."

Up for the challenge, William slid his twinkling gaze to Brand's brother. "Watch and learn, whelp."

Brand smiled but did not take his eyes off his wife as she made her way across the hall. She was beautiful to him. She sparkled with life, verdant, and as fresh as a spring morning. Every movement she made caused the soft velvet that so delightfully covered her to shift and expose more of the strong, shapely limbs that coiled around him the night before. He watched her through hungry, hooded eyes, and when she smiled at him, his body hardened in a rush that left him feeling powerfully stimulated. She was mysteriously sensuous, flooding every one of his senses with desire.

"This is a game she plays with me," Brand said more to himself than to the duke at his side.

William sipped his mead lazily before he replied. " 'Tis the only game with which to reach you."

"I will win, William." Brand practically growled, still watching her.

The brutish duke fixed his gaze on Brand. "What price the victory, *ami*?"

"Death," Brand answered. "My death if I lose."

"Mayhap, but what if her victory brings you life, eh?"

Brand sipped his drink, ignoring William's question as well as the unspoken concern that lined his friend's face. His eyes followed Brynna with a savage intensity as she drew closer to the table. When she finally reached them, it was William who smiled at her.

From the seat Brynna chose, she faced her husband directly from across the table. After returning William's affectionate wink and Dante's charming grin, she slanted her green eyes toward Brand and curled her lips into a sensuous, heated smile that made her husband shift uncomfortably in his chair.

"Have you fallen mute this morning, husband?" Her voice was a flame that licked across Brand's spine.

William's grin grew wide. "My lady," the duke said, leaning forward in his chair, "may I say how fantastically ravishing you are this morning?"

"You may, m'lord," Brynna replied, turning her face to look at him.

"You exhilarate the soul," William wooed. "Your hair is like molten bronze, fiery hot against the creamiest skin God so generously clothed you in."

Brynna's eyes sparkled as she smiled. "Such pretty words spoken by such a bloodthirsty savage."

"Oui." William nodded and cast Dante a confident smile. "And your eyes . . . my lady, there is no emerald in any land more brilliant, none more faceted with such verdant fire."

She blushed and was about to respond when Brand sat back in his chair and folded his arms across his chest, his narrowed eyes and tight jaw daring her to continue. Brynna almost backed down from the cool steel of her husband's gaze. Was he jealous again? With a fluttering heart, she hoped so and bestowed her most dazzling smile on William.

"And you, m'lord, are emblazoned with power and might. Aye, it seeps from every pore on your battle-hardened body. You frighten and render weak with one glance of your eyes, eyes the color of polished steel on the finest sword. Yet you are warm like a favored woolen blanket on a cold winter night."

William's smile had grown so wide that Brynna giggled, covering her mouth with her hand. Suddenly he slapped his massive palms on the table and stood up. "Leave this Norman rake and come away with me!"

Everyone in the great hall was startled out of their seats at William's thunderous outburst, but Brand's glinting azure gaze never left Brynna's face.

"But, sir, you are a Norman as well," Brynna reminded William, ignoring her husband's burning glare.

"Oui." William sighed sadly, then brightened again.

"I will renounce my throne and proclaim myself a Saxon!"

Brynna gasped in feigned shock. "Such treason!"

And finally William exploded with laughter, throwing his head back and holding his stomach. "Ah, you are a rare woman . . . rare indeed," he proclaimed as he sat down again. "See what you have here, Brand, or I *will* steal her from you."

Brand's slow smile scorched her soul. "A woman who can slay mighty men with just her tongue."

Brynna's heart hammered feverishly in her chest. The battle was on and she had run straight into it purposely. Now she had to be careful—but not too careful.

Forcing her smile to remain intact, she stared directly at her husband and delicately licked her lips. "A tongue, when used correctly, my lord, can be quite a deadly weapon."

William coughed up his drink, almost choked in fact, and then he slapped Brand on the back and rose from his chair. "Good luck to you," he said almost pitifully. "You are going to need it." He laughed again, a great, hearty laugh fit for a man of many passions, as the duke of Normandy was. He fit his large hand under Dante's arm and brought the younger knight to his feet. "Come," he said, wanting to give Brand and Brynna some time alone. "We need to discuss Graycliff Castle."

"Why?"

"Because you will be living there."

Brynna watched the duke pull Dante away; then she returned her gaze to Brand and was about to say something when she caught her breath at the way he was staring at her.

Brand's smile was dark, sensuous, and riddled with raw male intent when he cast it upon his wife. The sight of her tongue could not have been more arousing to him if it had been stroked across his own flesh, but he controlled his emotions as well as his growing desire for her.

"I have warned you before about how dangerously you play, wife. Seducing other men right before my eyes." His voice was silky smooth while his fingertips grazed lightly over the rim of his goblet. His powerful gaze left her for a moment to admire the smooth finish of the golden cup. Then he lifted his eyes again and stared at her. "Fortunately, the feel of something so fine under my fingers makes me forget my anger."

Brynna watched his hand. Long, callused fingers tracing, savoring, the cool metal. She shuddered from imagining it was the swell of her breast he relished beneath his tender touch. He mentioned seduction, but it was the raw desire in his eyes, the quirk of his sensual mouth, his passionate smile, that worked so well at seducing her. Careful, Brynna, she warned herself, lifting a piece of bread to her lips with shaky fingers. "Then truly it is a good thing my husband delights in fondling his goblet, else his anger might frighten me so that I would hasten to our room and cower in our bed awaiting my punishment."

Brand studied her for a moment, his eyes were aqua pools of crystalline calm, and then he flashed her a grin that set her world on edge. It was real and unguarded, and every time he graced her with those kinds of smiles, she felt closer to him, like she was touching the ice and melting it. She amused him, made him laugh, and it delighted her. She returned his smile, feeling what she was sure was real affection reaching for her from across the table.

They shared the precious moment in silence, and then Brand rose to his feet and held his hand out to her. "Come riding with me."

"But my garden, I should—"

"I've already sent Alysia and Lily to the task. Come," he beckoned, his voice a sorcerer's whisper drawing her to him. "Your land is unfamiliar to me. If I am to keep Avarloch safe, I must learn every hill, see each road, and know where they lead."

Brynna couldn't refuse him, and she didn't want to. She left her chair and fit her hand into his. He didn't let her go again even as they walked together to the stables. When she tried to mount one of her horses, he stopped her and lifted her to his stallion instead.

"The weather is brisk," he told her, leaping into the saddle next. "We will keep warm if we ride together." His breath behind her ear was enough to frazzle Brynna's nerve endings. When he slipped his arms around her and grasped the reins, she snuggled comfortably into the hard planes of his chest.

The bite in the autumn air numbed Brynna's cheeks as Brand rode them past the outer bailey and beyond her mother's garden. The dazzling swath of blue sky soon disappeared above a canopy of leaves painted gold and green and deep crimson. Brand followed her directions that wound them through the labyrinth of trees and over stony gorges. He noted each winding path she pointed out, though he found himself so captivated by the sweet dips and swells of her voice that twice he missed what she was showing him. Every dew-covered hill held her in awe of its beauty. Each bubbling stream they crossed brought a squeal of delight from her lips as icy water splashed over her legs.

"Oh, there is a place I would show you that will steal your breath!" Brynna said, and her husband smiled at the thrill that laced her words. "My father used to bring me there. Of course, we never dared tell my mother. She would have skinned my poor papa alive."

"And why is that?"

Turning her head, Brynna graced him with an impish smile he had the urge to kiss right off her mouth. "You will see. Follow that steep incline and keep going up."

Brand guided his horse up what he was beginning to think was the side of a mountain. Twice his stallion almost lost its footing on the rocky slope, but Brynna only paused her carefree chatter for an instant to tell him they were almost there.

"You should have let me take my horse, Brand. Your stallion tires easily."

He was about to give that remark the laugh it deserved when the beast slipped again. An instant before they finally reached the top, Brynna shifted around so fast they would have plunged back down if Brand hadn't commanded such control over his steed.

"Close your eyes!" she commanded.

"What? Woman, you're as daft as a—"

"Please, Brand. Close your eyes or you shall spoil the surprise."

He didn't want to close his eyes. He wanted to curse and mayhap even throttle his wife for being so careless. He set his hard gaze on her, ready to deny her foolish request, but damn her, her cheeks were so rosy, and her eyes so wide and pleading, that he scowled, ground his teeth together, and closed his eyes.

"Now get off the horse. Nay, don't open your eyes! Do as I say and stop looking so frightened."

That got his goat. "The only thing I'm frightened of is flinging you over the side of this behemoth hill of yours." He heard her giggle and he scowled even harder.

"Take my hand," she instructed him after she dismounted. "You must trust me."

Brand stopped moving. He kept his eyes closed, but he didn't take another step.

Brynna yanked on his hand. Her laughter filled his ears. "Come, husband. I promise not to let you fall."

"Brynna." He was suddenly assaulted with images from his dreams of falling off the edge of a precipice. He opened his eyes, but Brynna covered them again with her hand and pressed her body to his.

"Just follow me."

"No." She had no idea what she was asking of him.

"Please," her lips whispered against his. "Really, Brand, you are taking all the fun out of this."

She tugged on his hand again and this time he moved. He let her lead him a few paces while his heart hammered awake and alive in his chest.

"Now sit down. There, that's better, isn't it?" she soothed. "My father had me do this when I was nine years old, and I tell you it was the most magical day of my life."

"Can I open my eyes now?" He nearly growled at her.

"Not yet." The wailing wind snapped a lock of her hair across his cheek when she sat down beside him. "First you must lie flat on your belly." She giggled again. "My, you certainly have a mean scowl when you put your mind to it." She pulled on his sleeve until everything but his face was pressed flat against the cold rock beneath him. "You can open them now."

He did, and what he saw stilled his heart. "My God." He could barely breathe looking straight down at frothy waves crashing against the cliff side at least two hundred feet below.

"Is it not magnificent?" Brynna smiled, staring down. "With your head over the side like this, doesn't it feel like you're flying?" He didn't answer, but Brynna wasn't really expecting him to. "Do you hear the way the waves sound as they blend with the wind? It still gives me gooseflesh."

Gooseflesh wasn't the word Brand would have chosen to describe what he was feeling poised over the edge of the world. Exhilaration that made his blood sweep through his veins like fire, that was more like it. Heart-stopping awe that snatched away any meager words, had he the audacity to utter them. Graycliff was built upon the high cliffs of Dover, but he had never felt suspended in midair this way.

Brynna turned her head to look at him and saw the wonder in his smile. She smiled with him. "Now do you see why Mother would have been angry?"

He laughed softly; then he clamped his fingers around the back of her head and kissed her. When he retreated, Brynna felt light-headed looking into his eyes.

"Every day that I know you better makes me thank God that I didn't take your father's life."

Brynna blinked into his gaze. She was thankful too, but they had never spoken of it. She didn't know why he did now. "Why didn't you?"

"Because he is brave. He is a great warrior and I respected him even as his sword came down on mine."

She nodded her head and watched him turn back to the waves. "Why does knowing me make you thank God that you spared him?"

"If I killed him, you would have hated me."

Brynna bit her bottom lip to stifle the myriad of questions that reply ignited in her, but she had pushed him enough for one day. "I would not have hated you for long, though." When he raised an eyebrow at her, she slanted her lips into a regretful frown. "I would have shot you dead with an arrow long before you had a chance to pine over me."

Brand's laughter was swift, rich, and deep. It carried on the wind mingling with the powerful roar of the sea below her. Brynna was certain nothing would ever sound more sweet to her ears, until a moment later when he told her he wanted to take her home and make love to her in a warm bed.

❈

Sauntering down the steps and about to take a chunk out of a fresh apple, Dante was the first to greet them when they entered Avarloch. He grinned, flashing his famous dimple as he passed them on his way to the great hall. "William is looking for your head."

"Why?" Brand called out after him.

"Your hounds arrived from Graycliff," Dante replied over his shoulder, and continued walking. "They terrorized his men for almost a full hour before he stormed into the hall and bellowed loud enough to scare the fur off poor Shredder."

"*Merde.* Where are they now?" Brand asked, following him.

Dante didn't reply but pointed to the two thick doors

just ahead of them. An instant later he pushed one of the doors open, pressed his back against the wooden frame, and swung his arm across his waist. "After you."

Brand found his dogs the moment he entered the great hall; two of them padded around benches, snapping food right out of the owners' trenchers. Brand's mouth hooked into a half smile while he turned to his brother and Brynna at his side. "William's men look about to wet their pants."

"They look quite savage." Brynna took a step behind Dante and peeked around his arm to watch the enormous hounds.

"They can be," Brand replied, and then puckered his lips and released a short whistle that snapped the dogs' muzzles up out of their stolen meals.

At the sight of Brand, one of the hounds, a large silver beast, bolted to him, much to the relief of the knight who sat still as a statue while the creature had licked his trencher clean. Brand bent forward as if to gather the great dog in his arms, but instead, the hound stretched upward on its hind legs almost knocking Brand to the floor.

"You have missed me, then, Whisper?" Brand asked, clutching the dog's loose jowls. "And I have missed you too, fair lady." He tilted the hound's massive head and planted a firm kiss within the sleek silver fur.

"Whisper, eh?"

Brand looked up to find William strolling toward him, a large tankard of ale clutched within his fingers. "Her incessant barking meant nothing to you when you named her?" When he stepped closer to Brand, the dog growled and bared her fangs.

"*Ce qui?*" William growled right back at her. "What's

that you say? You should be whimpering at my feet for not skinning your hide for a new winter blanket." He cast his menacing glare at Brand next. "If your mongrels disable one of my men, it's coming out of your coffers."

When Dante sunk his teeth into his apple to stop the grin spreading over his face, William mumbled under his breath and went back to his seat.

"Brynna," Brand said, turning to look at her. "Come pet my dog."

"No thank you."

"You must make friends with her. Give her a morsel of food from that plate beside you, lest she dislike you and tear at your throat when you come near me."

Brynna stared at him while her disbelief turned to anger. The thought of putting her fingers to the beast's mouth terrified her, but the amusement dancing in her husband's eyes told her that was exactly what he meant to do.

Not willing to be defeated by a dog, Brynna lifted a slice of mutton to the hound. She eyed Brand defiantly, wanting to curse him vehemently, but she thought better of it when eyes as dark as a nightmare turned on her.

"Easy, Whisper," Brand soothed. He had taunted Brynna, knowing that Whisper was as docile as a kitten, but his wife didn't know it. If he didn't spark her anger, she would constantly live in fear of his giant hounds. He smiled when Brynna rose to his challenge, as he knew she would, and put her fingers to the beast's mouth. The meat was plucked almost daintily from Brynna's fingers by large white fangs.

"What about the other two?" Brynna challenged after a scared swallow.

Brand shrugged his shoulders and continued to stroke Whisper's head. "They are scoundrels and will take what they want without asking."

"Hmmm, just like their master," Brynna said curtly. Eyeing the other two dogs, she had no doubt that Brand spoke the truth. "What are their names?"

He smiled. "Chaos and Shredder. But you need not touch them. They are hunters by nature, not pets."

That certainly sent a shiver down her spine, but Brynna was determined to win the battle her husband had begun with his hounds. Closing her eyes, she breathed a silent prayer, then took more mutton and held it out to two beasts now drooling at Dante's side. "Easy," she breathily commanded as they came near. She sensed the change in Brand's stance immediately. He looked ready to subdue the hounds if either tried to take a bite out of her. Brynna smiled. Her husband wasn't willing to let harm come to her as his callous manner had suggested. Heat and saliva touched her skin. Then, closing her eyes again, she lifted her hand slowly and patted Chaos on the head. The dark hound lapped her fingers with its tongue and Brynna allowed herself to exhale.

With a look filled with astonishment, Brand released Whisper and turned to Dante. "We should bring my lady into battle with us. She has a tongue *and* a touch that soothes the most savage beast."

"Nay, m'lord." Brynna shot him a seductive glance, deciding to keep the battle going. "*You* are the most savage beast of all, and I have yet to soothe you."

"It is true," Brand replied huskily. He bent his face to hers and traced her lower lip with his thumb. "You make me feel more like a savage than ever before."

Brynna blushed and turned to Dante, but he was already gone. She curled her lips and moved past her husband, brushing the delicate curves of her body against his solid muscles.

He breathed in the scent of her. He let the velvet of her gown caress him, the soft suppleness of her flesh beneath arouse him before he gave Brynna a smile that made her tremble before she turned to leave. He watched her. He couldn't take his eyes off her as she walked toward the doors. Her body called to him, invited him to follow. He basked in her delicious curves with eyes that devoured. Shaking with desire for her, he took off after her and pulled her into his arms. His kiss was racked with a fevered moan.

"Excuse me, m'lord."

Brand looked up, a bit perturbed at the interruption from the young squire. "What is it, can't you see I'm kissing my wife?"

The squire's cheeks paled to a sickly white. "I'm sorry, m'lord." He twisted the hem of his tunic nervously. "The tower guard sent me to inform you that there are riders approaching."

Brand tore his sultry smile away from Brynna for a moment. "Do they carry banners?"

"Nay, m'lord."

"All right." Brand sighed, casting Brynna an apologetic frown. "Alert the garrison. I will be there shortly."

"Send Dante," Brynna suggested with a purr, lifting her warm breath to his neck. "I am in need of you now."

He closed his eyes against the velvety seduction of her voice and the heated promise that came with it. Brynna could feel his body tighten and smiled at the power she had over him.

"Dante!" Brand bellowed. His brother looked up from the chair he had taken and tossed his apple core to Chaos. "There are riders approaching, see to them and let me know who they are. I am retiring with Brynna to our chambers." He turned to leave with one hand against the small of her back.

In his haste to get Brynna into bed, he hardly noticed two of his hounds racing past him to the castle doors. Only when Whisper began her low whimpering did the lord of Avarloch look up.

Brand's face went paler than the moon on a cold winter night. There was only one person who produced such anxiety in his dog; one person who made this dog cower at his feet as though a disaster were about to strike that only Whisper, with her keen nose and sharp hearing, could sense.

With a quick, deep intake of breath, Brand left Brynna's side and met Dante in two great strides just before his brother opened the castle doors. "Wait," he shouted. Dante stopped and turned to look at him. Brand seemed to gather what strength he had left in one last, slow breath, then nodded and stepped away from the doors. The hounds settled quickly at his feet. They were silent except for Whisper's low whines.

William strolled out of the hall to see what the commotion was just as Dante swung the wide doors open. William tossed Brynna a questioning glance, but she shrugged her shoulders and returned her gaze to Brand. Whoever was out there made her husband recoil as if he were afraid to see what he somehow already knew.

Brynna's heart suddenly began to beat a thunderous tattoo in her chest. "Brand?" She went to him and placed a delicate hand on his arm, but he did not look at her. His eyes were already set on the dark figure riding closer to Avarloch.

"God have mercy." William's voice behind Brynna made her skin crawl and her heart cry out. She was about to turn to him when a low groan from her husband stilled her. She looked at him, afraid to look anywhere else, afraid to see what her heart told her. Brand's eyes were closed now, as if in denial of whom he saw, and finally Brynna turned to see for herself.

A rider approached the outer gate on horseback, shrouded in a mantle as black as Brynna's hope when she realized who it must be. Surrounded by a company of at least fifteen men, the rider's delicate features became clearer from under the shadow of the hooded mantle. The stark, shocked silence of Brand's men, including William, told Brynna what her mind refused to accept.

"What should I do?" Dante's deep voice broke the silence.

Staring at the rider as though his aching heart were about to burst from his chest, Brand barely breathed, never blinked. "Meet her at the gate and see what she wants."

Dante hesitated, then walked away to do his brother's bidding.

"Brand, just slam the damn door in her face!"

Brand held his hand up to quiet William. Brynna turned to the duke, searching his smoldering eyes. But he looked away from her, hopelessness plaguing him. She wanted to cry, to scream out. She ached to run to the doors and slam them shut as William had demanded, but she did nothing. She could barely move, watching Dante leap to his saddle just outside the doors.

"Don't be a fool, Brand," came the tight warning of the duke of Normandy. But Brand did not acknowledge what he heard. His eyes never left the dark woman outside. The color did not return to his face, nor did he seem to breathe at all. He just watched, as if, in his silence, he might capture a word spoken on the wind outside.

Brynna had stopped breathing as well, and she realized it suddenly when her head began to spin from lack of oxygen. She drew in a deep breath, and then stopped again when Dante returned to the castle. His eyes darted to Brynna before he spoke to his brother.

"She wants to take refuge here from her father."

"Why?" Brand asked quietly.

"She would not say, only that she wished to speak with you."

Avarloch went silent for what seemed an eternity. No one spoke. No one breathed. The only sound came from Whisper, who continued her low whining at her master's feet. The world seemed to shift, to age, in that space of silence it took for Brand to decide. It was one of those times when mere seconds slipped into hours, while the mind fought to deny some cataclysmic change that the heart knew was about to occur. And Brynna was sure that everyone in the hall had felt it.

Brand's gaze had never left the figure waiting outside. Finally he spoke the words that echoed through Brynna's heart like thunder, sweeping her away on endless waves of sorrow and torment. "Allow her entry." He spoke clearly, with a command in his voice that no one dared to question.

No one but Brynna.

She turned on her heel to face him, grasping his arm. Her eyes pinned him, demanding that he look at her. "I have no need to inquire if the woman outside is Colette de Marson. For clearly, by the clattering of your heart, it is she who approaches my home. But I do ask you, husband, why do you allow her entry? Why would you carelessly disregard my feelings so?" Clenching her teeth, Brynna answered her own question. "You love her. You love her still and you will flaunt that love before me like—"

"Silence!" Brand snapped, cutting off her words. His face was carved from granite, his eyes as hard as steel. Then he blinked slowly and seemed to gather himself, shielding himself once again with layer upon layer of solid stone. "You will be silent, or I will have you removed."

Brynna glared at him, fighting the waves of tears and fury that overwhelmed her. "Very well. Silence you shall have," she promised in a voice filled with quiet determination.

For the first time since the doors were opened, sea blue eyes finally left the woman now awaiting entry into Avarloch. Brand turned to follow Brynna as she stepped around him and stood with William and her father.

"All will be well with us, Brynna." It was almost a whisper, as if he were afraid to say it, afraid to promise her anything. His eyes searched hers, but Brynna turned away, silent.

Colette de Marson entered Avarloch upon a gust of cool air, her black mantle riding the wind behind her. When she reached Brand, she stopped and slowly turned her hood back until it fell like liquid down her pale, silken hair.

"Fool!" William could contain his disgust no longer and stormed out of the castle, slamming his massive shoulder into one of Colette's men as he went, almost knocking the man off his feet.

Colette did not flinch at the duke of Normandy's seething fury; in fact, her composure and grace, not to mention the striking, angelic beauty of her face, astounded Brynna, who watched her with careful, blazing eyes.

"My lord." Colette de Marson's voice was the sound of a sigh spoken on the wind. She pinched the thick pleats of her velvet gown and curtsied slightly before Brand. When she straightened, she revealed large, dark eyes that glistened with tears. She lifted a dainty hand toward his cheek, but he caught her by the wrist with the speed of a serpent, stopping her.

"Why are you here?" he asked flatly.

Sable eyes, as searing as burning coals, scanned the hall and came to rest on Brynna. "I would speak to my lord in private." Slowly she brought her gaze back to Brand and waited.

He stared at her for a long time, and Brynna could almost hear the questions he longed to ask her and the pain that laced each one.

"Very well," he answered finally.

Colette smiled at him and waited for Brand to return the gesture. He didn't.

Seething with anger, Brynna failed to recognize the frigidity that drifted across her husband's features while he stared at Colette.

Untying the laces of her mantle, Colette turned, inviting Brand's hands alone to remove it from her shoulders.

When he did, hair so flaxen it seemed to brighten all of Avarloch spilled onto his fingers. And if Brynna had not fled the hall in that instant, she might have seen her husband turn to look for her instead of inhaling the clean scent of rose that used to haunt his dreams.

Chapter Seventeen

❋

William stormed past the gatehouse, slicing the air with his presence while curses spilled forth from his mouth. His thick legs carried him swiftly across the fields that surrounded Avarloch. He headed toward the forest. His terrible anger defied the cold as it sought to bite at his flesh. He felt nothing, could think of nothing except snapping the French bitch's little neck like a dried twig. He thought he would never see Lady Colette de Marson again, but she was here! It was bad enough having to watch one of the greatest warriors he had ever known grow weak and fall under the power of the seductress, but now Lady Brynna would be destroyed as well.

William thought of Lord Richard Dumont's daughter while he battered weeds and grass under his heavy leather boots. He saw her face in the blossoms that defied the cold. There was no woman like her in all of England, William was certain of it. Such life, such fire and passion, to be given to a man who would stomp on it as though it were naught—given to a man he loved like his own son, the blasted fool. He flung the goblet he still carried at a tree. "Curse you, Colette de Marson. I will not let you destroy them." The dark promise resonated through the forest and the birds that nestled in the branches high above screeched in fear and took flight. The duke of Normandy hardly noticed, his smoldering gray eyes seeing beyond the forest. "*Non*, never."

※

Brynna exploded into her room and tore her gown from her body. She hurried to her wardrobe and searched through her clothes until she found a brown riding dress and a heavy woolen tunic.

"Brynna!" Her father's voice boomed from behind the door before he knocked.

"A moment, please," she called out, slipping into her new clothes. She roughly wiped the tears from her eyes with the back of her hands and headed for the door. When Richard saw his daughter, his heart shattered. "Brynna . . ."

She stepped away from his outstretched arms and turned to search for her boots. She moved quickly, without thinking—it had to be that way, for if she allowed her mind to think . . . "Where are my boots?" she cried, her words cracked as her agony betrayed her.

"Brynnafar—"

"I can fight a ghost, Father." Before she could stop them, the words poured from her lips. "But not a woman of flesh and blood who will live in my own home. A woman he loves with all the heart he has left."

Without knowing how she got there, Brynna was in her father's arms, consumed by a love she had almost forgotten existed.

"Daughter," he whispered, and she let her tears flow into the broad shoulder of the only man who loved her.

"I will take you to Normandy with me. You do not have to stay here and—"

"Nay, nay," she cried, wiping her eyes with a determination her father recognized and admired. "I love him, Father. I must stay."

Lord Richard smiled gently, holding his daughter away to look into her eyes. "Then you will fight for him?"

Brynna's lips turned up wryly. "You have spent too much time around Duke William already." She sighed, letting her smile grow with his. "I will try." She had no other choice really. To leave Brand would turn her into what her merman had become . . . though to stay might do the same.

"Truly, you are your mother's daughter, Brynnafar Grenalyn."

Smiling at the full name her mother had given her, Brynna kissed her father's rough cheek and left his arms. "Right now, though, I need to ride—to be away from here and gather my senseless thoughts." She tied a leather belt around her waist and wove her hair into a thick copper braid down her back.

"Take Dante with you, daughter, or one of my men."

Brynna cast her father a delicate frown. "Since when do I need an escort to ride through my own land?"

"You don't, but do it to make me happy." The concern he offered her warmed her heart. She took a step forward and threw her arms around his neck. "All right, I will find someone. I promise."

Lord Richard nodded; then, before he could say another word, and because she had to leave quickly else she would not go at all, he watched his daughter leave her room. He sighed deeply and decided to head for the

kitchen for something to eat. His heart told him to find
Lord Brand Risande, but his mind rebuked the idea, realizing that for the Norman knight's own safety, getting
something to fill his belly was better for everyone involved.

Brynna slipped out of Avarloch Castle, but in keeping
with her promise to her father, she did not go alone.
Treading closely at her heels was Brand's hound, Chaos.

✳

With eyes as sharp as a hawk's, Brand watched Colette as
she paced the solar. He did not miss a single movement
she made, including the fingers that clutched and released
the velvet of her gown. He caught the tight, nervous
twitch of her lips and the silky pale tresses that fanned
outward when she turned quickly, continuing her frantic
march.

"Well?" Brand asked her quietly.

Colette paused for just an instant before she threw her
hands up to her face and wept. "My father has promised
me to a beast, Brand."

"So?" he answered vaguely. Hadn't Brynna been
forced to marry a beast as well? And hadn't she faced her
fate with no tears? "Many women are forced to marry
men they do not love."

Colette peeked at him from over trembling hands. "I
cannot. I cannot! He is a savage!"

Brand found a high-backed chair and fell into it. For an
instant he thought about going to her, soothing her. But he
realized quickly that it was the comforting familiarity he
felt around her that made him even consider holding her.
He actually had no desire at all to feel her flesh in his arms

again. He thought if he ever saw her again, he might be tempted to forgive her. When he allowed her entry into Avarloch, he thought it might do him good to put the questions to her that tormented him. But here she was and all he could think about was Brynna. *Enfer,* but his wife made him feel alive again. A faint smile touched the edges of his mouth as he recalled how ridiculously good it felt to kiss her with the freezing wind beating their faces and threatening to hurl them into the clouds. He closed his eyes to the memory of her full lips as she spat poison at him. She had a spitfire temper indeed, but she did not argue or hurl her foulest words at him when he shouted for her silence earlier. She simply looked at him as though he'd ripped her heart out of her chest and held the bloody mess to her face. Christ, he hurt her. He dragged out a low breath. Why were women's sensibilities so delicate? Men were better off without them, he decided. *Oui,* then he would not have to worry about making rash decisions that he regretted five breaths later.

"You must return to your father," he told Colette. "You cannot stay here. I made a mis—"

"Nay, nay, please, my lord!" She sprang at him and collapsed at his feet. "Let me stay until the spring, I pray you. By then, my father will have forgotten about marrying me to that beast and you can ride back with me and speak to him."

"And tell him what?" Brand shouted suddenly. His eyes blazed into her like lightning through a tree. "What shall I tell your father? Should I request that he pardon yet another shame his own daughter has brought upon his name? Should I tell him to forget that your heart belongs to no one? That he should erase from his mind the fact that she spreads her legs for any man who wants her?"

Oddly, his words did not sting the woman at his feet, nor did she realize or even care that what she was hearing were his own heartfelt accusations. And if Brand had been less consumed by the deep anger that seethed within him, anger he needed to feel in order to heal, he might have noticed that Colette did not seem to care at all what he thought of her.

Rising on her knees, she settled her eyes directly on his. "You sent me away once before. I beg you, do not do it again. For this time I will not make it to the front doors before I take my own life."

"You will not take your own life. You love yourself far too much."

Gazing at him, Colette marveled. He was as breathtaking as the sky before a storm. But she had known a different Brand Risande. She had known Lord Brand the Passionate, a man whose zest for life consumed him, made him so alive that she always felt like she had to run to catch up with him. She remembered the love in his aqua gaze that used to wash over her so tenderly, the gentle caress of his powerful arms, and the sweet feel of his mouth when he kissed her. *Oui,* she had power over him. She just had to remind him of it.

"Brand." Her voice was a low purr. She let her dark, haunting eyes sweep over his face. She saw the anger there when he returned her gaze, but she ignored it. She lifted her hand to his cheek. "If you ever loved me, help me now."

"Do not speak to me of love. I owe you nothing. I have wed another and wish to be free of you." The moment he spoke the words, Brand knew they were true. He did not want to dream of her anymore. She was here, and he did not want her.

"I know you're wed, Brand." She touched the tip of her finger to his lips to silence him, ignoring his wishes. "Talk of your battle with Sir Richard Dumont spread quickly throughout the country. I know that you were forced to marry his Saxon daughter in order to keep this land—"

"I wanted to marry her," Brand interrupted, fighting to gather his thoughts as the familiar scent of Colette assailed his senses.

"Do you love her?"

Silence.

"She is lovely." Colette's body drifted upward like a cloud until her waist was nestled between his muscular thighs. Brand closed his eyes at the sight of her face so close to his, at the lips he once ravished while savoring the taste of her. "Colette." He breathed her name and it sounded foreign to his ears.

"I love you, Brand."

He tilted his head to the soft fingers that stroked his cheek. He opened his eyes. For a moment he expected to see hair the color of burnished bronze tangling around his fingers as he lifted them to the beautiful face before him. He was almost surprised to see Colette. He snatched his hands away.

"May I stay, my lord. Please?" The sweet heat of her breath caressed him, flooding him with unwanted memories of their days together.

"*Non,* Colette." He stood to his feet, pushing her away from him. "You will leave in the morn."

"I cannot!" She wailed and threw herself at his feet.

"Please don't send me away. 'Tis freezing and I shall die before I reach Canterbury." She quieted for a moment, listening for a response from him. When nothing came, she continued. "Oh, please, Brand. My betrothed has already beaten me. I fear going home."

Brand looked down at her pale yellow hair. He had the urge to touch it. Damn her, and damn Brynna too. He was not a heartless bastard. "Very well. You may stay until I figure out what to do with you. But, Colette, while you are here, stay away from me, and stay away from my wife. I do not want her feelings hurt any more than they already are by your presence here."

Colette wiped her eyes and stared up at him with a sudden spark of anger in her eyes. "If I didn't know any better, I would think you were in love with your Saxon wife."

Brand left her without giving her an answer. She didn't deserve one, but that was not the reason for his silence. His heart was pounding too fiercely in his chest for him to speak. Seeing Colette in the flesh had proved to him that there was still room in his heart to love a woman. And he broke out in a cold sweat on his way to her room. Love! God's blood, he might as well just toss himself onto his sword now and be done with it—that is, if falling in love with his beautiful wife didn't kill him first.

Brynna rode hard. The cool wind tore at her lungs and whipped through her hair, snapping her braid against her back like a whip urging her to ride faster. Chaos kept the frantic pace beside her horse. She entered the forest without slowing and her tears stung her face moments before they were snatched away by the wind. Her mount tore at the earth with hooves that thundered across the forest floor, giving dreadful warning to the smaller creatures to flee or be trampled underfoot. Soft white ribbons rose from her stallion's nostrils before disappearing into the frigid air. And still Brynna pushed the horse harder, dodging trees and low branches, eager to escape the pain that always seemed to be lurking one step behind her since lord Brand Risande stepped into Avarloch.

The stallion suddenly reared up on muscular hind legs, startled by something in its path. Brynna tried to hold on, but the animal had been going too fast, the stop too sudden, and both horse and rider fell with an earth-shattering crash to the cold, carpeted floor.

Brynna woke hours later, warmed by a fire that burned inches from where she lay. A large figure hulked over her. She was about to scream, but then a fresh burst of pain exploded into brilliant colors through her head.

"Easy, fair lady, 'tis only me." William whispered close to her face. He gave her his warmest smile. "You took quite a spill off your horse."

Brynna lifted her hand to her head and groaned. "Is that what happened? I dreamed I was thrown from Heaven."

William laughed softly. "*Non,* that would never happen." He returned to the fire, pouring his attention over a slab of meat he had roasting on a makeshift spit. He tore a piece off with his fingers and offered it to her.

"Here, eat."

"What is it?"

"Rabbit."

Brynna eyed the offer for a moment, then tried to sit up. Fire roared up before her eyes and she fell back against the cloak William had rolled into a pillow.

"You need to lie still until help arrives, Brynna," William ordered gently.

"You killed it?"

"What?" He looked at her over the firelight with eyes that shone like polished silver.

"What did you kill the rabbit with?"

The Norman duke smiled savagely, holding the meat up to his face to examine it. "Why do you ask that?" Before she had time to answer, he shrugged his massive shoulders. "To be a true warrior, one must make use of all the resources God has given him."

Brynna looked around the small bonfire, but as she suspected, she saw neither dagger nor sword, nor bow. She remembered the duke storming out of Avarloch with naught in his hands but a goblet. "Did Chaos kill it?" she asked with a growing reverential respect for the man she had called a monster.

At the sound of his name, the large black hound lifted his head from his lazy slumber and looked at her.

"Non." William licked his fingers and continued chewing the meat he had tossed into his mouth. "If I told you that my hands killed the animal, would you think less of me?" he asked.

"Nay," Brynna answered, staring at him. "Mayhap I just need to know how dangerous my new friend can really be."

William laughed, tossing a piece of the meat to Chaos. Brynna watched the duke and envisioned him running through the thick trees like some untamed beast chasing his prey. "I can be quite dangerous, fair lady, but never to you."

Brynna smiled. She believed him. He looked positively

uncivilized against the wild growth of dense bush and thick tree trunks. The shadows that danced across his face and eyes from the fire lent to his savage appearance, but his voice was gentle, his large fingers almost delicate as they tore the roasted meat from the rabbit carcass. "What are you doing out here?" she asked him.

"I might ask you the same question."

Her gaze drifted to the darkening sky above her. A slow sigh escaped her as her thoughts turned to Brand. She wondered what he was doing at that moment. Was he with Colette?

"I had to get away for a while."

"So did I," William told her, understanding the pain he saw in her eyes.

Brynna tried to sit up again, but William stopped her with a large hand on her shoulder. "Be still."

"Nay, I have to return," she said, fighting to free herself from the brick wall that stopped her from moving.

"You will return, Brynna, but not right now. We have no horse, and 'tis too long a way to walk."

She stopped. "No horse? But"—she looked around the small clearing—"where is my stallion?"

William remained silent for a moment, staring into her eyes; then he sat back on his haunches and shifted his gaze into the fire. "Your horse twisted its neck in the fall."

As he suspected, Brynna closed her eyes to stop the rush of tears that ached to flow. "I should not have pushed him so hard." She sobbed, unable to contain the sorrow that tormented her.

William stared into the flames, silently respecting her tears, knowing they did not merely fall for her horse. And as the woman he admired more than any other cursed her own sorrow, his anger toward Brand and Colette was once again kindled. "Brynna," he began slowly, carefully, letting his silvery eyes find her in the semidarkness. "When you return to Avarloch, you must gather all the strength that I know you possess. Use the feminine wiles God has blessed you with. And believe me, woman"—William sighed, looking at her—"he has blessed you with much. Ready yourself for battle now."

"But—"

"*Non.*" He stopped her. "Ready yourself right now, Brynna, else do not bother to return. I know how much of his heart he gave Colette de Marson. I know not how much of it remains with her, so best prepare yourself for full battle." A wolfish cast crept over his lips. "You could give up, surrender. But you will not."

Brynna wiped her eyes and stared at the brutish warrior. She nodded with a new determination blazing in her eyes and William nodded back. He offered her a fresh piece of rabbit and this time she accepted.

"You have a monstrous reputation, m'lord William," she told him suddenly.

He threw his head back and laughed. "I have earned it."

Brynna studied him. Muscles danced in his jaw and throat as he chewed, ripping at the succulent meat. He was sitting now with one leg bent to his chest, his arm dangling over his knee, and Brynna realized what a striking man he was under all that hair and rough demeanor. He caught her surveying him and lifted one corner of his bearded mouth into a crooked grin.

"Tell me about your battles, William."

The duke tossed more meat to Chaos. He paused for a moment as if turning something over in his mind; then he lifted his smoky gaze and let it wash over her until she shivered at the ferocity she saw there. "Swear fealty to me, Brynna Risande, and I shall tell you a story that your children will tell their children."

"Fealty." She laughed, but the hungry glint in his eyes told her that he was serious. "But I am no knight," she reminded him incredulously.

"True, but you are a warrior nonetheless. It runs in your blood. I have seen it. You are loyal to your father and to your home. I know you will be loyal to Brand. Now I am asking you to be loyal to me and I will share something with you that no one else knows. Not even your husband."

"But I'm Saxon," Brynna reminded him, a new sparkle gleaming in her eyes.

William smiled gently and again Brynna was struck by the tender nature of this renowned savage. "Soon it will not matter what anyone calls himself. Will you swear to me, fair lady?"

Caught up in the fire of his eyes and the soft golden glow from the fire that bathed him in an eerie, majestic light, Brynna grew serious. "Aye, I will swear."

The Norman duke lifted his hefty body and knelt before her. He eased her up slowly into a sitting position, asking her if she was comfortable. She assured him that she was, excited and a bit dazed by what he was asking her to do. "There," he said when she was steady enough to sit without his help. Brynna had to remind herself twice that they were not two children secretly swearing by blood to be friends forever. He set his gaze squarely on hers and she had the feeling that all this was a dream. Here she was about to swear allegiance to a Norman!—a man who appeared before her in the firelight as menacing and domineering as he was reputed to be. But he was much more than that, she told herself, vaguely aware that Chaos had risen from his resting place to sit beside the dark warrior. Duke William of Normandy was a man ruled by wit and wisdom first, brawn and strength after that, not the other way around.

"Repeat after me," William said against the crackling of the fire. "I, Lady Brynna Risande, wife of Lord Brand Risande of Avarloch, do swear fealty to Duke William of Normandy. I pledge loyalty and honor on my life in the sight of God."

Brynna repeated the oath, and when she was finished, William took her hands in both of his and kissed each one.

Brynna sighed. "I feel silly."

"Non," he whispered. A passion flared in his hungry gaze that Brynna had only seen in one other man. When William spoke again, his voice was deep and low, and Brynna swore she heard his heart drumming in his chest.

"Brynna," he confided wickedly, "have you ever heard of a small village in the south called Hastings?"

Chapter Eighteen

Brand stormed the castle halls. Torches that burned on either side of him wavered and weakened when he passed. He searched for Lord Richard, hoping, for the older knight's sake, that he had a good reason for allowing his daughter to go riding off with only a hound at her side. Brynna had been gone far too long, and as each new moment passed, Brand grew more infuriated with her father. He knew he had been too harsh with his wife when he told her he would have her removed from the hall. But, hell, he had needed time to think clearly and could not do so with her going on about how much he loved Colette. God's teeth, his wife's eyes had burned so green he wanted to lose himself in them forever. He had seen sorrow in them, as well as defiance, and he cursed himself. He did not understand why she had so much trouble trusting him. Did she think that just because he allowed Colette into Avarloch it meant that he was going to run off with her as well? He recalled her wrath when she found her handmaiden Rebecca bathing him. She accused him of wanting Alysia as well. Damn her for never believing him. One would think, by her untrusting nature, that his wife had been the one betrayed instead of him. He would have to have a talk with her about it. She loved him. He needed to reassure her that he would never betray that love.

His skin warmed as though a tongue of fire had swept over him at the thought of her loving him. He thought her beautiful when he first saw her, but the irresistible combination of tenderness and passion she offered him made his guts go soft. His heart quickened when he thought of her sensual gaze, her beautiful smile that made him forget his past and think of no one but her. He sighed deeply, remembering the languid groans he pulled from her.

Making his way down the stairs, he spotted Lord Richard entering the castle. "Where have you been?" Brand asked him sharply, poised midway in his descent.

"In the stables." Lord Richard looked up at him impassively before continuing on his way to the great hall.

"Where is my wife?" Brand continued his slow descent, giving no heed to the fact that Richard had only stopped briefly to look at him. "Peter told me that she left here alone, save for one of my dogs."

The sight of Brand was a bit unnerving to Lord Richard Dumont. Living in the castle with him, sharing wine and laughter, had almost made Brynna's father forget the cunning, merciless warrior he had met on the battlefield. But he could not forget, especially not now, seeing Brand's eyes as deadly as his sword. Looking at him was like seeing the calm before the storm hit—a storm that could destroy everything in its path.

"Where did she go?" Brand asked again. Hard cerulean eyes pinned Richard to his spot until Brand finally reached him.

"She went riding." Richard faced his son by marriage straight on. Senses honed to perfection, he was acutely aware of every movement the younger knight made, no matter how slight. He watched the skilled hands hanging at Brand's sides, close to his sword.

"Riding." It was more of a statement than a question, and the bleak smile Brand offered him told Richard that the dark knight did not believe him.

"My daughter needed to rid herself of the dishonor you brought upon her today, Lord Brand," Richard said between clenched teeth, not caring what the consequences were.

For a moment the warrior faded and understanding, and then regret, flooded Brand. But he fought his emotions as savagely as if they were an enemy he faced in battle. He might be falling in love with his wife, but he would never let that emotion rule him again. In the space of one moment, the battle Brand fought with himself played out clearly on his face. He had to stop what he felt for Brynna before it was too late. *Oui,* he had to stop himself because he was sure if he allowed it, he could love her even more deeply, more passionately than he had loved Colette.

Lord Richard marveled, watching his daughter's husband become undone and then restored again before his very eyes. He watched as a self-control born only to conquer was itself conquered. But it lasted for only an instant before the victorious warrior returned. And now the warrior did nothing to disguise his anger.

"Where did she go and why has she not returned yet?" Brand demanded.

"Why? Why do you ask?" Richard seethed, narrowing his eyes to deadly slits. "You do not care if she returns or not." He hated himself at that moment for losing to this man and having to hand his daughter over to such a heartless rogue. He had hoped that Brand would come to love his daughter, that Brynna would somehow manage to overcome his defense, but as he gazed into the vast depths of Brand's eyes, his hopes faded. "Is it not what you wanted all along, Lord Brand? Not to have to marry my daughter?"

"I will *not* be disgraced by a wife who has left me because her feelings were hurt," Brand retorted hotly.

Richard glared at him. He wanted to hate this Norman bastard, to run him through with his sword, but his heart was too broken with the knowledge of how he had failed his daughter to do anything but stare into Brand's frosty gaze. "If she is as strong as I taught her to be, she will never return to you," he spat out. "She will ride and keep on riding, and never come back."

Richard was too angry now to recognize the panic in Brand's eyes, brought about by his words. "Pray," Brand warned in a thoroughly chilling voice, "that she does return to me, else you will never see Normandy."

"Are you threatening me, Brand?"

Brand nodded, his eyes seared into Richard's with unblinking intensity. "*Oui.* And this time I might not show you mercy."

Two hours later Brand's orders could be heard thundering through the corridors and passageways of Avarloch. He wanted Dante prepared to ride and his two remaining hounds readied, now! He was sorry he hurt his wife's feelings, but he wasn't about to let her leave him over it. He would find her, and after he throttled her for making him pace the battlements all day, he would kiss her senseless, damn her.

Colette left the castle when the men were readying to leave the bailey. She gathered her cloak tightly around her shoulders to shield against the freezing cold while she watched Brand vault onto a stallion as black as the curls that fell loosely over its rider's forehead. His crimson mantle lifted off his shoulders as the wind howled in the bailey. She pulled her hood over her head and ran to him, but the wind blew the hood off again. Her hair spilled out behind her like a halo around her head.

Atop his horse, Brand watched her with hooded eyes as the winter bit his flesh. He traveled back in time to a day when he was leaving Graycliff to battle Baron Hawthorn's men, to a time when having to leave Colette tore at his soul. She had raced out of Graycliff, looking much the way she did now to bid him one last farewell. Leaping from the saddle of his warhorse, he had gathered her up in his arms to cherish the scent of her, to relish the feel of her body pressed so tightly against his own, and to whisper his love into her ear. Now he ground his teeth at the holdup.

"Brand!" she called out, hurrying to reach him before he left Avarloch. When she did, she placed a small, gloved hand on his thigh and looked up at him with wide, haunting eyes. "I will miss you, my beloved."

Brand laughed, but there was no trace of mirth in the mocking sound.

"Why do you chase after this woman? Let her go, Brand, and stay with me."

"Go back inside, Colette."

"You have not answered my question. Why do you chase after her?" she repeated, trying to keep the honey in her voice.

A thin smile curled his lips when he looked down at her from his horse. "Because, Colette, the scent of her ravishes me."

The slight flaring of her nostrils told Brand that his words had the effect he wanted, but then her beguiling smile matched his. "William is gone as well, my lord. Have you not noticed? Mayhap they are together."

Brand's stallion reared and protested the sudden vise-like pressure of its rider's thighs. "That does not matter," Brand challenged. "Not all women have trouble keeping their legs closed." He flapped his reins sharply to leave. "And, Colette," he added acidly, whirling his mount around to face her again, "the next time you call me 'your beloved,' I will have your tongue cut from your mouth."

Unfazed by his threat, Colette de Marson cast her be-witching smile on Brand's powerfully built brother. In return, Dante offered her a scornful smile that dimpled his cheek. A cool breeze blew a black strand of hair across the shimmering glitter of his eyes, concealing, for just an instant, the disgust he felt.

The forest loomed before Brand like a thousand echoing doors, calling . . . beckoning. He shook his head to clear his thoughts, but the image of long, winding corridors only changed into Colette's face. The face of an angel sent to destroy him, Brand thought angrily. There were no more tears to shed over her—though once they did fall like rain, flooding his heart, his very soul. There was no more urge to shout like a Norse berserker, driven to mad-ness with suppressed anger. The pain that had utterly con-sumed him was gone. There was nothing left but the deadly numbness that covered his heart, trying to shield him from love that had become his enemy.

Dante rode up beside him and, seeing the familiar shadows in his brother's eyes, remained silent. He would have disagreed with anyone who told him that Brand no longer felt any passion. Indeed, one only had to look beyond the turbulent blue-green oceans to see the fire that once had blazed so brightly. Dante knew firsthand why Brand was called "the Passionate." Like a double-edged sword, he cut through life, letting its energy fill his veins until his laughter rang out rich and real, causing those around him to join in his joy. But his darkness was as deadly as his light was exhilarating. When Brand rode into battle, his passion was not exhumed but ignited, and anyone who fought alongside him, as Dante had, could feel the life he cherished pulsing through him. The warrior still lived, Dante knew, recalling the skill and fury his brother had used to conquer Lord Richard's army. Emotions still raged within him. Brand had only replaced his laughter with sorrow, but he could still feel. He still lived. Somewhere the fire still burned. And because Dante knew him so well, he was the only one who recognized the flames flickering again whenever Brand set eyes on his wife.

"I am worried something has happened to her," Dante ventured, keeping his horse at a quick canter alongside Brand's.

Brand kept his gaze steady on the tangle of trees just ahead. "Her father assures me that she knows these woods as if they were part of her own room."

"*Oui*, but I still worry."

Silence, then, "So do I, Dante."

✳

Hearty laughter rang out in the silence of twilight, rever-
berating against dark, heavy branches and finding its
way to the ears of the men who traveled the moist, leaf-
covered ground.

Brand stopped his horse, listening.

William.

"This way," he ordered, snapping his reins and leading
his horse toward the familiar sound.

"Mayhap they are together." Colette's voice taunted
him.

Whisper and Shredder howled and barked in a frenzy
of discovery while Chaos answered their call just over a
slight ridge in the distance.

"We are found." William squatted by the fire and
looked at the fine woman sitting next to him. He smiled,
though the hint of disappointment in his voice was not
lost on Brynna. "Remember, fairest of all my loyal warriors," he whispered gently as the thundering of horses
grew louder, "a battle awaits you, and I await your
victory."

"Aye, my lord." Brynna squeezed his much larger
hand, then quickly planted a kiss on his cheek. "And I
await yours as well."

William lifted a finger to her lips and pressed it there.
For a moment Brynna thought he meant to quiet her, but
the eyes she once thought so savage rested like petals on
her face, drinking her in as if he were looking at her for
the last time. "Brynna, know that you will always be precious to me, and if you ever feel unloved, remember that
your future king does love you indeed."

Tears filled her eyes, and William drew in a deep breath before he rose to his feet to tower over her. "Wipe your tears, lady, your husband approaches." His voice had changed in the space of a breath. Brynna's friend was gone, and in his place stood a man of majestic authority studying the semidarkness of the forest for the accusation he knew was about to descend on him.

Brynna tried to stand when she saw Brand, but the pain from her head wound made her reel. She closed her eyes to the darkness that threatened to overtake her. She heard her husband's voice like a blast of freezing air against her skin.

"This looks cozy, William," Brand said as he reined into the small, firelit clearing. His gaze came to rest on Brynna sitting before the flames, looking quite dazed.

"*Oui*, 'tis." William smiled, but his voice was stark and as crisp as the winter air. "But, unfortunately, not for your wife. She was thrown from her horse and is injured."

Brand was out of his saddle in an instant and kneeling beside Brynna the next. "How badly are you hurt?"

The tender concern in his eyes made her want to reassure him that the wound was not serious. "It is only my head," she told him quietly.

Lifting his fingers to her scalp, he searched gently while heavy folds of burnished copper buried his hand. "There is no open wound, only a knot the size of my fist."

The warm breath of his mouth fell against Brynna's cheek and she longed to turn her head for a kiss, but her husband was already back on his feet. He faced William with a hard edge in his eyes that made Dante slip from his saddle and approach his brother cautiously.

"Why didn't you return her to Avarloch, William?" Brand asked, his voice a menacing growl.

The two warriors regarded each other for a moment before William answered. "I left on foot, and the lady's horse died in the fall."

"How long have you been here with her?"

William tossed his friend a benign smile, but there was a fire in his deep gray eyes—fire that William hoped would keep their friendship burning. This scene was familiar to Brand, and William knew what his friend was thinking. He had to put an end to those thoughts quickly; not by trying to convince Brand of the truth, but by allowing him to make his own conclusion.

"Long enough to do to her the one thing you dread."

Brynna made a sound to protest, but the deadly swish of Brand's sword being ripped from its scabbard paralyzed her. Polished steel, gleaming like liquid wrath, was pointed with both hands at the Norman duke.

"Brand, put away your sword!" Dante took a step toward his brother, unable to believe what he was seeing. But William drew him back, his eyes never leaving Brand's face.

Brand's eyes were wild with fear and rage, his hands shook, causing the blade to wobble before him. Not Brynna, please. His heart beat so furiously in his chest he thought he might retch.

"Did you, William? Tell me."

"*Non,* friend," William replied quietly, calmly. "You tell me."

Silence hung like an ominous shroud while Brand stared over his blade at the person he had trusted since he was a boy. Faced with the demons that betrayal had created, he teetered at the edge of the precipice again. But this was William. Would his dearest friend truly betray him? Brand knew the answer immediately.

He lowered his sword. "I beg you forgive me, William."

With one step William reached him and slapped his cheek affectionately. "Already done, *ami*." He turned, patted Dante's arm reassuringly, then headed toward the horses. "But try me not again, lest I gut you before your wife's beautiful eyes," he called out over his shoulder.

Sheathing his sword, Brand looked down at Brynna. He heard his brother's footsteps leaving the clearing. His heart wrenched with something he tried very hard to deny. God help him, he was losing. He ran his hand down his mouth and closed his eyes. Was it dangerous to let himself love her? He recoiled, understanding again that the depth of love he could feel for Brynna would be far more intense than anything he had felt for Colette. But Brynna was not Colette. She was not a selfish, spoiled brat. She'd proved her loyalty to her home and all the people in her father's care. She had been patient and loving to him, even when he behaved like the barbarian she called him. Hell, she already took him to the edge of the world, and he had followed her. Blindly, no less! But instead of falling, she showed him what it was like to fly.

He knelt beside her and brought her hand to his lips. "And you? Will you forgive me as well, Brynna?"

"Aye," she whispered instantly, almost breathless from his tender gaze. She wanted to tell him how the sight of him melted her like sun-warmed honey. "Brand, I—" When she would have said more, his fingers brushed over her lips.

"Ssh. Let's go home, Brynna. You will need looking after for a few days." He slipped his arms under her, lifting her from the cold ground as if she were weightless. He rubbed his cheek against the top of her head, and then let his lips linger there in a long, sweet kiss. He should be throttling her for making him worry so, but he was too relieved to have her back in his arms.

Cradled securely against his chest, Brynna closed her eyes and let the masculine scent of him fill her, and fill her it did, awakening all her senses, igniting small fires that burned and then melted her until she nearly went limp in his arms. She breathed deeply, resting her head in the hollow of his shoulder. She turned her face slightly upward to bathe in the velvet warmth of his neck.

Brand could feel his wife's lips against his flesh. It sent tongues of heat down his spine. He moaned softly, carrying her to his horse, wanting to dismiss William and his brother so that he could take her right where he stood. Testing the supple firmness of her thighs with one hand, he squeezed and then stroked. Heat burned from his navel to his knees. "Brynna," he whispered, slowing his pace. The word sounded as though it had been ripped from him against his will. He wanted to tell her how happy he was that he had found her, and how the thought that she might have left him had driven him mad.

Brynna waited for him to continue, but he said nothing more. He only held her tighter, pressing his cheek against her head. His voice had been heavy with the whipcord tightness of desire burning to be released. Desire, not love, she told herself.

"Is Colette still at Avarloch?" she asked without lifting her head.

"She is," Brand replied. He felt Brynna stiffen in his arms and he sighed. "And I'll not have my wife running off on her own every time I speak to the wench. You and I must have a talk about your lack of trust, Brynna."

Fury boiled in a flash of emerald as Brynna lifted her head and glared at him. "*My* lack of . . ." She was so angry she could not finish. She found her voice after another instant passed, though. "What reasons have you given me to trust you? Not only do you try to hide the truth that you still love Colette, but you took my home, and then you made me your wife simply to satisfy the lust in your savage Norman loins, and now you mock me by bringing your beloved to my home so she can laugh in my face as well."

Brand stopped and glared down at her. He was tempted to drop her. "I told you I do not love her. You seem to have difficulty believing me—another talk we shall need to have soon." He picked up his steps again. "I will forgive you for accusing me of mocking you, or allowing anyone else to do so because I understand that the bump on your head has made you daft."

Brand reached his horse and lifted Brynna to his saddle. He was somewhat gentle, but the quick movement made her head ache to the point she thought she might retch. She tried to move away from him when he fit her between his strong thighs, but he curled his arm around her waist and dragged her back to him.

"I will have Alysia tend to you as soon as we return." His voice was cold and flat. "Stop wiggling in my lap. I would regret making love to you and hurting you further."

Brynna wanted to scream.

Another horse trotted alongside Brand's slowly. She

looked up. Steel gray eyes met hers in silence, but William's message was clear, and boomed in Brynna's aching head.

"Remember, fairest of all my loyal warriors, a battle awaits you, and I await your victory."

Chapter Nineteen

❋

Brynna sulked in her bed while Alysia sighed over her mistress's uneaten dinner.

"You must eat to regain your strength, m'lady." The handmaiden sighed again when the tray she pushed toward Brynna was pushed back to her.

"I have strength already." Brynna fumed. "Strength enough to go downstairs and claw that witch Colette's eyes right from her head."

Alysia's large eyes opened even wider, but then a wistful smile formed on her full lips. "I think every woman in Avarloch would give her firstborn babe to see you do it."

Brynna turned her head on the thick pillow that propped her and looked at her handmaiden. "Is she that bad already?"

"Aye." Alysia nodded and took a seat at the edge of Brynna's bed. "When she sees Dante, she radiates like iron tossed into the flames. The only man she does not pay any attention to is Duke William."

Brynna did not know whether to curse the trollop or weep over the pain the trollop's behavior was probably causing her husband. She would not weep, she decided quickly. Brand chose to let Colette stay at Avarloch, no matter the torment she caused him. Just as long as he could gaze at her satiny, flaxen hair, her sable brown eyes. . . . Brynna fought to control the fury that welled up inside her. How could she ever battle Colette de Marson? Brand loved her, he always would. He was too busy pining over his beloved to even visit his wife since he brought her home.

Brynna seethed at the memory of being carried like a helpless babe past the amused smile of the hellwitch. Brand had brought her straight to her bed and deposited her there without a word. She tightened her fists into the cool sheets of her bed now, clenching her teeth against a flood of tears that ached to wash her away. Let him spend his days with that seductress, she lamented. Let Colette break what was left of his heart. He deserved it.

"I do not want to know what he's doing with her, Alysia, do you hear?"

"But, m'lady, he has not even—"

"Do you hear?" Brynna's voice was dagger sharp.

"Aye."

"Good. You may go. And take this tray with you."

Alysia nodded and lifted the tray from the bed. She could see Brynna's pain reflected in the glistening of her eyes and the tight, drawn lips that quivered holding back her sorrow. "Is there someone I can send for? Your father mayhap?"

"Nay," Brynna answered. She was tired of constantly letting her father see her grief. It was hard enough for him knowing that he was the reason Brand was here in the first place. She would not torture him further. She thought of eyes the color of steel and soft as velvet. "Send for Duke William. I would like to speak with him."

"He left, m'lady."

"Left?" Brynna sat up in her bed. Her eyes were huge saucers when she blinked. Her fingers clenched the sheets until they went numb. "When?"

"Early this morn. He spoke to Lord Brand for a while and then he gathered his men and left."

Alysia wanted to put the tray down and run to her mistress. Never had the handmaiden seen such emptiness in anyone's eyes the way it haunted Brynna's at that moment. But just as quickly as it had come, it was gone.

"Thank you, Alysia," Brynna said with all the composure she could muster. She dismissed the girl with a curt nod of her head.

As soon as the handmaiden was gone, Brynna threw her head into her pillow. So, the Norman brute left Avarloch without so much as a farewell. How could he? Brynna tried to halt her tears, but she no longer could. She told herself that William of Normandy was naught but a savage. She was right about him all along. He was cold, just like her husband. Well, she could be like them and care for no one as well. Brynna told herself these things, but her heart raged against her thoughts, and no matter how hard she tried, her tears fell hard until the darkness that consumed her made her sleep.

Brand sat in a chair of white oak whose cushioned seat and back were embroidered in the rich greens and yellows of Lord Dumont's emblem. Despite the roaring fire in the central hearth, the great hall of Avarloch was cold.

The fingers of one of Brand's hands traced the elaborate etchings of a silver goblet that sat idly on the table in front of him, while his other hand slowly raked through his hair. He was alone but for Whisper, who lay in a deep slumber at his feet. Brand's eyes fixed vaguely on the etchings of the goblet. The silver was finely crafted, carved with the figure of a woman, her head thrown back in ecstasy while her lover's body bent over her, ravishing her neck with kisses. Flowers blossomed with invisible colors around the couple while branches tangled over-head like the lover's embrace. They were making love in the woods, Brand thought, just as he had wanted to do with Brynna before he brought her home. Just like Colette had done with Alexander before Brand killed him. Shad-ows danced in his eyes as his mind brought him back to the place where he lost who he once was.

Colette.

Betrayal.

"You bitch." His hand shot out against the goblet, hurl-ing it into the wall behind him. Whisper jumped to her feet and whined softly before circling the floor and lying back down.

"Brand?"

The voice was pure silk, like an angel sighing. Brand knew the sound, had heard it many times, and dreamed it after that. He looked up from the hands now covering his face.

"Colette, leave me."

"Nay, my lord." The music of her voice echoed through the hall with sweet innocence and silken feminin-ity that drenched his soul and left him weary.

"You have not visited me since I came here, my lord, nor have you summoned me to your chambers." Colette moved toward him as if gliding. "Pray, tell me why?"

Brand watched her with hooded, tired eyes. The air around her seemed to dance as though permeated with heat.

"Why do you deny what is so obvious to everyone here, even to your wife?" Colette asked gently as she came closer, circling the table to reach him, her finger tracing its surface.

"I deny nothing," Brand said, but she glided closer . . . closer. . . . She was like a dream coming into existence as the firelight cast its golden glow upon her hair.

"Colette"—the sound of his voice drew another whimper from the hound at his feet—"why did you betray me?"

"I did not betray our love, Brand. I never stopped loving you." Like an apparition, she came to him, bending to her knees before his chair. "I have thought of no one but you since you forced me to leave Graycliff. Betray? Nay, my love, 'tis you who betrayed me by marrying another." She stroked his thigh as she spoke, smiling up at him softly.

Brand closed his eyes. There was no fire raging within him to take her. . . . There was nothing. Even his anger had deserted him.

Brynna.

His mind reeled, became heady with the sweet wine he had been drinking all night. "I cannot give her my heart because of you, Colette."

"Because your heart belongs to me, Brand," she corrected.

He opened his eyes, watching her slide between his legs, up his body until her face was close to his, until he could look directly into the eyes he dreamed of so many nights. Slowly he lifted his hand to her face and brushed her cheek with the back of his fingers. The touch brought a soft sigh from Colette. She was about to move closer to kiss him when the bleak emptiness that filled him became visible in the glistening of his turquoise eyes. She stopped, stricken by the unspeakable sorrow that cried out louder than if a crash of thunder had filled the great hall. "You took so much from me, Colette."

"Love me again, Brand, and I will cease all the pain I have caused you. Make your wife leave. Do away with her. I care not. Fill me with your love again, and I promise—"

But even as she spoke, Brand was already shaking his head. He rested a finger to her lips to quiet her. "*Non*, Colette. That's what I am trying to tell you. I refuse to love anyone. Not even you." He lifted her hand from his thigh and rose from his chair.

"Brand!" Colette sprang to her feet as he started to leave the hall. "If you cannot love me, then make love to me at least. Remember?" she pleaded, pulling his arm so that he would turn to look at her. "Remember how I felt under you?"

Brand searched her eyes with his and then laughed softly, but the sound brought another low whimper from Whisper. He spoke slowly, quietly, just now discovering a great truth so simple he felt foolish for not knowing it sooner. "My wife will never be satisfied with my lust alone because she desires my love as well, while love was never enough for you, Colette. You are happy just to have someone's sword in your delicate sheath. Anyone's sword." He stepped away from her. "I fear I have become like you, my sweet angel, only I have not yet grown so loathsome as to want *you*." A beauty so deadly that it gave

Brand the power to slay with a smile illuminated his face and took Colette's breath away, even though the curse of it was directed at her.

"I will find another to warm my bed," she promised him. "And it will tear at your heart tonight."

He shook his head, still smiling. "I have no heart, Colette. Enjoy yourself."

As if a command had been spoken, Whisper followed her master out of the great hall and up the long winding staircase to Brynna's bedroom door.

Brand entered his wife's room just as he had the night before after she had fallen asleep. He gazed at her sleeping soundly in her own bed. The hearth fire died down to glowing embers, but he could still see her. Moonlight filtered through wooden shutters casting its silvery beams upon the sheer chemise that clung to full curves and sensuous angles. Thick copper hair caressed her face. Brand's fingers moved over her to touch it, to feel the fire that enveloped her. But he dropped his hand to his side. He feared he could never give Brynna what she wanted— what she deserved. She wanted sweet promises whispered while his body ravished her, and he could not speak them. She wanted love and he was sure he was too afraid to give it. Yet his body trembled at the mere sight of her. His heart hammered when she looked at him from across a room. Her face haunted him every moment he was awake.

Brand closed his eyes and drew in a deep breath. He had told himself that he would not take Brynna again tonight or any other night. He would not cause her to lose her heart to a man who could never give her what she needed. But looking at her now, he knew he could never resist her. He wanted her already. He reluctantly moved away from her bed and went to the hearth. He placed with care more wood on the dying embers and watched the flames lick hungrily at the thin slices of timber. A new warmth filled the room as he took up his usual place in a chair facing Brynna's bed to watch her while she dreamed. He did not want to think about why he felt the need to be here with her, nor did he question it. He simply watched her. Azure eyes drinking in the length of her, remembering the soft scent of jasmine that washed his senses when she was near and the sparkling of her eyes so filled with passion, honesty, and a love for life that he had lost. He listened to the song of her deep, rhythmic breathing and soon fell asleep in the chair.

Brand made his way down dark, winding corridors. His boots tapping lightly, kicking up swirls of dust and a musty odor that clung to him along with the scents of rose and gardenia.

She was here somewhere.

Colette.

The door at the end of the hall stood open like the gaping mouth of a dragon waiting to swallow up his trust and love, while doors on either side of him called with haunted voices, beckoning him to enter.

Eyes set, Brand strode directly toward the last door. This time, when he reached it, he did not fall upon his knees at the sight of his angel crouched demurely in the grass.

You took everything from me.

Someone was moving in the trees and Brand looked up, expecting to see Alexander.

"Wake up, Brand." It was Brynna. He smiled, looking at her. "Wake up and I will make you live again." She handed him a perfect rose. Her fingers moved softly over his, shielding him from the thorns.

Something stirred within his soul at her touch, at her words spoken with such meaning.

"Wake up and let me love you. Wake up."

Brand opened his eyes. It was morning and he was staring into endless fields of emerald green. He sighed, losing himself to the love he found in Brynna's eyes. Her hair fell like flames over his pale knuckles clutching the arm of his chair. He smiled at her leaning over him.

"Your sleep is haunted," she said knowingly.

"Oui."

Brynna studied him for a moment, her eyes tender with concern; then emerald darkened into olive as shadows filled her and she turned away in a flurry of flowing gauze. She went to her bed and sat down, facing the window. Without looking at him again, she picked up a comb and ran it through her thick hair. "What are you doing in here?"

Brand watched her. He watched her hair clinging to her breasts and he wanted to play with the fiery locks, to touch her as seductively as her hair touched her. "I am your husband. Where else should I spend the night?"

"In my bed mayhap?" she shot back curtly before looking at him. "Or with Colette."

"Brynna." Brand spoke her name with such tenderness she wanted to weep at the sweet sound. "I don't want Colette. If I did, I would have been honest with you from the beginning. Lying leads to mistrust, and I value trust too much. How can you not know that by now?" She lifted her eyes to him while he spoke and her beauty called to him from across the room, drawing him to her. "I am here with you. This is where I want to be."

"But you dream of her. What does that mean, Brand?" The honest and painful curiosity in her voice made his heart wrench. "Tell me, I beg you. Why do you let your goddess haunt me as well as you?"

Brand shook his head. "You are the goddess, fair Brynna." He watched her with eyes that yearned for something lost and longed for. Her breath hesitated. The hunger in him summoned her, but she did not move from her bed. "Your hair is like hungry flames that burn when it touches my skin," he said huskily, rising from his chair. Brynna felt her resolve melt when he stood over her a moment later, his beautiful eyes burning into hers. "Your smile renews my soul."

The touch of his gaze was almost physical as it moved over her until she felt dizzy. Breath labored, she closed her eyes in self-defense of the passion that once drove him, that still did. He knelt before her and lifted her hand to his lips. He brushed a kiss against the underside of her wrist. "You are so beautiful."

"Nay."

"*Oui.*" His voice covered hers, seductive, raw, and fully male. His fingertips glided from her cheek to the soft curve of her lips. "I want to taste the nectar of these lips. I want to drench myself in the passion for life that pulses within you. Will you help me, Brynna?" He pressed in closer to her until his lips brushed hers and then his tongue began to taste her as he said he would.

Brynna was lost to a kiss that was completely Brand— intimate, intense, fierce, and tender.

"Brand . . ." she breathily responded as his mouth drank her in further, then traversed a scorching path down the length of her neck. "You must know that if you take me and I lose you, my heart will be as broken as yours is."

Drinking in her cries, Brand lifted his powerful body over hers, shivering with a sensual hunger that was as great as his restraint. He stopped kissing her long enough to speak, and as he did, his lips moved over her forehead, her nose, her cheeks, and then to her lips again. "I do know the hurt I would cause you." His mouth whispered over her eyelashes, capturing the crystal tears she tried to deny. "That's why I stay away. I ask only for your help."

Brynna gazed into his eyes when he withdrew to look at her. The dark shadows she saw there were as real as his desire for her. Dear God, she loved this man. "Tell me how to help you, Brand, and I shall do whatever you ask. I love you so, husband."

His smile was a beautiful dawn awakening. "I know you love me." His smile faded a bit. "But I don't know how to reclaim what her betrayal took from me."

"Very well," Brynna whispered. "I thank you for speaking only the truth to me from the beginning." She let a smile grace her face, then blushed when Brand inhaled sharply. "Am I renewing your soul, husband?"

Low laughter and sensual arousal tangled in his throat. "You are." He rose to his feet with a self-control that surprised even him and took her hands in his.

"Are you well enough to breakfast with me this morn?" he asked. His eyes poured over her, touching her like a profound caress. Brynna nodded while he smoothed back a wisp of copper hair that had fallen against her cheek. "I will await you outside your door while you dress."

"You have no need to go," she protested. "You are my husband."

Brand stepped away from her. "*Oui*, but the mere memory of your breasts rakes at my loins, burning me with a fire I fear I would not be able to control if I see them again and cannot taste them." A fire of her own leaped up in Brynna at his words, the passion in his voice. He flashed her a lecherous grin. "I will wait outside." Without waiting for her reply, Brand left the room.

Brynna's heart beat frantically in her chest. Brand had stayed away to protect her from himself. The thought made her love him even more. And it was her love for him that made her passion burn like a wild fire, blazing through her, making every nerve tingle. She ached to be taken by him, to feel him cutting through her flesh with his raw, primitive power. To hear him speak her name while he moved her the way the ocean moves against a rocky cliff. Hope stirred once again in Brynna. Something told her that the high battlement walls Brand had built around his heart were beginning to fall. Dear Lord, those walls were thick. But she understood why when she looked into his eyes. Brand gave all of himself in everything he did, including loving Colette. Brynna realized with eye-opening clarity that she probably would not have fallen in love with him if she had not witnessed the total giving of himself that day at the lake. She would not have loved him as she did if he were able to give up Colette so easily. She wanted to be loved with that kind of complete commitment, with trust and loyalty, and she would give it in return. Oh, he was worth the fight, worth her patience. His was the kind of heart that if she could win, it would belong to her forever. And she would be victorious. But great victories took time to win. All fair and loyal warriors knew that.

She leaped from her bed and dressed in a gown of soft crimson velvet. She weaved her hair into a thick braid that fell down her back and finished with a thin circlet of tiny rubies that dangled softly around her forehead. When she was done dressing, she clothed herself in the strength she would need to see the battle to its end, then quietly left the room.

Brand sat outside her chambers on a small bench against the wall, his long legs stretched out before him. When she opened the door, he greeted her with a warm grin and rose to his feet, ready to escort his wife to the morning table for the first time since they were wed.

Looking up at him, Brynna encountered the fathomless pools of blue-green eyes that drank her in so intently. His gaze traveled over her face, studying her soft contours. "You are so lovely that you snatch the breath from my body," Brand told her, lifting her hand to his lips.

"And you take mine, husband."

He looked up from her hand and Brynna almost gasped with desire for him at the sensuous stare he gave her.

"Then we had best not look at each other, lest we fall faint on the way down the stairs."

She laughed at the vision he conjured up in her mind, but then almost stopped when her husband began to laugh with her. His face changed, radiating with a joy that made Brynna's heart accelerate. She wondered if she could ever survive gazing at this man's happiness when he truly found it again.

"Good lord, sir, but you are so strangely beautiful." She barely breathed.

Brand raised a raven eyebrow in amusement and surprise. Then, taking a step back, he bowed to her, a real, modest smile curling his lips. "Thank you . . . I think." He pulled her to him, molding her supple warmth to his body.

He slipped his arms around her waist until she could feel the thundering of his heart against her own. His eyes were vast oceans, depthless pools. But no longer were they void. Indeed, the emotion that poured through him was so powerful that for a moment Brynna thought she would die in his arms, and be content to go.

He trembled as he spoke, fearing that whatever it was he was feeling at that moment would flee before he could tell her. "Promise never to take your smile from me, Brynna. Gaze at me always the way you do right now, basking me in the sunlight of spring. I swear to you, wife, I can feel your love summoning me. And I promise I will ever be faithful to that love."

Brynna ran her fingertips over his lips and watched as he kissed them, knowing he spoke the truth. He would always be faithful to her. Aye, she was breaking those walls. Defiantly, she dared to hope. And at that moment it did not matter, she only knew that she never wanted to be apart from him again, not even for a moment. No matter if he loved her or not, the sight of him, the scent of him, gave her life.

"And I will ever be faithful to my love for you, my beautiful warrior. I promise this to you with all my heart."

Brand kissed her, and finally the voices that haunted him were silent.

Chapter Twenty

The great hall bristled with people. The sounds of laughter blended with lute and harp as knights and ladies ate and vassals and serfs clanged goblets in various toasts of goodwill. The aroma of sweetbread permeated the air, along with the scent of freshly roasted pheasant.

Brynna surveyed the enormous hall and then glanced up at the man who walked beside her, his arm locked in hers. Ranks and stations meant little to Lord Brand Risande, a fact he had made quite obvious even to the king. Brand's respect was a thing not given lightly; having to be earned rather than owed, and he gave all the opportunity to earn it, treating everyone at Avarloch fairly.

Brynna smiled up at her husband as he led her through the hall. This was her home, and though her father was a just and fair man, she never remembered Avarloch so filled with life.

Brand's gaze swept over the many faces, searching the crowd for Lord Richard. When he found him, he laced Brynna's fingers through his and led her to her father.

Lord Richard Dumont watched the approaching couple with narrowed eyes and wondered if the smile his daughter wore was genuine. He doubted it was after leaving her miserable in her room just the morning before. But, Richard thought with bewilderment creasing his brows, there was nothing hidden, nothing calculating in the warm smile that Lord Brand offered him. The man positively radiated happiness, leaving Richard Dumont to wonder what had transpired between his daughter and her husband in the last twenty-four hours.

"Lord Richard," Brand greeted quietly when they reached him.

"Sir." Brynna's father gave him a curt nod, then turned his attention to his daughter. "Brynnafar." He gripped her arms and pulled his daughter in gently for a kiss. "How goes it with you?"

"I am well, Father." Her eyes darted to both men. She frowned, sensing anger from her father. "What is it?" she asked carefully.

Brand answered her, taking a step forward to face her father squarely. "I fear I was more than disrespectful to your father the other day. Lord Richard, I ask you to accept my apology for the way I spoke to you. I have no excuse for my anger."

Richard eyed her husband for what seemed an eternity to Brynna. She could almost see her father searching for Brand's sincerity.

"If I thought that mayhap you were worried about my daughter at the time, I would have—"

"I was," Brand interrupted. "Much more than I cared to admit." He turned his meaningful gaze to Brynna. "So much more."

Richard looked at Brynna, but his daughter had no idea what they were talking about, so she could offer him no answers. Struck by Brand's apology and admission of some emotion for his daughter, Lord Richard was at a loss for something to say, so he cleared his throat. "Very well, then. I accept your apology."

Brand flashed him a bright smile, one that made Brynna swoon. He whispered into her ear that he needed to speak to Dante, and then left her alone with her father.

"What happened between you two?" Richard asked his daughter the moment Brand was out of earshot. "I swear, he looked at you like a lovesick squire."

Brynna's heart leaped at her father's words while her eyes clung to Brand, now taking a seat beside his brother. "I think my husband is turning into a merman." She turned to look up at her father and the warm tears in her eyes moved him, though he clearly had no idea what she was talking about. "I love him, Father," she explained. "And I think he is beginning to return my love."

Her father smiled gently and slipped his arm around her shoulder. "That should be quite easy, Brynnafar."

"Nay," Brynna told him. She finally believed that Brand no longer loved Colette de Marson. His heart was not held captive by love, but by fear of loving again. "Her betrayal holds him prisoner."

Richard turned to follow his daughter's gaze.

Colette de Marson entered the hall on the arm of Sir Jeffrey Hamlin, one of the men who had escorted her to Avarloch. Her hair was the color of sun-bleached wheat, coiled loosely around her head like a crown. Her eyes held within them the charm and innocence of a child. Watching the petite figure entering the hall, Brynna could understand why Brand had loved her so.

The two women's eyes met for a brief moment and Colette smiled before casting her eyes downward.

Brynna's blood boiled. "She does not fool me with her angelic beauty. William told me how she . . ." Suddenly Brynna's eyes opened wide on her father. "You did not go with him!"

"Who?"

"The duke—you were supposed to go back to Normandy with him. He left without you!"

Her father leaned in closer to her. "My dear," he whispered as Colette passed him. "William did not return to Normandy. Your most loyal servant, the duke, has gone off to fight for you."

Brynna stared at her father. Her eyebrows knit in confusion. But before she could question him further, the sound of sweet laughter assaulted her ears. She turned just in time to see Colette throw her head back, inviting her escort to bury his face deeper into the neck he was laving. With half-closed eyes, Colette moaned loudly, loud enough for everyone in the great hall to look at her. Everyone, including Brand.

"No biting, Jeffrey!" Colette giggled, pushing the man away. "Save that for the bedroom." She turned her head purposely in Brand's direction.

Brynna stood rooted to her spot, watching her husband's reaction, which was quite different from what she had expected it to be. Brand merely looked up with vague interest at the passionate couple and continued his conversation with Dante. Brynna wanted to claw the woman's eyes out.

"She tries to make a fool of my husband in front of his men," Brynna observed seethingly, more to herself than to her father. But Lord Richard answered her anyway.

"Then go make him feel like the man he is, Brynnafar.

Show him that he married a woman, and not a spoiled child."

Battle. War. Brynna's eyes blazed and her shoulders straightened with single determination. She loved Brand. Loved him from the very first moment she saw him, alive and rhapsodic. She knew what he wanted, knew how to make her husband feel fierce and alive. The only thing he had not lost to Colette's treachery was his desire. And so, with a sensual smile forming on her full lips, Brynna slipped the combs from her hair and gracefully made her way across the room.

Energy infused the air with feral sensuality that made every head turn to look at Brynna as she passed, her silken waves cascading over her shoulders and breasts as she walked. Brand saw his wife coming and the sensuous hook of his lips told her that everyone else in the hall was utterly forgotten, including Colette. Brynna's passion summoned her husband the way a falcon is summoned by its master's whistle.

Brand's eyes darkened and he watched her with a nakedly male grin. He rose from his chair to welcome her. When she stood close, his nostrils flared, breathing in her achingly familiar scent of jasmine. Slipping his hand around the small of her back, he offered her a seat next to his. His eyes never left hers as hunger hung like a mist around them both.

"Do you have much business here this morn, husband?" Brynna's lips grazed his ear as he sat.

Brand's expression changed slightly to one of surprise when her intentions became clear; then he smiled rather fiercely. "Naught that cannot wait, wife. But I thought we agreed that—"

"Wonderful. Make haste with Dante, please." Brynna cut off the rest of his words.

The erotic catch in her voice sent a stroke of heat through Brand's body. What was she doing? he wondered. Why were her eyes begging him to carry her off to their room? He had not wanted to use her body without giving her everything she needed, and he knew she did not want that either. He watched her lift a biscuit to her mouth. Honey dripped along her lower lip and she swiped it up with her tongue. Brand inhaled sharply, knowing he had to have her.

As if reading her husband's thoughts, Brynna's eyes slanted sideways, catching his hungry appraisal of her.

"What is it, Brynna?"

"What is what, husband?"

He smiled. But beyond his savage thirst, Brynna could see the confusion in his eyes. "Why do you tempt me so?"

When he spoke, Colette giggled again as her lover gripped her inner thigh under the table. Understanding washed over Brand's face suddenly and his smile faded. "You do this only so that I will pay no attention to her," he accused Brynna quietly.

"Ha!" Brynna laughed and went back to chewing her biscuit. "It is I who holds all your attention, m'lord." She lowered her voice so that no one else could hear but her husband. "It is my body that will delight in your hot desire. My flesh that will feel you pulsing through me in our bed. Remember," she added with a twinkle in her eye, "you swore faithfulness to me."

Brand studied his wife suspiciously while he fought to control the aching hardness growing uncomfortably under the table. The certainty in her voice assured him that she believed what she said. "You do this out of pity for me," he concluded, slapping his hand lightly on the table. "Do not pity me, Brynna."

She turned in her seat to face her husband fully. Her eyes were blazing embers as she leaned in close to his face. Brand could almost feel the heat coming from her, the longing that made her voice tremble, and the hot need that made her breasts rise heavily above her gown when she breathed, then fall again as if in exhaustion.

"I do not pity you, my love. I want to pleasure you. I want to look into your eyes and you in mine while our hearts hammer against each other and our bodies strain to the point of bursting. I want to feel the satin coolness of your hair coiled around my fingers while you use your tongue to quicken the pulse at my throat." Her voice was a sensuous whisper that teased and taunted and pulled Brand as tight as a whip. She smiled wickedly, seeing him shift in his seat, then continued to torture him further. "I want to caress your hardness in my palm, stroke your silken flesh, and then . . . I want to taste you," she finished, relishing the effect she had on her husband. She leaned in closer still and kissed the smile that lingered on his lips.

Turning in his seat, Brand leaned his elbow on the table and balled his fist under his chin. He sat that way as seconds passed into minutes and Brynna wondered if she had gone too far.

"Are you angry with me, Brand?"

He slid his brilliant eyes at her. *"Non,"* he said simply, "but I need a few moments to . . . relax before I carry you upstairs and ravage you thoroughly." He was silent for another moment, then stood up.

One corner of Brynna's mouth curled into a delighted smile when she saw that his body had not fully "relaxed" quite yet.

Brand pulled her chair out in one swift motion and lifted her out of her seat, tossing her legs over his arm. "We are retiring," he called out to the shocked faces without letting his savage gaze leave his wife's eyes. "Enjoy the rest of your day, everyone."

Brynna giggled and swung her arms around her husband's neck as he carried her out of the great hall.

❃

Brand kicked the door closed behind him and brought Brynna to the large, canopied bed. She stared into his eyes as he laid her gently on the down mattress, his powerful body bending to kiss her passionately.

"I ache just looking at you," she whispered when he pulled back slowly.

"Where?" He lifted her crimson skirts and brushed his fingers against the velvet mound that rose slightly to meet his silken touch. "Do you ache here?"

She nodded, watching his eyes. She moved her hips, increasing the pressure of his fingers. The low moan Brand pulled from her made his body tighten with pleasure that was almost violent in its throbbing need to be in her.

"You spoke of pleasuring me, but let me please you first, Brynna." His voice was hardly recognizable under the strain of anticipation pouring through him. His fingers worked with agonizing delicacy unlacing the front of her gown. Once loosened, he slipped his hands under the fabric, brushing his palms against the satin of her breasts and the sensitive buds that hardened at his touch. The gown slipped from her shoulders down her waist, caressing her knees until Brand lifted his hands and simply looked at the beauty he had exposed.

"You look quite savage, husband." She groaned, soaking up his male power.

"I feel quite savage." The smile he gave her was as untamed as the caress of his teeth against her flesh. "You delight my tongue with the sweetest honey." He licked down the valley between her breasts. "Like spring itself." The end of his tongue circled her nipple and then he slowly enveloped the tip of her breast with his lips to drink in her splendor. The caress of his mouth changed from gentle to intense hunger. Heat cascaded through her—drawing low, languid moans from the back of her throat.

"Do I please you?" Brand asked, watching his wife's reaction as he sent fire to her neck with sweet brushes of his tongue. "Do I make you burn?"

Brynna couldn't answer him. She could hardly breathe as the liquid flames of his fingers continued a blazing path to the coppery mound between her legs. Rough fingers became soft as he probed the delicate folds that molded to him. He drew the tips of his fingers slowly over the hidden ruby making her body shudder as thunder crashed through her. Still, he probed, farther beyond the sleek petals that pulsed with desire.

"You blossom for me so quickly."

"Aye." She gasped through a moan that was as sultry as the liquid that drenched his fingers.

Brand sucked in air through clenched teeth. His pleasure was turning to agony as his swelling flesh fought for release from his trousers. He rose to his feet, looking like a hunter who had spotted his prey.

Brynna watched with widening eyes as Brand undressed. He was fully aroused, so tight he looked about to burst. She smiled languidly at his powerful body gleaming with hunger for her.

"You are beautiful . . . magnificent."

"*Non.*" Brand shook his head. "It is you who is beautiful. I cannot describe what you are to me, Brynna."

"Then show me, beautiful knight." She beckoned to him and he went.

Light touches of her fingers sent fire down his muscular thigh as he pushed her legs apart and knelt between them. His heaving manhood rested against her flesh, hot and alive with need. She ran her fingers over it, then closed her hand, delicately caressing the velvet steel.

"Take what you want," she whispered sensuously. "I can wait no longer to feel this strength inside me."

Brand closed his eyes and made a sound like his passion was being wonderfully ripped from him. He covered her hand with his and caressed it tighter. He rose up on his knees to his full height above her. A smile transformed his savage face into one of complete ecstasy. He slid her hand down and then up again, over and over, until Brynna thought he would explode in her hand. Then he opened his eyes and grinned so wickedly that she would have grown frightened, had she not felt the same way.

"Open for me," he commanded.

She obeyed, winding her legs around him as he lowered himself into her. His eyes pinned her when he entered her. Slowly, teasing, sending wave upon wave of hot convulsions through her; then the muscular thrusts of his body became more urgent, deliciously primitive. He rocked her, tightening his fingers through her hair, searching her mouth with his tongue as both parts of his body claimed her ravenously, then retreated. She clung to him with her legs, her fingernails, and it seemed the tighter she clung, the more intense his desire became until pleasure continuously exploded in Brynna, making her sway as she cried out his name.

Savoring every bit of her warmth, Brand withdrew slowly, then slid within her again, filling her to bursting. He teased her as her tight body caressed every inch of him. He relished every pulsing spasm that clenched, then loosened, around the sword that devoured her. He watched her, his eyes penetrating her as deeply as his body did. He was silent as he claimed her, almost emotionless while his body swept her against solid rock and cliff like a great turbulent tide.

And it was in his silence that Brynna heard his heart. She had longed to gaze upon that sinful, sensually dark smile of his. To see the ecstasy that once undid her while he swam, and then again when he took her so savagely. Brynna had thought her triumph would come in that smile. But it was here, in the subtle arch of his brow, in the quiet yearning of his eyes as he drank in her face, that told her that taking her was not enough anymore. He wanted to give.

In the silence of Brand's passion, Brynna could hear his heart beating into sweet surrender.

Later she lay tangled in his arms, one of his powerful legs tossed over hers. He had not spoken a word, even after he lay spent and shaking on top of her. He gathered her up in his arms, kissing her forehead, her cheeks, her lips, each with exquisite care.

Closing her eyes against the strength of his chest, Brynna wondered if what she had seen in his eyes was real or only her stubborn hope stirring again. She wanted to ask him, but did not dare, fearing she was wrong.

"I'm hungry," she whispered, stroking the fine lines of his chest with her fingertips.

Brand shifted in the bed, pulling her closer, "So am I," he replied huskily.

Lifting her head to look at him, Brynna smiled as the gentle gleam in his eyes deepened into a hungry blaze.

"The warrior awakens again."

"*Oui.*"

Beneath the bedcovers, delicate fingers whispered over him, measuring his aroused flesh.

"Let me pleasure you the way I promised." She caressed his rigid organ and smiled, feeling the whipcord tight shudder that lanced through her husband.

"Where did you learn to please a man so?" Brand groaned, closing his eyes under the beloved stroking of her hand.

"Alysia has told me many things. She is Turkish, you know. She lived in a sultan's harem before my father brought her here."

"That explains why Dante is always smiling."

"As you will be tomorrow, my warrior." Brynna pressed her lips against the warm, muscular pillar of his neck. Her tongue burned a fiery path to his chest. The taste of his salty masculine scent made her heady as if she were drinking fine wine. She remembered how he drank so sweetly from her nipples, drawing her in with insatiable yet delicate kisses. Her tongue flitted over his nipples and then she sucked and grinned secretly at the tight groan she pulled from him.

Brand's body stiffened against the savage passion surging through him at each caress from his wife's hand.

"How could an instrument of such splendid velvet grow so hard within my fingers?"

"It grows at the mere sight of you, woman," Brand told her raggedly, watching her coppery crown move farther down his body.

"Truly?" Brynna asked, licking fire along his inner thigh. "I thought it had to be touched at least." She paused, lifting her face from his flesh to give him a dark smile. "Mayhap, even kissed."

Fire raged untamable, quaking Brand's body as her lips caressed him and heat pulsed upward from her silken touches. Her tongue traced the length of him before she embraced his passion in the warmth of her mouth.

Brand groaned as bursts of ecstasy jolted his body, tightening muscles to the point of pure, blissful agony. Grasping her head within his palms, he guided her, directed her slowly, and then to more meaningful thrusts.

Brynna never imagined that giving pleasure could be as wonderful as receiving it, but feeling the thick muscles of his thighs convulsing under her, hearing the low, rough growls torn from her husband's throat, made her passion spring anew.

Suddenly, when Brand thought he could take not a single moment more of this delightful agony, he lifted her head. "Come here."

"Where?"

Effortlessly he lifted her. His hands snaked under her arms. "Right . . . here." Gently he lowered his wife onto his throbbing flesh. "Claim me as deeply as I claimed you."

"Oui," he whispered as she slid down, taking his sword to the hilt.

His name was drawn from Brynna with a rough harshness that matched his thrusts. Her hair spilled onto his chest like molten fire. And as if fire had indeed licked his flesh, he groaned with languid pleasure. He pulled her down, wanting her closer, needing her closer. And behind the curtain of copper hair, his hungry mouth found hers.

Time ceased to exist as bodies moved in perfect rhythm. Hot, sleek moisture covered them, igniting bursts of heat into minute explosions as pure pleasure drenched them inside and out. Brynna threw her head back, racked with spasms so tantalizingly sinful she thought she might die impaled upon him. Brand rose up to meet her, finding her taut, erect nipples and biting them tenderly.

"Let your perfume drench me, Brynna," he whispered.

She cried his name again, digging her nails into his muscled shoulders as explosions became unbearable, shaking, convulsing her into a feverish rapture against him. And Brand savored every hard, full thrust. He relished the grip she claimed him with that closed around him more tightly than his own flesh, until finally he cried out, filling her with all he had to give. They slept finally as night covered Avarloch like a smoky fog. And for once Brand did not dream.

Chapter Twenty-one

✳

"Wake up, Brand!"

Brand sat up so quickly that Brynna near fell off the edge of the bed, where she had been sitting. Her husband caught her with quick, strong hands.

Brynna gave him a wry smirk and shook her head. "Do you always wake up like that?"

"Like what?" Out of habit Brand glanced at the hearth. Flames licked hungrily at thin slabs of timber. It was not an unusual sight when he awoke from his dreams. The unusual thing was that Brand was not cold. He looked at the window next. The sun hung like a giant sunflower in the sky greeting the day. Dawn had passed and grew into late morn while he slumbered peacefully.

"Like someone had stolen into your room in the night and was waiting for you to awaken before they killed you."

"How long has the sun been up?" He ignored her question and rubbed the sleep from his eyes. It had been so long since he slept past dawn that he could not believe his eyes and looked out the window again.

"It is late, husband. I am afraid we slept most of the morn away."

"Truly?" Brand looked at her, his gaze locked on hers and then, slowly, he smiled. "That is good news."

"Nay!" Brynna's face burst into a huge grin that made Brand want to laugh. As if the sun were not bright enough, her smile drenched him with warmth. He loved her smile. "William has returned while we slept the day away."

"And?" Brand asked, touching his fingers to her lips and tracing her happiness. "Why are *you* so happy about that?"

"Because I have missed him, silly," she sang merrily. "Come, get dressed."

Brand looked at her as though he were dreaming. He must be dreaming. "You've missed William? The savage of all savages?"

Brynna waved his words away with a swipe of her hand. "William is as harmless as Squeak's kittens in the stable."

"*Non,* beauty." Brand laughed easily and leaned up on his elbow. "He is more dangerous then a den of hungry lions."

"Not to me." Brynna sprung from the edge of the bed and hunted for her ruby circlet she had flung away the night before. She spotted it near the window and bent to pick it up. She slipped it over her head to hold back the masses of auburn hair that fell around her shoulders, and when she turned back to Brand, he was watching her.

He took her in—all of her—from the top of her head, down the length of her crimson gown, to her feet. The rich sunlight from the window spilled over her, bathing her in light. But she needed no sunshine to glow, Brand thought. To him, Brynna was the most beautiful woman he had ever seen, and no one would argue with him when they looked at her. But Brand also saw a different kind of beauty in his wife. She was fresh with life, like spring waking the earth from its winter slumber. Spring that beckoned seeds to burst forth from the ground into tiny sprouts and reach up toward the promise of hope and the life-giving warmth of the sun.

Brynna smiled at the way he looked at her. "Are you getting up?"

"Oh, *oui*, I am."

She lifted an eyebrow. "You will keep William waiting?"

"What exactly did happen between you two all those hours you spent alone in the woods?" The slight knit of his raven brows made him look dangerous, but Brynna recognized the tiny smile that curled the corners of his mouth.

"Oh, nothing," she sang. "We talked of battles and royalty and other such boring things. You have no need to worry, my love." She went back to him and fell into his waiting arms. "William is far too hairy for me." She giggled and Brand drank in her happiness, imprinting into his mind the perfect arch of her brow, her small, straight nose, and the fresh life in the verdant blaze of her eyes.

"It's a good thing. I was afraid I would have to let my hair grow to my elbows to please you."

"Would you?" Brynna sighed into his mouth.

He nodded and his gaze held her still. She was amazed that before this moment she had no idea how piercing his eyes were. Had they changed? She remembered haunting shadows, depthless pools of hidden or lost emotion. She had seen tempest waves wrought with anger and agony; calculated innocence that was as beautiful as the sky before a storm, but never had she seen his eyes reaching out to her, speaking to her the way they did now.

"You are my beloved," Brynna whispered close to his face. Something . . . something moved in him, his eyes told her, but she wasn't sure what it was. Something alive, she told herself, a reaction to her love.

"Go on, woman." Brand brushed his smile over hers. "Go greet your favored warrior before I keep him waiting for you another two hours."

Brynna waited another moment, but whatever she saw in his gaze was gone now. She rose reluctantly from the warmth of his bare chest, kissing his chin as she went. She smoothed the velvet of her skirts and fretted over the many wrinkles left there from spending the night crumpled in a ball on the floor. "Why have my ladies not brought my gowns into my marriage chamber yet? I cannot continue wearing your clothes or the same gown two days in a row."

"They are all probably too frightened to step foot in here. That temper of yours is fearsome," Brand teased, remembering poor Rebecca.

Brynna snapped her tongue and waved her hand at him again. "Silly," she said. Nothing could spoil her mood today. Her king had returned and she was anxious to tell him of her victories, no matter how small.

"I will send William your apologies and tell him you are too worn out by your wife's passion to come down and greet him properly."

Brand laughed, catching the triumphant glance she threw him over her shoulder. "In that case, my love, tell him I need ten more hours of sleep at least," he agreed, and fell into his pillow as the door closed behind his wife.

Brynna stopped in her tracks on the other side of the door. Had he just called her his love? It was the first time he had ever used the word with her. She clutched her chest and breathed a deep gasp. "Good Lord." Her face broke into a wide grin, and then she raced down the winding stairs and toward the great hall, the way a child rushes to see what gifts await her upon her father's return from a long journey. Her cheeks were flushed and her breath was quick when she stopped at the enormous doorway.

William stood a few feet away, engaged in quiet conversation with Dante while dozens of people threaded around him. The huge goblet he held looked puny in his hand. His dark, gray-streaked hair was pulled back into a loose tail, exposing the hard angles that were usually hidden by the wild mane. He shifted his gaze as though he could feel her eyes on him. His eyes met hers with a smile so tender it felt like an embrace.

"Spring has returned to the earth," William said in awe, and loud enough for her to hear. "Like a breeze that stirs the fallen leaves, she renews my weary spirit."

The massive arm he held around Dante's shoulder lifted and met the other in an invitation for Brynna to be consumed by warm fur and raw muscle.

She went to him in a rush of crimson and copper, surprising herself at how much she missed the brutish rogue who teased her so mercilessly when he had first come to Avarloch. "My king," she whispered whimsically, close to his ear as his arms closed around her like tree trunks.

A hearty laugh rang out, coming from deep within the hefty duke, and he sighed, letting the scent of her fill him.

"How does my most beautiful warrior fare?" He gave her a long, measuring look; then he smiled wolfishly at the gleam in her eyes. "That well, eh?" he stated admiringly. "And so quickly. My dear, I must bring you to my next battle. We will have England in no time at all."

Brynna laughed, holding a delicate finger to her lips to caution him to silence. Dante was close enough to hear them, but if he did, he made no reaction to William's treasonous declaration.

William winked at her playfully, then looked over her shoulder. "Where is he?"

"In bed." Brynna's cheeks blushed pink, but the devious glint in her eyes gave her away.

"Where you left him." The duke grinned proudly. "Ah, good work." He slapped her shoulder slightly and downed the rest of his ale.

"Brand is sleeping? Now?" Dante finally spoke, gazing at Brynna with such admiration, she dropped her eyes shamed by what he must be thinking.

"Lady Brynna, pardon me." The handsome knight repented, seeing her discomfort. "It's just that he has not slept well in so long. . . ."

William patted Dante's back. "She is doing well by him, *non*?"

"Oui," Dante agreed, with a tender smile creasing his lips.

"Well"—William slapped his large hands together and Shredder and Chaos came running—"what I have to tell him can wait a few more hours. I would much rather spend my time with his wife anyway."

Brynna cast him a hard glare. "It was quiet here without you, m'lord. And you left without so much as a farewell."

William pouted through his beard. "Forgiveness is a blessed virtue, sweeting, and I had a pressing issue to attend to."

"Fighting for me." It was not a question and Brynna answered William's smoky, hooded gaze. "My father told me."

"I'll have his head."

"Nay, you will not!" She slapped his muscular arm, but he drew her in under it, pulling her closer.

"For you only, will I spare his life."

"I thank you."

"Ah, spring." William breathed at the beautiful smile she bestowed upon him, then led her to the table, where the aromas of the morning meal called to him like a long-lost lover.

❉

Brand took his time getting dressed, knowing that whatever news William had for him could wait.

The Norman duke had gone to Canterbury to find out from Colette's father the truth about Colette's betrothal. But Brand didn't care about her betrothal, or if she had lied to him as William suspected. He didn't care if he ever saw her again. Brand stopped in the middle of slipping into his black tunic and smiled, letting his freedom from Colette fill him. Brynna had accused him of still loving Colette. But he knew he no longer did. He had not even considered it. He thought he could not love anyone after what she had done. But he was wrong. He was glad Colette had come to Avarloch, though. Seeing her outside of his dreams had made him realize that whatever he had felt for her was gone.

Brand closed the door to his room, feeling like a man who had been set free from a dungeon. He started for the stairs, drawn by the delicious aroma of fresh bread and the thought of setting his eyes on the woman who stirred his soul back to life.

"My lord?"

Brand stopped before he reached the stairs. He turned just as Colette entered the hall from her room. She smiled angelically and tossed a lock of pale yellow hair over her shoulder. His eyes roamed the length of her body as she made her way to him and settled on the milky breasts barely hidden beneath turquoise silk.

"Once, not so long ago," she teased, "the sight of me in this gown caused your blood to turn to fire." When she reached him, he lifted his gaze to her eyes and smiled thinly. "I see it still has the same effect on you." She circled him like a cat. "I always knew that you would forgive me, Brand. That the memory of how I felt in your arms would call you back to me." She came full circle and faced him, lifting a small finger to trace his lips. "I understand how much I have hurt you."

Brand shook his head as her scent filled his lungs, suffocating him. "You understand nothing, Colette. I was a fool to allow you to stay here."

A provocative smile curved her lips. She took a step closer to him until he could feel the heat of her words against his face. She was hypnotic in her movements, the slow blink of her eyes, the way her fingers played over the laces of his tunic. She entranced, bewitched, subtly took control over the senses until she rendered men weak. Everything about Colette de Marson was too lovely for any man to resist, but Brand saw something in her eyes that he never noticed before, though he was sure it was always there. She was selfish, hungry for her own good. Did she ever really care about him? Or had she simply told him all the things he wanted to hear just to stay away from her father's tight rule? The realization surprised him. He had been blind indeed not to see it before. He had been willing to give her anything she wanted. And he did. He had given her his world.

And now he wanted it back.

"You allow me to stay because you desire me still, my lord." She slid her hands up his chest, to his shoulders, measuring his strength and muscle. "You want to taste the sweet flavor of my lips. Your heart aches for me as much as your body does." Suddenly she pouted, looking up at him with huge, sad eyes. "I was so angry with you for sending me away, my love, but you know now that it was a mistake, do you not?"

"*Non.*"

"Liar," Colette whispered close to his ear. "Why else would you take Dumont's daughter to your bed but to satisfy the savage lust you have for me."

Brand smiled faintly when Colette's lips moved across his cheek as delicately as the petals of a rose. But it was not a smile of pleasure, rather of another simple truth he had foolishly refused to see.

"What you insinuate cannot be true, Colette," he said succinctly. He let his fingers touch her, lightly over the flesh just above her breasts. His fingertips moved with slow deliberation, melting her like butter, while his dark penetrating gaze pinned her. "Beautiful Colette," he said breathily. "You enrapture men's hearts with your false angelic innocence. Your hair falls like gossamer wings over shoulders made of fine alabaster meant for anyone to touch." Colette trembled beneath his touch. His beautiful lips curled with menace while he moved his hand over the curve of her neck. For an instant Colette's eyes widened with fear as his fingers tightened around her throat. His large hand could break her instantly. His fingers could squeeze the life from her before she could even scream. "Your lips pout for kisses, hungry yet gentle while they pour out lies."

"Brand—"

"But invoke a savage lust in me?" His voice overrode hers, and the dark passion in his eyes faded into nothing more than amusement. "You have never done that to me. You are lovely, my lady, but savage lust is the one thing you never made me feel. You are, and always have been, as dead inside as you made me. Gather your men, Colette, you're going home."

Leaving Colette alone with her stunned humiliation, Brand bowed to her slightly and continued on his way to the great hall.

Laughter invaded his thoughts before he reached the doors of the hall. Recognizing the rich, hearty sound of William's joy, Brand could not help but smile to himself. It was the sound of life—life he missed, life he wanted back. He knew that he truly no longer loved Colette. He was not even angry with her anymore. She had brought death to him. *Oui,* he did love her once, and seeing her, smelling her, made even death tempting. But life called to him the way the moon called to the sea, beckoning him to remember the warmth of the sun as it bathed him in its glorious light. Tempting him as even Colette never could, to feel the passion of laughing again. To savor the wind in his face as his horse thundered across fields emblazoned with color as brilliant as . . . Brynna's eyes. Brand smiled, thinking of his wife. His heart ached to live again. And he knew now where to begin.

✳

The instant Brand entered the crowded hall, his eyes found her. The smile that graced Brynna's face was real, open, and more splendid to him than the breathtaking shores of Normandy. He stood, simply watching her at the table with William and Dante on either side of her. He studied the elegance of her fingers when she lifted her goblet to her lips, the way the leap of flames from the hearth ran like sunlight through her flowing hair.

Drawn to her, Brand took a step toward the table.

"Finally our warrior has awakened from his slumber," William cheerfully called out, without realizing how true his words really were.

Brynna lifted her verdant gaze to her husband and smiled as though glowing from within. "You did not sleep long, m'lord," she said when he reached her.

"I dreamed of fire and fields so green I wanted to bask in their beauty forever." As Brand spoke, his eyes poured over his wife's face. "I awoke ravenously hungry," he added huskily.

"And we thank you for gracing us with your presence, mighty lord of Avarloch," William interrupted before Brynna had a chance to blush. A crooked grin lifted the duke's smile to his ear. Brand shook his head, caught in his friend's dry but cheerful humor a moment before William pushed his chair out from under him. He enveloped Brand with arms so massive and strong that for a moment Brand lost his breath.

"Easy rake. You don't know your own strength."

Holding Brand at arm's length, William stepped back and offered him a confident, thin smile. "*Oui,* but I do. She could never love me while you live."

"She could never love you anyway, you are too hairy." Brand flashed his wife a playful wink, then pushed past the brutish duke and reached for her hand.

"I have missed you." The brush of her husband's lips inside her palm made Brynna shudder in her seat.

Without releasing her, Brand sat in the chair Dante had occupied before moving over a space. His brother was more than happy to oblige, seeing a spark of happiness in Brand's eyes he had doubted he would ever see again.

"So you will not be returning to Graycliff with me?" Dante asked Brand with a sly grin.

"*Non.* My children will live at Avarloch."

"Children?" Brynna repeated, delicately raising a brow, then blushed a deep shade of red when Brand looked at her, his smile darkened his eyes with emotion.

"Many children," he said thickly. "As many as we can stand making."

On the other side of Brynna, William grumbled exasperatedly, "Normans!"

"Aye," Alysia cried out next to Dante. She raised her goblet to them all. "The finest bunch of savages ever to come to Avarloch!"

The hall came alive with laughter and shouts of agreement from William's and Brand's men alike.

Later, when all that remained of the morning feast were crumbs and empty goblets, William rose from his chair with an enormous stretch that seemed to reach from floor to ceiling just before he slapped Brand gently on the back.

"I am weary from my journey. Enjoy the rest of your day . . . and your wife. We will talk later."

Brand wanted nothing to upset his mood this day, so he ignored the smoky haze that shrouded William's eyes. He hardly cared at all about what his friend had discovered in his quest to find out the truth about Colette. Brand wanted her out of Avarloch by nightfall regardless.

"Do you know why William rode to Canterbury, husband?"

Strong fingers closed around a more delicate hand. "*Oui,* I do," Brand told her. "But you need not worry, Brynna." He gazed deeply into her eyes. "What I felt for Colette is a memory that fades with each passing day."

"Truly?" Brynna asked, afraid to breathe.

Tracing her lips with the tip of his finger, Brand filled himself with the vision of her. She was a ray of sunlight against his heart, a ray of hope. "Truly," he answered, and then he kissed her in a way that left no room for doubt.

Chapter Twenty-two

✻

Nordic wind howled across the fields that now belonged to Lord Brand Risande, bringing with it the promise of a brutal winter. As if to prove its point, winter's first frost clung to the sheaves of the stable where Brynna, Brand, and Peter knelt in the thick hay waiting, as if in defiance of that promise, for life to spring forth from Brynna's pregnant mare.

"She went down with the sun," Peter told them breathlessly, clawing at the hay with his fingers to prepare a soft pillow for the foal to arrive in.

"Easy, not too much." Brand's voice was low, soothing as he knelt at the mare's head, stroking her gently.

"She seems more agitated than the others when they delivered," Brynna informed her husband with worry creasing her brow.

"Non," Brand whispered confidently, shaking his head. "She's strong. She will be fine." His hand never left the mare, nor did the tone in which he spoke to her change. "She has promised to let me ride her when spring arrives, and no promises shall ever be broken in Avarloch." He smiled and lifted his gaze to Brynna for a moment before returning it to the chestnut mare he so delicately stroked.

Brynna watched her husband in the golden light of the candle flames. He was serene, calm, magnificent, and the effect he had on her horse was amazing. The rise and fall of the mare's swollen belly actually appeared to fall into a gentle rhythm with his voice as he praised her.

"You are a fine horse," he whispered. "The finest I have ever seen. Your legs are strong and swift and your will is like iron, not to be beaten by the cold, nor the blistering heat, nor the torment of life that must come."

Brynna sat listening to him, lulled by the calm, entranced by the black curls that fell over his brow. . . .

"Brynna?"

She realized suddenly by the gentle grin on her husband's face that he had spoken her name more than once.

"You have done this before, I trust?"

"Aye, many times."

"Good, then you should position yourself at her rear. I think she will need some help. But not too close to her legs. Peter, stay close."

Suddenly the mare lifted her head. She clawed at the hay with her front hooves and tried to stand.

"She is in distress, Brand," Brynna cried out.

"Let your babe arrive, fair lady," Brand whispered close to the mare's ear. "You cannot stop life when it decides to come. No matter how you fight it, it comes. Trust me," he added in a soft whisper. "For I know what I speak."

The mare kicked and tried to rise to her feet again. A powerful back hoof missed Brynna by a hair.

Brand cursed out loud, his face paled to a sickly shade of white. "Move away from her legs, Brynna!" he shouted between more curses, steadying the horse's massive body under soothing hands. Then, seeing that his wife suffered no harm, he went back to speaking kindly to the mare.

Brynna saw a spot of white atop a newborn head protruding from between the mare's legs. "Brand! It comes!"

The mare swallowed, making the muscles in her thick neck dance while her tongue shot out in search of water.

"She thirsts, Bryn."

"In a moment."

Brand gently lifted the mare's head and placed it in his lap. He spoke to her so quietly Brynna could not hear what he was saying. The mare calmed again and the foal slid out almost into Brynna's lap.

Immediately the mare was on her feet, forgetting the man who soothed her with such tender care.

Scooting her body to Brand, Brynna took her husband's face in her hands and kissed him passionately. "When our babe is born, I want you there with me."

"I will be there," he promised. His eyes poured over every inch of her face and he sighed out loud as his heart wrenched within his chest.

Satisfied that the mare and her foal were doing fine, Peter slipped out of the stable.

Brynna ran her fingers over his mouth. "What is it, my beloved?"

He wanted to tell her . . . tell her what? That he never wanted to be without her? That just gazing at her face, her smile, was enough to make him want to give up his life for her? He had done that once before and it was worse than dying a slow death on the battlefield. He could not tell her that he was afraid of that dying, more afraid of it than of death itself, so he shifted his gaze away from her and smiled at the foal. The tiny creature tried to stand on wobbly legs that were no thicker than the meager twigs in the central hearth, while its mother cleaned him to a polished chestnut.

"He is beautiful," Brand announced breathily.

"Already magnificent," Brynna agreed quietly. She had heard the wonder in her husband's voice and gazed at his strong profile outlined against the firelight.

"Does a small, weak foal strike such awe in a warrior?"

For a moment Brand did not answer her as tidal waves of emotion crashed against his long-forgotten heart. Then he pulled his wife within the circle of his arms. "It's life, Brynna. It's life that I miss. I used to relish it, savor every moment like the finest cuisine upon my tongue." She nodded, knowing. He drew in a deep breath as if the memory were too much for him to bear. "And then I let it all go. I let her take my life from me and I didn't know how to get it back." He ran his fingers lightly over her hair, smoothing it away from her face. "I didn't even know if I wanted it back, Brynna . . . until I saw the light in your eyes. Until I held you in my arms."

Tears waited at the delicate fringes of Brynna's lashes, and when she blinked, they stole down her cheeks and onto his fingers. "I'll help you trust again, Brand," she promised him. "And then I'll claim your heart and love you until you can stand it no longer."

For a time he simply gazed at her, soaking in the way she loved him, and then he drew her closer and his tongue stole softly around her mouth.

"Does life also make you amorous?" His wife smiled.

His only answer was a smile hotter than fire before laying her down in the cool hay.

❋

The castle was silent by the time Brand and Brynna returned, half-frozen, from the short walk from the stable. A
soft glow filtering from the bottom of the doors of the
solar drew Brand's attention.

"Brynna"—he pulled her into his arms—"go upstairs
and prepare a bath for us. I will clean you thoroughly," he
promised with a hungry smile before he kissed her.

"Are you not coming up with me?"

"I will be there shortly."

Brynna did not want to go without him. She wondered
if it was Colette that he wanted to see before coming to
their bed. "All right," she conceded, trusting him to his
promise of faithfulness . . . if not love. "Please come to
me quickly."

He nodded and watched her slow ascent up the winding stairs. He waited until she was gone before he headed
to the solar, where he knew William was waiting for him.

"How is the mare?" William asked when Brand entered the softly lit chamber.

"She is well and so is her foal." Brand unclasped his
cloak and tossed it onto a nearby chair. His cerulean eyes
glittered against the firelight of the hearth.

"Are you waiting up for me, William?"

The duke's voice was low. *"Oui."*

"She has deceived me again, then?"

"Oui, mon ami."

"It matters not, William," Brand quietly assured his
dearest friend. He could see the worry creasing William's
brow and the pain it took the Norman duke to tell him
what he had found out. He chose a velvet high-backed

chair and fell into it. "Tell me. Let's get this over with so that I may rid Avarloch of her and get back to my wife."

"A drink?" William offered first, holding up his goblet.

Brand shook his head. Then, because he could wait no longer, he said, "She lied to me." It was a statement spoken with certainty.

William drew in a massive breath before he began. "*Oui,* she lied. There is no betrothed, savage or otherwise." William's hulking form was silhouetted against the crackling flames as he sat forward in his chair. "There is no way to say what I'm going to tell you in an easy way, or one that will spare you more pain." He sighed a great sigh and gazed into his goblet. "I am afraid this time she has betrayed you even worse than the first time."

Brand remained silent, his fingers tapping on the arm of his chair.

"I found Lord de Marson where I expected to find him, in Canterbury," William continued. "He was quite terrified when he saw me, Brand. Shaking in his boots, as a matter of fact."

Brand's eyes burned like molten fire as he considered what William told him. "Why would he be afraid of you, William? He knows you well enough to know that you would not harm him, unless . . ."

The duke's smile was emotionless. "That is what I asked him, but his only reply was that King Edward had informed him that I had returned to Normandy." William's eyes narrowed into slits. "Now, if he had been simply surprised to see me, that would have sparked my curiosity in itself, since every person in England, including Lord de Marson, knew that I was coming here. But no one knew that I hadn't left when the king did. And since Edward was not here to see me leave, he must have informed de Marson that I returned to Normandy." Still, Brand said nothing and William continued, a bit uneasily. "I would have to wonder why the king would find it so important to contact de Marson about my whereabouts, *non*?" He did not wait for Brand to answer. "But he was afraid, Brand, scared senseless when he saw me, so I pressed him further. And as I suspected, it was because of you that he feared me. It seems Lady Colette was residing at the king's castle due to an . . . incident with a local knight in Canterbury who was already wed."

The duke's voice trailed off as Brand smiled, but Brand's eyes told William that he was nothing more than disgusted with the woman who had once been his betrothed.

"There's more, *ami*," William told him regretfully. "Colette was sent to Winchester to serve the queen and hopefully make better with her life. But when Edward returned, he found better use for the girl. You are not a favorite of the king's, Brand," William added ruefully, and with a silver glint in his eyes that was sharper than any sword. "I want you to know that I have taken care of this matter—"

"Tell me, William."

William lifted the goblet to his mouth, quaffed his ale, then rose from his chair, unable to remain confined to his seat a moment longer. "There is a plot against you, Brand. Just as there was a plot against Richard, made by Edward and Harold and played out by Colette with blessings from her father."

Eyes as fiery as brimstone stared unblinking into the hearth fire as Brand took in William's words.

"She was promised land and a marriage to one of Edward's wealthiest knights. Her task was to come here and lead you away from Brynna."

"Why?" Brand asked quietly.

"Think, man!" William strode toward Brand and leaned over his chair. He placed a large, tender hand on his friend's shoulder. "Edward knows the flaxen-haired wench was your weakness. He hoped that once Colette arrived here, you would cast Brynna to the dogs. And since you made it perfectly clear to him that you might just do that anyway. . . ." He let the idea drift over Brand, waving his large hand in the air. "His treachery extends far beyond what he did to Richard. Edward does not give a rat's arse about alliances, as the witan council believes. The Saxons would never stand for your bringing a Norman lady to Avarloch. They threatened to take Avarloch back by force if you didn't marry Brynna, but to throw her out for a Norman . . . ? War would be inevitable, Brand. And there was not supposed to be anyone here to aid you. *That* is why de Marson was so afraid to find me still in England." William stepped away from Brand's chair with a proud, concluding smile on his face. "After you were dead, Edward would claim Avarloch. Harold of Wessex has assured the king of his aid, should I come against him. So you see, the plan was almost foolproof."

Brand sat stock-still in his chair, digesting all that William had told him. A plot to do away with him . . . and Colette, willing to watch him die.

William let out a great sigh and returned to the table for more ale. "I have sent messengers to Edward informing him that I know everything and if one hair on your head is so much as vexed, I will take his precious Harold's head."

The only sound in the great hall came from outside. Wind howled and wailed, banging against the shutters, as though the arctic cold was demanding entrance into Avarloch.

Brand did not blink, nor did he look at William when he spoke. And when he finally did, the duke was sure his favored knight must be the one holding back the winter storm. But soon . . . soon the storm would come.

"Bring her to me."

※

Brynna stared at the thick wisps of steam rising from the bath in front of her bed. She folded her arms across her chest and then unfolded them waiting for Brand. Finally she slapped her hands against her thighs and left the room.

From the top of the stairs, she saw William leave the solar, looking even more tormented than Brand had looked when he first arrived at Avarloch.

The duke climbed the steps slowly, staring at Brynna all the way up. He smiled at her, but she could see, even in the semidarkness, the dismay in his eyes.

"What is it, William?" she asked quietly, not really wanting an answer.

The brutish duke obliged her and laid a tender hand to her cheek. "Go to bed, fair Brynna. He will come to you shortly."

Brynna nodded but did not move from her spot as William walked the long corridors to Colette's room. Quietly she made her way down the stairs, walking on the tips of her feet to the doors, where Brand waited on the other side. A chill licked her spine as she cracked the doors open, filling her with a sense of foreboding that made her skin crawl.

Brand sat facing the fire, watching the flames that reflected over and over in his eyes.

"Brand?"

He did not answer her. He did not move, except for his fingers clenching and unclenching the arms of his chair. In the silence that stretched on, Brynna watched her husband with alarm rising in her like sour bile. Something was terribly wrong. What news had William brought him that turned Brand's eyes to flaming swords, his mouth to a thin line of hatred and fury?

"My love?" she whispered. She took a step closer to where he sat.

William's voice behind her startled her almost out of her slippers. "Return to your bed, Brynna."

Brynna spun around to face him. He held a writhing Colette by the elbow. "What is going on?" she demanded.

"Please, Brynna," William ordered gently. "Go back to your room."

"She stays, Will." The sound of Brand's voice made Brynna turn back to him slowly. Despite his nearly tangible anger, his tone was mild. "Shut the door, William, please."

The moment William released Colette, she rushed to Brand and collapsed at his feet. "Whatever he says I have done, do not believe him, my lord." She wailed like a woman giving birth. "You know he has always hated me."

"Oui," Brand said silkily. "He is a man of great wisdom and has never been as foolish as I."

The sight of Colette's pale hair tangled around her husband's feet angered Brynna. She took another step forward, but Brand's eyes stopped her.

"You still think me a heartless savage, wife?"

"Nay, my love." Brynna melted at the way he looked at her. For his fury had vanished, the moment their gazes met.

"I am not heartless, Brynna," he said, as if trying to convince her. He looked down at the woman huddled at his feet. "But Colette de Marson has conspired against my life. Should I not cut her lying tongue from her mouth? I will do as you say." Brynna didn't answer him but held her breath while Colette's sobs grew louder. "She is the demon that has possessed me." Her husband continued looking down again at Colette. "Should I kill her and be done with it all?"

"Nay." Brynna choked back her tears, seeing the emotion that raged within the man she loved—the emotion that burned like a blazing fire within him. Here was her merman, back from the dead. "You loved her once," Brynna told him. "Remember it as an honor you bestowed upon an ungrateful heart and nothing more, and then give it to me, Brand, for I will treasure it with my life. I have seen how you love. All the riches in the world could not be compared to it. It is a priceless treasure I battle for. And if I ever hold it, I will die rather than let it go again."

Brand fixed his eyes on his wife. The firelight that danced in his gaze reflected something so tender, so unreserved, that even William saw it and stifled a tight groan as though it were his own emotions being pulled from him.

"You know not what surrendering your heart can do to your life, Brynna," Brand told her softly.

She took a step toward him. "I trust you to treat my heart tenderly, husband."

And then, as though driven by the immeasurable force of her love, Brand rose to his feet and stepped around Colette's slumping body. He reached his wife in two long strides and cupped her face in his tender palms. He tilted her face up to his. "I tried to fight what I was feeling for you, but you fought harder than I. You ask for my love?" His eyes devoured her, his breath eager with staggering emotion. "It is already yours. I do love you, Brynna; *oui*, with all my heart do I love you." He bent his head to her and captured her mouth with his.

Behind them William breathed a great sigh of relief. "Victory at last." He waited another moment while his favored knight kissed his beloved before clearing his throat. When Brand withdrew slightly from his wife, the duke motioned with his chin toward Colette. "What is to be done with her?" he asked, eager to rid her from the couple's life.

Still clutching Brynna within the circle of his arms, Brand turned to look at Colette. "My wife has spared your life, but I want you out of Avarloch tonight. Take your men and your horses and let God decide your fate."

Colette sat up and stared at him in stunned disbelief. "But 'tis freezing outside. . . ."

Brand nodded. "As I said, let God decide." Without another word or a glance in her direction, he led Brynna out of the great hall.

"Come, wench," William ordered. Taking three giant strides toward the woman glaring at him with black contempt spilling from her eyes, he lifted her by the elbow and yanked her to her feet.

"My father will watch you die," Colette spat out venomously.

"I doubt it," the Norman duke replied sarcastically while he dragged her out of the hall. "When I left him, he was introducing himself to his Creator." He lowered his sharp silver eyes to her. "You see, my dear, I am not as merciful as Lord Brand of Avarloch. Or his wife."

Chapter Twenty-three

Brand couldn't sleep. With Brynna tucked snugly against the curve of his body, he lifted his fingers and traced the smooth outline of her shoulder, down her arm, and then over the voluptuous swell of her derriere. His touch drew a faint moan from her throat while she slept, making him want to wake her and make love to her again. He sighed, thinking how easily she had slipped past his defenses. He had vowed never to become a fool for love again, but only a fool could resist this incredible woman. Pulling her closer, he felt his body tighten when she wiggled her rump into the crook of his embrace.

"Brand?" she whispered, half-awake.

But he quieted her with kisses. "Sleep, my love." And soon the relaxed rhythmic breathing of sleep returned to her.

Brand stayed awake until the sun rose, holding her, stroking her hair, and kissing her delicately so as not to wake her again. Christ, he loved her. There was no fear in it, only exhilaration. He clutched her tighter and finally fell asleep.

Brynna awoke shortly after he fell back to sleep. Although frost laced the thick shutters of her window, sunlight poured into the room, urging her to begin her day. Reluctantly, and with a soft kiss to her husband's parted lips, she left the warmth of his arms. She dressed quietly, not wanting to disturb her husband's peaceful slumber. She smiled, watching him, while she brushed her hair, remembering the passion in his eyes when he made love to her the night before. It was a passion that was more intense than any she had ever known. He had given her his heart as fully as he gave her his body, and Brynna luxuriated in the memory of it.

Brand shifted in the bed, feeling for her.

"Rest, husband." She went to him, kissing his eyelids closed.

"Where are you going?" he asked groggily.

"To the barn to see the foal."

No matter how he tried, Brand could not keep his eyes open. "Make haste back to me."

Brynna smiled at the black fringe of lashes curling slightly against his cheeks, stepped over Whisper, and then left the room.

She was busy tying the laces of her mantle and looked up just in time to avoid crashing into Dante's chest.

"*Bonjour, belle.* Where are you off to in such a hurry?"

"To see my foal. He came last eve," she explained with a cheerful exuberance, which made Dante smile.

"I have yet to see him. Let me get my mantle and I'll join you."

He disappeared down the hall and Brynna watched him, thinking how sad Alysia was going to be when he left Avarloch. Brynna would miss him too, she realized a few moments later when he came striding toward her again with an indigo cloak tied around his broad shoulders and a beguiling grin spreading across his handsome face. His easygoing nature and carefree smiles made even the gloomiest days seem brighter.

"And just what is in Graycliff Castle that compels you to leave us all?" Brynna snapped at him before she could stop herself.

"My sister." Dante's grin remained intact despite her unexpected outburst.

Brynna blinked up at him, and then laced her arm through his when he offered it. "I didn't even know you had a sister."

"Katherine is thirteen years old. I brought her to England with me four years ago."

"And your parents?" Brynna asked while they descended the stairs.

"My mother left this earth giving birth to Katherine. It was a late pregnancy for her and too difficult. My father died in service to King Philip."

"Oh, I'm so sorry." She patted his arm and bit her lower lip, realizing she knew nothing about her husband's life. "You and Brand must miss your father terribly."

"Non." Dante shook his head and flashed his dimple at Rebecca when she waved at him from the great hall. "Brand was sent to serve William as his page when he was seven. I was sent three years after that. We scarcely saw our father."

He pulled the heavy doors open and a gust of wind blew Brynna's hair away from her face. They made their way toward the stable while crisp ice snapped at Dante's mantle, lifting it with indigo wings. He said something about a warm body, but his words were carried away on the wind. Brynna guessed he was talking about Alysia, but then she remembered the sensual curl of Dante's lips when he saw Rebecca.

He wrestled the stable door open against the driving gale that fought to keep it closed. It screeched against the bitter cold.

"I doubt it will be any warmer inside," he said upon entering.

"Surely not as warm as Alysia . . . or whoever's body you were just referring to." Brynna giggled behind him.

Dante turned to offer her an amused smirk, but the black hair that blew across his countenance made him look more like a lethal warrior than the charming rogue he was.

"You . . ." His words were lost to the howl of a fierce gust of wind. And the flash of a dagger sinking into his back. Glittering gray eyes speckled with green met emerald ones before Dante's body collapsed to the ground.

In the instant that followed, Brynna was swept away as if by the swirling gusts around her. She was there, shocked beyond screaming. And then she was gone.

✳

Brand woke sometime later to a scream that pierced his very soul. The sound seared through his veins, reaching his throat, where a harsh cry exploded from his lips. Without lacing his trousers, he fled his room and entered the chaos that had descended upon Avarloch.

William was already on his way to Brand's room when the two men spotted each other in the hall, which was crowded with knights from both garrisons running toward the stairs.

" 'Tis Dante." William reached his friend in two great strides.

Brand's mind reeled as images of his brother filled his thoughts. "Dante?" he asked, fighting to clear his mind.

William's massive hands rolled down his face, and when he looked at Brand, there was fury in his eyes.

"He was found in the barn, Brand; a dagger was in his back. He lives, *mon ami*," the duke added quickly, seeing the horror and stark disbelief on Brand's face. "The blade pierced between his shoulder blades, but he is unconscious and near freezing."

The barn! A whole new horror lit Brand's eyes. "Where is Brynna?" He grasped William's tunic while panic encased itself around him, gripped his heart with cold, deadly fingers. "Where is she, William?"

"Brynna?" For a brief, merciful moment William did not understand Brand's fear and panic. He looked over Brand's shoulder to the door of his room. "Is she not with you?"

Pain seemed to invade Brand as he threw his head back, longing to scream.

William's face paled of all color. Terror crept up on the mighty duke of Normandy. It gripped his heart in a way that made his mind rebel because terror was completely foreign to him. All around him people were scurrying to and fro. Knights were commanding serfs to bring their swords; one of their brothers was attacked by an unseen enemy. But William heard none of it, he only heard the brutal pounding of his heart. He saw no one but the man before him.

Black fury, mixed with unbridled, unspeakable fear, engulfed Brand. And the pale mask of fear he wore on his face was enough to convince William that the terror he himself felt was indeed real.

"Why is Brynna not with you?" William's voice thundered through the halls of Avarloch. "Where is she, Brand?" The sound was followed by a growl deeper and more lethal than any listener could withstand when Brand uttered his next words.

"She went to the barn."

❋

Brynna was led through the woods blindfolded and half-frozen. Her mantle had been torn from her body by the same savage hands that felled Dante. Her face and arms bled from the stiff branches that clawed at her, pulling her deeper and deeper into the forest. She did not speak, nor did she cry out. She only spoke to tell her captors that their fate was now worse than the most merciless death. They laughed, one walking behind her, pushing her onward, while others rode on horseback.

Hours later, when she could no longer stand on her numb and exhausted legs, she collapsed to the cold earth.

"Get up!" a man's voice demanded high above her.

"Nay," someone else said. "'Tis as good a place as any to ambush him when he comes for her. We stop here."

"Colette." Beneath the darkness of her blindfold, Brynna recognized the woman's soft voice. The aggravating sweetness was gone from it now. Or was it only that Brynna could not see the woman's angelic face—could not see the innocent smile that masked the true evil in her heart—that made Colette's true character so apparent.

"You do not sound surprised that it is me." Colette slid from her horse and nodded to two of her men.

Rough hands closed around Brynna's wrists.

"How can anything you do surprise me, Colette?" Brynna shot back venomously while she was dragged along the cold ground and lifted painfully to her feet.

"I surprised Brand." Colette laughed, pulling the blindfold from Brynna's eyes. "He had no idea of my plans until the bastard William told him."

Brynna's eyes adjusted to the filtered light of the forest and she glared at the woman wrapped in a black mantle like an ominous cocoon. The angelic beauty was gone from Colette's dark, hateful eyes, her sweet smile erased by the cold.

"You killed Dante." Brynna spat as her hands were tied with thick ropes to the tree behind her.

"Nay, Clyde only wounded him. It would take more than a dagger to kill that one, and we hadn't the time."

Brynna studied the cold expression, searching for something, any trace of human empathy. There was none. "You know, Colette, you are almost ugly out here in the open."

A hand came around like a whip cracking against Brynna's already numb cheek.

Fighting viciously against the ropes that bound her, Brynna promised to rake the eyes from Colette's face the moment she was free. But her captor only laughed and turned away from her.

"By the way, my lady," Colette called over her shoulder. "Thank you for sparing my life from that beast you call a husband."

"Careful, Colette," Brynna warned darkly. "You have more than used up all the mercy I had to give you."

"Dare not threaten me, dear, or I shall be forced to kill

you before Brand gets here." Colette moved within the circle of men who had accompanied her to Avarloch.

"We need a fire," she told them.

"Nay," one of the men said. "It will give away our position."

"But we will freeze to death."

"I will keep you warm." The man's hand came out to touch a strand of pale yellow hair that had fallen loose from under Colette's black hood. Brynna recognized him from the castle. It was Sir Jeffrey, Colette's lover. Colette pushed his hand away, snapping at him in a low voice.

"She used you to get to him, fool," Brynna explained pitifully, but the hatred in her eyes was as hot as molten steel. "She used you, and now that Brand is not here to see, she pushes you away."

Colette turned to face Brynna again, her eyes wide and blazing, a tight smile curving her lips. "Brand is going to die. And so are you." Suddenly her face softened as a thoughtful expression drifted across her eyes. "Pity really, I am fond of Brand. Oh, well," she sang, shrugging her petite shoulders.

Sir Jeffrey had not taken his eyes off Brynna since she spoke to him. He stepped up to her now and eyed her under long, thick lashes. For an instant Brynna could not read his expression. Then he lifted his hand to stroke her cheek. "You are fair." He toyed with her like a cat. "Would *you* like to use me?"

"Touch her and I will rip out your heart, Jeffrey," Colette promised ferociously, rising from the rock she had been sitting on.

Brynna smiled into Jeffrey's hungry brown eyes. "She jests not, for I have seen her do it," she assured him. "But touch me and what I will rip from you will be much more painful."

He chuckled softly, thoroughly amused by Brynna's temper. "Let's untie her, Colette," he called out without turning. "Let's see if her fire can muzzle you."

Colette's expression was so angelic when Jeffrey finally looked at her, he seemed to melt before Brynna's eyes. "You try my patience, sir knight." She purred. "But I will forgive you if you come here to me and show her who you really want."

Jeffrey practically leaped over a fallen branch to get to her. Colette opened her arms to receive him and threw her head back as he bent over her, biting her neck.

The dagger appeared for only an instant, but Brynna saw it. She tried to scream out, but it was too late. Colette sliced the short blade across Jeffrey's cheek. It was merely a flesh wound, and the blood trickling down her lover's face only made his eyes burn with more hunger.

"Later, Jeffrey," she said simply when he tried to kiss her again.

"Watch where you stick your blade, wench." A man with pocked skin and a long scar across one eye stood up and glared at Colette. "Or I'll bring your head to King Edward."

"The only head you will be bringing to the king will be Brand's, Clyde." Colette's empty expression had not changed except to reveal a hint of amusement hidden beneath her frustration. "So the plan has changed a bit. All the king wanted was Brand's death, and he shall still get it."

"And Duke William's head?" Clyde asked through clenched teeth. "If, by some miraculous intervention, we kill him as well, you will bring war upon England. Have you not thought of that?"

Colette closed her eyes, frustration now clearly creasing her brow. "We . . . we will wound the duke so that he cannot fight or pursue us."

Someone laughed and Colette raked her hateful gaze across each face. "You can all return now if you like. I will do this myself and the reward will be mine alone. Edward doesn't care who kills Brand, just as long as he dies."

Brynna's blood turned cold listening to her. Colette was a madwoman capable of anything. And Edward—oh, she prayed William would kill him quickly when he invaded England. "What happened in your life that caused your soul to become so wretched?" Brynna asked her, almost pitying the young woman.

"Shut up!" Colette screamed, pointing her dagger at Brynna. "You keep quiet. You are already dead."

Brynna's eyes burned. Her blood boiled. "You didn't betray Brand, did you, Colette?" she asked calmly, understanding the woman now. "You cannot betray love when you do not even know what love is."

"Oh, but I do," Colette drawled, her rage seemingly forgotten once again as she moved toward Brynna. "I love power. The power my beauty has over men." She held the tip of her dagger to Brynna's throat, letting it glide over her flesh. Brynna closed her eyes and Colette leaned in close as if to kiss her. "I love the power not caring for a single soul gives me," she whispered, watching her blade trace the contours of Brynna's cheekbone.

Brynna knew she should remain silent, but fury charged through her, and if she had to hold her tongue for an instant longer, she would bite it off. "You hate Brand because you had no power to convince him to take you back." Brynna opened her eyes, casting a hard emerald glare at Colette. The woman blinked and Brynna's lips curled into a thin smile. "That is it, is it not? He was the one man who defeated you."

"Not quite." Colette pulled herself together quickly, but the hand that held the dagger dropped to her side. "I will see him dead."

Having heard enough, Brynna clenched her teeth until they hurt. "How could Brand have ever loved you?"

Colette's only reply was a radiant smile as if that in itself was answer enough.

"You will not kill him." Brynna's voice was a low growl. "It is you who will die this night." Her promise was spoken with such terrible conviction that Colette almost believed her.

"Silence!" Colette turned to the man closest to her. "If she so much as sighs, kill her."

Chapter Twenty-four

Four knights followed Brand's, William's, and Lord Richard's thundering horses into the forest. They rode like warriors entering battle, with faces set in stark determination, hard and powerful, ready to cut down their enemies with a single swipe of their mighty swords. Only the presence of Chaos and the absence of helm and armor revealed that they rode toward a hunt and not a battle.

Deciding to wait for the cover of darkness, and to take only one hound was William's idea. His well-trained, tactical mind reasoned that Brynna had been taken for one reason only, to make Brand follow. Brand's face had been cold and unreadable when William explained to him that he believed it was Colette de Marson and her men who wounded Dante and took Brynna.

"They mean to kill you, make up a story to Edward of your treachery, which he would be only too happy to believe if this fantasy of theirs had even a chance of coming to pass."

"I'm going to kill them slowly," Brand promised with deadly confidence.

"Oui." William had nodded, his expression mirroring Brand's. Then, "We take one hound to help us find them; then we keep it quiet as we approach."

Brand nodded his agreement. "We get Brynna; then we massacre the rest."

Night descended early in the forest, against pale-trunked trees that lifted their countless, nearly bare branches to the sky. Frost clung to the dying leaves that remained, but Brand did not feel the cold under his black mantle. Fury drove his horse hard, ignited a fire in him that would not be extinguished until Brynna's abductors were all dead. He did not doubt that he would get Brynna back alive. He could not doubt it, for if he did, then he might as well plunge his sword into his own heart after he killed Colette.

It did not take the men long to find Colette's camp. From quite a distance away smoke could be seen rising high above the thin canopy of branches.

"Fools." William smiled savagely.

"It could be a trick," Lord Richard offered.

"Non." The Norman duke shook his head, turning to Brynna's father. "They had to make a fire. 'Tis freezing. They are there, or they are frozen to death."

"They are there," Brand agreed. "Chaos leads us." He pointed to the hound, which had run on ahead in the exact direction of the smoke, then stopped to look at the riders as if wondering what the holdup was.

Without waiting for his companions, Brand flapped his reins and rode on with William and the others closely behind him.

✳

Colette paced near the fire, wringing her hands around the thick wool of her mantle. Every few minutes the sound of an animal scurrying through the underbrush pulled her attention away from Brynna. "He should have been here already. I heard him tell you that he loves you. Why has he not come?"

Brynna's eyes searched the trees looking for any sign of movement.

"I heard the bastard say he loves no one." Clyde grunted, adjusting the sword at his side. "Mayhap he does not care if she lives or dies. The fire will lead him straight to us if he does come, though."

"Let it." Colette glared at him. "The sooner he dies, the quicker we can return to Edward."

Brynna closed her eyes, not wanting them to see her tears. Mayhap they were right. Mayhap Brand did not care. He said he never would. But Brynna could not stop the memory of his eyes when he looked at her, the flash of his genuine smile, the way his hand closed over hers, and the words he had spoken to her the night before. He would come for her. He would come with her father and William. And they would fall right into Colette's trap. Suddenly a thought came to her through the panic that wrenched anew in her stomach—a way to save all the men she loved.

"Brand will not come for me, Colette. You destroyed him. He does not love me. He cannot."

Colette stopped her pacing and looked at Brynna through narrowed eyes. "He told you that he did, I heard him myself."

Brynna shook her head. "Do you know why William came here? Brand had to be commanded to take me as his wife," she answered before Colette could. "Brand would rather have fought a battle than marry me. He told William and my father that he would never love me." Brynna's feigned tears bit her flesh and glistened like frost on her cheeks. "I did everything I could, but I could not make him love me. He will not come, so you best kill me right now and be gone."

A few feet away, hidden in the dense bush of mulberry and currant, Brand listened to his wife's testimony and a tremor coursed through his soul. He vowed to spend the rest of his life convincing his wife of his love.

In the darkness Brand turned to William and nodded. The duke lifted the hood of his black mantle over his head and crawled silently out of the bush, blending with the shadows and the men of Colette's company at the same time. He went unnoticed as he sat on a large severed trunk and whittled a thick twig with his dagger.

Soon another figure, as black as the first, entered the small clearing like a phantom, hooded mantle pulled tightly around him against the bitter cold.

"We will wait until morning and then kill her and return to King Edward." Colette sulked, realizing that Brynna was probably right. Nothing had gone as planned anyway, and Clyde was certainly right about William. The Normans would attack England if any harm came to the bastard duke. Mayhap the king would still reward her. She would tell him that Brand had murdered his wife, and once word reached the Saxon nobles, the same result would occur. Brand would be killed, and the king could have his land and she would have hers.

With a low growl that sounded more like a wild animal than an angel, Colette kicked dirt into the fire. Flames danced, casting shadows along the thick tree trunks, over the carpeted ground, and across her men, whose number had grown to three more.

Clyde stood up, pulling his mantle tighter around his shoulders. "I am cold and in need of a woman's warmth." His eyes shifted toward Brynna, one lid hanging past his dark pupil. He smiled. "I am taking her, Colette, and if you interrupt, I will take you as well . . . before I kill you."

"He may still show up, Clyde." Colette glared at him. "Why do you not wait and let him watch?"

"Nay, I am cold now," the pock-faced knight called over his shoulder, already reaching for Brynna.

"I have a feeling I will fit into you quite nicely." Clyde's leer of naked intent shook Brynna to her knees. She tried to kick out and almost caught him in the knee, but he moved back and sneered at her. "Mayhap I will just rip you apart."

Directly behind him, a shadow rose up. William tossed his mantle over his shoulders. In less time than it took to inhale, the duke of Normandy set his sword free. It flashed against the moonlight for an instant, and then disappeared into Clyde's back.

"And mayhap you will not," William said dryly, watching the man as he fell.

Time seemed to stand still as the duke lifted his smoky gaze to Brynna; then, he spun around so quickly the folds of his mantle flared and snapped around his legs.

"Colette! *Ma cher*!" he exclaimed cheerfully as the forest came alive around him. "How nice to see you again."

All at once, hoods were thrown back to reveal faces that Colette had seen at the castle, including Lord Richard's. It took a moment for the numb shock to wear off the faces of her men, and in the ominous glow of the firelight, Brynna watched William's eyes flash with the excitement of battle as steel clashed against steel.

The duke's blade slid smoothly, almost too easily, into the belly of an oncoming attacker. Before his victim fell to the ground, William withdrew his sword, wiped the blood on the man's mantle, and sheathed it in its scabbard as quickly as it had come out. He surveyed the small battle with a satisfied grin, then turned back to Brynna.

"Are you all right?" He slipped a dagger from his left boot and began to cut her free.

"Aye." She breathed deeply. The moment her hands were free, she threw her arms around his neck and clung to him.

"*Oui,* fairest of all women." The brutish Norman warrior closed his eyes against Brynna's copper hair. There was careful tenderness in the crushing weight of his arms as he held her, and such great relief in the deep sigh that escaped him that it sounded more like a groan than a sigh. "Thank the God of the saints that you are all right."

"Does Dante live?"

"*Oui,* he does. When we left him, three of your handmaidens were tending to him like love-starved waifs."

"Where is Brand?" Brynna asked as he released her.

The duke untied the laces at his neck and with a flick of his wrist sent his mantle swirling around Brynna. He pointed to a shadow that moved in a blur of speed as he fought. "He is there. The one whose blade sheds the most blood. *Merde,* but he is a merciless bastard, is he not?" William sounded appalled, but the grin on his face told a whole different story of what he thought of his favored friend.

Brynna's eyes widened as they focused on the lithe, agile form of her husband. His sword shone savagely as it descended, slicing the air and sending blood spewing forth in every direction. If his fury had not been so terrifying, he would have been beautiful to watch. He was so sure, so quick, so lethal as he spun, swinging his heavy blade with both hands and making the steel dance at his command. His eyes blazed in the darkness, merciless in their destruction, untamable passion set free. And although to an enemy, he was a nightmare come to life, to Brynna, he was breathtakingly magnificent.

"I trained him," William said proudly.

Behind his towering form Brynna felt quite protected from the fighting taking place all around her and shifted the duke a quick, sardonic side-glance. "Should you not be fighting with him?"

"But there is practically no one left to fight!" William argued presenting the small battlefield to her.

Brynna pointed to Colette, who was about to mount her horse and flee. William smiled brightly, then took off.

There were only two of Colette's men left alive and Lord Richard was making a quick end of them when Brand lowered his sword and turned his savage eyes on his wife. Instantly his gaze softened. His eyes called to her from across the fire. His tight shoulders relaxed as though the very sight of her made him human again.

"I did everything I could, but I could not make him love me."

But I do, Brynna. His heart cried out to her.

He treaded his way toward her, over bodies and branches, aching to take her in his arms, to tell her that she meant more to him than life itself.

He was inches away when a figure leaped out from the trees behind Brynna.

Terror utterly consumed Brand as an arm coiled around

his wife's neck. A dagger at the end of it gleamed against her throat.

Instantly Brand's sword came up. The hilt was held in both hands parallel above his shoulder and even with his eye. "Release her, and I will not cut you to pieces," Brand promised her captor. His voice was low and more deadly than any weapon forged in fire. The point of his blade remained so still it appeared to be an illusion to the eye.

Brynna's attacker shook his head as Lord Richard and the others moved slowly toward him behind Brand. "Get me a horse and time to flee, or I will kill her slowly," her attacker countered.

Silence. Not a muscle moved in Brand's body. His eyes seared like terrible flames of fire. There was no brilliant, calculating smile when he spoke, only rage so black it sliced the very air, cutting through his clenched teeth. "Release her now."

Wild fear passed over her assailant's face. He frowned, ready to kill her. "So be it. She dies."

Brand only growled. With lightning speed that shocked even Lord Richard, his sword flew like an arrow shot straight from its bow. It cut the air as it whistled a hair away from Brynna's face and landed into her attacker's throat, pinning him to the tree behind her.

Every fiber in Brynna's body came undone as she turned slowly to see how close the blade had come to her. Then she looked at her husband and fainted.

❊

The first thing Brynna was aware of when she awoke was the warmth of Brand's body. She lay in his lap. His hand moved over her hair, stroking, caressing her as if she were more precious to him than the air he took into his lungs. She opened her eyes and he smiled down at her, and then frowned.

"Forgive me for frightening you. The blade would never have struck you," he promised in a whisper.

Lifting her fingers to his rough jaw, Brynna let her gaze drift over her husband's face. His eyes spoke to her, drenching her with the passion she longed for. In his perfect cerulean gaze, Brand told her of his fear of losing her and of his overwhelming joy that he hadn't. They told of a masculine need to protect her, not because she belonged to him, but because he could no longer live without her. And in the quietness of a moment that passed sweetly between them, Brand's eyes told her how much he loved her.

"I know that you would never have allowed him to hurt me, Brand," Brynna told him softly.

Regret drifted across his eyes. "But I hurt you, Brynna. I never meant to."

"Brand—"

"*Non.*" He quieted her, bending his face to hers. "Just kiss me and let me give my heart to you." He traced her smile with his lips. "I love you, Brynna." His lips were sunlight and darkness together, a tender caress and a primal yearning as they drew her in deeper, deeper, until she felt the pumping of his heart and claimed it.

Chapter Twenty-five

William paced the small clearing, dragging Colette with him while he waited for Brynna to finish embracing her father.

"*Merde,* I am freezing!" the Norman warrior called out impatiently, casting Brand a savage look at the same time. "Not a hair on her head was injured. Can we go?"

Brand laughed, and as he neared William, he mumbled loud enough for his friend to hear. "How will you ever manage to survive in this country if you take it, you whining babe?"

The curt response on William's tongue was halted by Colette's soft plea. "What are you going to do with me?"

Brynna joined her husband. His arm came around her tenderly. "My lord," Brynna said to William while her crystal green eyes met Colette's, "were you aware that the only thing this creature loves is the power her beauty has over men?" Without waiting for William's response, Brynna tossed him a deadly smile. "What kind of power do you think she could wield over you, 'William the Conqueror'?"

William's wicked grin was fierce and fully male as he sized up Colette de Marson in a whole new way. "It might take me a long time to find out, but what a satisfying game it will be."

Brynna's gaze drifted over the length and breadth of William's muscular body and then at his hard, steel eyes. "Colette?" she said with a shiver. "Now I really do pity you."

Offering William a delicate curtsy, Brynna turned to leave the clearing with Brand, who did naught to hide his admiration toward his wife.

"Wait!" William took a giant step to stop them. With a quick gesture to one of Brand's men, Colette was led away and tossed over the duke's saddle, kicking and screaming heedlessly. William's eyes spoke of a tender, deep love when he took Brynna's hand. "Are you sure you were not . . . hurt by any of those bastards?"

Brynna smiled, reaching up to kiss his cheek. "I am sure."

"Good." He let out a breath; then with a refreshed grin and a proud shrug of his massive shoulders, he said, "You know, I like what you called me before, 'William the Conqueror.' It fits me, does it not?"

Brynna's eyes gleamed brilliantly. "Of course, that is why I said it."

The duke's laughter echoed through the dark woods and he threw his arm around Brynna's neck, almost knocking her to the ground. "Lady, the world is much brighter for me because you are in it."

"Thank you," she said sincerely, knowing this man would forever be her friend. "My king," she added with an impish wink.

"King?" Brand mocked with a grin. "Does my wife know something the rest of England does not know?"

"*Non*," William said as innocently as a child. "I have always told you that I would rule England someday, have I not?"

Brand nodded, dismissing the secret look that passed between his dearest friend and his wife. He wanted to take her home to Avarloch and begin their life together. Let the nobles fight over the land, he had much more pleasant duties to attend to. "Let's go home and make some heirs," he whispered deeply into Brynna's ear. He leaped into his saddle and then lifted her into his lap. His arms closed around her while taking hold of the reins.

"Did you really doubt that I would come for you, my love?" he asked against her ear as they headed out of the clearing.

Sighing at the warmth of his breath and the chill it sent down her spine, Brynna pulled his arms tighter around her. "Not even for a moment." She could feel his smile against her neck and his chest expanding behind her as he drew in her scent.

Above them, the moon hung low in the velvet sky casting its silver light upon the thin frost that covered the branches. To their right, a lake glittered like crystal under the light and Brynna gazed at it, remembering a beautiful merman she had fallen in love with.

"Brand?"

His answer was a low moan while he relished her scent and the sound of his name on her lips.

"There is something I want to do when summer returns."

"What is it?" he asked, kissing her neck.

Brynna closed her eyes and let his lips drive out the cold. "I want to learn how to swim."

Epilogue

The wind was favorable, blowing the storm west. The sun rose over the horizon while a battle horn trumpeted in the new day, and the great cavalry assembled on the shore, ready for war.

William sat upon his destrier studying the distant hills that would lead his army toward victory. The helmet he wore on his head flattened his thick hair, while a thinner piece of the hard metal covered his nose. His steel gray eyes swept over the channel, where his ships had already set sail for Hastings and his countrymen would meet up with Dante and the four hundred soldiers now under his command.

"Looks like as good a day as any."

"Oui," came the powerful affirmation of his most loyal knight waiting beside him.

"I'm glad you are here," William said, staring straight ahead at the land that spread before him like a lover's waiting arms.

"I would not be anywhere else but here with you." Brand turned to him and smiled, his eyes a deep turquoise beneath the silver of his Norman helmet.

"Your babe is due to come any day now," William reminded him.

"Then we shall have to make a quick end of Harold's army." A grin as sinister as William's careful plans to take over England, graced Brand's face.

William laughed, finally turning to look at him. "That we shall, my friend. That we shall."

After thinking of his fiery-haired warrior, the duke grew serious. "How is she, Brand? How is my dear Brynna?"

His hard gaze softened and a gentle smile replaced Brand's calculating grin. He appeared, to William, to drift away to her. For the way Brand drew in his breath suggested that he could smell her even here, amidst thousands of muddy, sweating horses. "She is more breathtaking than the sea," Brand said huskily, as if Brynna could hear him praise her. "She is perfectly beautiful. She stills my heart every time I look at her."

William sardonically lifted an eyebrow. "So, what you are trying to say is you love her." He jested, but the life bursting forth in his friend's eyes warmed William's heart too much for him to tease him.

"I love her beyond all reason, William."

William sighed happily. "'Tis good for the heart to love so deeply," the mighty duke said in all seriousness, then turned his gaze longingly toward the fields and hills before him.

"Shall we, Brand?"

"*Oui,* my lord," Brand said, fixing his hungry gaze toward Hastings.

William lifted his hand in a silent signal that commanded his men to follow. And just before he kicked his horse into a full gallop, he glanced once more at the man he loved like a son. Passion for battle coursed so fiercely through Brand's blood that William could almost taste it, and his own dark smile mirrored Brand's as their eyes met.

William snapped his reins with a mighty flick of his wrists and thunder echoed beneath his horse's hooves. "For Brynna!" he called over his shoulder, lifting his fierce Norman sword to the sky. "For she has been awaiting my victory as eagerly as I awaited hers!"

Wind whipped through the ends of William's hair and stung his cheeks and he raised his face toward the sun to relish the feel of it as he rode. He smiled, hearing the deep, joyous laughter of his dearest friend behind him, knowing as Brand shouted out to him that victory would no doubt be theirs.

"You told her about Hastings before you told me? You are a bastard, William the Conqueror!"

About the Author

I live in the busy and beautiful city of Manhattan with my childhood sweetheart who made me his wife sixteen years ago. We have three children, two dogs, and too many reptiles to count. I am an avid reader of both romance and science fiction and have been writing since I was eleven. I love all things medieval and have a special affinity for the Highlands of Scotland. I would love to hear from you at Paula Quinn c/o Warner Books, 1271 Avenue of the Americas, New York, NY 10020.

More Paula Quinn!

Please turn this page
for a preview of

Lord of Temptation

AVAILABLE IN MASS MARKET

February 2006

CHAPTER
I
———

Gianelle twisted the heavy rope into one more knot, pulled both ends as tightly as she could, and then tossed the rope out the window. She rushed back to the small bed she shared with Casey and double-checked the thick knot tied to one of the four legs. She tugged, bracing her weight against it. It would hold. She hoped.

"Are you ready, Casey?" She turned to the trembling girl, who hovered in a shadowy corner of the room even paler now, recognizing the determined glint in Gianelle's eyes.

"Nay, Gia. I—I don't want to." But even before she spoke, Casey knew it was no use. Gianelle was going, and she would never leave Devonshire Castle without her. Casey sniffled, bringing her apron to her nose to wipe it, trying desperately to control the rush of tears and the tight aching scream rising up in her like a powerful spring. "He . . . he will have us. . . ."

Gianelle rushed toward her and gripped Casey's shoulders tightly. "*Non,* he won't!" she snapped, looking as fierce in her thin cotton overdress as any warrior in the heat of battle. She pulled Casey by the arm toward the window. "He won't come to the room tonight. You saw how drunk he was earlier. By now, he is slumped over his soup and hopefully drowning." She tugged her friend harder. "We must go, Casey."

Somewhere in the golden fire of Gianelle's huge, round eyes, Casey could see their freedom. It was there, just beyond their reach like a treasured jewel guarded by a savage dragon. Freedom, a treasure more precious and longed for by Gianelle than the greenest, most fertile land was to a conquering king. But freedom frightened Casey. Born the daughter of a wealthy Saxon noble, Casey had led a much happier life than Gianelle until her family lost their land and their lives in the conquest that delivered England into William of Normandy's hands. She was but twelve years of age when Baron Bryce Dermott rescued her from the burning ruins that had been her home and made her his servant. He was a foul man, indeed, but he also owned Gianelle, and while the years spent in his care were terrible ones, Gia had made them bearable. Happily, the unfortunate baron met his demise while he slept, after taking Gianelle to his bed. Casey often wondered if Gianelle was responsible for murdering the brute.

"We must go," Gianelle urged, her delicate, slippered feet treading hastily toward the narrow, arched window in their room.

As if on signal, Casey took a cautious step forward just as their bedroom door burst open. Leaping toward Gianelle, Casey screamed and cowered against her friend's breast. Alponte had come. They should have known the evil in his heart would give strength and lucidity to his drunken stupor. Casey could do naught but whimper at the sight of his stout, heavy form leaning against the door.

Gianelle shoved Casey toward the window as arms, heavy with the thick black hair of a bear, closed around her.

"What is this? Do you think to escape yet again?" Lord Alponte breathed his foul breath onto Gianelle's neck while she writhed and screamed for Casey to run.

"Don't stop! Flee, Casey!" Gianelle fought heedlessly against her master's tight embrace. Her hair, as golden as a summer sunset, tumbled in thick cascading waves over her face, tangling within the fat fingers that imprisoned her. She was small and thin and no match for the hunger that gave their master his strength.

Casey watched in horror, unable to move her feet. She should do something, rush at the drunken brute and . . . and . . . do what? Gianelle was shouting at her. The window was so close. But Casey couldn't leave her, she just couldn't. How would she survive without Gianelle? She was Casey's protector, her friend, her mother. Casey squeezed her eyes shut and shook her head. She could never leave her. Gianelle screamed again, warning her with a flurry of vile oaths to leave now or face her wrath. Casey moved closer to the window and the two women's eyes met for the briefest moment. Huge, luminous amber eyes penetrated Casey's blue eyes and seemed to bid her farewell. And then Casey gripped the rope and disappeared over the edge of the window.

Still imprisoned in her master's arms, Gianelle smiled just before she was dragged out of the room by her long golden tresses.

Casey thought it a pure and merciful act of God when her feet touched the ground outside the castle. She thanked her kind Lord and did not wait to see what else He had planned for her before she hiked her skirts over her ankles and raced toward the safety of the forest. She prayed for Gianelle while she ran; she prayed that the same Lord who had helped her escape would now help her find a way to rescue her dear friend. With feet that she was sure had sprouted wings, and hands clasped to her mouth in fervid prayer, Casey ran and ran until her legs grew weak beneath her. Her chest felt as if it were being crushed beneath stone. Driven by pure fear and the need to find help, she broke through Bainwood Forest like an arrow exploding through straw.

She never heard the approach of horses, did not feel the vibration of thunder beneath her moth-eaten slippers. With her eyes squeezed shut in her holy benediction, Casey never saw the enormous black stallion until she crashed into the stirruped leather boot of its rider.

"Whoa! What in hell is this?" the rider roared, quaking tree and earth and sending the poor girl at his feet into an hysterical delirium of flailing arms and tangled reins. One of her small hands struck the stallion's snout and with a great and feverish snort, the beast bucked and rose up on its hind legs. The rider tried to hold fast to the reins. He shouted curses into the air while he slipped from the saddle. The thunder of his voice and the vehemence of his oaths made Casey cover her ears and crumple to her knees, certain that God had changed His mind and her untimely death was imminent.

"*Rien,* woman! You had best tell me it's the Devil that pursues you or those prayers you utter will be said face-to-face with your Creator." The rider rose to his feet, rubbing his backside. He glared down at the kneeling girl. "Are you mute?" he demanded. One of his men muffled a snicker behind him and he turned his head around slowly and sent each of them a black glare that wiped even the most concealed smirk clean off their faces.

Huddled at his feet, Casey raised her gaze, and continued

to raise it, traveling over fine black kid leather boots and farther up tight hose that barely concealed, even under the filtered moonlight, thighs of steel. She squeaked in terror, realizing she could never outrun this man. By the time she lifted her head enough to absorb the great expanses of his mailed chest and broad shoulders, her mouth had fallen open.

"Be ye monster or God?" she managed, gape-mouthed.

"Neither," the rider admitted, no longer shouting. His voice was deep, so deep in fact that the very sound of it was almost oppressive to Casey's poor ears. "I am Lord Dante Risande of King William's royal guard."

Casey risked a glance to his face and then quickly lowered her eyes. Seconds passed; then another flurry of prayers issued into the night when the huge beast bent toward her, gripped her at the top of her arms and hoisted her to her feet to face him fully.

"Stop that sniveling," Lord Dante demanded, scowling at her. "No one here is going to hurt—" He stopped suddenly, staring into her face, a face as sweet and innocent as his sister Katherine's had been. He swallowed hard enough to cause the thick muscles in his neck to dance. It looked to Casey like he was about to throw his head back and howl in agony. She recoiled, awaiting the awful sound and the hard slap that was sure to follow. But only a faint moan escaped through his lips when he released her, dropping his arms to his sides. "My God, who are you?" His rich, husky voice faded to a choking whisper. He stepped away from her, lifting his gloved fingers to her face at the same time.

Unable to move, be it from fear or the gentle way his fingers touched her cheek, Casey could only stare in mute silence at this man's breathtaking torment and the power in his silvery gaze as his eyes swept over her face. "My—my name is Casey, my lord." She finally breathed.

"Casey." He repeated her name as if he had never heard such a profound sound before. His fingertips were like sighs against her flesh. Never had she been touched so. "You look just like . . ." He did not finish but turned instead to one of his companions.

Finally shrinking from his touch, Casey stumbled back as the man he had spoken to dismounted and stepped toward her. Stunned by the lead rider's awesome presence, she had forgotten the small army of men behind him. His companion was a bit smaller than Lord Dante, but then, Casey reasoned, Goliath himself would appear frail next to this silver-eyed dragon.

The man examined her for a moment and nodded. "If her hair were longer . . . *Oui,* she looks like our sweet Katherine."

Lowering her eyes in shame, Casey lifted her hand to her cropped locks. "I—I did not cut it myself. Gianelle did it to protect me from Alponte's bed."

Gathering whatever emotions he had lost control of a moment earlier, Dante stepped forward again, looking even bigger and more dangerous than before. "His bed?" he repeated, his brows a dark slash against the brilliance of his eyes. "Indeed, it is the Devil you flee from."

Casey lifted her eyes to him and nodded. "Aye, my lord. And he holds my dearest friend captive."

THE EDITOR'S DIARY

Dear Reader,

An old nursery rhyme told us "first comes love, then comes marriage." But passion never follows the rules, even if they are Mother Goose's. So pick up a copy of our two Warner Forever titles this August and take part in a love revolution.

Most mothers are dying to marry their daughters off, but what if your mother never wants you to tie the knot? Eve Farrel from **Kimberly Raye's SWEET AS SUGAR, HOT AS SPICE** knows she's in a pickle. By day Eve creates red-hot how-to videos as owner and operator of Sugar & Spice Sinema, and by night she tries to stay sane by dodging her famous feminist mother at her every turn. Her only solution is the ultimate rebellion: get married. One of NASCAR's hottest drivers, Linc Adams just wants to race. The last thing he cares to do is follow in his father's footsteps of becoming mayor of his Georgia town. So he hatches a full-proof plan to blow his chances starring Eve, the one woman whose steamy career could shock the pants off his conservative town. Eve and Linc agree to marry in name only, but they're about to find out that love knows no rules and attraction knows no limits. Grab a copy now and find out why *New York Times* bestselling author Vicki Lewis Thompson raves, "Kimberly Raye is hot, hot, hot!"

And I'd like to introduce a debut novel from an exciting and sensual new voice at Warner Forever, **Paula Quinn's LORD OF DESIRE**. Lady Brynnafar Dumont is having difficulties of her own. When Lord Brand "the Passionate" Risande ruthlessly defeats her father's army, almost killing her father in the process, Brynna knows she has to keep her wits about her. For her goal now is to protect her people and she'll do whatever is necessary to ensure their safety . . . even if it means seducing Lord Brand, the savage Norman knight. The only problem is that he wants absolutely nothing to do with her. But Brynna refuses to be ignored. Since King Edward decreed they must marry, they will. Yet one look at Lord Brand's broad shoulders and bedroom eyes leaves Brynna wondering if having his name is enough. For now she wants his heart . . .

To find out more about Warner Forever, these titles, and the author, visit us at www.warnerforever.com.

With warmest wishes,

Karen Kosztolnyik

Karen Kosztolnyik, Senior Editor

P.S. A little feistiness never did a girl any harm in these two irresistible novels: **Kathryn Caskie** delivers a tantalizing battle of wits and will when a cad meets his match in a beautiful young writer in **A LADY'S GUIDE TO RAKES**; and **Robin T. Popp** tells the sensual and spellbinding tale of a spunky woman searching for her father and the sexy half-man, half-vampire who comes to her aid in **OUT OF THE NIGHT**.